A HOUSE BY THE SEA

www.rbooks.co.uk

A HOUSE BY THE SEA

ELVI RHODES

BANTAM PRESS

LONDON · TORONTO · SYDNEY · AUCKLAND · JOHANNESBURG

TRANSWORLD PUBLISHERS
61–63 Uxbridge Road, London W5 5SA
A Random House Group Company
www.rbooks.co.uk

First published in Great Britain
in 2008 by Bantam Press
an imprint of Transworld Publishers

A CIP catalogue record for this book
is available from the British Library.

ISBN 9780593060094

Addresses for Random House Group Ltd companies outside the UK
can be found at: www.randomhouse.co.uk
The Random House Group Ltd Reg. No. 954009

The Random House Group Limited supports The Forest Stewardship
Council (FSC), the leading international forest-certification organization.
All our titles that are printed on Greenpeace-approved FSC-certified
paper carry the FSC logo. Our paper procurement policy can
be found at www.rbooks.co.uk/environment

Typeset in 12/14½pt Plantin by
Kestrel Data, Exeter, Devon
Printed in the UK by
CPI Mackays, Chatham, ME5 8TD

2 4 6 8 10 9 7 5 3 1

Mixed Sources
Product group from well-managed
forests and other controlled sources
www.fsc.org Cert no. TT-COC-2139
FSC © 1996 Forest Stewardship Council

This book is for my great-granddaughter,
Hermia Rhodes,
and her parents, Paul and Netty, with much love

PART ONE

ONE

The afternoon surgery was almost over. It had been a particularly busy one, not only with those who really needed to see one of the three doctors but with individuals with the most minor of ailments who would have been much better off seeing the practice nurse. It was the duty of Caroline, or whichever receptionists were on duty, politely to try to keep such patients away from the doctors dealing with life and death and divert them to the nurse's kind, knowledgeable, even if sometimes brisk, ministrations.

Eventually the surgery slowly began to empty until the only patient left was Mrs Fawcett, one of Doctor Meadows's most faithful regulars.

The buzzer sounded.

'There you are, Mrs Fawcett,' Caroline said. 'Doctor Meadows is free.'

She hoped the lady wouldn't be too long-winded, but it was probably a vain hope. Caroline couldn't leave until the last patient was off the premises, and this afternoon she had shopping to do.

It was almost fifteen minutes before Mrs Fawcett emerged, smiling and satisfied. How could she possibly take so long, Caroline asked herself? Staff were not encouraged to peruse patients' notes but Mrs Fawcett looked the picture of health. 'Good-bye, dear!' she said amicably to Caroline. 'Take care!'

'Good-bye, Mrs Fawcett,' Caroline said. She saw her to the door and locked it firmly behind her. She gathered her things together then picked up the phone and buzzed Doctor Meadows. 'Unless there's anything else,' she said, 'I'm just off.'

The heat hit her as she stepped out of the surgery. She turned the corner and walked along Great Pulteney Street, crossed the bridge, busy with visitors looking into the windows of the small shops which were built on it. There was never a month in the year when Bath didn't have visitors, but now, in September, they were thick on the ground. At the end of the Pulteney bridge she turned left into Grand Parade. The river, on her left, looked cool and inviting. She would have liked to have sat there, watching the world go by, or if Peter had been with her perhaps to have taken a boat out, but this afternoon she had more pressing things to do. And Peter was not with her, and never would be again. It was a year ago now, and it still hurt, she thought about him so often.

She walked the streets quickly, cutting through to Marks & Spencer's. She had persuaded herself she wanted a new dress. Wanted, rather than needed, she reminded herself. She had a wardrobe full of clothes, she wasn't going any-where special, she didn't have a date on the horizon: in fact she wasn't going anywhere at all except to the Sales to buy a dress she didn't need.

She found the dress within the first few minutes in the store. She was a quick shopper, partly because she was usually able to make up her mind almost at once about what she didn't like, or what wasn't suitable. For instance, she never even looked at anything sleeveless; her arms were not her best point, being, to her way of thinking, too thin. She was too thin in most ways, she thought. She could eat like a horse, eat anything – cream cakes, fried potatoes, chocolate – and never put on an ounce, let alone the few pounds she would have welcomed. Peter, however, she thought sadly, had maintained that thin was elegant.

She wished, oh, so much, that Peter was with her right now, that he was here to help her to choose. Not that he would have been. On a Monday afternoon he would have been beavering away in the legal practice twelve miles away in Bristol, where he was a solicitor. And when, later, he'd arrived home she would have poured them both a gin and tonic with lots of ice and they would have sat down to drink it, and talk about how the day had gone. But, she reminded herself now, he had never taken much part in helping her to choose clothes. He appreciated what she wore, he liked her to be well dressed, but shopping for clothes, especially, as now, among crowds of women, he hated. On the rare occasions when he had accompanied her, he had always stood apart, as if not belonging to any of it. But he himself had always been well turned out. He had had a natural affinity with clothes, and with his height, an inch or two over six feet, and his slender figure, he had looked good in anything. Oh, Peter, she thought, why did you leave me?

She managed not to say the words out loud, though if she had been at home, she thought, she would have done so, and not for the first time in the year since he had died. She had been so full of anger, anger at what Peter had suffered as the cancer took over everything. Anger that he had died; left her alone. Anger, even, at her own anger, with which she didn't know how to deal and had found her, in the first few months, shouting at the walls. It was quite normal, Doctor Meadows had said. And better out than in.

The dress she had found on the rail was a pale lilac colour, of fine, soft cotton, with a deep V-neck. It was a colour she was fond of. It went well with her fair skin and her dark blond hair. 'I could turn you into a redhead,' her hairdresser had said. More than once. 'It would suit you!' She had so far refused his offer, but as a few grey hairs were now beginning to show through the dark blond, who knew? She was directed to a cubicle and put on the dress then surveyed herself in the long mirror. She was frowning slightly. Not a suitable expression for one buying new clothes, she thought, trying to look more pleased. There was no reason not to be pleased with the dress. It fitted well over her shoulders and breasts and the softness of the material, slightly draped, somehow camouflaged the fact that her waist wasn't as slim as the rest of her. The skirt flared gently to mid-calf length, which suited her long legs and slender ankles. Would Peter have liked it, she thought with a stab of pain? Probably he would. The colour certainly suited her, she thought.

She queued at the cash point to pay then, remembering that she'd not planned anything for her supper, she picked up some soup in the Food Hall. It would do very well: no cooking. She had fallen out with cooking since Peter had died; it was no fun cooking for one and she had actually lost her appetite for a while. Still, she knew it was high time to make an effort to start again. She promised herself she would do so when the weather cooled down.

She left the store and began the walk home. She never minded walking anywhere in Bath, it was such a pleasant city, in whatever direction one looked, and the pale stone of which much of the city had been built had now turned to gold in the afternoon sun. Less than fifteen minutes' walking brought her back to the house she had shared with Peter for more than twenty years. It held so many memories: of Peter playing the piano, which he did most evenings after they had had their gin and tonic, and before they ate; of Rosie's childhood. Rosie had been a rumbustious child, she had made the house come alive, but now that her daughter was grown-up and lived and worked in London – though she came to Bath when she could spare the time – all that was gone too. She had tried to get out of the habit of half-listening for Peter's key in the door, though she still sometimes found herself doing so. Now she went into the kitchen, made herself a mug of tea, no milk, no sugar, and sat at the kitchen table with it. Peter would not have done that. He was a china teapot man; Earl Grey tea left to brew for five minutes before being poured. I am turning into a slob, she thought as she ate and drank.

What would she do with the evening? It stretched before her endlessly. There was no housework to be done, and she didn't want to be alone with her thoughts.

I could ring Marion, she thought. Marion was a good friend. On the other hand, she was the half of Marion and Nicholas. That was the case with most of her friends. They had husbands or partners, or children still at home. She had developed a dislike of breaking in on them, though she knew that that was her fault, not theirs. They would have made her welcome. And of course if she were in any real trouble or difficulty, she *would* turn to them and they would help; but would any of them want to hear that she had just returned from buying a dress in Marks & Spencer's, together with a description of it?

She switched on the television, quickly grew tired of it, and turned it off again. Yet another programme on how to transform an entire garden in a matter of five hours while the lady of the house had gone to visit her mother in the next town. She knew exactly what would happen. The team would move in, they would spend an inordinate amount of money on mature plants, containers, garden furniture, trellising and ceramic slabs (decking seemed mercifully to have gone out of fashion). Towards the end there would be moments of panic because the wife was due to walk in at the door in precisely seven minutes' time. And indeed she would arrive on the dot, seconds after the last shrub had been planted. No late trains, no hold-ups of any kind, ever delayed her. She would take one look at the scene before her, then scream with surprise and delight – after which they would all have a glass of champagne.

She concluded that it would have to be an early night, and shortly afterwards – it was still light – went to bed. But bed, she decided, was even now where she missed Peter most of all. She still wanted his arms around her, his body against hers and to see his kind, smiling face first thing in the morning.

She chose a book from the small untidy heap on the bedside table, tried to read, and failed, then switched off the light and willed herself to go to sleep. It didn't work. Sleep eluded her. Even covered by a thin cotton sheet and with the window wide open, the room was too hot. She switched on the light again and turned on the television.

It was in the middle of a programme which featured Brighton. There, filling the screen, was the pier – now called Brighton Pier but to her it would always be Palace Pier, since she had known it as a small child, from the time when she had wondered if she might fall through the spaces between the wooden planks of which the pier was fashioned. And if she did, if the tide was high, she would fall straight into the sea and her father would have to jump over the side and rescue her because she couldn't swim. And of course he would have done so. She had no doubt at all about that. Her father would save her from anything.

Her memories of Brighton were all happy ones: collecting pebbles, paddling near the edge of the sea, visiting the mysteriously dark aquarium where strange-looking fishes swam in tanks. She had continued to live in Brighton, the only child of loving parents, until she had gone away to university, and there she had met Peter, whom, after they had both graduated, she had married in St Peter's church in Brighton. Peter had been her first serious boyfriend. And my last, she thought now. And if his job had not taken him to Bath, and from there to Bristol, they most likely would be in Brighton still.

They had gone back regularly to visit her parents until, two years ago, both her mother and her father died within a few months of each other. Caroline had inherited their house of which, over the last few years, and to augment their pensions, her parents had let the upper floor to students. There were always students in Brighton, looking for somewhere to live in term time. Her mother had enjoyed having them coming and going, and her father hadn't minded much except for their choice of music, played at full blast.

When she had inherited the house Peter's idea had been to sell it, but she hadn't wanted to do that. It was not because of the house itself; it was not the one she had grown up in, her parents had moved since then. It was, she admitted to Peter, because it was in Brighton. It was a little bit of the place from which she had never quite torn herself away.

'Let's not sell it just yet,' she'd said. 'The rents from the students pay the expenses, and you and I have a place to go when we want a change. And Rosie might well like to use it from time to time. She could take her friends there.'

Peter had been persuaded, not only because he, too, liked Brighton, but because of George Clarke, a good neighbour to Caroline's parents, who kept an eye on the house, and on the students in term time.

They hadn't gone down to Brighton nearly as often as she'd wanted to and when Peter was ill it had become nigh on impossible. Since he had died Caroline had only been down twice. Perhaps now was the time to rectify that.

Caroline lay awake a long time, thinking about Brighton and her childhood there, thinking about Peter, thinking about her parents, whom she had loved, and still missed.

The thoughts went round and round in her head and she fell asleep with all these things jumbled in her mind. When she awakened it was still dark. She looked at the clock. Half past four. She had slept little more than an hour and her head was as full of thoughts as it had been before she slept. The truth was, she was not happy. Her life was not working for her.

She got up, and went into the kitchen. She made herself a mug of tea, then sat at the kitchen table with it, watching the early light filtering through the blind. 'What am I going to do?' She was astonished to hear herself express it out loud. Am I going potty, she thought, talking to myself? And why am I feeling like this a year on, when I should at least be starting to get over things? But if there was an answer, she didn't know what it was.

She finished her tea, and told herself that she must go back to bed, try to get a little more sleep. She was on duty at the morning surgery and she must be there at eight for an eight-thirty start. She went back to bed, set the alarm for seven, then slept fitfully for a while before falling into a deep sleep just fifteen minutes before the alarm woke her.

It started off as one of those days when things didn't go well. The surgery was crowded, which was nothing new, though hayfever had taken the place of coughs and colds. Two fractious toddlers squabbled loudly over a small wooden truck from the toy box: a small baby screamed and wouldn't be pacified. Worst of all, to Caroline's mind, she sent the wrong notes in for a patient. Doctor Meadows marched into the surgery and demanded the correct ones, which were lying on Caroline's desk. She felt harassed and stressed and perilously close to tears. He looked at her keenly, raising his eyebrows but saying nothing. But in the end everyone was seen to and the waiting room emptied.

Doctor Meadows buzzed her. 'Can you come in for a minute?' he said.

She went at once, apologizing the minute she set foot in his room. 'I'm very sorry . . .' she began.

He waved away her apologies. 'Sit down, Caroline,' he said. As she did so, he gave her a long look. 'Are you all right?' he asked. 'Is there anything wrong?'

'I'm sorry about the notes . . . And the baby.'

'Caroline, we all know you're the best receptionist this practice has had in years but I sense there's something wrong,' he said. 'Am I right? Is there anything I can do?'

Caroline shook her head. 'Not really. I didn't sleep much last night, I haven't for a week or two. That's all.'

'We can do something about the sleeping,' Doctor Meadows said. 'It's *why* you're not sleeping that's the question.' Naturally, he knew about her bereavement, but until the last week or two she'd seemed to be progressing normally, whatever 'normally' meant in the circumstances. Whatever difficulties she had, she didn't bring them to her job. 'So do you know why? Is there anything special?'

Caroline shook her head. 'Too much thinking,' she said. 'I thought I'd more or less done all my thinking, but it seems not. It comes back at me. And then last night I watched a programme about Brighton. That unsettled me.'

'Why Brighton?' he asked.

'I was born and brought up there,' she told him.

'I didn't know that. But you've lived in Bath a long time now?'

'Twenty years,' she said. 'And happily. But now it's not the same, for obvious reasons. But in any case I've always loved Brighton. I kept in close touch with my parents when they were alive, and I go back to what was their house, and which now belongs to me – though I don't go as often as I should; I've hardly been at all in the last few months. And I miss it.'

17

'So what was it about, the TV programme?' he asked.

'It showed all the places I've known since I was a small child,' Caroline answered. 'I felt I was living there.'

He looked at her for a long moment, without speaking. In the end he said, 'Are you telling me you're homesick for Brighton? Would you put it as strongly as that?'

Caroline also hesitated, for several seconds, then she said, 'I don't know. It sounds ridiculous, but I think I might be. Oh, I do love Bath and I've been so happy here. But it's different now, especially without Peter.'

'It's bound to be,' Doctor Meadows said sensibly. 'It stands to reason. But may I make a suggestion?'

'Please do.'

'Why not take a few days off . . .' He waved away her protests. 'We'll manage. Take yourself to Brighton, spend a few days there. See how it goes. It might have been just the programme which upset you, caught you at a bad time when you hadn't been sleeping. But seeing the places again might settle you. So relax; take your time.'

'I will,' she said. 'You're very kind.'

'Not at all,' he replied. 'So just do as I say. Doctor's orders!'

TWO

I will do as Doctor Meadows suggested, Caroline thought as she walked home after the surgery was over. I will spend a few days in Brighton, relax, take things as they come. She still had the whole of her three-week holiday to come; she had taken none of it so far, partly because she hadn't been able to decide what to do with it, and a trip to Brighton would work perfectly.

Back at home, she phoned George Clarke. 'How are you, George?' she asked. 'How's Emmie?' His wife had recently returned from hospital after a hip replacement.

'She's fine,' George said. 'She had a little walk along the road earlier on.'

'Good. But don't let her overdo it. You know what she's like!'

'I do! And I won't,' George promised. 'But thank you for asking. Is everything all right with you?'

'Yes,' Caroline said. 'In fact, I'm calling to tell you I'm coming down to Brighton for a few days. Tomorrow, actually.'

'Fine!' George answered. 'One thing is sure, you won't want me to turn the heat on. It's real hot here!'

'And probably hotter still here,' Caroline told him. Bath was in a hollow, surrounded by hills, which kept the temperature reasonable in the winter months but sometimes too hot in the summer. In Brighton, hopefully, there would be a sea breeze. 'I'll be down around lunch time. Don't bother to get anything in. I'll do a shop here before I leave. See you, then!'

She phoned Marion to tell her. 'I'll be away about a week,' she said. 'I felt like a change. In any case, there'll be some clearing up to do. All the students left at the end of June. They've finished their courses, so they won't be back.'

'Very well, but don't work too hard,' Marion said. 'And you must come to supper when you get back. It's been ages!'

It had, Caroline thought. And she hadn't particularly enjoyed it last time. Everyone in couples – though by now she should be used to that.

Most of the journey to Brighton was on the motorway. She stopped mid-morning at a service station for petrol, coffee and a doughnut, and was in Brighton before lunch. It looked clean and bright and busy, as in her mind it always did. She parked in front of her parents' house, which was one of a terrace of identical houses solidly built in mid-Victorian times. It was not close to the sea, which was a pity, but a mile or so inland and adjacent to the park. When her parents decided to move house – it was after she had left Brighton and she never quite understood why they wanted to do that – they had elected to be somewhere near to Preston Park. From one point of view it was a good choice since her father, especially after he had retired, had been an inveterate bowler and the greens were close at hand.

'Far *too* close,' her mother sometimes said, though that was before she herself was inveigled into the game and took to it in a big way, joining the ladies' section, and soon becoming as addicted as her husband. In no time at all she was in the team, travelling, in her pleated skirt, trim blouse, blazer and her white panama hat with a ribbon band, to compete with other clubs in Sussex.

When Caroline reached the house George was already there, waiting for her. 'I've laid in the basics,' he said, 'bread, butter, tea, milk. I know you said you might get them, but just in case. And I won't stay, in case Emmie might need me. But I'll be round tomorrow, first thing.'

As soon as he had left she went over the whole house, top to bottom, with the exception of the loft, as its ladder was very rickety. Also, she felt sure, it would be full of all kinds of junk. Her parents had been great hoarders. She and Peter had meant to do something about the loft, but there had always been more urgent things to see to, so the loft, they reckoned, could wait for another day: a day which had so far not dawned. Right now, she felt unable to face the task, and did it really matter? The rooms on the first floor, two large ones and a small one, had been the students' domain. She had expected, as she went into them now, to find them untidy, perhaps messy, but she was wrong. They had been left in quite reasonable order, even the rugs vacuumed and, as far as she could see, nothing left behind. So, apart from the fact that I could let the rooms to students again, what should I do with them now, she asked herself? It depended, of course, what she wanted to do with the rest of the house. Did she want to live in it herself, or didn't she? She didn't know. It was all in the air. The bigger question was, was there anywhere at all, anywhere in the world, she wanted to live, without Peter? And the sad but inevitable answer was that she would have to do so. She had no choice.

After lunch – no more than a sandwich, it was too hot – she took a walk in the park, which went a little way towards clearing her head.

Back at the house, she made up the bed and then sat

for a while in the garden, which was in a fairly neglected state. She couldn't however shake off a restless desire to be down by the sea. It was not even visible from her parents' house, indeed it was a longish walk, but it was a nice day so she set off, crossing Preston Circus, continuing down the road, passing St Peter's church, through the Steine gardens and across two roads to the pier, the pier of beloved memory. Nevertheless, she decided not to go on the pier at the moment. She would save that for another day, perhaps tomorrow. Instead she turned left and walked eastward towards the marina.

It was almost high tide now, but a calm and gentle tide on this autumn day. She had always preferred the tides in winter when they thumped against the sea wall, or occasionally dashed over on to the promenade. As a small child she had run away from the waves, shouting, running ostensibly to keep dry, but always hoping that the wave would catch up with her and she would get slightly wet.

A leisurely walk half an hour later found her at the marina. She remembered this place before anything had been built on it. When she was young her father had taken her as a special treat to the rock pools there, pointing out all the little, and sometimes strange, creatures which dwelt in them. He knew the names of each one of them and when the plans were mooted to build the marina his was one of the many voices which had protested loudly at what was feared would be the wildlife irrevocably lost to nature if the marina were to be built. But in spite of the protests, built it had been, and in many other ways a great asset it had become. And not only commercially. There was beauty, as well as interest, she thought, in the craft, large and small, which came from near and far-flung places, and which at this moment were gently bobbing about on the water, their sails furled, while outside the marina other craft waited to come in.

She sat in the warmth of the sun, sipping a coffee in a

pavement café: for longer than she had intended. All around her it was a busy scene, alive with holidaymakers – parents, small children, a not surprising number of foreign students: Brighton was a Mecca for them. There was no traffic since the place she had chosen to sit was in a pedestrian area. It was not until the waitress stopped by her table and asked was there anything else she would like that she became aware how much time had passed. It was a long way from being dark, but the light had changed.

'No thank you,' she said. 'I must be going.' Not that time mattered to her; she had nowhere particular to go, no place where she had to be by a certain time. She had the blessing of being as free as the air, though with the drawback of no one waiting for her to arrive anywhere. She wondered what Rosie was doing. She had intended to phone her, before she left Bath, tell her she planned to go to Brighton for a few days, but in the end she hadn't done so. She would, though, this evening.

She left the marina and walked back towards the pier. The sun was dipping over the horizon and there were the beginnings of one of those wonderful Brighton sunsets she remembered so well; the sky, and a wide path across the sea, turning to red-gold. So, a fine day tomorrow, she thought. She walked back to the pier, then crossed to the Steine and took a bus back to Preston Park. In fact, she got off the bus before it reached the park. Walking down earlier she had passed an Italian restaurant which, she'd noted, did takeaways. It would be just the thing for her supper – she enjoyed Italian food – and after that she'd have an early night.

True to her plan, she was in bed by nine o'clock. As she went to draw her bedroom curtains she looked out. It was amazing how the flowers stood out, sharp and clear in the light from the street. And as she stood there she saw a fox crossing the lawn. He stopped in his tracks, and stared at her, his ears alert, his eyes wide and shining. He was not in the least abashed that she was there in his territory. She stared back at him; he was rather beautiful, such a delicately formed face, red and white, and his tail a long, thick brush, white-tipped. He held her gaze until, suddenly, he turned, and disappeared into the bushes at the far end. He had seemed very much at home: she wondered if he was a regular visitor, though she had never seen him on any previous occasion. She drew the curtains reluctantly, leaving only a small gap through which she might catch sight of the fox if he returned, though common sense told her she wouldn't see him; it was almost dark already.

In bed sleep once again didn't come. She lay awake, wondering what she would do with her life. At the moment, she was drifting and drifting was not in her nature; never had been. She thought about her grandmother, her mother's mother. She was a woman who always knew where she was going. On her dining-room wall she had had a framed motto, 'Home is where the heart is.' Caroline had been a small girl then, not long able to read. She didn't altogether understand it. 'It means,' her grandmother had said, 'that your heart will always speak to you. It will tell you where you belong.' I wish my heart *would* speak to me, Caroline thought desperately. She pummelled her pillow into subjugation, and finally fell into a deep and dreamless sleep.

George arrived just after nine o'clock in the morning. Caroline was up and dressed, feeling better and more focused than she had done for ages. She made a cup of coffee for herself and George and they sipped together in the sunny kitchen.

'The house seems empty without the students here,' George observed. 'A month before they come back.'

'They won't be back,' Caroline reminded him. 'Not the

same ones, anyway. They've finished with university; they'll be out in the big wide world now, looking for jobs.'

'I know,' George said, 'but you'll easily get others to take their place, won't you? I could keep an eye on them in between your visits.'

It was probably as he spoke that she realized she didn't want students again. Not that she had anything against them in principle, and this year's had been good enough, but if she wanted to make the best use of the house, and if she needed some extra income, which now she did, then an arrangement which meant that for ten weeks or so in the year she was without them made no sense. She said as much to George. 'I'm not sure. I could divide the house into two flats and let them both, though not to students. Or . . .' she heard herself saying the words as if it were another person '. . . or, I could live in the bottom one myself and let the top one.'

George looked at her open-mouthed. 'You mean you'd leave Bath, come to live in Brighton?'

'Well,' she said. 'That's what I *could* do. It's not that there's anything wrong with Bath, but it's just not the same now.'

'It can't be,' George said. 'Not without your husband. I'm very sorry about that, and so is Emmie. He liked coming to Brighton, didn't he?'

Caroline nodded, swallowing hard. She still found it quite difficult to talk about Peter. 'He did. Though never as much as I did. But then I was born here. Not in this house, as you know, but in Brighton. And I do love it.'

'I understand that. Me and Emmie came here when we were first married. We wouldn't want to be anywhere else. But do you really think you could be happy here?'

'I really believe I might be,' Caroline said. 'I wouldn't want the whole house to myself. In fact, I couldn't afford it. But there'd be quite a lot to be done to it first.'

'You're right,' George said. 'Proper kitchen, new bathroom and all that.'

'And perhaps a separate entrance,' Caroline said. 'It would be a good idea to look out for someone who could advise me. Do you happen to know of anyone?'

'Well, there's been quite a few conversions of houses into flats around here. People don't want a big house unless they've got a family.'

'So who do you know?'

'There's Stanley Merritt. He's a builder, he's done a few jobs locally. I don't know him personally but I've not heard of any complaints. I could get his number. And then there's Alec Barker. He started up for himself not long ago. It might be worthwhile talking to one of them. You could give them an idea of what you had in mind. See what they come up with. But are you serious about this?'

'I reckon so,' Caroline said. And where was the harm in seeing one of them, or preferably both? She wouldn't be committing herself to anything by talking to them: not even to leaving Bath. 'So, if you can arrange it, I'll start with Mr Merritt, since you mentioned him first, and after that I'll see Mr Barker. Best to consult two people. Will you ask if they can come this week? I have to go back to Bath at the end of the week.'

'I've got Stanley Merritt's number at home so I can call him this morning,' George said. 'And I know how to get hold of Alec Barker, too. Leave it to me!'

'George,' she said, giving him an impulsive hug, 'what would I do without you!'

THREE

George rang Caroline later that morning. 'I've had a word with Stanley Merritt,' he said. 'He can come this afternoon if that's convenient.'

'Super, thank you, George,' Caroline said. 'And did you speak to Mr Barker?'

'I didn't get to speak to him, but I left a message. I gave your phone number.'

He phoned around midday. 'Alec Barker,' he said. 'I hope this isn't an inconvenient time. I've been out on a job and only just got back.'

'Not at all,' answered Caroline, then told him, briefly, what she had in mind. 'Though,' she added, 'it's a fairly new idea to me and it might come to nothing. I'd just like to know if what I'm thinking of is feasible – I think it is – and then of course how long it would take and what it would cost.'

'Of course!' he agreed. 'And once I know what you want I'll tell you what I think. I'd like to have your ideas. I'm sure you will have some. Also, it would be useful for me to know if there's something you actually don't want or like. You might like to give some thought to that.'

'Oh, I will!' Caroline assured him.

'Right!' he said. 'Would this evening suit you? It would have to be around seven; I'm working on another job but I should be through by then.'

'That's fine,' Caroline said.

He had a pleasant voice, she thought. Deep yet clear, and with an accent which wasn't from any part of the south of England, certainly not Sussex. The difference was in the vowels, which she thought were northern, and probably seemed accentuated because he was speaking over the phone and not face to face. She couldn't place which part of the North.

That afternoon she phoned Rosie. 'Hi!' she said. 'I'm in Brighton. How are you?'

'I'm fine,' Rosie said. 'Except that it's too hot in London. It must be cooler in Brighton. But why are you there?'

'I thought I'd like a change,' Caroline said. 'Get a few sea breezes.' She wasn't going to tell Rosie what she had suddenly decided, not yet, not until she'd taken it a step or two further – and perhaps never if the whole idea came to nothing. Perhaps she shouldn't have phoned her. She'd done so on an impulse. Impulsiveness was a fault she was prone to. Peter used to say she acted first and thought later, but she was trying, really trying, to remedy that.

'Well, lucky you!' Rosie said. 'And I'd love to say I'll come down for the day tomorrow, but I can't. We're unspeakably busy. Too many people away on holiday, of course!'

'Yes, and quite a few of them in Brighton.' But Caroline liked that. She liked the buzz it gave to the place.

For once, she was glad Rosie couldn't make it, even though being so made her feel guilty. She didn't usually keep things from Rosie – and nor would she the minute she herself was certain what she was going to do.

'I'm going back to Bath tomorrow,' she said. 'I'll ring you from there.'

★   ★   ★

Caroline spent some time before Stanley Merritt was due to arrive walking around the house, in and out of every room, notebook in hand. Peering into every cupboard. There were a lot of those, some of them still containing odds and ends of no particular value which had belonged to her parents and she'd not so far managed to deal with, though she knew she must eventually. It was one of the worst parts of loved ones dying. She had found it almost unbearable dealing with Peter's things, especially his clothes, of which there were a great many. He had been a dressy man. His suits had smelled of the expensive cologne he'd used – one of his small extravagances. Was anything more evocative than smell?

If I were to take the plunge, she thought as she moved around looking at everything with new eyes, if I *were* to leave Bath and move to Brighton, and if I *were* to divide this house into two flats, then I would definitely keep the ground floor one for myself. The rooms were slightly bigger and it would mean that she would have the garden.

At three o'clock in the afternoon, a long, persistent ring on the doorbell heralded Mr Merritt's arrival, forty minutes late, she noted with slight annoyance. He stood on the top step, a short, plump, balding man with a red face. He wore a white T-shirt which strained over his ample belly and paint-splashed grey flannels.

'Do come in!' Caroline said, but he was already over the doorstep. 'Shall we sit down and talk over what I have in mind before I show you round? Basically, I want to make the house into two self-contained flats.'

He shook his head. 'No need to tell me more, love!' he said confidently. 'I know these houses like the back of my hand. If I've done one I've done a dozen in my time. All the houses in this terrace were put up by the same builder. We'll start at the top, shall we?' He led the way up the stairs. They were halfway up when his mobile phone rang. He came to a stop, Caroline on the stair behind him, took it out of his pocket and answered it. 'Hello, mate!' he said. 'How's everything? Good! Oh yes, busy, busy busy! Been at it all day!' He paused briefly to listen. 'Well, if I were you, chum, I'd not do it that way! You'll meet yourself coming back. Oh, I can get the paint for you, no prob. But I thought you were going on holiday? No, not me! No time, no peace for the wicked, eh? Ethel's not pleased, I can tell you! Might get away for a day or two at the end of the month. No, we'll go to Spain. How's Joan? And the kids? They all right?'

There was more to come. Caroline ostentatiously looked at her watch but he was too engrossed to notice. Eventually, the conversation ended and Mr Merritt put the phone back in his pocket. 'Well, now,' he said to her, 'on we go!'

'I do have some ideas I'd like to tell you about,' Caroline said, by now extremely irritated with Mr Merritt. 'I've jotted down a few notes. One or two must-haves.'

The words were hardly out of her mouth, they had reached the top of the flight, when his phone rang again. He took it out of his pocket and gave it his full attention. While still listening attentively he lowered his voice and spoke to Caroline. 'It's the wife! She wants me to do a bit of shopping on the way home. You ladies! You're all the same.' He fished through his pockets, found a scrap of paper, and as his wife dictated, made out the shopping list.

That done, he put his phone away and turned to Caroline. 'Now where were we?' he asked.

'Actually, nowhere!' Caroline said. 'I'd just told you I had some ideas and I'd made a few notes.'

'Well, let's take a quick look around,' he said. 'Then if you've any questions . . . It won't take long,' he added. 'As I said before, I know the inside of these houses like the back of my hand. I reckon I can more or less guess what you want.'

He was quite right about the survey not taking long. It was a case of popping his head around doors, or at the most venturing a few feet into some of the rooms, nodding sagely, and retreating. 'Some of the woodwork needs attention,' he said. 'And I don't like the look of this ceiling!'

'And there's the loft . . .' Caroline said when he'd finished his quick tour of the bedrooms.

'We'll not bother with the loft at the moment,' he said. 'Everybody's loft is like everybody else's, full of junk!'

'Do you want to take some measurements?' Caroline asked in surprise. 'I mean in the rooms.'

He smiled. 'No need to as yet, my dear!' he said. 'One look and I've got it all up here!' He tapped the side of his head with his pencil. 'Experience tells! We can do the finer stuff later.'

They went downstairs. He was even quicker there. When she saw him out – he had been in the house, she reckoned, fifteen minutes – he said, 'I'll let you have an estimate.'

'Tell me,' Caroline said as he stood on the doorstep, 'if you did get the job, when would you be able to start?'

He sucked in his breath, pursed his lips again. 'Can't say exactly,' he admitted. 'There's a lot going on. But not to worry! I'd fit you in somewhere!'

She watched him walk down the path. As he reached the gate he fished out his mobile and was still conversing as he inched into his car.

Alec Barker arrived late that evening, held up by roadworks but full of apologies.

Caroline showed him to a chair in the sitting room. She wanted to take charge but at the same time couldn't help noticing that he was quite attractive, around her age, with dark hair and nice clothes. She forced her mind back to the interview. Never mind what he looked like, she had to decide whether they would be able to work together.

He opened his mouth as if to speak and was interrupted by his mobile phone. 'I'm sorry,' he said. 'I thought I'd switched it off before I came in. Would you mind if I dealt with it?'

She nodded assent – what else could she do? – and sat back in her chair, ready to grin and bear it.

He listened for a few seconds, then he said, 'Sorry! It will have to wait. I really can't talk to you right now. I'm engaged. Business. I'll call you back as soon as I can.' He switched off the phone and put it in his pocket.

'I do apologize,' he said to Caroline. 'Mobile phones can be a nuisance but I couldn't quite manage without one. I work alone. I don't have an office and I need to keep in touch.'

It hadn't sounded like a business call, Caroline thought. There'd been a more intimate tone in his voice. Wife? Girl-friend?

'That's all right,' she said. 'So, I'll tell you what I have in mind – and you can tell me if it's feasible.'

'Of course,' he said.

'I spent most of this afternoon walking around the house and garden,' she said. 'Looking at things, saying a lot of "what ifs" to myself. And I made some notes, measurements and a few sketches – not that I'm much good at that . . .'

'Then shall I take a look at all that?' he suggested.

'Certainly,' she said. Then on an impulse she added, 'I was just going to have a cup of coffee. Would you like one? You could be looking at my notes while I make it.'

'I'd appreciate that.'

She made the coffee and took it back into the sitting room.

'Your notes are helpful,' he said. 'So does this mean you'd sell up in Bath, and you'd move here, lock, stock and barrel? And let half the house?'

She nodded. 'At least, that's the possibility. I've not decided. It's a big step.'

'It certainly is,' he agreed. 'Not that it's any of my business, of course.'

32

Then, as they drank their coffee, she found herself opening up to him, how she had been brought up in Brighton and yes, she had always been happy in Bath, but now with her husband's death her circumstances had changed and she might – or might not – come back to Brighton.

He was extremely easy to talk to. She even found herself telling him how much she missed Peter, something she didn't dwell on with other people as they seemed to find it uncomfortable. Perhaps, she thought now, it was just easier to talk to strangers.

'I don't doubt you've given it a lot of thought?' he said.

'Oh, I have. And everyone tells you you shouldn't make big decisions too soon after you've been bereaved, which is probably true – though most of the people who tell you that haven't actually been there. They mean well, of course they do, but they haven't experienced that feeling you suddenly have of not belonging anywhere any more. That's when you want to run away. Particularly, you want to run *back* to somewhere, somewhere familiar, where you've been happy. And for me, that's Brighton,' she said. 'Growing up in Brighton was wonderful. If Peter's job hadn't taken him to Bath we might well have stayed here.'

What am I doing, she thought? Why am I saying all this? I hardly know the man. 'Anyway,' she said, rather more briskly, 'that's the big idea. I could make this house into two flats, live in one of them myself and let the other. My parents let the top floor to students, but I'm not sure I'd want that. There'd be too many weeks of the year when they weren't here and I wouldn't be drawing any rents. So I thought perhaps business people, or nurses, or teachers perhaps. Or even a family. I wouldn't mind children around.' It had been a disappointment both to herself and Peter that they'd had had no more children after Rosie.

'So I take it from these notes that you'd have the ground-floor flat,' Alec said.

'Yes,' she said. 'I'd like the garden. And I would like to have separate entrances made for each flat if that's possible.'

'Most things are possible,' he said and went on to discuss the practicalities of the flat and the budget she had for renovating it. Caroline realized that she hadn't thought far enough ahead at all and was relieved when Alec suggested taking a look around.

He looked at everything, including things she hadn't even thought about, all the while taking measurements and discussing finer detail. 'I have a few reservations,' he said. 'You'd definitely need a better bathroom, for example.'

'Oh, you're right about that,' Caroline agreed. 'My parents haven't done anything to the house for years and I have my house in Bath to sell so I shall do all the redecorating I can afford to.' She stopped suddenly, realizing that she was talking as if the whole thing was a decision already made. Which it wasn't. Not yet anyway . . .

'Tell me,' Alec said, 'is there anything you *don't* like about the house? Anything you'd specifically like to change – because now would be the time to deal with that.'

'Of course,' Caroline said. 'And there's nothing I've thought of so far that can't be changed. Except . . .' She hesitated.

'Except?'

'I do like the house. It's fine. It will be even better when it's been reorganized. But there's one thing I don't particularly like . . .'

'And that is?' he asked.

'Its position. I don't really like where it's situated. Oh, I know it's a very nice part of Brighton, but to me Brighton means the sea. I love the sight and smell and sound of the sea, I love it in all its moods. It's near the seafront where Brighton is most alive, most itself. But one

34

can't have everything, and I suppose I'd get used to living here.'

'I suppose so,' Alec agreed. 'As you say, here is where the house is. Perhaps you'll feel differently when you see the plans for the conversion. I have several ideas. But before we go any further,' he continued, 'I should take a look at the loft, see what that offers. I take it one gets at the loft through the panel in the landing ceiling?'

'That's right,' Caroline said. 'You pull down a very rickety ladder when you open the trap door. Do be careful, it is precarious.'

'I'll be careful,' Alec said, smiling at her worried face. 'I'll take a quick look around and report back. I'm guessing you don't want to come up with me?!'

She watched while he opened the trap door and, with some difficulty, pulled down the ladder, climbed up and disappeared from view.

'There's a load of stuff up here!' he called out. 'You're going to have a high old time sorting this out! For the moment I'm just going to take some measurements, if I can find my way through everything!'

Except for the sound of him moving around there was silence for a while, and then suddenly a loud shout.

'WOW!'

'What is it?' Caroline called. 'Are you all right?'

'I'm perfectly all right. It's just that . . .' He hesitated. 'I can't believe it! I've found something really great, really exciting! I can't believe it!'

'Nor can I,' Caroline said. 'What in the world . . . ?'

'There are two wonderful old chairs . . .' he began. He had moved back to the opening, and now he could look down at her.

'These are amazing,' he said. 'If I'm right they're William Morris chairs, original nineteenth-century. Known as Sussex chairs, rush-seated. Of course I know there were a lot of reproductions made, but I do think these might be the real thing. My goodness, what a find! Do you want to come up and take a look? Once you've climbed the ladder it's all right up here.'

'I'll take your word for it,' Caroline said nervously. 'Could you bring the chairs down, do you think?' She wondered how he knew all this. He spoke with authority.

'OK then,' Alec said. 'Watch out below, the chairs are coming down.'

When both chairs were down he placed them side by side, then stood back to admire them. 'There!' he said. 'Aren't they lovely?'

Caroline surveyed them. Apart from the fact that they were thick with dust, and the rush seats were worse for wear, they were nice enough, but she could see nothing remarkable about them. They were straight-up-and-down chairs, no fancy curves. The only concession to design were vertical struts in a line across the back and two rows of fine wood running between the narrow, slightly tapering legs.

'Oh!' Caroline gasped. 'I remember my mother telling me about these. I'm fairly sure that my grandfather gave them to my grandmother as a wedding present. She really treasured them and so did my mother when my grandmother gave them to her. How sad that they've ended up in the loft all covered in cobwebs.'

She touched the top of one of the chairs absentmindedly, remembering her grandparents, how happy they'd been, how in love, and mused how sad it was, that this emblem of their union had been so neglected. She thought how nice it would be to give the chairs to her daughter, Rosie, should she ever meet the right man. But Rosie, at twenty-eight, was still so spirited and fiery, and showed no sign at all of settling down.

'They're absolutely typical of Morris's Arts and Crafts movement,' Alec said excitedly. 'It was a movement

36

– he introduced it – in the second half of the nineteenth century.'

'Why?' Caroline asked, though she had vaguely heard of it. 'I mean, why did he?'

'It was partly as a result of the Industrial Revolution,' Alec said, 'which led to several things, furniture high amongst them, being produced by machines in factories. It ignored the skills of craftsmen, everything started to be produced by machine, and in separate parts; nothing the work of one man only. Chair legs, table tops, arms, seats, all manufactured in bulk, then assembled together. A carpenter, for instance, no longer made the whole piece, he no longer had the satisfaction of seeing the work of his hands. And if an artist, of whatever kind, doesn't have that, then what is he there for? Can you give me a duster?'

She found a duster and handed it to him. He began, almost lovingly, she thought, like a fond mother cleaning up a child after a fall, to remove the thick dust from each chair in turn, though still continuing to speak.

'So Morris and some of his friends – he was a member of the Pre-Raphaelite Brotherhood . . .'

'Oh, I know about them!' Caroline interrupted. 'They were painters, weren't they?'

'Not only painters,' Alec said. 'They were immersed in all the arts: architecture, stained glass, books, poetry – Morris himself was no mean poet. All the arts were important to them, as were artists of every kind, and they were of a social standing to make things happen – which was why they formed the Arts and Crafts Society, of which Morris was a leading light.' He broke off. 'Oh dear!' he said. 'Am I boring you? Once I get on my hobby horse . . .'

'No, do go on, it's fascinating,' Caroline assured him truthfully.

'The unfortunate thing was,' Alec continued, 'that though Morris and his friends fought for the rights of the artist and for his satisfaction in what he created, most things produced in the new factories could be made more cheaply . . .'

'So only people with enough money could buy the craftsman's work?' Caroline interrupted.

Alec nodded. 'That's right! And it's still the same, isn't it? Factory-produced is cheaper, the work of artists and craftsmen goes to those who can afford it.

'If I were you,' he went on, 'I suggest you keep the chairs up here in a bedroom,' he said. 'Don't let anyone sit on them until I've really examined them, checked they're in good condition.'

'There won't be anyone here *to* sit on them,' Caroline pointed out. 'The house will be empty after I go back to Bath.'

Alec looked thoughtful. 'Then would you like me to take them home with me, look after them until you know what you want to do?'

He saw her hesitation. 'I'm sorry,' he said. '*Not* a good idea! You don't know me well enough, do you? Shall I put them back in the loft?'

'Well, yes – if you think that's best,' Caroline said. She was reluctant to put the chairs back, especially as they had such sentimental value, but could see no other option.

'To change the subject slightly,' Alec said. 'There's no way you'll be able to make the loft another bedroom. Not enough head room, I'm afraid. The only way you could get that would be to raise the roof a bit – for which you might not get permission, and if it were to be allowed, it would be very expensive.'

'Oh,' Caroline said. She felt rather disappointed at this.

'But I do think you ought to go up there, see what there is. I can go up the ladder behind you; you'll be quite safe.'

'Perhaps another day,' Caroline said hastily. She had no

38

desire to wobble up that ladder. 'Shall we take the chairs outside and get rid of the dust from the rush seats?'

'Yes,' Alec said, looking at them thoughtfully. He had seen Caroline's face as she looked at them, and an idea was beginning to form. 'You go ahead to the garden,' he said to Caroline. 'I'll sort out the chairs.'

FOUR

On Friday afternoon Caroline returned to Bath, equipped with Alec's telephone number so that they could keep in touch about the house. Alec, in the meantime, was preparing an estimate so that she could get to grips with the finances of the project.

Though, she thought, there was far more to think about than just finances. She hoped that this move would change her life. She was conscious that she had to be careful that she was not simply running away from her problems.

Slowly she walked around the house in Bath, in and out of the rooms, all of which held memories of Peter, some of them still so sharp. His books, for instance, were everywhere. He had been such an avid reader and read voraciously on all subjects with a real passion. She now realized that some of the books would have to go, although this thought made her feel sad and somehow guilty; Peter would never have given his books away and it would be like giving away a part of Peter himself. Caroline swallowed, resolving at the same time to keep at least a few of the books herself.

Having been into every room in the house, feeling that at any moment she might miraculously find Peter, hear his voice, see his smile, she went dejectedly into the kitchen and made herself a cup of tea. She felt out of place without Peter in the house, as if half the equation was missing, though she knew she must not use that as an excuse to flee to Brighton. Perhaps if she stayed on in Bath, waited for more time to go by, she would get over this awful feeling of not quite belonging anywhere, and would eventually settle in again. Life would go on. But did she want to do that? Would she be settling for second best, simply giving way to apathy?

I'll ring Rosie, she thought – that would be a distraction and her daughter's voice could take her away from her own rather depressing thoughts. She could use Peter's books as an excuse.

She picked up the phone and tapped out the number. 'I'm back!' she announced.

'Good,' Rosie said. 'Did you have a nice break?'

'Very pleasant,' Caroline said. 'I *do* like Brighton!' She said nothing more of how she was feeling now.

'Me too!' Rosie agreed. 'I used to love visiting Grandma and Grandpa. I still miss them.'

'So do I,' Caroline admitted.

'I was looking at Dad's books,' she continued. 'I wondered if you would like to have any of them?'

'I might, but only a few. As you know, I don't have the room.'

'OK, darling,' Caroline said. 'There's no desperate hurry. Come and have a look whenever it suits you.'

'Actually,' Rosie said, 'and nothing to do with the books – I had been thinking I might go down to Brighton for a few days. I still have some holiday to come. I wondered if perhaps you might like to be there at the same time?'

'That's a good idea,' Caroline said carefully. 'Or you could come to Bath and we could sort out the books,' she suggested. She didn't, as yet, want to go into all that was in her mind, and being together in Brighton it was bound to come up. Why am I being so secretive, she asked herself? And the answer was that Rosie would try to put her off. She would say it was too premature. Also, she didn't want to go into the likelihood of Rosie meeting Alec, with its inevitable outcome of a three-cornered discussion. One's grown-up children, with the best intentions in the world – and Rosie was no exception – tended to be on the cautious side when it came to their elders, especially if they loved them. Instead of 'Go for it, Mum!' they were more likely to say 'This requires a lot of thought . . . Have you considered . . . ?' And Caroline, as much as she could see that Rosie did have the best intentions, felt quite old enough to risk making her own decisions. 'We'll sort something out,' she said to Rosie.

'Whatever!' Rosie responded. 'But fairly soon, if that's OK with you.'

And then there was Doctor Meadows, Caroline thought later. She knew his reason for advising her to spend a few days in Brighton had been to encourage her to clear her mind, and to a certain extent it had done so, but only in as far as she had realized that there *were* other possibilities open to her. If she planned to stay on in Bath then that was all right, there was nothing to discuss, she would simply inform him, and thank him for his concern. If, on the other hand, she was likely to up sticks and leave him, then he had a right to know. She had worked for him for a long time now; they knew each other's ways. He wouldn't want to be rushed into finding a replacement at the last minute.

She was about to go to bed, have an early night, when the phone rang. It was Marion.

'We're having a few people for lunch on Sunday,' she said. 'Nothing special, probably a buffet, and in the garden if it's fine. I wondered if you'd like to join us? Please do, Caroline!'

Caroline dithered for a moment and then accepted, as

Marion was a good friend and it would probably be a fun day.

The next day, Saturday, did not turn out quite as Caroline had expected. All she had definitely planned was to go into the town and do some household shopping. It was a lovely morning to be out so she decided to walk in.

It was while she was walking along the street that she saw the estate agent's place and wandered over to have a quick look in the window. There were lots of properties under offer and some were houses similar to her own. What amazed her was how high the prices were for all of them, even the smallest. Intrigued, she decided to go into the agency and speak to someone in the know.

She waited a moment at the counter before a young man appeared from nowhere and stood in front of her.

'I'm Trevor Carter,' he said pleasantly. 'Can I help you, madam? Is there something you're particularly interested in?'

He was very young, with a spiky hairstyle. What, she thought, could he know about buying and selling houses? She would rather have been seen by the grey-haired, dark-suited man behind the counter who was deep in conversation with a young couple.

'I'm not thinking of buying,' Caroline said firmly, 'but it's possible I might want to sell my house. I wondered . . . ?'

He nodded, 'And you wondered what it would fetch?' he said. 'Shall we go into my office, and I'll take some details.'

She followed him into a very small office, about the size of a cupboard. 'I'm not totally sure,' she said as she took the chair he offered her, 'that I actually want to sell. At least . . .'

'I understand, madam,' he said. 'Naturally, you need a few facts before you can decide,' he said. 'So whereabouts is your house? I presume it's in or near to Bath?'

43

'Oh yes!' Caroline said. 'It's not far from here. Just off Great Pulteney Street.' She gave him the address.

'Oh, I know it!' he said. 'Well, not the actual house, but I know the road. It's a very good road, nice houses. Have you lived there long?'

'Twenty-seven years. And it *is* a nice house.'

'I would think it is,' he said, 'though naturally we'd need to come and see it before we could give you a specific figure.'

'Of course!'

'So what about Tuesday?' he asked. 'Tuesday morning?'

'I'm sorry,' Caroline said. 'I have to be at work. But I could be home by five o'clock.'

He made a swift call, nodded his head, then said, 'That's fine, if that suits you, Mrs Denby. Our Mr Proctor will be with you then.'

She felt pleased about that. 'Our Mr Proctor' sounded mature, experienced.

Sunday dawned fine, and already, in the early morning, warm. So it did look like lunch in the garden, Caroline thought. Marion would be pleased: she was a devoted gardener, no weed ever dared show its face on her not inconsiderable patch of ground. She would enjoy showing it off. And if 'Our Mr Proctor' is coming to view this house on Tuesday, Caroline decided, I must do a bit of tidying up in *my* garden, and in the house. Make a good impression. It seemed ridiculous on the face of it that the state of the garden and the order or disorder inside the house should influence the selling price, though, she reasoned, perhaps a well-kept appearance means a house has been cared for. And this one had: Peter had always seen to that, she thought sadly. Nothing had ever been left to deteriorate. Peter, even when he was quite ill, had kept an eagle eye on things, seen that everything was kept up to scratch.

She looked at the house afresh, trying to see it through the eyes of 'Our Mr Proctor' and concluded it really was rather messy. She began tidying up. It seemed a rather arduous and relentless task and she couldn't help but feel that this was because Peter was not here to urge her on, to chat to her while she tidied. Perhaps a change was needed after all . . .

Sunday lunch was rather as she had expected it to be. There were a dozen or so people there and she knew several of them. Marion came forward to greet her. She looked cool in a pale-green linen dress, her dark hair drawn back in a pony-tail. 'Caroline!' she said. 'How are you?' Without waiting to hear, she continued to speak. 'I thought as it's such a beautiful day we'd take advantage of it and eat in the garden. I've laid out a buffet in the dining room.' Small tables were placed around the garden. Marion, Caroline thought, was one of those people who, if they suddenly needed half a dozen garden tables and twenty garden chairs, would immediately have them to hand, and they would all be in good condition.

Nicholas, Marion's husband, appeared and put a Pimms into her hand. 'You're looking well,' he said. 'And very pretty.' And then he was on his way again, being the perfect host to everyone. Peter, she thought, had been like that, except that he preferred smaller gatherings, a few people around the dinner table. She had quite got out of the habit of giving dinners.

She did know almost everyone present, except that two regulars had today each brought a visitor with them, and there was a sixty-ish man walking around, viewing the flower borders. She had not seen him before. Aside from him, most of the people there were younger than she was. They had children still at school, or in a few cases, at university. She listened to accounts of their offspring, how well they had done at seemingly everything in the last year. Marion came across to where Caroline was sitting, the older man whom she had noticed earlier in tow. 'Caroline,' she said, 'I don't think you've met Gordon Parsons before, have you? He is a second cousin of Nicholas's – if that's the right description; I find family trees quite baffling. He's in Bath attending a conference.' She turned to the man. 'Gordon, Caroline is an old friend.' At that moment someone called out to her. 'I'm sorry,' she said. 'I think I'm needed in the dining room. I'll leave you two to get to know each other.'

'What is the conference about?' Caroline asked Gordon.

'Packaging!' he replied.

'Oh! I'm afraid I don't know much about packaging,' she said brightly. It was quite the wrong thing to have said.

'There's quite a lot to packaging,' he informed her – and twenty minutes later was still informing her: the cost of materials, labelling, the rise of blister packing; the necessary anti-theft devices he needed to employ. Why, she wondered? Who would want to steal packaging? She didn't interrupt the flow to ask him, since he was now engaged in a recital of his many triumphs in the packaging world. In amongst his revelations she gathered that he was a widower. 'My wife always used to come with me to the conferences,' he said. 'Of course, not to the actual presentations. She would go shopping with the other wives. Yes,' he continued, 'this is my very last conference. I'm due to retire shortly. I've been kept on longer because I know what I'm talking about.' He tapped the side of his head as if it were all stored under his grey thatch. Caroline thought that his wife had probably died of terminal boredom – and then she admonished herself for being so rude, even in thought. 'Yes,' he went on, 'packaging is important. There are so many sides to it, and I can tell you, I've come across them all!' And if I sit here any longer he'll describe the rest of them, Caroline thought.

'Will you excuse me for a minute?' she said out of desperation. 'I've spotted someone I need to speak to rather urgently.'

He rose to his feet in mid-sentence – something about polystyrene. 'Certainly!' he said.

She went to the bathroom, where, in the hope that Cousin Gordon would grow tired of waiting for her and would latch on to someone else, she spent an inordinate amount of time washing and drying her hands. Why am I at this party, she wondered? They were all nice people – give or take Cousin Gordon – but she no longer fitted into their world and she felt rather removed from most of them.

Later, once she had left, she reflected that she had found the whole party something of an ordeal. What is the matter with me, she thought? Am I deliberately cutting myself off from people?

The next morning she felt full of resolve to talk to Doctor Meadows about her future in Bath.

As it turned out, it was not possible for her to speak to him before his surgery started. He had been called out on an urgent case and arrived at the surgery fifteen minutes late for his first appointment. This would mean she'd have to wait until the end of his appointments, which was annoying as it gave her more time to lose her nerve completely. Finally he buzzed her through.

'So,' he said when she sat down in front of him, 'how did your few days in Brighton work out?'

'Quite well,' Caroline said carefully. 'They gave me a lot to think about, and I've come to a conclusion of sorts. Whether it's right or wrong, only time will tell.'

'That's usually the case,' he said. 'So what *is* your conclusion?'

'I've decided that I *will* leave Bath, and that I'll go to Brighton. Don't ask me for a rational explanation because I

47

don't think I've got one. It's just a gut feeling.'

'All right, I won't,' he promised, though you could see the surprise written all over his face. He looked at her carefully for some seconds, then he said, 'You've made a decision which might, or might not, turn out to be the right one – but in my opinion it's better to have made a decision than to have meandered on without doing so. And if it turns out to be the wrong one, well then, you simply reverse it! Well, perhaps not simply, but it's not the end of the world. Of course I shall be very sorry to see you go. I mean for my own sake. We've worked well together.'

'And I've enjoyed it,' Caroline said.

'Thank you,' he said. 'So what will you do in Brighton?'

'I don't truly know,' she confessed. 'Apart from converting the house, that is. But I will certainly want to find a job.'

'Then why not look for a job you're already good at?' he suggested. 'There are loads of medics in Brighton and Hove – Hove is awash with consultants, and they all need someone to look after them. And you can be sure I'll give you a good reference. In fact, I might be able to do better than that. I do know one or two people in Sussex – I mean people in the medical profession. When the time's ripe I'd be happy to have a word with them.'

'Thank you, that would be extremely kind,' Caroline said. 'I'll bear that in mind. And I'm grateful to you for everything. I shall be sad to leave the practice.'

She waited until early evening to phone Alec to tell him what she'd decided. For some reason or other, although she had his home number, she didn't have that of his mobile. A woman answered the phone. She had a pleasant, cheerful voice.

'I'm sorry,' she said. 'Alec isn't in. Can I give him a message?'

'Oh yes, um, if you could get him to call Caroline about the house,' Caroline said, suddenly flustered, and gave the woman her number. As she put her phone down, her curiosity was piqued – who was the woman on the phone?

FIVE

The time has come, thought Caroline, to tell Rosie what I'm up to. It wasn't fair not to. She should have mentioned it long before this but she had put it off, knowing it wouldn't be easy. Rosie had doted on her father; she had always been a Daddy's girl. She is likely to think I'm deserting him, Caroline told herself: much in the way I felt when I gave away his clothes. But of course it wasn't like that. She would take Peter with her wherever she went. He would always be part of her life.

Perhaps I'll ring Rosie tomorrow, she thought. Perhaps I'll leave it for now. She was struggling against what she knew would be a cowardly decision when the phone rang. It *was* Rosie. I will tell her now. It has to be done and I will get it over.

'I want to come down to Bath this weekend,' Rosie said when the preliminaries of how are you and what's the weather like there were over. 'But, unfortunately, I'm involved in another conference so it won't be possible. But I'll get down as soon as I can.'

'That's all right,' Caroline said. 'It will be lovely to see you whenever, darling.'

They chatted about this and that, though Caroline could not concentrate on what Rosie was saying. Her head was full of what she had herself wanted to say. It was uncanny, she thought, that just when she had been thinking about Rosie, there she was on the line – as if it was meant to be. All the time Rosie was chattering away Caroline was thinking, now is the moment. It will be easier on the phone. Shorter. She waited for a space in the conversation but when it didn't come she took a deep breath and plunged in, trying to keep her voice normal, as though what she had to say was an everyday announcement. 'I'm really looking forward to seeing you,' she heard herself saying. 'I have an idea I'd like to discuss with you.' And that is not totally true, she reproached herself. Not any longer. She had made her decision. She had told Doctor Meadows she would be leaving her job, and come Tuesday she might well put up her house for sale.

'Oh yes?' Rosie said amiably. 'So what is it?'

Caroline took a deep breath; when her voice came it sounded almost normal, as if she were announcing a small, everyday decision, like redecorating the sitting room and buying new curtains. 'The thing is,' she said quickly, 'I'm considering moving to Brighton permanently. Selling this house and going to live in Grandma and Grandpa's house. I thought maybe I would have it properly converted into two flats, live in one of them myself, and let the other.' There was a moment's silence between them, before Rosie found her voice.

'*Leave Bath?*' she said. 'You *did* say "leave Bath"?'

'I did,' Caroline said. This was not going to be easy.

'What in the world . . . and why so suddenly?'

'It's not as sudden as it sounds,' Caroline said. 'I've been thinking of it on and off for a while now.'

'But you never said anything! Why didn't you mention it?' Rosie demanded.

'Because at first I wasn't sure,' Caroline admitted, 'but I've given it a great deal of thought, I really have, and I've come to the conclusion that it would be a good idea. And of course, I have the house in Brighton.'

'But for ages your life has been in Bath,' Rosie said. 'Since before I was born. Not that Brighton is the far side of the earth, but all your friends are in Bath. Is this a wise move, do you think? It all seems too quick to me. And what would Dad say?'

'If your father were here, we wouldn't be having this conversation, would we? But he's not, and he won't be. And friends are friends, but they don't take his place. And who is to say I wouldn't make friends in Brighton? I've lived more of my life in Brighton than I have in Bath. And you and I have both said, many times, how much we liked it.'

'Of course we do, Mum!' There was a touch of restrained impatience in Rosie's voice. 'It *is* a lovely place, but you've never talked about going back there. As I said, this is all a bit sudden. More than a bit.'

'I'm sorry if this is how it seems,' Caroline said. 'And I haven't just thought about it in the last ten minutes. It's been in my mind for some time.'

'Then I wish you'd mentioned it earlier,' Rosie said. 'We could at least have talked it over.'

'Perhaps I should have,' Caroline agreed. 'I think if I'd seen you I would have. But I've done so now.'

'You have!' Rosie said indignantly. 'And I'm not madly happy about it. And I'm not sure you will be when it comes to leaving your lovely house in Bath. But I'll come down as soon as I can, and we'll discuss it. It's not the same over the phone. And what about your job, for instance? You love your job!'

'I do,' Caroline said, 'but I daresay I'll find another. There are probably as many doctors in Brighton and Hove as there are in Bath. And I'm not without experience.'

'Well, you seem to have thought it all out,' Rosie said belligerently, 'but please don't do anything too rash. I am thinking of you. I do care about you and I want what's best for you.'

'I know you do, darling,' Caroline agreed, trying to pour oil on troubled waters.

'So keep in touch – I'll ring you during the week, and I'll get down to Bath as soon as I can.'

Once she had put down the phone Caroline was aware that she hadn't told Rosie that she had already spoken to the estate agent and he would be coming to value the house. It wasn't deliberate. The conversation hadn't taken that turn and while they'd been on the phone she hadn't given a thought to that particular development. But she would tell her when they spoke during the week. She wished she could see her. It would be so much easier.

Alec phoned back, as she had expected he would. 'I've made up my mind,' she told him. 'Well, almost. In fact I called in the local estate agent's on Saturday, just to suss out the position about selling the house here. He's coming to see me and he'll take a look at the house and give me a possible price.'

'My goodness!' Alec said. 'You haven't been letting the grass grow under your feet, have you? But do be a bit cautious, give yourself time to think.'

'Oh, I will,' she said. 'And I have.' How much longer do I need, she asked herself? She had considered it from every possible angle, or so it seemed to her. It had filled her mind to the extinction of almost everything else and she didn't know what more there was to think about. What remained now was to make a decision, one way or another. 'You sound like my daughter,' she said. 'She's just been on the phone to me.'

'And she didn't approve?'

'She didn't say that in so many words, but I reckon she thinks I'm mad.'

'I expect she's concerned for you,' Alec said. 'Anyway, don't feel you have to give me a quick answer. I shall have the estimate ready in the next few days; I'm just waiting for some figures. But we can put the whole idea on hold if that would suit you better. Or even forget about it altogether.'

'Oh, I'm not going to do the latter!' Caroline said firmly. 'I'm definitely going to explore the possibilities. In fact, I had been thinking I might come down this weekend and go through things with you. Would that be convenient for you? I'm sorry it has to break into your weekend but we're very busy in the surgery – people on holiday and so on – and I can't get the time off during the week.'

'That's all right,' Alec said. 'Whenever it suits you. And in the meantime would you like me to send you a copy of the estimate when it's completed? But I will need at some stage to walk around the house as we discuss it, point out physically what I have in mind.'

'Of course you will, and so shall I,' Caroline agreed. 'And if you could put it in the post then that would be fine. I could have a preliminary look, before I come to Brighton.'

'I'll do that,' Alec said. 'And perhaps you'll confirm about coming to Brighton?'

'Right!'

On Tuesday she was home at ten minutes to five. It had been a busy day in the surgery and she had done a double shift. She had hardly spoken to Doctor Meadows and certainly not about anything personal. In between surgeries he had been out on visits. Now she bustled around the house, making sure that everything was shipshape and tidy for 'Our Mr Proctor', who arrived at five minutes past five. He was a short, round man with a ready smile. He listened while she told him briefly what she had in mind. 'Though of course nothing's settled,' she said. 'I just need to go into the pros and cons.'

'Of course you do,' he said. 'That's the wise thing to do. So shall we make a start? Shall we begin at the top and work down?'

He went with her into every room, but spent very little time in any of them. That done, he walked around the garden and looked at the outside of the house. It was all over much more quickly than she had thought possible. They went back into the house and sat down in the kitchen.

'Well, Mrs Denby,' he said, 'it's a very nice house and I can see it's been kept in good condition. Houses in this area fetch a reasonable price – a good price, in fact. I would think . . .' He named a figure which astonished her. How pleased and proud Peter would have been, she thought. 'So perhaps you'd think it over and let us know what you want to do?' Mr Proctor said. 'It's a good time of year for selling. There are still a lot of visitors in Bath and will be for a few weeks yet. They're enjoying themselves and they think how nice it would be to live here. And I daresay, we'll find several people who are looking for a house like yours.'

'Well, that's encouraging,' Caroline said. 'I still haven't totally made up my mind, but the minute I do, whether it's one way or another, I'll get in touch with you.'

'Please do,' he said. 'I think we can get an excellent price for a house like this.'

In the evening Rosie rang her again.

'I just wanted to know you were OK,' Rosie said. 'I didn't want you to be too upset by anything I'd said, even if I do think you're moving a bit fast, and I *am* worried about you.'

'It was nice of you to ring,' Caroline said, mollified by Rosie's change in tack. 'And, in fact, in the spirit of keeping you in touch on everything, I do have a bit of news for you.

The estate agent came this afternoon to put a value on the house – I mean a selling price. You will never guess!' When she told her the figure there was an audible gasp at Rosie's end.

'Well,' her daughter said, 'you *are* moving rather quickly, but it is a decent price, more than I expected – though that's not to say you'll get it. But in any case, the money involved doesn't mean that the entire thing is a good idea. And you would have to make sure that you were getting a fair deal at the other end – I mean, whoever you found to do the conversion of Grandma's house.'

'Oh, I've already found someone!' Caroline announced. 'He was recommended to me by George Clarke. You and I both know how reliable George is. He recommended two people and I saw them both. The one I chose is far better than the other.'

'And do I get to meet him?' Rosie asked crossly. 'Or are you going to do the rest of this without reference to me?'

'Of course you can meet him,' Caroline replied calmly. 'I shall probably go down to Brighton at the weekend but you can't go with me because of your conference, otherwise I'd have suggested it. I only made the arrangement yesterday. But do let me know when you can go with me, so that I can tell Alec and make sure you can meet.'

'Alec?'

'The builder,' Caroline said. 'That's his name. You'll like him.' She wasn't sure Rosie would. She was probably determined not to. But at least she was now keeping her in the picture.

'I'll come to Bath as soon as I possibly can,' Rosie said rather sharply. 'The way you're rushing at things, who knows how many more times I'll have the chance? Bath is my home, remember!'

Caroline took a deep breath, then answered as quietly and as calmly as she could. 'No, Rosie, it isn't! It was, but you left to go to university and after that you never lived here. By choice – and quite rightly in my view. You started a new life. Your home is in London, and you're happy there. I'm pleased you think so fondly of Bath and you're happy to visit, but you know perfectly well you'd never come back to live here. You've moved on. And now I want to move on. Do you understand that?'

There was a long silence at Rosie's end of the phone, during which Caroline said nothing. Then, at last, Rosie spoke.

'It's just that I'm anxious about you,' she said finally. 'I don't want you to do something silly and then live to regret it.'

Caroline shook her head. 'I would be more likely to regret that I hadn't explored it,' she said.

'I want you to be happy, Mum,' Rosie said quietly. 'Of course I do. And I want you to be safe, even more so now that you're on your own. I know you'll be safe in Bath. I know you'll have friends to turn to. You won't know a soul in Brighton.'

'I know George and Emmie Clarke,' Caroline reminded her. 'They'll always look out for me if need be. But what makes you think I won't find friends in Brighton? Of course I will! I'm not in my dotage, not by a long chalk. I shall get a job, meet new people. There's no shortage of things to do in Brighton.'

'Well, I grant you that,' Rosie said. 'And I can see you've made up your mind . . .'

Caroline interrupted her. 'I haven't. Not yet. But I want the privilege of making up my own mind. And I'll be happy to consult with you all along the way. So now, Rosie love, just let me know when you're coming and I'll be delighted to see you.'

'Truly, Mum,' Rosie said, 'all I want is for you to be happy.'

'Thank you, darling. And I will be.'

'And promise you'll keep in touch. No matter what you say, I'm concerned about you.'

'I appreciate that, darling,' Caroline said. 'And of course I'll keep you up to date on everything, but you must allow me to do what I think is best for me. After all, it's not as though I'm going to be homeless in Brighton, is it? I do have the house there.'

'I can't stop you doing what you want, even if I do think you're mad – and certainly far too impulsive – but I just don't want you to do something you'll regret.'

'I don't think that will happen,' Caroline said.

The strange thing was, she thought later that evening, that her conversation with Rosie had made her quite certain that Brighton was where she wanted to be. And Peter had always loved Brighton. She would ring the estate agent the next day. So, goodbye, Bath, I shall never forget you – and hello, Brighton! And she was guiltily pleased that Rosie wouldn't be able to join her that weekend. She would be free to discuss things with Alec, go into details of the estimate and so on, without opposition – though that was perhaps too strong a word.

Mr Proctor was not slow to move. On Thursday he phoned to say that he had a client who was very interested in viewing the house, and would that afternoon be convenient? They were in Bath only for a short stay.

'Absolutely!' Caroline said. 'I could be home from one thirty onwards. In fact,' she added, 'I was going to ask you about viewing. I work different shifts and I can't always be here when you might want me. Would it be all right for you to have a key and to show people around when I'm not here? And would you yourself do it?'

'Of course!' he said. 'I'd make a point of that. And of

course I'd always phone you, at home or at work, before-hand.'

'Good!' Caroline said.

She rushed home from work at lunch time and was there ten minutes before Mr Proctor arrived with a middle-aged man and his wife. They went over every foot of the house, climbing up to the attic and down to the basement, seem-ingly pleased with everything, though they asked very few questions. When they left, Mr Proctor said, 'I'll be in touch, Mrs Denby!'

He phoned her later that afternoon. 'Sorry!' he said. 'No joy this time! Too many stairs, the wife said. It's usually the wife who decides. But no matter. It's early days and I'm very hopeful.'

On the Friday, Alec's estimate for the conversion of the house in Brighton arrived in the post, just as Caroline was leaving for the surgery. She was then frantically busy all morning and once work was over she couldn't get away fast enough. As soon as she was home she examined the estimate and was pleased by what Alec had proposed. As she studied it she walked, in her mind, around her parents' house. She looked forward to doing it in reality.

SIX

Caroline arrived in Brighton at half past five. It being Friday afternoon, the roads had been busier than usual. Going in, the house felt airless and before doing anything else she went around opening windows, her mind wandering as it so often did when she was there to her parents. They had spent some of the happiest years of their lives here, and they deserved those years, for they'd been good parents and she'd been close to them. Certainly she had been closer to them, and they to her, than she had been to Rosie. She wondered where she had gone wrong with Rosie, but even as she wondered she realized it was simply that she was not Peter.

At six thirty Alec arrived and they started at the top of the house and went into each room in turn, looking at everything with the view in mind of making a good flat, then they came downstairs and walked around what would be her domain. She made some coffee, and she and Alec sat at the table with the plans and estimates spread out before them.

'In my part of the house,' Caroline said, 'which must be the ground floor because I don't want to give up the garden – my father was fond of his garden – I want my living room as large as possible. I'm happy with the other rooms being small; I don't need this large kitchen or a big bathroom.' She broke off, noticing the look on his face. 'Oh dear!' she said. 'I should have mentioned this sooner, shouldn't I? How very stupid of me!'

'You should,' Alec agreed. 'It will make a difference. I don't mean it can't be done, but it will mean allotting the space quite differently.'

'I'm sorry!' Caroline said, embarrassed. 'I must be mad.'

'Well, at least you've thought of it before we've actually started,' he said. 'So, is there anything else? We need to know.'

'Well,' she said. 'I do need a second bedroom. I hope to have people stay from time to time, most particularly my daughter, Rosie. She works in London. I hope she'll come often, though I have to say she's very much against my coming here.'

'That's a pity,' Alec said. 'Perhaps she'll feel differently when she sees you installed, and happy.'

'Let's hope so. I think it's to do with her strong attachment to her father. They loved each other to bits.'

They pored over the plans for a while.

'Everything seems great,' Caroline said after a while. 'The only thing is . . .' She sighed. 'I do so wish the house were nearer to the sea. It's a stupid thing to say, isn't it, but there's no point anywhere in it from which I can get even a glimpse of the sea. I know there was no sea in Bath, I didn't even think about it, but Bath is Bath and Brighton is Brighton. I was brought up close to the sea; I saw it every day of my life. I wanted to get back to it but of course it will be a bus ride away.'

Alec shook his head. 'I'm sorry . . .' he began.

'I know,' she said. '*I'm* sorry, and I'm being stupid. But one can't have everything, and I've said my say. And it *is* a nice house; it will be wonderful when it's all done.'

'Are you unhappy about leaving Bath?' Alec asked.

'Surprisingly I'm not. Of course there are things I shall miss, and a few people, but I'm looking forward to Brighton. And the good news is that the estate agent thinks I might not have to wait long for a buyer. So the minute I get one I shall move to Brighton, even if you're still working on this house. I really would like to finalize things. In any case, I'll need some of the money to pay for the conversion. I want it to be a good one. I want the upstairs flat to be good also.'

'That's where quite a bit of the money will have to go,' Alec said. 'There are very few facilities there at the moment.'

'And then as soon as I move to Brighton I shall look for a job. Part-time,' Caroline said. She told him what her job was in Bath. 'My boss doesn't think I'll have much difficulty in finding something similar here,' she added.

They talked on and on and time seemed to fly by until Alec glanced at his watch and rose to his feet. 'Well, then,' he said, 'I'll leave you to it. When will you be down again?'

'I can't be sure,' Caroline said, a little sad he was leaving. 'It will depend on who's coming to look at the house, and when. I can't leave it all to Mr Proctor. But I'll be down every weekend I can. I'm afraid it will have to be weekends because of my job.'

'I'll look forward to seeing you whenever it is,' Alec said. 'Just give me a ring.'

'I will,' Caroline promised. Then, she hesitated a moment before blurting, 'Doesn't your wife mind you working at weekends? Or is she used to it?'

Alec smiled. 'She's not my wife. I'm not married. I was once, but not now.'

'I'm sorry . . .' Caroline said.

'It was a long time ago,' Alec said. 'We were both young, far too young, though in fact we'd known each other most of our lives, we'd been at school together, always lived in Whitby.'

62

So that was where his slight accent came from, Caroline thought. She'd recognized it as northern, though it was softer, less harsh than some other northern accents.

'It was more or less expected we'd marry, eventually,' Alec continued. 'But we jumped the gun and Jenny was pregnant. I was nineteen, Jenny was eighteen. We got married before the baby was born.'

'So you have a child?'

'A son. Jack, after Jenny's father. No longer a child, of course. He's in his mid-twenties.'

'So where . . . ?' Caroline began, but he interrupted her.

'I don't know where he is. Just before his third birthday Jenny went off with another man and took Jack with her. I didn't try to get him back, though my mother wanted me to. She would have looked after him. But I thought, and I still do, that when it comes to the pinch a child's place is with its mother.'

'And do you ever hear from him?' Caroline asked, feeling suddenly sorry for Alec.

'Not any longer,' Alec said, his face stricken. 'They emigrated to Australia. I think Jenny's parents kept in touch, and my mother had the occasional Christmas card.' He paused, then said, 'I suppose I could be a grandfather by now!' He smiled at the thought. 'Imagine it! A grandfather at forty-six!'

'Nothing wrong with that,' Caroline said, smiling. 'I'd be happy to be a grandmother, but Rosie shows no inclination to make me one!'

'But at least you'd know if she did, I mean if you were. Sorry!' he added. 'Listen to me rambling on. I don't mean to sound sorry for myself. Anyway, I'd probably not have been any good at it.'

'*I'm* sorry,' Caroline said. 'I shouldn't be asking all these questions.'

'That's all right,' Alec said. 'And to complete the family

saga, my mother's still alive and I have two younger brothers, still in Whitby. My dad died a few years ago. I go up to see my mother – not as often as I should – but I'd never go back to live there. Nothing wrong with Whitby, but mine was a fishing family – my dad had his own boat – and I never liked the fishing life. I wasn't cut out for it. It needs to be in your bones and it never was in mine.'

'So, unlike me, you don't have this desire to be by the sea?' Caroline asked.

'Actually, I do,' Alec admitted. 'Which I suppose is why I eventually ended up in Brighton. But that's another story. I'm sorry, I shouldn't be going on like this. I don't usually.'

'Don't apologize,' Caroline said. She realized how much she enjoyed listening to him.

'Paula, the woman on the phone, is my girlfriend,' he said. 'We've been friends for some time now. She's a photographer, freelance. She works for local newspapers and magazines. Occasionally she gets something in the nationals. She also photographs local bands for the entertainment bit of magazines. Her main claim to fame right now is that she's the photographer for the Sledges. Have you heard of them?'

'I'm sorry, I haven't,' Caroline admitted.

'Nor had I,' Alec said. 'Not my kind of music. But apparently the kids are crazy about them. Well, that's what Paula does, and she's good at it.'

'She sounds interesting,' Caroline said, choosing her words carefully.

'She is,' Alec agreed. 'And now I must be off, if you'll excuse me. I have another call to make before I finish. When are you leaving?'

'I thought on Sunday, after an early lunch,' she said. 'But there's nothing hard and fast about it.'

'Right,' Alec said. 'And if I get the catalogues tomorrow

I'll drop them in on you on Sunday morning. I'll be here around ten. If not, I'll put them in the post.'

Shortly after ten o'clock that evening, the phone rang. She thought it would be Rosie – who else knew she was here? – but to her surprise it was Alec.

'I'm sorry to ring so late,' he said, 'but I have had an idea which I'd like to put to you and I don't want to do it on the phone. I know I'm due to see you on Sunday, but would it be possible for me to come around tomorrow morning?'

'Of course!' Caroline said. 'But I'm happy to listen now. You're not interrupting anything.'

'If you don't mind, I'd rather see you,' Alec said. 'It would be easier to explain. Would around ten o'clock be OK?'

'Fine!' Caroline agreed, suddenly feeling inexplicably happy. 'And once again, I *am* sorry I messed up the plans.' That, she told herself firmly, she thought, was what he wanted to talk about.

'Please don't be,' he said. 'I'll see you in the morning.'

The next morning the sun streamed through all the windows. It really was a beautiful day and Caroline stood at the kitchen window admiring the majestic horse-chestnut tree which had always given her mother such pleasure. 'It changes so beautifully over the seasons,' she had said. 'One colour after another! It makes washing up a pleasure!'

Her reverie was interrupted by the sound of the doorbell. It would be Alec.

'I can't help thinking,' she said as she let him in, 'that my stupidity is causing problems, and that's why you're here to see me.'

'It wasn't stupidity,' Alec said. 'And it can all be dealt with. But it *was* something you said.' He followed her into the kitchen and they sat at the table.

'So what is it, this new idea?' she asked.

'Prepare yourself,' Alec said. 'It won't be what you expect, but at least listen to it.'

She looked at him, puzzled. 'Of course I'll listen,' she said.

He looked more than a mite uncomfortable. 'What I'm about to suggest is a radical change of plan,' he warned her, 'but hear me out.'

'Of course,' she agreed with some trepidation, wishing he would come to the point.

'By your own admission,' Alec said, 'you really don't like the situation of this nice house, do you? And whatever's done to it, you won't. It's going to cost quite a bit of money to carry out everything you have in mind for it – and even when it's done, and all the money's been spent on it, it won't be your ideal place to live.'

'I daresay you're right,' Caroline acknowledged. She had no idea where he was going. 'But I don't have a better idea.'

'In fact, I do,' Alec said. 'It came to me when I'd left you yesterday, and I've really given it a lot of thought.'

'And?'

There was a pause before he replied, then he said, 'My advice to you – though it's only my opinion and you're free to reject it out of hand, but please at least think about it – is that if you intend to come to live in Brighton, it might be best to sell this house more or less as it stands, and go for something which is in the place you really want to be.'

She stared at him in disbelief. 'Look for another house?' she said. 'Are you serious? You can't be!'

He nodded. 'Yes, I am! Oh, I know this is a good house, a pleasant house – there's no denying that, but from your point of view whatever you do to it, however much time and money you spend on it, in the end it won't satisfy you, will it? Be honest!'

'I can't quite . . .' she began. 'I never thought . . .'

66

She had given so much thought to what she would do to her parents' house, to how they would have loved the idea of her living in it, and now Alec, whom she hardly knew, was suggesting that she should abandon it. 'I had set my mind on a new beginning,' she said. 'This was to be it.'

'But that's part of the problem. It wouldn't be, would it?' he reasoned. 'Not really. You would be taking on something which happened to be there, which you had inherited, something chosen by your parents, which you yourself might not have chosen. The house, maybe – but not where it is. The place is where your parents wanted to be and in your heart you don't. Isn't that the truth?'

'So you're saying . . .' she began.

'I'm *suggesting*,' Alec said, 'and not totally easily because I don't know you all that well and I haven't the right, that at this point in your life you should do what will give you what you really and truly want in the end – a place to live in Brighton which is within sight of the sea. Isn't that the reason you wanted to come here?'

'It's one of them,' Caroline conceded. She had been wonderfully happy with Peter, she would have wished that to continue to the end, but that life was no longer possible. Nor did she – and she had seen it happen with friends and acquaintances – intend to make a profession of being a widow. 'But even if I was prepared to do what you suggest,' she said, 'I'm not at all sure how I'd begin. It seems so daunting.'

'Oh, you'd find the way!' Alec said. 'And that brings me to the next bit of my suggestion – about which I'm extremely embarrassed.'

'Why?' Caroline asked.

'Well,' he began – then broke off.

'Do go on,' Caroline said.

'The thing is,' he said, 'I know of a house in Kemp Town. A Regency house, four storeys plus a basement. When the last owner died – it had been a family home until then – it was put on the market and was snapped up by a man whose intention was to convert it into four, possibly five, flats for letting. I don't know if you've been to Kemp Town recently, but this has happened a lot.'

'I know the kind of houses you mean,' Caroline said. 'They're beautiful, though I've never been inside one.'

'And they remain beautiful,' Alec said. 'And quite rightly, there are strict rules about what can and what can't be done to them.'

'And the house you're talking about,' Caroline prompted him. 'What's the story there? I mean, since it was bought by the present owner?'

'Sad,' Alec said. 'Though I daresay a not uncommon one. The man set out on the conversion and before it was completed or ready to take tenants, he ran out of money. He hadn't done his sums properly – not uncommon with people buying property.'

'So are you actually suggesting,' Caroline said slowly, 'that I should buy this house – and then, I suppose, finish the conversion and let the flats? Because if you are, I don't have that kind of money, nor even a smidgeon of the expertise. It would be beyond me on both counts.'

'Whoever does buy the house is likely to get a bargain,' Alec said. 'The owner needs a quick sale: he still has bills to pay in connection with the conversion so far. There's not a great deal left to do to it and what's done has been well done.'

'Who did the conversion?' Caroline asked.

Alec looked decidedly uncomfortable. 'That's the most embarrassing part,' he admitted. 'I did. And that's the reason why I found it difficult to put the idea to you. In fact, I almost didn't, but in the end I changed my mind because it seemed it might be exactly right for you. I was struck by your strong misgivings about the position of this house. I thought it might, just might, interest you. Anyway, I thought I should tell you.'

There was a longish silence, broken, in the end, by Alec. 'I'm sorry,' he said, looking awkward. 'I'm being too presumptuous. You don't know me at all. I could be leading you up the garden path.'

Caroline nodded. That was true of course. He could. She didn't think he would be, but that was only a feeling and this was no time for being naïve. 'But that's not the only thing,' she said, 'where on earth would I find the money to buy a house like that, and then pay for the conversion to be completed?'

'You know best about that,' Alec said. 'I couldn't judge. But I know you would have two houses to sell and if the house in Bath is anything like your parents' house, then they are both good ones. You might also be able to get a loan. The money would come back to you when you let the flats – and I've no doubt you'd be able to do that. It's a good area.'

'And would you expect to be in charge of the conversion?' she asked. 'I mean, if I were to go ahead – which I must say seems a large undertaking for me.'

'I wouldn't expect it at all,' Alec said. 'I would be happy to be considered, but happier still if you made it your business to find out something more about me. In fact, I would prefer you to do so. Start from the beginning, so to speak; as you would with anyone else who was in line for doing a big job for you. Naturally, I would give you references – people I've done work for, including the present owner of the house. I've been in this sort of business for a few years now. And of course I'll give you a bank reference. And I would want you to take up every one of them. Even so,' he added, 'don't consider any of it if you don't want to.'

'Oh, I'll think about it,' Caroline said. 'I'll certainly do that.'

'In the meantime,' he added, 'would you like to see the

house? Would it help? I have a key. But don't say yes if you'd rather not.'

Caroline thought for a moment. She was not inclined to rush, the whole idea was so new to her and she felt slightly nervous about it, but on the other hand what harm was there in seeing the property? If nothing else, she could judge if it was, indeed, where she would want to live.

'Why not?' she said. 'But what would I do about all this?' She indicated the plans and estimates on the table.

'Whatever you wished to do,' Alec said. 'If you want my opinion and you did decide to sell it then I wouldn't go to the expense of converting it. I'd spend a bit of money on doing it up, sand and polish the floors on this level, a lick of paint here and there, and so on. Put in a new bathroom. Then I'd market it as a family house. It's in a prime position for that with the park and two schools near by.'

She was silent for a minute, not sure what to say, which way to go.

'Then since you're going back to Bath tomorrow afternoon, would you like to see the house today?' Alec asked. 'This afternoon, perhaps – or even right now if that suits you better.'

'I think this afternoon,' she said. It would give her a little more time to think, to come down to earth and collect her thoughts. At the moment she felt as if she were perched on a cloud, high above everything, and where nothing seemed real.

'That's fine,' Alec said smiling. 'Shall I pick you up around two o'clock?'

SEVEN

Caroline answered the door at almost the same moment as Alec pressed on the bell push. She had been standing by the window, eagerly watching for his arrival, though her eagerness was tinged with apprehension and more than a small degree of doubt. Was she doing the right thing? Or was she quite mad? But even as she went to the door, having seen him park his car, she told herself firmly that all she was doing at this point was going to look at a property. She need do nothing more than that and she was quite open-minded about it all. In a way that was true, though she knew that in her heart she was already leaning towards something more decisive. It was exciting, as well as intimidating.

'I'm glad it's a fine day,' Alec said, climbing into the car. 'You'll see the place at its best.'

'Though in a way,' Caroline said as she fastened her seatbelt, 'it might be even better to see a place at its worst: stormy weather, pouring rain and so on. Anyway, I'm looking forward to this though I'm determined to look at it with a critical eye and a cool head.'

'I wouldn't want you to do otherwise,' Alec said.

He drove down the busy London road and through the

Steine, then, turning left to drive to Kemp Town, waited patiently while a large group of overseas students streamed over the crossing, chattering and laughing, so full of life, so happy to be in a new country. While she sat there her eye was caught by what she still thought of as the aquarium, though it was now called something like 'Sea Life'. 'I used to love going to the aquarium,' she told Alec as he drove off again, 'but never on my own. It was very dark, and scary, with all those weird-looking fishes and sea creatures. Have you ever been there?'

'No,' Alec admitted. 'Maybe I should try it?'

'I suppose, next to being a child, and you're too late for that, then the next best thing is to take one,' Caroline said. 'Perhaps you could borrow one?'

He drove along, the sea on his right and now almost at high tide, and to his left the long stretch of what he thought of as the most beautiful line of houses he had ever seen in any city except perhaps London. He said as much to Caroline.

'Or Bath,' she replied.

'Perhaps,' he conceded. 'Though here one has the sea as well.' It looked particularly good today, sparkling in the afternoon sun, reflecting the brightness of the sky.

He took a left turn, not far short of Lewes Crescent. 'We're almost there,' he said.

The streets here ran at absolute right angles to the sea-front and were criss-crossed further back by streets which ran parallel to the sea, as if it had all been mapped out to the last yard – which perhaps it had, Caroline thought. Much of it, her father had told her, had been built by one man – hence its name, 'Kemp Town'. Some of the parallel streets were home to all kinds of small shops, nothing at all of any size. It was another world from the centre of the city, though less than a mile away.

'It's a matter of finding a place to park,' Alec said as

he drove around slowly. 'It always is. No garages to speak of. This area wasn't built for cars. Everything's parked in the street.' He slowed down, approaching another corner, then gave a sudden whoop of delight. 'Down there!' he said. 'Right where we want it to be.' He drove forward and manoeuvred carefully into the space.

Caroline got out of the car and looked around. Alec locked the car and joined her. It was a pleasant street, lined on both sides with trees set near to the edges of the pavement at regular intervals. Alec parked about a third of the way from the bottom of the street, in front of a tall white house which was one of a short row of three almost the same, all with semicircular bay windows. 'Is this it?' Caroline asked. 'It looks lovely!'

'No,' Alec said. 'Number seventeen is on the other side of the road, exactly opposite to where we're standing. But from here you get the best view of the outside of the house.'

It was one of two almost identical houses standing very close to each other. She was slightly disappointed, at first, that it didn't have the striking bay windows of the house behind her. It, and the neighbouring house, were flat-fronted, with a double column of large windows rising up to four storeys high, under a level roof. And then her eye was caught by the elegant black-painted, intricately wrought iron railings fronting the narrow balcony which ran across the width of the house at first-floor level. Why was it always called first-floor level when it was a storey up from the ground, she asked herself? But never mind that, she thought. It was quite beautiful – though whether the balcony served any purpose other than decorative she was not sure. At this distance it seemed quite narrow.

In front of number seventeen, separating the house from the narrow pavement in front of it, was a low wall, and at the end of the wall steps led down to what was the basement. Looking along the street it was obvious that this was the case with every house. 'The tradesmen's entrance,' Alec said. 'The front door for family and friends, the basement door for the butcher and the baker – not that it would be called a basement now. In estate agents' speak it's the "lower ground floor". And, in fact, just about every house in the street has a lower-ground-floor flat either let or for sale! You can also get down to it from a door in the hall.' That number seventeen had at one time had someone living in the lower part of the house was apparent from the fact that a small garden of sorts had been made, though the space from the house to the wall was no more than six feet across, and paved over. It was a garden of pots and containers, the plants in them now neglected; dead or dying. And to extend the garden every foot of the surrounding wall had been utilized for hanging plants or baskets. 'It was very pretty earlier in the summer,' Alec said, 'quite a feature, but it's had no attention since then. Shall we go in? I have the front-door key, and one to the basement.'

'Then let's go in by the front door,' Caroline said, wanting to see the house at its best.

The door was impressive: heavy, solid, with a fanlight over it. It was painted black, with an imposing brass door knob and letter box. She felt a thrill, almost physical, as Alec held open the door for her to go before him into the house. It was as if she belonged here – which of course was ridiculous, she told herself, and she must not let such ideas go to her head. They stood now in a long hall, generously wide in this first part, and within eight feet of the front door an elegant stair-case rising on the right. The ceiling was high, with moulded cornices, and on the left of the hall, a few feet from where they stood, was a closed door. 'That's to the drawing room,' Alec said. 'The dining room is further back and the kitchens and so on beyond that. Let's look round now. I think if we go from bottom to top that would be best.'

The basement flat was small, taking up no more than half

the space, the rest being given over to utility rooms. One was fitted as a laundry, another a storeroom. There were closets, and various cupboards. 'You'll see,' Alec said, 'that the basement flat has at some stage already been converted. It has all the necessary services. Of course it will need smartening up and decorating.'

'But it would be somewhere for me to camp out, so to speak, while I was waiting for my own bit of the house to be made ready,' Caroline said. 'And it's quite pleasant.'

'You'd have no difficulty at all in letting it,' Alec said. 'When you're ready, and probably to a single person.'

Leaving the basement, they climbed to the ground floor. 'From here on up,' Alec told her, 'each floor is one flat, amply large enough for two or three people, and the flats are more or less identical with each other. And in every case the basic work has been done – walls, wiring, plumbing. What remains to be done is fitting up the kitchens, bathrooms, and of course all the decorating, all the usual finishing things, which I daresay you'd like a hand in choosing.'

'Oh, I would like that,' Caroline agreed. 'That's something I've always been interested in.'

They were on the first floor now. The moment they entered the room at the front of the house Caroline rushed out on to the balcony. 'The sea!' she cried. 'Oh, isn't it just so beautiful! And so calm!'

'But not always so calm,' Alec said. 'As I know you're aware.'

'Oh, I am!' she agreed. 'But I love the sea whatever it's like.' And here, she thought, I would be able to see it in its every mood: sunny, flat calm, turbulent and angry. There it was and always would be. She wondered how many people, since the house was built, had stood on this spot and watched the sea. In the end, she turned and went back into the house and to the next level, identical in layout, but without the balcony.

75

'And now for the top floor,' Alec said. 'I guess you'll like that. It being the attic, the room at the moment isn't up to much, but the view is wonderful.'

'How did you get into converting houses?' Caroline asked as they climbed the stairs, which here were narrower and steeper than in the rest of the house. 'Was it something you'd always had in mind?'

'Not really,' Alec answered. 'It was partly, as I told you before, that I was never cut out for the fishing, I didn't fit in with either the job or the life. It takes over the whole of life. You're at the mercy of the elements and you have to cope with what they dictate. But also I'd always been keen on designing and making things, mostly things around the house, and I wanted to do more of that kind of thing. I'd like to have gone to art school but it was never on the cards.'

They had reached the door at the top. When he opened it, it led into one large room, which was the whole of the top floor. It was light; there were four good windows, though not nearly as large as those in the rest of the house. The floor was covered in dark-brown linoleum which had seen better days and there were sundry pieces of furniture around: a washstand, a small table, two upright chairs, tea chests filled with who knew what. 'I expect once upon a time this was the servants' room,' Alec said. 'There were two single beds in here when I first saw it but the owner – his name is Frank Teasdale – took those away.'

'What's that door in the far corner?' Caroline asked. 'I mean, where does it lead?'

'I'll show you,' Alec said. 'And you'll like this bit!'

The door opened on to a small, square landing from which yet more stairs rose.

'Where . . . ?' Caroline began.

'To the roof. There's a flat roof, quite sizeable – and whoever lives in this top part of the house gets to use the roof because this is the only way up to it. Do you want to see it?'

'Of course I do,' Caroline said. 'Lead on!'

It was not simply a flat roof, an open space. A chimney stack rose in the middle of it and at one side there were two large water tanks. It was surrounded by a low stone wall, and what caught Caroline's eye was that in one corner a section of iron staircase led down, joining the ones from the other floors, to the small garden at the back of the house.

'But whoever has this top flat,' she said, 'could have the whole roof space as a garden!' She turned to Alec. 'That would be possible, wouldn't it?'

'Possibly,' he agreed. 'But you couldn't bring any depth of soil up here. It wouldn't take the weight.'

'But perhaps enough for one or two raised beds, and things in containers,' Caroline said excitedly. 'Like the garden of the basement flat, only on a larger scale.'

'I suppose so,' Alec said. 'It would be very windy. You'd get the full blast. And you know how the wind can blow in Brighton.'

'But one could build windbreaks,' Caroline pointed out. 'And choose suitable plants.' She could see it all. It was rapidly taking place in her mind's eye. A low table or two . . . a comfortable chair . . . drinks on a summer evening. And the view of the sea. And since the road ran gently uphill from the coast road to where number seventeen was situated she looked down now on the wide stretch of sea from the pier in the distance to her right to the marina on her left; and beyond that to the grass-covered tops of the chalk cliffs which extended to Rottingdean and beyond. Standing there, she felt herself on the same height as the seagulls which swooped and circled and called over the top of the cliffs.

'If I do go ahead,' she said, 'this is the bit of the house I'd want for myself. I know it's not as grand as the lower parts

77

– no ornamental cornices or elaborate ceilings, and the woodwork isn't as good – but it would suit me beautifully. I can imagine myself here. And I would definitely make a garden.'

Alec nodded, without speaking.

'Of course,' she continued, 'I would have to stop myself wasting time, just looking at the view!'

'So on the whole,' Alec said, 'you like the idea?'

'Oh, I do!' Caroline said. 'Much more interesting than converting my parents' house and, more importantly, in an area where I'd want to live. You were absolutely right about that. There's such an atmosphere here. I don't quite know how to describe it: perhaps as if its history still lives on, but without holding it back or separating it from the present.'

'I think I know what you mean,' Alec said.

'Of course there are things I'd have to ask. I have a lot of questions,' she said. 'It would be a big step for me to take and there's still a lot I don't know.'

'Quite right,' Alec said. 'You must ask about everything.'

'So what—' Caroline said, 'I mean, if you have the time right now, what if we went and got a cup of tea somewhere? Would that be OK?'

'Absolutely!' Alec said. 'I do have another job to go to, but not for an hour or so. And there's a small café in what they call the village. I used to go there most days when I was working on this house.'

'Great!' Caroline said. 'Let's go.'

They climbed back down the stairs. Again she noticed how the flight up to the top floor and then the roof were so steep and narrow, compared to the broad, shallow steps of the rest of the house. One style for the masters and a different one for the servants, she thought. But in this case she was willing to be with the servants, though how often had they had time to look at the view?

The café was not more than ten minutes' walk away, a

small, darkish place serving a variety of snacks. They settled for a pot of tea and toasted teacakes. 'So fire away!' Alec said. 'What can I tell you?'

'Well, first of all I have to tell you that I can't contemplate any of this until I've sold my house in Bath, and my parents' house also. I don't have enough money floating around.'

'That's OK,' Alec said. 'But you'll have to move quickly, otherwise you might lose the opportunity. The property hasn't been put on the market yet, but it will be quite soon and you could just miss it. In any case, if you came in now you might get an advantage on the price.'

'Of course,' Caroline said. 'And for my part I'd need to move in here as soon as I'd sold my parents' house. So how would I do that? I wouldn't want to be left high and dry.'

'Well, as you yourself said,' Alec replied, 'you could camp out in the basement flat until the top flat was ready. It might be a bit dusty and dirty, not to mention noisy, living down there while there was work going on in the house, but if you wouldn't mind that . . .'

'I'm sure I could put up with it,' Caroline said. 'And I'd really like to be around while the work was going on.'

'Very well then,' Alec said. 'So the next time you're down, and it would be as well to make that as soon as possible if you decide to go ahead and make an offer, we could go over things and work out exactly what you'd want and what it would be likely to cost.'

There was a pause in the conversation. Caroline poured more tea then, looking for something to say, asked, 'How long have you been in Brighton? Did you come straight here from Whitby?'

'Oh, no!' Alec said. 'I wanted to leave Whitby. It was no longer my world – and I wanted to see more of what I thought of as the real world. I'd seen very little, and I was free to go. So off I went – and a long way too. First I went to Canada. I had no difficulty in finding work there – odd jobs, a lot of them, and mostly in the construction business. I never stayed long in one place – Toronto, Calgary, Vancouver – I particularly liked Vancouver. Then I moved into the US – Seattle, Portland, Oregon, and then to San Francisco.'

'And did you make the proverbial fortune?' Caroline asked.

He smiled at that. 'No!' he said. 'But that didn't bother me. I got by. I might have been there yet, or who knows where, except that I got word that my mother was ill, so I went back to Whitby. I hadn't been home in five years. Thankfully, she recovered, and I'd got rid of some of my wanderlust by then, so I decided to stay on.'

'Did you go back into fishing?' Caroline asked.

'No way!' he said emphatically. 'I just took whatever jobs were handy, usually in building or carpentry. I liked carpentry most of all. But in the end there weren't enough jobs of my kind so once again I decided to leave.'

'And was that when you came to Brighton?' Caroline said. 'Did you have a reason for choosing Brighton?'

'Well, as I told you earlier, I've always liked to be near the sea – a bit like you in that – but after seeing some of the world's great cities I couldn't see myself settling down in some quiet seaside town, devoted only to holidaymakers. And Brighton, with its proximity to London – apart from the fact that Brighton is, one has to admit it, cosmopolitan – filled the bill. There was a lot of construction work going on and it was no trouble getting a job. In fact, I was doing so well in the firm I was working for that there was the possibility I'd be made a partner and would take over when the boss retired. It didn't work out. In the end his son was promoted. "A family thing, you understand," was what they said to me. And he took over, so I left. Now I'm freelance, and that's how I like it.'

He looked at his watch. 'I'm sorry,' he said. 'I've been going on too long! I hope I haven't bored you?'

'Not at all,' Caroline assured him. 'But I know you have another appointment, so if you'd just drop me back at Preston Park I'd be most grateful.'

'Right away,' he said.

He left her at her gate. She walked into the house and as she did so the phone was ringing. She hurried to answer it.

EIGHT

'Hi, Mum!' Rosie said. 'I thought I'd give you a quick call. How are you?'

'Quite well!' Caroline said. 'And you?'

'I'm OK,' Rosie answered. 'Just busy, but that's good! So have you decided what you're going to do in Grandpa's house? Is it beginning to take shape? I'm sorry I can't be there to go through it all with you, but I will be as soon as I can.'

Caroline felt decidedly uncomfortable. Not, she thought, because she had done anything wrong, but because she had made, or was about to make, a sudden and what would probably seem to Rosie an extraordinary change of plan, and without the slightest warning. It might have been better, certainly more tactful, to at least have said something to Rosie before taking such a positive stance with Alec. On the other hand, it had all happened so quickly. When she'd met with Alec this morning the last thing in her mind had been to consider new plans, radical plans, and to change her mind-set so quickly, so unexpectedly.

'As a matter of fact,' she said now to Rosie, 'I've gone over with Alec what I'd intended to do, in some detail, but for the moment it's on hold.'

'On hold?' Rosie queried. 'Why? What's the problem? I thought it was all pretty straightforward.'

'Well, it was – and it wasn't,' Caroline hedged. She was far from sure how to put it, which way to tell Rosie exactly how she had spent the afternoon and what had transpired – or what might transpire. All the same, she would have to tell her sooner or later, especially if she was to go through with it, and that, she knew in her heart, seemed already more than a possibility.

'The fact is,' she said, 'I've had another idea, and a better one.'

'Oh, that's OK,' Rosie said equably. 'I expect new ideas will crop up all the time. It's bound to happen when you're changing things around. So what is it in particular?'

Caroline took a deep breath. This was not going to be easy, however logical it seemed to her. 'Well,' she said, 'I've been looking at another house. In Kemp Town actually. A lovely old house. It's in the process of being converted into flats . . .'

'So you're thinking of renting a flat?' Rosie chipped in. 'Well, I suppose it's not a bad idea if you don't want the responsibility of a whole house . . . and tenants.'

'It's not quite that,' Caroline said. 'Not exactly.' She paused for a moment. 'The fact is, I'm considering buying the property: living in one of the flats and renting out the rest.' Once started, the words came out in a rush, and were followed by a sudden total silence – though that did not last long.

'*What* did you say?' her daughter asked, her voice rising an octave. 'Tell me I'm dreaming. Tell me you *didn't* say you'd been to look at another house and you're actually considering buying it? The whole house?'

'No, you're not dreaming.' Caroline kept her voice steady,

though, stated in plain words by Rosie, what she had just said sounded quite impossible. 'That's what I said.'

'What on *earth* for?' Rosie said. 'I'm bewildered! I don't understand. Buy another house? Why would you want to do that? You already have a perfectly good house in Brighton, you've made plans for it. I thought it was all going ahead.'

'I know,' Caroline said quickly. 'But I've realized that, pleasant though it is, living here in Grandpa's house is not where I want to be. Not only would it be a less than perfect conversion, I wouldn't be at all near the sea. It wouldn't be the Brighton I know, and always remembered. I might as well stay in Bath – well, not quite, but almost . . . So I would sell it.'

'I cannot believe what I'm hearing,' Rosie said. 'I just can't! How did all this happen? How did this other house come into the picture? What in the world led you to it?'

'Alec did,' Caroline said. 'He knew I wasn't happy about the position of Grandpa's house . . .'

'Ah! I might have known!' Rosie cried fiercely. 'And I suppose he just happened to know of something which would be just the ticket for you, and it just happened that it was in exactly the right place and, moreover, he just happened to know the owner – or maybe he *is* the owner – and if you did it all through him, he persuaded you, it would be a real snip . . .'

Caroline interrupted her. 'He did *not* persuade me. It wasn't at all like that . . .'

Rosie didn't even listen. Her voice had got louder; she was shouting down the phone now. 'Who is this bloody Alec?' she demanded. 'I haven't even met him! Oh, Mum, can't you see that it's all a set-up? It's a trap and you've walked right into it. Are you *mad*?'

Caroline interrupted her. 'Stop it!' she said sharply. 'That's enough! It's not like that. If *you* would just listen instead of flying off the handle . . . Alec is a perfectly decent man. As you well know, he was recommended to me by George Clarke. It so happened that he, I mean Alec, was engaged on the house in Kemp Town, converting it into three or four flats, working on it for the owner, when the owner was forced to back out, so the property came up for sale.'

'I'll bet it did!' Rosie said. 'And you were conveniently to hand.'

'It's not like that at all!' Caroline protested. 'Why are you so against it? Why are you so distrusting?'

'And why are you so gullible?' Rosie demanded. 'And if I am against it, which is absolutely true, could it be because you hardly know this man? He doesn't work for a company. He's not even a bona fide estate agent. He's a one-man band, practically a stranger, and you're considering buying a house through him. A house you didn't even know you wanted. You *didn't* want until today. Of course I'm worried. I have every reason to be. He's seen you coming!'

'Will you please calm down!' Caroline said. She tried to speak calmly, but her insides were churning. 'If you were to meet the man – which you can do as soon as ever you wish to – and if you were at least to *see* the property and listen to what I thought I might do with it, then I think you might realize that I have not in any way taken leave of my senses. It's a perfectly sound and economic idea. I don't think you're seeing my side of it at all. You're just saying what *you* think is right.'

'That's not true!' Rosie protested.

'Oh yes it is,' Caroline retorted, 'and I think we'd better leave this conversation for the time being. We're getting nowhere. I'll speak with you tomorrow, when you've calmed down and we've both done more thinking. After all, I haven't said that I'm definitely going to do it. I've seen the house, I've thought of the pros and cons, I love the area it's in – and now I'm considering it: sensibly, I hope.'

'You seem totally out of your senses to me,' Rosie said

sharply. 'But I agree, we'll talk tomorrow.' Then she changed her tone of voice, spoke softly. 'I do only want what's best for you, Mum! Can't you see that?'

'I'm sure you do,' Caroline agreed, 'but it's possible you don't always know what's best for me. Anyway, as I said, we'll end this conversation and speak again tomorrow. I can't bear quarrelling with you. I love you far too much for that.'

'And I love you,' Rosie said, 'which is precisely why I'm worried. If you were someone else's mother I could look on without turning a hair. But you're not. You're mine! I want you to be safe and secure.'

'Which I'm sure I will be,' responded Caroline. 'So for now we'll say goodnight and God bless, and I'll call you tomorrow.'

'I'll call *you*, early evening. I'm going to be in and out all day. Promise me you won't do anything silly between now and then!'

'I promise!' Caroline said.

She put the phone down gently and then, without warning, burst into tears. Why, she asked herself, when everything seemed to be going well, did it suddenly all turn sour? Perhaps Rosie is right, she thought. Perhaps I *am* mad? But no, she didn't think so. She went into the kitchen. She knew she ought to eat, but now she realized she couldn't face food. She turned on the television to distract herself – and almost immediately turned it off again. It was a load of rubbish. She would have a warm bath, go to bed, and read herself to sleep.

It didn't work out. She lay in the bath, thinking, until she was aware that the water had started to cool. She got out and dried herself, then went to bed with a new book she had brought with her from Bath, but now not even Ruth Rendell could satisfy or distract her. She tossed and turned, hoping for sleep, but sleep didn't come. For a start it was far too early but also her mind was too full of thoughts, whirling around and conflicting with each other. *Am* I doing the right thing, she asked herself? And why is Rosie being so difficult? Or is she right, and am I wrong? The truth was, she supposed, that she was not used to making decisions of this nature. Big decisions – and sometimes even less important ones – had been made together with Peter.

I do miss you, Peter, she thought – and almost said out loud – and then her train of thought was broken as the telephone on her bedside table shrilled through the silence. It was Rosie.

'I wanted to talk to you,' her daughter said. 'I wanted to know you were all right. What are you doing?'

'At the moment,' Caroline admitted, 'I'm in bed. Yes, I know it's far too early, but I was tired.'

'Well, don't get into the habit of going to bed early every night,' Rosie said. 'It's a waste of life. Anyway, I'm sorry I upset you and I'm sorry we argued, though I still think I am right and you're wrong.'

'So is that what you called to say?' Caroline said shortly. 'Because if it is there's no need. You made yourself quite plain. There's no need to repeat it.'

'It's not exactly that,' Rosie said. 'I mean, that's not why I phoned. The fact is, I've been thinking things over and I have an idea. I don't mean I have a solution, I mean exactly what I said. I have an idea.'

'So?' Caroline said.

'Don't sound so dubious. Wait until you've heard it.'

'I'm waiting!' But not with bated breath, thought Caroline. She was surprised at how raw she still felt after the earlier altercation with Rosie.

'I wondered,' Rosie ventured, 'would it be a good thing if you and I were to pay a visit to Aunt Patience? I mean, if we were to put the problem to her? You know how wise she is. And we both love her, and she loves us.'

I didn't know I had a problem until you saw it as one, Caroline thought, but did not say.

Patience Denby was Peter's sister, senior to him by several years, and now well on in her sixties. She had never married and lived in a small cottage in the High Street of the Surrey village of Latchley where, until her retirement, she had been headmistress of Latchley Primary School. In Latchley she took part in everything that went on, from the Parochial Church Council, of which she was secretary, to the Ladies' Bowls Club, at which last year she had won the cup. Incredibly, she also managed to be liked by everyone.

'I'm not at all sure about that,' Caroline said. 'I'm not convinced it's necessary. Of course I'm very fond of Aunt Patience. She was wonderful to me when your dad was ill, as you probably remember. All the same, I don't see what she could do about *this*.'

'Perhaps nothing,' Rosie conceded. 'But she'd be another voice; and because she loves us equally she wouldn't be biased.' Privately, Rosie thought Aunt Patience would be as horrified as she was. 'So I thought,' she continued, 'that we might give her a ring, say we plan to visit, and then mention something like we have a family problem on which we'd appreciate her views.'

'Very well.' Caroline hesitated, then in the end said, 'I'll do that.' She didn't see how Aunt Patience could be of any help, but at least it would do no harm. 'So when shall we go?' she asked.

'Next Saturday,' Rosie suggested. 'I'd come by train from London and get a taxi to Latchley.'

'OK, if that fits in with Patience,' Caroline said. 'You know how busy she always is. I'll speak to her and give you a ring.' She had little faith in this as a solution. On the matter they proposed to put to Aunt Patience the two of them were diametrically opposed. But if it pleased Rosie . . .

★   ★   ★

'What a lovely surprise!' Patience said when Caroline phoned a couple of days later. 'It's ages since I saw either of you!'

'We're looking forward to it, and as I mentioned, we have a small problem about which we can't quite agree. Your opinion would be such a help.' Caroline wasn't sure she believed a word she was saying.

'Well!' Patience said. 'I've never thought of myself as a solver of problems but if there's anything I can do . . . Are you sure you wouldn't like to tell me a bit about it on the phone?'

'Not really,' Caroline said. 'Rosie and I don't exactly see eye to eye on it, so I think it would be fairer if we explained when we see you together.'

'As you wish,' Aunt Patience said. 'Then do come in good time for lunch and we'll have a nice, long afternoon.'

As she had promised, Caroline rang Rosie back. 'All fixed,' she said. 'I must say, it made me feel guilty turning to her when I've been so long without a word.'

'I agree!' Rosie said. 'But I'm sure she won't mind. She's such a dear, isn't she? I wonder why she never married? Do you know why? She must have been really pretty when she was young.'

She was changing the subject, Caroline thought. But never mind. 'No, I don't know why,' she admitted. 'It was never mentioned, except once when Grandma let slip something about a lover who had run off with someone else at the last moment. I never heard it spoken of again, not even by your father.'

'Well, anyway, I'm pleased we're going to see her,' Rosie said. 'And will you do one more thing for me, Mum?'

'I expect so,' Caroline said. 'It depends what it is.'

'Will you promise not to make any further moves until we've met together, and seen Aunt Patience?'

'I don't see why I . . .' Caroline began.

89

'*Please!* It's only a couple of days!'

'All right, then,' Caroline agreed, feeling as if she'd been backed into a corner. But after that, she told herself firmly, I shall do what seems best for me.

The journey to Latchley was slower than she had expected. There were hold-ups for no discernible reason. She had hoped to reach there before Rosie, not in order to steal a march on her but simply so that Rosie would not blurt out the whole thing – or her interpretation of it – in advance. She would not do that maliciously, of course, nothing like that, but it was in Rosie's nature to be, well, spontaneous. 'And we all know which parent she gets that from!' Peter had said once. 'Not from her dad!' That was true. Peter had weighed things up, thought them through, before he made decisions.

Now, as Caroline drove down Latchley's broad High Street, the church clock was already striking twelve.

As she pulled up outside Patience's cottage she realized that Patience must have been looking out of the window watching for her, since even before Caroline had finished parking her car she had opened her cottage door and was standing on the step, smiling a welcome. She was a small, slight woman with untidy white hair, who looked as though a stiff breeze might blow her clean off her feet. She came forward, a wide smile on her face, her bright blue eyes shining, her arms outstretched to greet her sister-in-law.

'You've beaten Rosie to it!' she said. Her voice was surprisingly deep for so small a person, with a trace of the Surrey accent which she had never lost. 'Probably her train was late,' she added as she led Caroline into the house.

'Sit down, dear,' she said. 'It's quite a drive, isn't it? I'm going to pour you a glass of sherry.'

In no time at all Caroline had been made to feel utterly at

home and was drinking a fine dry sherry from an exquisite Waterford glass. Rosie blew in before she was halfway through it. At least, Caroline thought as Patience poured a drink for Rosie, neither one of us has arrived long enough before the other to start spilling the beans. Though to be fair, she thought, Patience would probably have discouraged that if either of them had attempted it.

'I've made a *coq-au-vin* for lunch,' Patience said. 'I hope you both like that. It's something I don't often get the chance to do. It's not worth it for one person, is it? But I do get quite bored with lamb chops and sausages. And I know . . .' she joined on the sentence without a pause . . . 'you've come to see me about something in particular. I'm quite intrigued, but I suggest we all leave that until after we've eaten. Things always seem worse on an empty stomach, don't you think?'

'*Coq-au-vin* sounds wonderful,' Caroline said. 'And I seldom have it, I suppose for the same reason as you.'

'It smells heavenly!' Rosie added.

'Then I'll just see to it,' Patience said. 'Can I top up your sherry?'

'Not for me, thank you,' Rosie said.

'I think I will, please,' Caroline said. 'It's particularly good.'

Patience refilled Caroline's glass, then left the two of them and went into the kitchen. The table, in front of the window, was already laid for lunch, there being no separate dining room in the small cottage. By an unspoken decision, and perhaps in the spirit of Patience's words, neither Caroline nor Rosie said a word about why they were here. Patience brought in the food and they took their places at the table. 'It's rather nice, having the table in the window,' Rosie said. 'You can watch everything that's going on in the High Street.'

'Oh yes! And I do!' Patience replied.

The talk was general as they ate, and mostly contributed by Patience.

As she listened, Caroline thought about what a kind woman Patience was. She felt sure Patience would understand what she had in mind. She had come here only to please Rosie, not at all keen to talk about things, and now, surprisingly, she no longer minded doing that. The more she listened to Patience discussing other things, the more reassured she felt.

The moment came when they had moved away from the table and were sitting drinking coffee. 'Are you still working for your doctors?' Patience asked Caroline.

'I am,' Caroline said. Then added, 'But not for much longer.'

'And why is that?' Patience enquired. 'Are they moving away?'

'No. But I am,' Caroline said. 'I'm going to live in Brighton!'

Patience raised her eyebrows. 'Well, you do surprise me!' she said. 'Bath is such a lovely place. I thought you were settled there for ever.'

'We were,' Caroline said. 'But circumstances change, don't they? I suppose if Peter was still there it wouldn't have entered my head to leave. But he's not, and I had the urge to go back to Brighton. I wanted to live by the sea again.'

Patience nodded. 'And of course you have your parents' house there! Was that the problem you wanted to discuss? It doesn't seem a great problem to me.'

Rosie could contain herself no longer. 'That's because you haven't heard the half of it, Aunt Patience! You'll change your mind when you hear the whole story!'

Patience turned to Caroline.

'I was going to live in my parents' house,' Caroline said. 'Convert it into two flats, live in one and let the other. It's been let to students since my parents died. I suppose it was partly because I had to visit the house from time to time, keep an eye on it, that gave me the idea to move back there. I'm very fond of Brighton. As you know, I was born there, though not in the house which is now mine. You remember when I was younger we lived near the sea?'

'Of course I do,' Patience said. 'I always loved coming to see you. But you said you *were* going to live in your parents' house – have your plans changed?'

'Have *they*?' said Rosie. 'The fact is, my mother has completely gone off the idea of living in Grandpa's house. Had she stuck to that it might have been more or less reasonable – though how she could bear to leave all her friends and her job in Bath I can't understand – but she's now about to buy a large house in Kemp Town, Brighton, convert it into flats, live in one herself and let the rest. To do so she'll have to sell the house in Bath *and* Grandpa's house in Brighton! She's risking everything she has, and the point is, the big point is, she's doing this under the influence of a man she met only a very few weeks ago . . .'

'That's not . . .' Caroline again tried to break in, but Rosie would not be silenced.

'. . . She knows very little, if anything, about him. He doesn't have an employer or a company behind him. He could swindle her out of every penny, leave her with nothing, even leave her in massive debt, if it comes to that!'

'Of course it won't come to that,' Caroline said. 'Don't be so silly, Rosie!'

It was at this moment that it suddenly seemed to Caroline that Patience was hardly listening. She was looking through the window, though not apparently at anything special. It was as if she had opted out.

'I'm sorry,' Caroline said. 'We shouldn't be going on like this.'

Patience waved her protests aside. 'My fault,' she said. 'I was just thinking of something long past, when I was a

93

young teacher, never dreamed of being a head. There was a chance of a job abroad, in Canada. Indeed, more than a chance; it was highly likely it would be mine if I chose. I turned it down. My father was ill at the time.'

'And what happened?' Caroline asked.

'Oh, he recovered,' Patience said. 'And I went on with my teaching here, and in time I was made headmistress.'

Caroline listened politely. It was interesting, but she couldn't quite see what all that had to do with the present problem.

'There you are, you see!' Rosie said. 'And it all worked out in the end!'

'You could say that,' Patience said. 'Though I've often wondered how it would have been if I'd gone to Canada. Who is to know? But I do think . . .' and now she was looking directly at Caroline '. . . that there are important moments when we must take charge of our own lives. It might be the one chance we will have. The years can slide by almost without notice.'

'But one can make the wrong choice!' Rosie persisted.

'Certainly,' Patience agreed. 'But sometimes I think it's not the opportunities we take – I mean the ones which don't turn out well – which cause the most regrets: it's the ones we didn't take.'

'Dad certainly wouldn't have approved what Mum's contemplating,' Rosie said.

'You're quite right about that,' Patience said. 'My brother liked a straight path through life. Not too many twists and turns. But he was a fair-minded man, wasn't he?' She turned to Caroline. 'I don't think he would have found it wrong for you to do what seems best to you now, in the present circumstances. Which doesn't mean you don't have to think very carefully about it. Very carefully indeed. You're not old, Caroline,' she continued. 'You've got many years in front of you, and you have to live them, not just exist. I think what you're considering sounds quite exciting. It's obviously a risk: it might not work out as you expect. But there are times in one's life when it's right to take a risk.'

'It's not the end of the world if it doesn't work out,' Caroline said. 'On the other hand it could turn out tremendously well.'

'And it could be disastrous!' Rosie said shrilly.

Patience changed the subject. 'Well,' she said, 'as far as today is concerned it's the village Fair Day and there are all sorts of high jinks going on in the school field. I can't not put in an appearance – so shall we walk down and take a look?'

NINE

It was a fine afternoon, with a blue sky and a slight breeze stirring the leaves on the sycamores.

The fete was in full swing. It was in a sizeable field and there were a great many stalls, as well as a roundabout for children, a bran tub, several games with prizes to be won and, in a booth in a small corner, with a heavy chenille curtain drawn across for privacy, lurked Madame Gloriana, the fortune teller. I wonder what she would tell me, Caroline thought. It might be helpful to have a glimpse of the future, providing, of course, that it was revealed as reassuring.

Rosie won a bottle of tomato ketchup on the bottle stall, and in the raffle – they all bought tickets – Caroline won a box of particularly nice soaps. 'My lucky day!' she said to Patience.

All the same, in spite of the fun and games going on around them, in spite of Patience doing her best to jolly them along, Caroline felt a constraint between herself and Rosie. Her daughter was not enjoying herself. Conversation between them had almost dried up. And then, at one point, standing by the cake stall where Caroline was trying to decide between a Swiss roll and some tempting-looking lemon curd tarts, Rosie drifted away. She did it quietly, not saying anything. One minute she was there – Caroline, having finally decided on the lemon curd tarts, was fishing in her purse for the right change – and the next she was not.

'Where is . . . ?' she began to ask Patience.

'Let her go,' Patience said. She had seen her niece slip away. 'Don't try to follow her, dear. I think she needs a few minutes on her own. We all do sometimes, don't we? And things are not turning out quite as she'd hoped. So let's give her some breathing space.'

'I didn't want it to be like this!' Caroline protested. 'I really didn't!' She was scanning the crowds, searching for a sight of Rosie, but without success. And then, a few minutes later, she saw her. Rosie was standing on the bank of the stream which flowed down the side of the field, gazing into the water. She looked so still, so alone. Caroline's first thought was to go to her, but Patience put a restraining hand on her arm.

'No!' she said. 'You stay with me. Why don't we go and watch the maypole dancing! You wouldn't think anyone danced around the maypole these days, would you? But they still do it in Latchley. The Guides and the Brownies. Of course I like it most of all when they make the wrong moves and get all the ribbons twisted. Somehow, they never fail to do that!'

Caroline allowed herself to be led away, though not without another glance towards the spot where Rosie had been standing. She was no longer there. There was no sign of her. She followed Patience to the dancers, applauded enthusiastically when the dance ended, and then let herself be led off again. 'We must visit every stall, or at least I must,' Patience said. 'I would never live it down if I missed one out.' In the end they reached the potted plants stall. 'Do look at these beautiful cyclamens!' Patience enthused. She is determined not to let me go, Caroline thought. 'I can never manage to grow cyclamens, can you? Not that I'm much good with any pot plants. I forget to water them.'

Caroline made an effort to concentrate on the plants. It really was a wonderful display. 'Then I think that I have that in common with you,' she said to Patience. 'I'm quite good at gardening, but I definitely need to try harder with pot plants!'

They pondered and discussed for several minutes. In the end, though her mind was not on it, Caroline bought two pots of African violets. It was while she was being served – she was standing with her back to the crowd – that she suddenly felt a hand being slipped gently through her arm. 'Hello, Mum!' Rosie said quietly.

'Hello, darling,' Caroline replied with some relief as she turned around.

Rosie gave her mother a small smile, then together they set off and walked at a leisurely pace around the fair, not really choosing where they were going. Nothing was said. Nothing, for the moment, needed to be. Patience had disappeared, she was nowhere to be seen.

Eventually they ran across her. She was rummaging through the second-hand clothes, all nicely displayed to their best advantage on hangers. 'One can get some really good bargains here,' she said as they joined her. 'The only thing is, we meet each other in the village, wearing the other person's dress. Frequently they look better in it than you did! You think, why did I ever part with it? And now, dears, I think we should go home and have a quick cup of tea before you have to leave.'

Over tea – and lemon curd tart – Patience said to Caroline, 'I think it might be a good idea, love, if you were to ask Roger Pym to look over things for you – I mean all the legal bits – before you finally commit yourself, don't you? I'm not suggesting that there will be anything untoward, but if there is he'll spot it, and be able to advise you. Do it before you finally make up your mind.'

Roger Pym was a partner in Peter's firm of solicitors. He was well known to all the family and trusted by them. Caroline had naturally seen less of him since Peter had died, but he kept in touch and, if business brought him from Bristol to Bath, he always took her out to lunch.

'I expect he'd be quite happy to come to Brighton to take a look at things,' Patience said.

Caroline turned to Rosie. 'Would that make you happy?' she asked.

'Happier,' Rosie said.

'Right!' Caroline said. 'I'll do that. I'll give him a ring – that is, when I've made up my mind what I actually want to do. You know I haven't finally done that.'

'Thank you, Mum,' Rosie said. 'And now I'd better be going if I'm not to miss my train. Thank you, Aunt Patience. It's been lovely, seeing you.'

'I'll drop you at the station on my way home,' Caroline said.

Not a lot was said between them as Caroline drove to the station. In the end it was Rosie who broke the silence.

'I have to admit,' she said, 'that Aunt Patience's reaction wasn't quite what I expected!' In fact, she had thought that Patience's attitude would be very like her own and, if anything, even more cautious. Her aunt was elderly, wise but not worldly, and probably set in her ways. She would not be in favour of what seemed to be, on the part of her sister-in-law, some sort of mid-life crisis. It was certainly an ill-considered decision, Rosie thought, made by her mother on the spur of the moment. But perhaps Aunt Patience had simply been looking back with nostalgia – and foggy glasses – to what might have been. Perhaps she had not faced the realities of what her sister-in-law was contemplating.

'But even though I don't approve,' she said now '– and there's no point in pretending I do – I hope we can keep in touch about this. You won't shut me out and go off alone on your wild-goose chase, will you?'

'I never had it in mind to do that,' Caroline said. 'I'll keep you informed about everything. And when I've seen Roger I'll let you know exactly what he thinks.'

'I'd be glad of that,' Rosie said.

'Though perhaps,' Caroline continued, 'the best idea would be if you were to come down to Brighton; take a look at the Kemp Town house, hear what I have in mind. And most of all, meet Alec Barker. You seem to have cast him as the villain of the piece, leading your mother astray. He's not the least bit like that.'

'The fact remains that you know next to nothing about him,' Rosie said. 'However, I *will* come down and I *will* meet him.'

They were at the station entrance now. 'I'll drop you here, if that's all right,' Caroline said. 'I'm not sure where to park.'

'And my train's due in ten minutes,' Rosie said. 'So good-bye for now, Mum. I'll give you a ring, probably tomorrow.'

It being Saturday evening, there was very little traffic on the road. She should have a straight run through to Bath and hopefully arrive before it was quite dark. She enjoyed driving on a reasonably quiet road at this time of day. The visit to Latchley and Aunt Patience had been a good one, though setting off this morning she had not looked forward to it, she had been more than a little apprehensive about Rosie, wondering about the outcome, while knowing that she was not to be swayed or diverted by her daughter's opposition.

She loved Rosie, of course she did, and she was sure Rosie cared about her, but Rosie had always been a Daddy's girl.

Since she was a baby it had always been Peter to whom she had turned. It was not that she and Rosie didn't get on with each other; but there was never the same closeness as there had been between father and daughter. On the other hand, and to be fair, she thought, Peter had never taken advantage of the fact that he could do no wrong.

If we had had a son, she thought – and not for the first time – would he and I have had the closeness that Peter and Rosie had? The sort of bond which mothers and sons were said to have? She would never know. After Rosie was born she and Peter had always hoped for a son. It had just never happened. Some mothers and daughters were spoken of as being 'more like sisters', and she had seen that in action, though it had never been so with herself and Rosie. They were mother and daughter. She had not wanted to be a sister to Rosie. In fact, she thought, there was something slightly disturbing about the closeness of such a relationship, almost, in some cases, as if the mother wished to relive her own life through her daughter. No, she thought, better for both to live their lives in whichever role they'd been given. She wished – perhaps it was what most mothers of grown-up sons and daughters wished – that Rosie would settle down. I suppose what I mean, she told herself now, is that I wish she'd find a good man, make a happy marriage, and give me two or three grandchildren I could spoil. Not that I *would* spoil them, she thought virtuously. No, she would be a model grandparent.

However, she thought as she drove down the long hill into the city, thinking – and not for the first time – how beautiful it all looked in the dusk, with the lights coming on one after another and illuminating the splendid buildings of which Bath had more than its fair share – there seemed no prospect of Rosie settling down. She showed no signs of it. She had had a few relationships which, to Caroline, had seemed promising, but in the end they had been terminated, mostly by Rosie herself, or they had gradually faded out. There had been, to Caroline's knowledge, no dramatic endings, no unpleasant quarrels or showdowns. Indeed, Rosie seemed still to be the best of friends with her former lovers, though they, too, had moved on. One was happily married, with twin boys; another lived with his new love in Sheffield. Rosie, it seemed, kept in touch with them and was still friendly. It seemed to be the way of the world now. Very civilized, Caroline thought, but slightly strange too.

Reaching home, she let herself in and checked her messages. There was one from Mr Proctor.

'Hello there!' he said. 'I thought you'd like to know I brought two people to view your house today. I knew you were away, but will you ring me as soon as you can? I'll give you my mobile number in case the agency is closed. I'd rather not leave this one until Monday morning.'

She called him at once. 'I've just got back,' she explained. 'So how did it go? What was the verdict? You sounded pretty pleased.'

'I am,' Mr Proctor said. 'They were very interested. A Mr and Mrs Matthews. It seems the house is what they wanted and where they wanted. They don't have to go through selling a house here, they've been living abroad, so they're ready to move quickly. They're staying in hotels for the moment. Which means there'd be no long delay.'

'That sounds wonderful!' Caroline said.

'It does!' Mr Proctor agreed. 'And naturally they want to see you. They have a few questions – like when would the house be available, and what you'd be taking with you and what you'd leave behind. They would actually like to see you tomorrow morning. I know it's Sunday, but I hope you'll agree to that. They have other places to see. In fact, on Monday morning they're moving on to Cheltenham, to look at properties there if they don't find one here.'

'Tomorrow morning would be fine,' Caroline assured him. 'No problem at all.'

'Then let's say around ten thirty,' Mr Proctor said.

The bell rang promptly at half past ten on Sunday morning. This, Caroline thought as she went to the door, is the moment for the smell of baking bread and the aroma of fine coffee. Well, there was no chance of the bread but the coffee was already on.

'Good morning!' Mr Proctor said cheerfully. 'May I introduce Mr and Mrs Matthews?'

Mr Matthews was tall, broad, rugged. Mrs Matthews was an inch over five feet, petite and slender in a delicate blonde sort of way. Mr Matthews had a voice to match his appearance, as did his wife.

'Do come in!' Caroline said.

'Thank you!' Mrs Matthews said. 'We just loved your house, didn't we, Herbie?' she said, turning to her husband.

He nodded. 'But we'd like to go through it again. I reckon one doesn't take in everything in the first go.'

'Of course!' Caroline agreed.

'Then shall we make a start at the top?' Mr Proctor suggested.

They climbed the stairs to the top of the house. I wish I'd kept the loft tidier, Caroline thought. Anything which was of no immediate use had tended to end up in the loft, awaiting its fate. From then on, as they descended, Mr Matthews examined everything carefully, poking and prodding, checking windows, talking about heating systems, gazing critically at ceilings, even switching switches. His wife stood in the middle of each room as they came to it, and gazed ecstatically around her. She is doing exactly what I would do, Caroline thought. She is seeing every room as it would be once she had got her way with it. New curtains, thick carpets, candelabra hanging from ceilings and pictures on the walls. Mr Proctor was totally professional and never lacked an answer to Mr Matthews's many questions. Thank heaven for 'Our Mr Proctor', Caroline thought.

In the end, when every single thing had been looked over, including the garden shed, they went into the kitchen. 'It's a lovely kitchen!' Mrs Matthews said, turning to her husband. 'Don't you think so, dear?' she asked.

'If you say so, honey!' he said. 'It's your domain, not mine. As long as you like it . . .'

It was at that moment that Caroline realized that this blond wisp of a woman with her tiny voice had this larger-than-life man completely in her power. Not that he was going to concede this in front of everyone present.

'Well then,' Mr Matthews asked his wife, 'is there anything else you'd like to see? Anything you'd like to take another look at, or ask about?'

'Not in the house,' Mrs Matthews answered. 'It's all lovely. But I just wondered . . .' She hesitated, then turned to Caroline. 'I wondered, once you sell the house, how long will it be before you can leave? I mean, do you have to look for somewhere else to live?'

'Oh no!' Caroline assured her. 'Not at all! I have a house in Brighton. I inherited it from my parents. I shall be moving there. There'll be no delay at all once the legalities of the sale are dealt with. Of course, I won't move until they are. After that I can be as quick as you like.'

Mr Matthews cut the conversation short. 'Right!' he said. 'So thank you for showing us around. We'll think it over and let you know. And naturally, any decision we make will be subject to a satisfactory survey.'

His wife looked apprehensive. She, it was clear to Caroline, would have liked to clinch the deal there and then.

The Matthews left, Caroline seeing them to the door. Mr Proctor remained behind. 'So what do you think?' Caroline asked him the moment she had closed the door.

'I think they're quite keen,' he said. 'There is one other house they have in view, in Bath, but yours is certainly the front runner.'

'And what about Cheltenham?' Caroline asked. 'You mentioned Cheltenham.'

'Oh, I don't think that will come to anything!' Mr Proctor said. 'Mr Matthews has a bit of an inclination to it, he's a racing man, but his wife finds Bath more sophisticated. And I'd put my money on her!'

'So would I,' Caroline agreed.

'I reckon we'll hear tomorrow morning,' Mr Proctor said. 'I can usually tell.'

'I shall be at work,' Caroline said. 'Will you ring me there? I'll be dying to know.'

When Mr Proctor had left Caroline wanted to tell someone about the Matthews's visit. She was excited about it, she didn't want to keep the news – even though it wasn't firm news – to herself; but when she considered who she should ring she realized that she had not told a single one of her friends in Bath – not even Marion – what she was contemplating. How could she now, in the middle of Sunday morning, phone and say, 'How are you? And by the way, I've just sold my house! I'm off to Brighton!' She couldn't – though whether this particular sale went through or not it really was time to let them into her new plans. She couldn't think why she had been so secretive – that was what Rosie had called her. And with the thought of Rosie she decided that she would definitely give *her* a ring.

She waited a longer time than usual for the phone to be answered, and when it was, Rosie sounded half asleep.

'Are you in bed?' Caroline asked. 'Are you all right?'

'Perfectly all right,' Rosie answered. 'The thing is, I went out with friends after I got home from Latchley. We had a late night – and now I'm having a lie-in.'

'I'm sorry!' Caroline said. 'Why don't you give me a ring later when it's more convenient?'

'It's convenient right now,' Rosie said. 'I didn't plan to sleep so late. Did you ring for something special?'

Caroline gave her the news. 'Not that anything is certain,' she said. 'But I've a feeling it will be. It looks hopeful. And I did promise to keep you in touch, didn't I?'

'You did. And at least I'm pleased you're doing that,' Rosie said.

They chatted for a minute or two. 'Think about whether there's anything here you'd like to have before I move,' Caroline said. 'Books, perhaps. Or a painting or two?'

'Thinking about it, I really don't have room for any more books,' Rosie said. 'But there is a watercolour I've always liked. It's the one in the hall, a view of Bath, painted from the higher ground outside the city.'

'I know the one,' Caroline said. 'Your dad and I bought that together from a gallery in Bath. At the time it was more than we could really afford, but we thought it was so lovely.' In fact, it was a painting she would particularly like to take with her when she went to Brighton, but she would not say so now. If Rosie wanted it, then she should have it.

'Then it's yours!' she said. A small peace offering, she thought.

TEN

On Sunday afternoon, having given them time to recover from their lunch, which, on this day of the week, was always a fully fledged affair – Caroline telephoned Marion. After a few polite preliminaries she broke the news that she was leaving Bath for Brighton and that she had put up her house for sale, though not saying anything about the Matthews. That could wait until she knew the outcome!

'You dark horse!' Marion said. 'You never hinted at it. Did you tell anyone else?'

'Of course not!' Caroline said. 'Obviously I would tell you first – and you can feel yourself free to pass on the news.' Marion would enjoy that. 'And I shall get in touch with everyone else in the next few days. I've been so busy!'

'Well, I know you've always loved Brighton, and you have ties with it, but I *am* surprised,' Marion said. 'So have you had anyone to view your house? Or any offers?' She would like to have enquired what the asking price was. Her own house was slightly bigger, with a larger garden, and though no way were she and her husband thinking of selling, it would be nice to know how much they were sitting on.

'No offers so far.' It was strictly true, wasn't it?

'You'll have to leave your job,' Marion said. 'I thought you loved your job.'

'I do,' Caroline said. 'But I'll get another. Or perhaps I'll take a short break.'

'And you'll live in your parents' house in Brighton, I suppose?' Marion asked.

'Yes!' Caroline answered. There was no need to go into anything else. The rest could wait.

'Well, you'll be missed!' Marion said. 'That's for sure.'

'Thank you, and I'll miss everyone too of course. But you'll come to see me in Brighton?'

'Absolutely,' Marion said. 'Anyway, keep in touch. Let me know what's happening. And if there's anything I can do. We must have a little dinner party soon. Or there's a new restaurant opened, near the Abbey. We might go there. I'll sort something out.'

'Lovely!' Caroline said.

Monday morning was grey and wet, the sky dark, full of heavy, low clouds, the rain falling steadily. She knew it had rained most of the night. She had lain awake in bed listening to it pattering on the window, a background to the thoughts which chased around in her head. Not that they were gloomy thoughts, it was more that she was not able to do anything constructive about them. Everything at the moment depended on someone else's decision, and most of all on what the Matthews would decide.

The morning surgery was crowded, busy with people who had finally resolved, over the weekend, that yes, they must take whatever ailed them to the doctor. Caroline glanced at her watch, though knowing full well that nine o'clock was too early to expect the call she was hoping for from Mr Proctor. Mr and Mrs Matthews were probably at this very moment having a substantial breakfast in their hotel before setting out for the day – she sincerely hoped not for

Cheltenham, but rather to see Mr Proctor. He would be, to her, the bearer of news, whether good or bad. She had had no idea that selling a house was like this, all these to-ings and fro-ings, all this going through the right channels, speaking with the right intermediary. It was a quarter of a century since they had bought the house in Bath, and then Peter had taken care of everything legal while she had sorted out what should go with them from their tiny flat in Whiteladies Road in Bristol, handy then for Peter's office, and where they would put it in the Bath home. She had also been pregnant with Rosie.

She was glad Rosie had come around to her point of view about Brighton, though even as she thought that, she knew it wasn't true – well, not quite. Rosie had accepted, more or less, the move to Brighton, but there was still the Kemp Town business – and Alec.

She must put it out of her mind right now, she admonished herself. She had to concentrate on what she was supposed to be doing: which was seeing to patients arriving.

Just as the surgery was finishing, the hoped-for call from Mr Proctor came. He sounded pleased with himself. 'Good news!' he said. 'The Matthews have put in an offer! It's a little less than you were asking . . .' he mentioned a figure '. . . but that's not too bad, is it? What do you think?'

'Oh, that's quite acceptable!' Caroline said in relief. 'I expected to have to come down a bit. In fact, it's wonderful, and so *quick*!'

'Yes, you were lucky there,' Mr Proctor said. 'Of course they want to know when you will move out and they can move in.'

'Look! I'm terribly sorry, but I can't discuss it right now,' Caroline said. 'The surgery is still busy. I have two people standing in front of me, waiting to be attended to. Can I call you later or, better still, can I pop in and see you and we can discuss the details?'

'Sure!' Mr Proctor said. 'This afternoon then. Give me a ring first to make sure I'm in.'

Later that day, she walked home and made an appointment with Mr Proctor's secretary to see him at three. The journey home was a short distance, a journey she had made countless times, but today it seemed different. It was as though she were seeing all the familiar places she passed, the corners she turned, the roads she crossed, not exactly for the last time but in the knowledge that her familiarity with them was finite; it would soon come to an end. It was a strange feeling.

When Caroline arrived at his office, a beaming Mr Proctor was waiting to see her. 'This is wonderful,' she said, as she sat down opposite to him. 'I can hardly believe it!'

'Well, it's true!' he said. 'And now we have to sort out how soon the Matthews can take possession. They're very keen, very eager! So you should consult your solicitor and I can get things moving. Oh! The Matthews did ask me if you'd be agreeable to them coming to take measurements, and so on. They want to check where everything will fit.'

'That's fine,' Caroline said. 'They'll just need to ring me to make sure I'll be there. I work different shifts at the surgery.'

'I'll see that they do that,' he promised.

She rang Roger Pym, her solicitor, the moment she reached home. She got through immediately and they spent a few pleasant minutes catching up.

She had always been fond of Roger and his wife, and when Peter was alive the two couples had seen each other often. Roger had been a rock during Peter's illness. She would never forget that. And then, somehow, in the year after Peter's death they had drifted apart. It was during this time that

Roger's wife, Bettina, had, without warning – it had come out of the blue – left him for another man. Roger had taken that hard and there had been a messy divorce. After that, he had become withdrawn, not really wanting to see anyone and politely dropping his friends. It was unfortunate that they had never had children. Or was it, Caroline had asked herself then? It was difficult to say, except that Bettina's new man had two children of his own, who lived with his ex-wife. But now, on the telephone, Roger sounded his normal, happy self. Caroline was pleased by that. Perhaps he, as well as Bettina, had found a new love?

'I'm selling my house!' she told him.

There was silence at his end of the line. Then he said, 'Did I hear you aright? It sounded as though you said you were selling your house.'

'I did!' she told him.

'Well, you do surprise me,' he said. 'I thought you were happy there.'

'I was,' Caroline agreed. 'And I'm not moving out because I'm unhappy. Not really unhappy, but things don't stay the same, do they? So I'm going to live in Brighton. I like Brighton. I was brought up there. My parents left me their house.'

It was not the time to tell him more than that. It might never be, though she had promised both Patience and Rosie that she would consult Roger if she went ahead with the Kemp Town idea – and of course she would do so. 'Anyway,' she continued, 'I've got a buyer here – subject to survey and contract and all that. So who else would I ask to see me through it? Oh, I know it's not your usual line, I know you're higher up in the world than that – but would you mind awfully? I'd be so grateful.'

'Certainly I will!' he said. 'Gladly! And I'll come to see you. We can have lunch and you can tell me all about it. When shall I come?'

'You fix the day,' she said. 'It's easier for me to fit in. I mostly work mornings only. But do make it as soon as you can. I do want this sale to go through and it would be so nice to see you too.'

They made a date, less than a week ahead. And now I must ring Rosie, Caroline thought: bring her up to date. And after that, call Alec to say when I'll come to Brighton.

'A quick call!' she said to Rosie. 'Just to put you in the picture. The Matthews came up with a good offer, subject to survey, which I've accepted, and I rang Roger Pym to ask if he'd act for me. I know it's not his usual line, but he's an old friend. Anyway, he agreed.'

'At least I'm pleased you got in touch with Roger,' Rosie said briskly. 'I've always liked him. And do I need to remind you that you promised to ask his advice about this Kemp Town nonsense?'

'You don't need to remind me,' Caroline said. 'And I'll certainly do what I promised, but today isn't the time. The immediate thing is the sale here. I'm seeing Roger for lunch on Wednesday and I daresay I'll talk to him about Kemp Town then. You must leave it to me. Actually, I do think it would be a good idea if you were to come to Brighton with me, look at the Kemp Town house, and meet Alec. You're making judgements without knowing the facts, or the people involved.'

There was a pause, then Rosie said, 'All right! I'll come. Will next Saturday be OK? I can be down by lunch time.'

'That's fine by me,' Caroline said. 'I'll check that Alec's available and let you know.'

'In the meantime,' Rosie said, 'give my best to Roger – though he'll hardly remember me.'

'Of course he will, and I'll do that,' Caroline promised.

★　　★　　★

She called Alec on his mobile. This was turning out to be a rather exhausting day of phone calls, she thought, but it was good to deal with them all, get them out of the way. 'Where are you?' she asked him.

'I'm working on a job in Worthing,' he answered. 'Did you want me for something special?'

'Only that the world and his wife seem likely to be visiting Brighton, which also includes meeting you. I wanted to be sure when you'd be available. I also wanted you to know that I've had an offer on my house here, which I've accepted.'

'That's fantastic news!' Alec said.

'I've been in contact with my solicitor here – or actually in Bristol,' Caroline said. 'He's an old friend and I think it would be a good thing – if he's agreeable – if he came to Brighton and the three of us could discuss the Kemp Town idea.'

'Absolutely fine!' Alec said. 'I've told you all along that I'd prefer it if you'd do something like that – for my sake as well as yours. I think you'd be foolish if you didn't. When would he come?'

'Not this weekend,' Caroline said. 'And not next. Rosie is coming to Brighton on Saturday week. I want her to meet you and to see the house. Is that OK with you? And with my solicitor it needn't be a weekend. So I'll let you know about that.'

'Right!' Alec said. 'Then I'll be with you on Saturday week, say, around two thirty.'

Roger called for her at the surgery, arriving on the dot of twelve thirty. There was only one patient left in the waiting room and Marilyn, the other receptionist, could well deal with her. 'I'll be through in a couple of minutes,' she said to Roger. 'Will you take a seat?'

'As long as I don't end up seeing the doctor!' he said.

'And where have you been hiding him?' Marilyn whispered

113

when he had moved to a seat at the back of the room. 'He's quite something, isn't he?'

I suppose he is, Caroline thought. He was tall, two or three inches over six feet, broad-shouldered but otherwise slim. His dark, crisp-looking hair had greyed becomingly at the temples since she had last seen him and he was immaculately dressed, as always.

'I've known him for ever,' she said to Marilyn. 'He and my husband were colleagues – and friends. I just haven't seen him for a while.'

'I've booked a table at the Stage Box,' Roger said as they left the surgery. The restaurant he had chosen was a small one they both knew, close to the theatre. It had been there for years, outlasting flashier restaurants, which had come and gone. 'I've parked my car near by,' he said, 'so are you happy to walk to the restaurant? You know how difficult it always is to park in the centre.'

'I'm perfectly happy to walk,' Caroline said. 'I do so most of the time in Bath. It's easier. And nothing is too far from anything else, is it?' But she had forgotten how long his stride was. Walking down Milsom Street she found herself doing a skip and a hop to keep up with him.

'I'm sorry!' he said. 'I'm going too fast for you! Bettina used to accuse me of the same thing.'

Caroline had heard that for a while after Bettina had left him he could hardly bear to utter her name, but now it tripped lightly off his tongue. She could never understand why Bettina had done what she had. Nor could Caroline understand why Roger had not been grabbed quickly by someone else. Perhaps that was not what he had wanted? Once bitten, twice shy.

They were shown to their table in the rather crowded restaurant and studied the menu. Both ordered sole, and Roger chose a bottle of Chablis. They slipped into easy conversation: what was he doing? What was she doing? Where had he been for his holiday – which was Italy – and the fact that she had not yet taken a holiday. 'You should,' he said. 'Everyone should take a holiday.'

'I did intend to,' Caroline said, 'but now, if I'm moving house, I suppose it will go by the board. Or at any rate I shall put it off.'

The conversation moved on to the sale of her house. He told her the ropes: what would happen, how long it might take. 'And I suppose your parents' house in Brighton is more or less ready to walk into?' he said. 'At least you'll have no delay there.'

'Actually,' Caroline said, 'there's something else I have to tell you about – and ask for your advice – at least I've been told I must do that!'

He raised his eyebrows. 'Do I take it you are asking me against your will?'

'It's not quite like that,' Caroline said. 'I'm happy to talk to you about it. It's just that Rosie, and to a lesser extent Patience – do you remember Patience? My sister-in-law?' He nodded. 'Well, neither of them seems to think I'm capable of being let loose on the property market.'

'They might have a point,' he said. 'It's not the smoothest of seas; in fact, it can be pretty rough. So tell me about it.' He refilled her glass and listened carefully while she talked.

'I understand their concern,' he said when she had finished. 'At the same time, if it worked out well it could be good – and very interesting to do. But would you be happy, letting off parts of your house to other people?'

'Oh yes! I reckon that's the part I'd like most. That, and seeing it restored and converted. It's a house which deserves to be looked after.'

'And am I right,' he asked, 'in guessing you'd like me to come to Brighton, see the house, meet with the builder, give them both the onceover?'

'That is *exactly* what I would like,' Caroline said. 'That

115

would set everyone's mind at rest. Either you'd say it was fine, or you'd throw it out.'

'And what if I threw it out?' Roger asked.

Caroline hesitated. 'Well . . . I'm not sure what I'd do. I mean, I *would* take notice of you, but I can't say for certain that I'd give up on the idea.'

'Fair enough,' he said. 'And of course I'll come. I won't necessarily give you the answer you'll like, but I will come, and I'll give you an honest opinion.'

'That is truly wonderful!'

ELEVEN

It seemed to Caroline, thinking about all the things which had to happen now that the house in Bath was on its way to being sold – she closed her mind firmly to what could possibly go wrong with that – that her first duty was to talk to Doctor Meadows, and this she determined she would do on Monday morning. She was not sure how long it would be before she must quit her job with him: the Matthews were in a hurry to move and, now that it seemed certain, so was she.

She was well aware that Doctor Meadows would have to find a replacement as soon as possible, and she owed it to him to give the longest notice she could, leave everything ship-shape and, hopefully, if he could find someone quickly enough, stay on for a week or so to show the new person the ropes.

'Well, Caroline, I'm truly sorry you're leaving!' Doctor Meadows said when she spoke to him after Monday morning's surgery was over. 'But though I'll be sorry to see you go, I'm not surprised. I realized that this was going to happen. I recognized that you had itchy feet, perhaps even before you did. And, of course, I hope that all will go well for you.'

'Thank you,' Caroline said. 'And I shall have to find another job in Brighton. A part-time one. You were kind enough to say you might be able to help me there.'

'I did,' Doctor Meadows said. 'And I have thought about it. There's Toby Freeman. We trained together and now he's a consultant, with a practice in Hove. A chest man. He does quite a bit of NHS stuff in the hospital but he has a fair number of private patients. I don't know what the position is as far as you would be concerned, but I'm happy to ask him – and if he doesn't have an opening he might know someone who will have.'

'I'd be most grateful,' Caroline said. 'And I'm aware I'll be fortunate if I find a job I've enjoyed as much as this one.'

'It won't be like working in a general practice,' Doctor Meadows pointed out. 'From your angle it will be very different. A bit of a rarefied atmosphere, and certainly not with the variety. And I daresay he wouldn't want you full-time.'

'I don't want to work full-time,' Caroline assured him. 'I expect life to be quite busy, once things start up in Brighton.'

He fell suddenly quiet. Caroline was not sure what to say next. Then he leaned back in his chair and gave her a long look. 'Are you sure about this?' he asked her in the end. 'It's your business, of course – but have you thought it through? I'm not talking now about you getting a part-time job in Brighton, I daresay that's the least of it. But are you sure about the rest? It's quite an undertaking. And it's not too late to change your mind.'

'I know,' Caroline said. 'But I really have given it a lot of thought. I'm sure it's what I want to do – and the beauty of it is, I'm free to do it.'

He nodded. 'That's true! It's not often the two things come together. One has ties. So when do you think you'd want to take off from Bath?'

'Probably in about six weeks,' Caroline said. 'That's what my solicitor reckons. He doesn't see any snags coming up.'

'Very well,' Doctor Meadows said. 'I'll give Toby Freeman a ring and we'll see what transpires. And perhaps you could see him on one of your trips to Brighton.'

'I'd be happy to do that,' Caroline said. 'Whenever it suits him.'

She spent the rest of the week, when she was not at the surgery, sorting things out in the house. She had hardly realized she had so many possessions. There was no way she could fit more than a fraction of them, the contents of a whole house, into her new flat. Why hadn't that occurred to her until now? And how could she discard so many of the things that had been part of her and Peter's life together, things which had supported her since his death? Was she really up to this? She became aware of tears sliding down her face and for several minutes she cried quietly. Then she wiped her eyes on her sleeve, and went in search of tissues. After that she took up a pad and pencil and started purposefully moving from room to room, listing the items she would have to take with her and, in another column, she would simply have to leave behind, no matter how she felt.

On the Wednesday of that week, and again on the Friday afternoon, she was interrupted by the Matthews. Mrs Matthews, armed with a tape measure, wanted to measure everything, with her husband holding the other end of the tape and noting down the figures as she called them out to him. It was clear that she already thought of the house as hers. 'I hope you don't mind?' she said to Caroline.

'Not at all,' Caroline assured her, squashing a stab of irritability. 'But if you need to come again it might save you a wasted journey if you were to ring me first. I'll be here in the afternoons for the rest of the week, and then I go away on Saturday morning for the weekend.'

She left Bath soon after breakfast on Saturday and was in Brighton an hour before Rosie arrived. She was nervous, almost anxious, about this meeting with Rosie, and even more so, though she was determined not to show it, about the two of them meeting with Alec. She would hold her ground, but she did so want things to go smoothly. While waiting for Rosie she checked that the beds were ready, and then she set about preparing lunch. They would go out for a meal this evening. She hoped it would be an amicable one.

Rosie arrived later than expected. 'I'm sorry,' she said. 'I meant to be here earlier than this but there was a hold-up on the train. No one said why, of course! We sat there without moving, just short of Haywards Heath, and then when we did reach Brighton I had to queue for a taxi.' She didn't, however, sound particularly put out by the delays, which Caroline took as a good sign.

'I'll do the lunch right away. It won't take long,' she said. 'Alec isn't due until half past two, so we'll be OK. I'm so glad you're going to meet him.'

'I wish it didn't arise,' Rosie said. 'I really don't understand why you're contemplating such a move. But if you must leave Bath then this is a very nice house, and I would think full of happy memories for you.'

'Of course it is. I know all that,' Caroline said. 'And of course you *do* know why I'm doing it. It's because this house is not where I want it to be. Also,' she added, 'I want something different in my life. I'm in a rut. A comfortable one, but still a rut. I want a challenge.'

Rosie said nothing to that. I hope she won't be awkward, Caroline thought, though without much hope. But even if she is, and even though I understand her motives, I shall stick to my guns. I am a grown woman and a long way from being in my dotage. And actually, she told herself, nor is Rosie, at heart, an awkward woman. She is being protective, wanting to be sure that I am not making a big mistake. I should be grateful for that.

Alec arrived on the dot of half past two. Introduced to Rosie, he saw an attractive young woman – not physically like her mother: sharper somehow – perhaps she took after her father. She was cool, certainly not effusive, but conventionally pleasant and well mannered. What Rosie saw was a man who was totally different from how she had imagined him to be. She had expected a glib salesman type of person, able to talk her mother into a lucrative ploy of his own devising, but he was not at all like that, at least not in this first meeting. He was quiet-voiced, with an accent she couldn't quite place. His manner was firm but polite and, as he continued to speak, it was clear that he was confident, that he knew what he was talking about. She would have to watch herself, she thought, not to be seduced by his attractive manner. Not that she saw herself as being easily hoodwinked.

'I'm pleased you could spare the time to come,' he said.

'Oh, I wouldn't have considered doing otherwise, not for a moment,' Rosie answered him. 'My mother's decision – not that at the moment it can be considered as anything as firm as a decision – came as quite a surprise to me. I would naturally like to know much more about it.'

'And I'm happy to tell you anything you want to know,' Alec said pleasantly. 'From my viewpoint, of course. Your mother will speak for herself.'

'Well,' Caroline interrupted, 'perhaps it would be as well if we went and looked at the property, and then discussed the pros and cons.'

'Quite right!' Alec said. 'Shall we go in my car, and then afterwards I can drop you back here?'

'Do you know Kemp Town?' he asked Rosie as they drove along the seafront.

'Not really,' Rosie admitted. 'Of course I know of it, I know where it's situated, and so on, but it was never part of my scene when I visited Brighton with my parents. As a child I was all for the beach and Palace Pier, especially the latter.'

'That's true,' Caroline said. 'If you'd been allowed I think you'd have spent all day in the amusement arcades on the pier. I had to drag you away from those games.'

'I know! But admit it, Mother, I nearly always won, didn't I?'

She had, Caroline remembered. She had been a lucky child, a happy one, and never particularly difficult, even though Peter had been inclined to spoil her.

'But I outgrew that,' Rosie said. 'When I was older and I came to visit Grandma and Grandpa on my own I was more interested in the town and the shopping. The Lanes, and the North Laine area – all those cool little shops. I never really knew Kemp Town.'

'There are still quite a few small interesting shops in Kemp Town,' Alec said as he turned off the seafront. 'It's different from other parts of Brighton. Like a little village. I think that's part of its attraction.'

There was a parking space immediately in front of number seventeen and he drove straight into it. 'That was lucky,' he said. He turned to Caroline. 'What would you like to do? Would you like me to go around with you and your daughter? Or would you rather go by yourselves and I'll be here if you want me, if you have any questions?'

It was Rosie who decided. 'Why don't my mother and I do it on our own?' she said quickly. 'If you're around we can always ask you anything we want to.'

'Oh, I will be around!' Alec said. 'There are several things I want to take care of. Just give me a shout if you need me.'

122

Caroline would have liked Alec to stay with them – he knew everything about the house – but for the moment she would let Rosie have her way. She was nervous about showing her the house. Will she like it, she asked herself? Will she see its potential as I do? If Rosie actually did like it, then that would be a bonus, though, she reminded herself, it will not be a matter of Rosie approving of the house itself as much as her disapproving of what I intend to do. But it will be *my* decision. She just hoped there wouldn't be too much dissension.

They started in the basement, which, Caroline told Rosie, would be where she would live until she had made her own part of the house ready to move into. Rosie's face was a picture of horror as she looked around her. 'I don't believe this is happening!' she cried. 'I don't believe you seriously intend to leave your lovely house in Bath and live in this . . .' she sought for the word. 'Squalor!' she said.

'Don't be so silly, Rosie,' Caroline said impatiently. 'If you call this squalor then you don't know the meaning of the word. All right, it's small, and it needs decorating, and some decent bits of furniture, but squalid it is not!'

'And you look out on to a blank wall and see people's legs as they walk by! What sort of a view is that? They probably throw empty cigarette packets and sweet wrappers – and goodness knows what else – as they walk by!'

'I don't see anything there now,' Caroline said. 'But in any case, as I've already told you, I'll only be here until my own place, on the top floor, is ready for me. Wait until you see that! And when I move out of this one it will be spruced up no end and it will make a very nice apartment for one person.'

'You have great imagination,' Rosie said.

'I daresay,' Caroline agreed. 'And in my case it's not clouded by prejudice. Shall we move on?'

123

They went, room by room, through the whole house. Once out of the basement, Rosie was less derogatory. She found fewer things to criticize and even admitted that some things were almost commendable. The proportions of the rooms were good, the original moulded ceilings and cornices were pleasant, the windows were large, and so on. She could not fault the balcony except to say that it needed re-painting.

They climbed the last few steps to the attic and Caroline opened the door on to the large, empty space. 'And this is where I shall live,' she announced.

'But there's nothing here!' Rosie objected.

'I know! All the better! All this space, and I shall be able to do exactly as I like with it! But you still haven't seen everything. Follow me!' She led Rosie through the doorway which led to the topmost flight of stairs, and then they were on the roof.

'Here,' Caroline said, 'I shall make a small roof garden. I can see it all in my mind's eye. I shall sit here on warm days and enjoy this truly wonderful view! Just look at it!'

For a moment, looking at the vista before them, everything bathed in the warm autumn light, the tide ebbing, leaving behind shining wet pebbles and newly washed sand, Caroline found herself wishing she didn't have to leave it and longing for the time when it would be settled, when it would be all hers.

Rosie brought her back to earth. 'Yes,' she said, 'the view is wonderful – but you can't live on that. And the house, given imagination – of which you have far more than I have – could be all right, I suppose. But that's not everything, is it? It's going to cost a mint of money – oh, I know you have two houses to sell – but you'll have to have tenants in every flat to make it pay. And how are you going to cope with tenants? You've never done anything like that in your life!'

'I know!' Caroline admitted. 'I think that's partly why I look forward to it. It will be something new, something creative. It will get me out of my comfortable rut. And I shall choose my tenants very carefully.'

They started back down the stairs. 'I shall be glad when Roger Pym has been and given everything the onceover,' Rosie said. 'I mean, financially and every other way. You must be sure to tell him everything.'

'Oh, I shall!' Caroline said. 'I certainly shall. I have great confidence in Roger. If there are any ifs and buts, any snags, he's the one to see them, and he won't hesitate to point them out. He's coming next weekend.'

'Yes,' Rosie said. 'I'm sorry I can't be here.'

Caroline was not certain whether or not she was sorry about that.

'Now, before we leave,' she said, 'is there anything else you want to see, or anything you'd like to ask Alec about? I think he'll be in the basement. He has a workroom set up down there, while he has things to do in the house.'

'I don't think so,' Rosie said. 'I take it for granted he'll be here when Roger comes?'

'Certainly. Since Roger will be acting for me he'll need to talk with Alec. So shall I give him a shout and tell him we're ready to leave?'

Alec drew up at the door of the Preston Park house. 'Then I'll leave you to it,' he said, 'unless there's anything else you want to ask me about.'

Caroline looked at Rosie warily. 'I don't think so, not at the moment,' Rosie said.

'Then thank you,' Caroline said to Alec. 'I'll be in touch with you quite soon. I'll call you from Bath if I need to, but in any case I'll see you next Saturday when Roger Pym, my solicitor, comes with me. Since you are the one who's in touch with the owner he'll need you to brief him on various things.' Alec could do that right now, she thought, indeed much of it he had already done, but she didn't want a three-cornered conversation with Rosie included. Her daughter had been surprisingly equable this afternoon, but depending where the conversation led, that might not last. She would prefer to wait for the rest until she had seen Roger.

'A cup of tea, I think,' she said, walking through to the kitchen, filling the kettle. 'So! What do you think?'

'A good idea!' Rosie said.

'I don't mean tea!' Rosie knew that perfectly well. 'I mean what do you think about the house, now that you've seen it – though of course not as it will be in the end, when everything's been done to it.' She spoke nonchalantly, busying herself with cups, taking the milk from the fridge, biscuits from the tin, determined not to show the anxiety she was feeling.

'Oh, I'm not faulting the house,' Rosie said. 'I can see it's a nice house – or has been in its heyday. And I liked the area. But the whole undertaking is just too big, too risky. I can't see you doing it, Mother. And of course it won't end when the conversion's done – in fact that might well be the easiest part.'

'So you no longer think Alec is out to cheat me?' Caroline asked. 'You've changed your mind about that?'

'I don't yet know enough about that,' Rosie said. 'But putting that aside, giving him the benefit of the doubt, I just think the whole thing is too much in every way. To begin with, it's going to cost a bomb. How will you possibly get that back, let alone make a profit? I assume a profit is part of your intention?'

'I wouldn't want to make a loss,' Caroline admitted. 'But I don't think that's likely. I'll get the money back, and more besides, from the lettings. I'll have three two-bedroom flats and a single basement flat. Have you any idea what rents flats in that area command?'

'Of course I haven't,' Rosie admitted.

'Then let me tell you, it's quite a lot. Once I let every flat – and I don't expect that to be difficult – the rents will pay all the expenses and leave me a reasonable profit to live on. I *have* done my sums. The sale of Grandpa's house, plus my house in Bath, will cover the purchase and the costs of finishing the conversion of number seventeen. Then once I've begun to draw in the rents I'll be fine. But you don't trust me to bring it off, do you?'

'It's something you've never experienced,' Rosie pointed out.

'It isn't exactly rocket science,' Caroline protested. 'I know I have a lot to learn, but you don't need an advanced degree to run this kind of business. And you can be sure I shall run it as a business. I'm not playing games.'

'What if the tenants don't work out well? What if they cheat on you? What if they're unpleasant to live with?' Rosie persisted.

'I don't intend to live with them,' Caroline said. 'I shall choose them carefully and I shall have proper legal agreements. Roger will make sure of that.'

'And what about Alec's costs? He'll have to employ a whole crew of people. I don't imagine he can do all this single-handed.'

'I know! I know all that, Rosie! I've gone over all the costs with him and I've budgeted for it. It's all in that plus a contingency for anything else which might crop up. Something is sure to. But I shall have considerable money quite quickly from the house in Bath to get things started – and then after that from this house. But none of this is just about money. It's about *me* wanting to do something. Something for myself!' Rosie, though she would be horrified to know it had, by her opposition, made Caroline even more determined to go ahead.

★　　★　　★

Eventually, the two of them called a truce, at least for the moment. It had all been said and in the evening they decided to go out for a meal. In the restaurant they talked a little about Alec. In spite of herself, Rosie had found him likable. 'Is he married?' she asked. 'No, but he once was,' Caroline told her. 'He has a girlfriend, though she doesn't share his house. She's involved in a mixture of PR and photography. At the moment, so Alec tells me, she's busy promoting a new group – the Sledges, I think they're called. Have you ever heard of them?'

'No,' Rosie said. 'Should I have?'

'I don't know,' Caroline said. 'Maybe we will. Alec tells me they're getting pretty big.'

'What will you do with yourself when all these alterations are taking place in the house – I mean, assuming you actually go through with it?' Rosie asked.

'I can't say entirely,' Caroline said. 'But I do plan to get a part-time job here. Doctor Meadows has a contact, a consultant, and he's promised to put in a word with him. But I shall be keeping a close eye on the house. Oh, Rosie darling, do wish me well! I'm so looking forward to it! And when it's finished it will be beautiful, perhaps almost as beautiful as it once was? And,' Caroline added in her best attempt at a North Country accent, 'one day, lass, all this will be yours!'

'Oh, very funny, Mum,' Rosie said with a grimace. 'But I'm not exactly looking to my inheritance right now. It's you I'm thinking about, Mother. Can't you see that?'

Caroline smiled. 'Yes, of course I can, really. But please try not to be over-anxious for me, love!'

Rosie left after breakfast next morning. 'Please let me know what Roger says,' she said. 'And promise me you'll follow his advice.'

'I probably will,' Caroline said. 'Certainly I shall listen to it very carefully.'

TWELVE

Rosie caught her train by the skin of her teeth. It shouldn't have been like that, but she had slept badly and stayed in bed until the last minute, and then Caroline had insisted that she must eat the proper breakfast which she had put in front of her rather than a cup of black coffee, which would have been more to her liking.

'I'm not used to breakfasts!' she complained.

'I could have guessed that,' Caroline said. 'You look thinner every time I see you.'

'I'm absolutely fine!' Rosie said. 'I'm never sick. I hardly ever have so much as a cold!'

There had been very little traffic on the way to the station, but every traffic light, it seemed, had turned red as they approached it, with the result that when her mother had dropped her at the station Rosie had almost had to run – hastily picking up a paper on the way, and taking her seat two minutes before the train left.

'It's been lovely seeing you. And I do appreciate your concerns,' Caroline had said as they parted company. 'Don't let it be too long before you come down again.'

Rosie had assured her mother that it wouldn't be and

129

she had meant it. Though the two of them seemed to have settled at an unstated truce, she was still far from happy about her mother's intentions. She'd never known her mother to be an impetuous woman, given to strange ideas, setting off at a tangent to do things she'd never done before and of which she had no experience whatsoever. No, she had on the whole seemed to have led a quiet, ordered life, and apparently been content with it. It's as if Daddy's death has completely changed her, Rosie thought. She supposed she had seen her mainly in her roles as wife and mother, but now she had become stronger, more self-sufficient. Was that what being widowed did to you? But the way I am going, she asked herself, shall I ever know? Would she even get as far as marrying, let alone having children? She was twenty-eight and there was no sign of Mr Right on the horizon. From time to time, on one or two occasions she had thought there was, but always in the end she had realized that this was not a relationship which would last a lifetime – except once, until it had turned out that he was already married. She opened her newspaper, took out the news review section and began to read, but quickly gave it up again, unable to concentrate.

Probably, she thought, when Roger comes down to Brighton next weekend, when he sees the place and goes into the details, his opinion will reinforce mine. She was sure his judgement would carry weight and she felt equally sure that, if he could help it, he would not let her mother do the wrong thing. So, there was nothing more she could do right now. She picked up her newspaper again and concentrated on it until the train drew into Victoria station. Wherever she had been, when she came back into London she felt she was coming home, and indeed it had been her home ever since her first term there at university. She would not like to live anywhere else.

★ ★ ★

After Rosie had left, Caroline did a few chores in the house, thought of ringing Alec, and then thought better of it. There was nothing more to be said at the moment. Also, it was Sunday. Perhaps he liked to spend Sunday with his girlfriend? The weekend had gone reasonably well, she thought. At least Rosie had liked the house and she seemed to have got along with Alec, insofar as she had had to. Even so, Caroline told herself, it wasn't going to be easy. Rosie clearly hated the whole project. But much as though she loved her daughter, if she herself thought she was doing the right thing then she would go ahead. A lot would depend on what Roger had to say. She would value his opinion, though even then not to the point of changing her mind completely. She was getting used to making her own decisions. She had not always liked that at first, but now she did.

Later in the evening, when she was back in Bath, Roger phoned.

'I was thinking about next Saturday,' he said. 'Why don't I pick you up and we'll go in my car? It's a bit silly to take two cars when most of it will be covering the same ground. What do you think?'

'Oh, I agree!' Caroline said. 'The only thing is, I rather want to stay overnight – I have a few things to do – and you probably want to go back the same day.'

'I'm happy to stay,' Roger said. 'I'll get my secretary to book me into an hotel and we'll travel back together on Sunday. I'm assuming you'll stay in your parents' house?'

'Of course!' Caroline said. 'But you could stay there too. There's plenty of room.'

'Well, if you're sure,' Roger said, 'then that would make sense.'

'I'm quite sure,' she said.

When he had rung off, she rang George Clarke and asked him to air the beds in two bedrooms. 'Mr Pym will be coming with me,' she said. 'I think you've met him before, though it was a long time ago.'

'That's right,' George said. 'I do remember him. A nice gentleman!'

On Monday morning she told Doctor Meadows how everything was going. 'But perhaps it would make sense if you didn't mention me to your friend in Brighton for a week or two,' she added. 'I can't be sure how free I'll be for a little while after I move to Brighton.'

'Very well,' he agreed. 'Though I think I must start to put out feelers for your replacement. I don't look forward to it.'

The survey on the house in Bath went well; there were no problems at all, which delighted the Matthews. She phoned Roger and gave him the news. 'No more than I expected,' he said. 'It should all go smoothly from now on. I'll see you on Saturday.'

He collected her at ten in the morning on what was a damp, drizzly day.

'How did last weekend go?' he asked as they drove along. 'I mean, with Rosie?'

'Unfortunately,' Caroline said, 'she still thinks I'm mad! Raving mad! She can't think why I would want to do such a thing. She sees so many risks – in fact, she sees nothing other than risks. The only bright thing is that though she certainly had believed that Alec Barker was about to cheat me wholesale, she seems to have changed her mind on that.'

'So he made a good impression on her?' Roger said.

'He seemed to. More or less. It's just that she mistrusts the whole operation. She still can't see why I would want to leave Bath. I think she wants to think of me nicely settled where she's always known me. It's all right for one's children to move away – to the far side of the world if they want to

– and of course that *is* right and proper, I wouldn't dispute it – but not for their parents, it seems. Oh! I'm sure she has my interests at heart, but I wish she'd be a bit more encouraging.'

'That's children for you, even when they're grown up,' Roger said. 'They don't always trust the older generation.'

'I'm fifty-four!' Caroline protested. 'I'm not that old!'

Roger nodded. 'Certainly not! But I think it's because parents stand for stability and continuity. It's a measure of love. They think they're responsible. And perhaps parents should be pleased that they care? Better than not giving a damn, don't you think?'

'Absolutely!' Caroline said. 'I tell myself that. But what do *you* think about all this? Do *you* think I'm mad? And do you think Alec Barker could be a con man?'

'How can I judge that?' Roger said. 'I haven't met him. I haven't seen his detailed proposals yet, so I intend to keep an open mind and a watchful eye and, obviously, your interests will be uppermost with me. But I see nothing intrinsically wrong with what you want to do. Quite the contrary. It might be just the thing for you. Especially if you mean to get really involved.'

'Oh, I do!' Caroline assured him. 'I'm not intending to stand aside and let someone else make all the decisions, have all the fun. I'll listen to others. I'll listen to you, and to Alec Barker. You both know what you're talking about, but I do have ideas and I want to take an active part – I don't just want to sign bits of paper and pay the bills. And when all the work is finished and the legal bits taken care of, well then, I shall have the tenants! That's something I'm looking forward to.'

'Of course,' Roger said. 'But you will have to be extra careful about that. You must take up references, draw up proper agreements. Leave nothing to chance. And you should never get too attached to your tenants.'

There speaks a lawyer, Caroline thought. He was right, and she would do as he said, though she would also trust her own instincts.

After having a quick lunch on the motorway they arrived at Preston Park in the early afternoon. Soon afterwards, Alec joined them, bringing with him his plans of the Kemp Town house, which Roger studied carefully. 'I did as you asked,' Alec said to Caroline. 'I spoke with Frank Teasdale and arranged we'd meet with him at the house at three thirty.' He turned to Roger. 'Teasdale is the owner,' he said. 'He is anxious for a quick, private sale, and if he has any difficulty in getting that, then he will definitely put the house on the market. He made no bones about that. But he's strapped for cash, so if we get in first he'll save time and we'll get a better price.'

Roger examined the plans and asked several questions, not only about the property as it stood for sale, but also what ideas Caroline envisaged for completing its conversion. He listened closely while she told him what she had in mind. 'All that sounds reasonable,' he said. 'Perhaps one or two queries.'

Alec looked at his watch. 'We must be off quite soon,' he said.

Shortly after they arrived at the house, so did Frank Teasdale. He was a large, plump man, his manner a mixture of apprehension and aggression. Caroline did not warm to him. He hurried through the preliminaries. 'I'd like this to be decided as soon as possible,' he said. 'And if you can't do that then I want to put it on the market without losing more time. So I need an answer pretty damned quick!'

'Naturally! And we'll get back to you as soon as we can.' Roger was firm, but courteous. 'But I still have to look around with my client and, of course, have more discussions with her.'

134

'Fair enough,' Teasdale said, 'but don't make it too long! Let's say by Monday at the latest.'

'We'll be in touch with you on Monday, Mr Teasdale,' said Roger calmly.

After Teasdale left them, Caroline, Alec and Roger spent a long time viewing the house, looking at everything, hopefully missing nothing.

Roger viewed the ways in which Caroline, together with Alec, had planned to divide the house into flats. 'Will these ideas work well?' he asked Alec. 'I mean, from a construction point of view.'

'Very well,' Alec said. 'I've given it a lot of thought.'

'And you?' Roger said, turning to Caroline. 'Are you sure you want to do this? Is it what you'd like?'

'Absolutely!' Caroline said. 'I've given it a great deal of thought too. As I've said, I shall have the top flat, which is definitely what I want, and the rest will be divided into three decent-sized flats, with a smaller one in the basement. I don't think I would have any difficulty in letting them all, and quite quickly.'

'Any questions you like to ask, I will try to answer,' Alec said. 'Or if you would prefer to, you could get a quote from someone else.'

'That might be sensible,' Roger said.

Caroline gave him a sharp look. There was antagonism in the air, though mostly from Roger's side.

'It might also mean that Mr Teasdale would rush to put it on the market,' she said. 'He's clearly anxious to lay hands on the money.'

'You must do whatever you think best,' Alec said, in a cool voice, and addressing his words to Caroline.

'I'm happy enough with what you suggest,' Caroline said to Alec. She was not quite sure why this *frisson* had arisen between the two men. 'I'm not sure I want to start again at the beginning.'

'And the cost?' Roger asked. 'Is that also feasible?' Alec had made a rough costing of the conversion to add to the buying price of the house, but he addressed the question to Caroline. 'What do *you* think? Perhaps we should go into this in more detail?'

'I reckon so,' Caroline said. 'I have two houses to sell. The first one is as good as sold, as you know, and with my parents' house I don't see any problem with selling. It should all work out well, even allowing for contingencies, which there are sure to be. And then I would soon be receiving rents. As I've told you, I would put the letting with an agency.'

'Who would charge you a commission,' Roger pointed out.

'I know,' Caroline said. 'But they would be much more efficient about it than I would be.'

'I think we should take some notice of Teasdale,' Alec said. 'If we – by which I mean you, of course,' he said, speaking directly to Caroline, 'don't move reasonably quickly, then this is one opportunity you'll lose. That's not to say that there won't be others, but it does seem to be what you want.'

'Have you done other conversions like this?' Roger asked.

'Yes, several, though no two are ever alike. I ran conversions for my old firm here in Brighton as well as in Hove and Eastbourne. But, as I'm sure you know, this is my first whole-house conversion in my own business. That's why my pricing is actually low. I want to do this job, do it well, do it in the budget and, frankly, use it as a way of establishing my own reputation as an independent contractor. So the stakes are high for me as well as for Caroline. And don't forget, I've been working on the house for Teasdale, so I know it has all been done well. The attic – Caroline's flat – will be all new construction and that's the only floor we haven't got the final plans for.'

Roger was silent for a moment. 'How would you feel about Caroline getting a competitive bid?' he asked.

Alec looked at Roger. 'Of course she could do that. But I think my pricing would be very hard to beat and I know no one could come close to my commitment to this project, or to Caroline. But, as I said, we'll have to decide quickly or we may lose out. There may be other opportunities, but I doubt any as good.'

Roger nodded. 'I take your point. But first I have to go over all the finances with Caroline. The purchase costs, the cost of the conversion, the potential rental income, everything. We'll get right down to it and talk to you tomorrow. Before we return to Bath?' He turned to Caroline. She nodded in agreement.

'Fine by me,' Alec said. 'And remember, *I'm* not the one looking for a quick decision. That's Teasdale. And now, if you'll excuse me, I have to look in on another job I'm handling. But if anything comes up, if there are any queries, give me a call.'

'I'll be here,' Roger said. 'I'm staying here until tomorrow. We go back to Bath late afternoon.'

'But don't hesitate to ring if you think of anything else. And thank you, especially for bringing in Mr Teasdale,' Caroline said to Alec.

'What shall we do for supper?' she asked Roger as soon as they got back. 'I have some food in, not a great variety but I could make an omelette, or something . . .'

'Let's eat out,' Roger interrupted. 'It's been quite a day; let's round it off with a nice meal – not that I'm suggesting you wouldn't do a good omelette . . .'

'Oh, I agree with you!' Caroline said. 'I'd much rather go out. There was a write-up last weekend of a new restaurant in the Lanes. It sounded interesting. But of course there are loads of good restaurants in Brighton.'

'Let's try the one you've mentioned,' Roger said. 'Where is it?'

'In Ship Street. I made a note of the number. We could ring and see if they can fit us in.' She found the number and Roger telephoned. 'That's fine!' he told her, putting down the phone. 'The very last table for two. Seven thirty.'

It was a small restaurant; well appointed, dimly lit and crowded. They were shown to a table in a corner and given handwritten and dated menus. 'I like that,' Roger said. 'It shows they don't serve the same food every day. What takes your fancy?'

'Almost everything on the menu,' Caroline laughed as she perused it.

'While we're deciding, I suggest we have some champagne,' Roger said. 'It's been an important day, possibly a landmark day. We should drink to it.'

'I'd love that!' It seemed ages since Caroline had celebrated anything: not that life had been hard but, when she thought of it, somewhat flat, with some hard decisions to make. Her thoughts must have shown on her face, for, as the waiter brought the champagne, Roger looked at her and said, 'Let's drink to decisions! But let's not make them until we've eaten!'

'I agree. In fact,' she added a little later as they ate, 'you haven't told me what you really think about it all. You've looked at everything, but you haven't really given me a firm opinion, or any advice. I mean, whether to do it or not to do it.'

'That's deliberate, so far,' Roger said. 'I want you to make up your own mind. I don't want you to be unduly influenced, in any direction, either by me or by anyone else.'

'But that was why I involved you in the first place,' Caroline reminded him. 'I promised Patience and Rosie that I'd give you the facts and ask for your opinion. They set

138

great store by that. They clearly trusted you more than they did me! So naturally I would like to know what you think, good or bad.'

He topped up her glass. 'Then I'll tell you!' he said. 'Pros and cons. Good and bad – or not-so-good!'

She put down her knife and fork. Suddenly she couldn't eat another bite. Then she picked up her glass and gulped down its contents. She felt – she didn't really know what she felt: she felt as if she were awaiting the result of some terribly important exam – she had always hated exams. Then she felt as if she were one of those women in Doctor Meadows's surgery, awaiting, perhaps dreading, his verdict. But why, she asked herself? Whatever Roger said, she was free to do as she liked, exactly as she pleased, though now, in this hour-long few seconds, she knew that what he said would matter a great deal.

He leaned across the table and covered her hand with his. 'Don't look so apprehensive,' he said.

She drew her hand away. 'Just tell me,' she said. 'Tell me what you think. I'm not asking *you* to make the decision. I'll do that myself. But tell me.'

'Right!' he said. 'I will!' He paused and she waited. 'In fact,' he said, 'I think what you propose to do is a very good idea. I think the plans are well thought out and the finances will work. Moreover, the more time I spend with you, the more I think it's just the thing for you. You would never be happy, not completely happy, spending your mornings in a doctor's waiting room and the rest of your day doing whatever happened to come to hand for the rest of your life. You have too much in your head for that. You have a good many years ahead of you and they have to have a purpose. You need a mountain to climb, if not this one, then you must look for another, but I sense you want to scale this one.'

'Oh, I do! I do!' Caroline cried. 'This one rather than another. I can see so much ahead. It could be so exciting!'

Roger smiled, raised his eyebrows. 'Not everyone's idea of excitement,' he said. 'You're not exactly taking on the Grand Hotel, are you?'

Caroline laughed. She felt free enough to laugh now, yet at the same time she wanted to cry. It was all too much. She felt her eyes brim with tears.

'Hey!' Roger said. 'Don't cry! Not here! People will think I'm upsetting you!'

She fished in her handbag and found a tissue. 'I'm sorry,' she said. 'You don't know what this means to me. Oh, I know it's small on a world scale – well, on almost any scale . . .'

Roger interrupted her. 'It's not small. It's not small to uproot yourself, to move from a place where you've lived happily for more than thirty years, and with a beloved partner, to take on something you've never done before. But I'm sure you can do it, and hopefully you'll be happier for it, though you'll have to watch out. It won't all be easy. And the part you're looking forward to, having the tenants, living on top of them, might be the most difficult bit. Rosie and Patience were not wrong to be apprehensive, but nor are you to want to do your own thing. And are you going to finish the food on your plate? And would you like a pudding?'

She smiled. 'I couldn't eat another bite!' she said. 'I'm up in the air!'

'You'll have to come down,' Roger said. 'Though I hope not with a bump!'

'Let's have coffee back at the house,' Caroline suggested. 'Or in my case, tea. Coffee keeps me awake.'

'That's fine by me,' Roger said.

They walked through to the Steine and were lucky enough to get a taxi right away. Back at the house she made the tea and poured it, and they sat in the kitchen to drink it.

'What a day!' Caroline said. 'It's been wonderful! I'm so grateful to you for coming.'

'It wasn't exactly a penance,' Roger answered. 'I wanted to come and I've enjoyed every minute – if "enjoy" is the right word for something so important.'

'The word suits what I feel,' Caroline said.

'We must see each other more often,' Roger said. 'We'd almost lost touch, and we mustn't do that.'

'You're right,' Caroline agreed. 'But Bristol and Bath are one thing, Bristol to Brighton is longer.'

He shrugged. 'It's nothing really. Though I must say, I'm pleased not to have to drive back tonight.'

There was a short silence, then Caroline said, 'How is everything with you? I've been so busy involving you in my affairs and I haven't asked a thing about yours.'

'Much the same,' he said. 'I never see Bettina, of course. That's really and truly a closed book.'

'Do you ever think of marrying again?' Caroline asked. He was an attractive man; prosperous, intelligent. 'I'm sorry, perhaps I shouldn't have said that.'

'It's OK,' he said. 'I've thought about it, if I met the right woman. But let's face it, I didn't make a success of my marriage to Bettina, did I? I reckon that was because I allowed myself to be too busy: worked too hard, played too little. I was building up my career. Well, now it's built up – but at the expense of my marriage. Bettina, I understand, is much more happily married than she ever was to me. And you?' he said. 'Do you think you will ever remarry? I'm sure you will have chances.'

'I can't believe I could ever find the right man,' Caroline said. Not that they had come flocking, she thought. She, too, had been wrapped up in herself, had ceased to go out and meet people. 'In fact, for a long time after Peter died I was numb,' she said.

'But not now?' Roger said. 'Not any longer?'

'No,' she said thoughtfully. 'I do believe, not now. One comes back to life, learns to live in the world again. It's absolutely necessary. And I'm doing it.' She knew that the changes she was about to make in the near future would be the start of a new life. She felt sure of it. She longed for it. 'I can't wait to start!'

'You have started,' Roger said. 'You now have to make the big decision, to make, or not take, the next step.'

'And you think I should do it?' she asked. 'You really do?'

'I think you *can* do it,' he said. 'I think you're more than capable. I also think it will be hard work and not without setbacks. But only you can decide.'

There was a lengthy silence between them, broken, in the end, by Caroline. 'I'll do it!' she said. 'I'll definitely do it. We'll make an offer to Frank Teasdale in the morning. I know it's Sunday, but we can phone him. After all, he wants a quick reply.'

'No!' Roger said, but he was smiling. 'We'll wait until Monday morning. Important decisions are best not taken late at night, especially after a good dinner, well lubricated with champagne!'

'Very well,' she said, though reluctantly. She wanted everything to happen right now. 'But I shall phone Alec and tell him. He'll be delighted.'

'Tomorrow,' Roger said gently. 'Not tonight.'

PART TWO

THIRTEEN

Six months had passed since Caroline had moved to Brighton and she was settling comfortably into her new life. Even in so short a time her life in Bath now seemed in another world, though one tenuous link she had made was in taking the part-time job as a receptionist to Toby Freeman in Hove. Doctor Meadows had arranged an interview for her, at which she had immediately been offered the post. Mornings only; he already had an afternoon receptionist.

It was a pleasant enough job, Doctor Freeman was easy to work for but, as Doctor Meadows had warned her, there was none of the variety she had experienced in general practice. No waiting room full of patients, many of them regulars, who had known her as she had known them; indeed she had frequently followed the progress of their ailments. These, now, were private consulting rooms, well furnished, fresh flowers around (for which she was responsible) and seldom more than one patient in the waiting room at a time; very few of them children or fractious babies. In fact there was not always enough to do and she would find herself tidying cupboards to pass the time – or even reading the upmarket glossy magazines provided for the patients. Nor did she see much of her new boss. He was immersed in his job and cared about his patients, so that a great deal of his time was spent in the hospitals, both private and National Health. Really, she had far too little to occupy her, and since, meanwhile, the work in number seventeen was progressing quickly she found herself wishing that she could be there, taking part in it. She felt sure there were several things she could do without getting under Alec's feet.

It was now mid-August; seven o'clock in the evening of a day on which the sun had shone from early morning, warming the air, so that in her cotton frock she could sit outside, high above the ground, without feeling the slightest chill.

From her rooftop she looked across and over the intervening buildings towards the sea. The tide was on the turn, lapping lazily, as though reluctant to recede. The sky to the west, in the direction of the Palace pier, was a softer blue than earlier in the day, and just beginning to streak with pink. Then, she knew, for she watched it most evenings, would come the deeper, darker shades of blue and grey, and sometimes crimson and purple, until the night came, blotting out the colours, leaving only the lights outlining the pier and the seafront. Most fine evenings, while it was still light, she observed the snowy-white vapour trails from the planes which regularly crossed the Channel towards the Continent around this time. She presumed they came from Gatwick. As the planes, themselves scarcely visible, disappeared into the distance the trails would broaden, into what looked like teased-out cotton wool, before they vanished altogether, absorbed into the rest of the sky. She sighed in contentment, feeling at peace and relaxed – though there had been a few times over the last few months when she had stopped whatever she was doing and had asked herself, 'Am I *mad*?' But such moods had never lasted long. And if she hadn't quite pulled herself out of them then Alec

– or sometimes it had been Roger – had done that for her. How could I ever have managed without either one of them, she asked herself now? She thought back to what was her outstanding memory. It had happened on the day she had finally moved up from the basement.

It was true that the basic conversion of the house into flats had been almost completed on three of the floors when she had first set eyes on it, but there had still been the basement, and more importantly the top floor to be dealt with, and several necessary things, small and not so small, on all the floors: bathrooms and kitchens to fit, shelves to position; light fittings, floor coverings, and then the decorating to consider and carry out.

As soon as she had sold her parents' house, and to the delight of the buyers, she had decided that she would immediately move out of there and into the basement of number seventeen. She had told Rosie of her intention when they were actually standing in the Kemp Town basement. She herself had known for some time that this was what she would do; she had discussed it with Alec, who had said it made sense, even if it might not be madly comfortable, but she had not previously said anything to Rosie and it had not come up in conversation.

'How *can* you, Mother?' Rosie cried. 'How can you come from your lovely home in Bath to . . .' words failed her as she looked around '. . . and even *think* of living in this squalid mess? At least you could have stayed in Grandpa's house until this one was actually ready to move into!'

'That's not what I wanted to do,' Caroline had said. 'I like the idea of being here while it's all happening. And anyway, this is not a squalid mess. It looks that way because Alec and the other men working on the upstairs rooms with him kept everything in here. It can be cleared in no time at all. They can use one of the other basement rooms.'

147

'Which right now are chock-a-block with furniture from Bath.'

'They are not chock-a-block,' Caroline said firmly. 'As you well know, I brought only what I thought I could use here, and the rest I sold. For quite good prices, actually. And I did offer to give you anything you really wanted.'

'It wouldn't have gone well in my flat,' Rosie said.

'Exactly!' Caroline said. 'And nor would it here. This will be a different lifestyle. And I don't expect to be living in the basement for long. I've asked Alec to tidy it up, make it fit to live in, and after that to work on the top floor, on what will be my very own place. Those two things are to be given priority before anything else in the house is done, and as soon as the top floor is habitable I shall move in. And when it's had a lick of paint I shall put this basement – I beg its pardon, lower ground floor – flat up for renting.'

'Another thing about which you know nothing,' Rosie reminded her.

'And which is why I have asked Roger's advice,' Caroline said. 'Roger will advise me on everything legal, including a good letting agency. It was a brilliant idea on Patience's part to involve him.'

Alec consulted her on everything, and listened to her ideas, which, though it was no more than her due, pleased her greatly as she felt that by her interest and her efforts she was helping to give personality to the building itself.

'I'd thought all the walls and paintwork could be white,' Alec had said one day as they discussed the decorating. 'It goes with anything.'

'Oh no!' she disagreed. 'Yes, it goes with most things, but it can be too cold, too clinical. I think perhaps shades of cream. Still neutral, but warmer. Or better still, slightly different shades in each flat to make them more individual. But muted shades which would blend with most furnishings.'

Alec smiled, and waved his hand. 'OK! You're the boss!'

'I'm not trying to be bossy,' Caroline said. 'I enjoy thinking about all the details.' And as the weeks had gone by more and more ideas had come to her. Small things, some of them. Others more significant.

'I hadn't realized – I mean, at first – that you were so interested – and so full of ideas,' Alec said.

'Nor had I!' Caroline told him. She had surprised herself. Of course she had had a hand in furnishing and decorating her home in Bath, but it had been Peter's home also, and he had had traditional and conventional tastes, with which at the time she had been happy enough to agree.

Now, though, she seemed to be straying away from these conventional tastes and had a whole well of ideas that she wanted to share with Alec.

She leaned back in her chair, and looked around her. This space would eventually be her roof garden. She looked forward enormously to designing that, choosing the plants, furnishing it. It would be the place for small, intimate parties of chosen friends, friends who, as yet, still had to be made. On evenings like this, what could be better?

The day of the removal from Bath had not been easy, certainly not emotionally. Rosie had taken time off to come down the previous evening to be with her and to give her a hand. Almost, Caroline wished she had not done so, she wished she could have been left to herself and to the highly competent removal men, who arrived dead on time on the day itself and required nothing more than a constant flow of tea to keep them going. But one way and another she had got through it.

Quite soon after it was put on the market her parents' house had been sold, with no difficulty at all, and much of the furniture in it had been willingly bought by the buyers of the house, who were taking on the property largely to let it to students. The arrangement had suited both them and Caroline. She was relieved not to be burdened with so many decisions about what to keep and what to let go. What kept her going through it all was the thought of the time – not far distant, she told herself – when she would be firmly installed in number seventeen, everything in place and her new future ahead of her. What she had not bargained for was how difficult that last night in Bath had been, with the rooms stripped of all except bare essentials, not even a picture on a wall to remind her of her life there. She had been taken by surprise by the strength of her emotion. In some ways she felt almost worse than when Peter had died. Then she had buried him; but now she was deserting him. At one point guilt swept over her. She could say nothing of this to Rosie; Rosie, she was sure, felt it all intensely and who would *she* blame? Me, of course, Caroline thought unhappily. Who else?

Outwardly, everything had gone without a hitch. In the few minutes after the removal van left and before she locked the house door for the last time, while Rosie waited outside in the car for her, Caroline went alone around the house, ostensibly to see that nothing had been left behind, though there was more to it than that and she could not have borne to have anyone with her as she went in and out of each room. There were too many memories, happy and sad. She found herself touching things: walls, doors – the sitting-room curtains which she had chosen with such care at the time and now, being of no use in number seventeen, were to be left behind. She felt almost as if she were saying good-bye to people. Tears had pricked at her eyes.

'Stop it!' she'd told herself, as she'd gone to join Rosie. Nothing had been said as they'd driven away, and indeed not for several miles. What was there to say? But, she had reminded herself, I am leaving of my own free will to do something I want to do.

And now here she was, sitting on the roof, drinking her wine and feeling as if she had been here for ever. As if it was where she truly belonged.

She saw Alec most, though not all, afternoons when she was back from work. While there was always someone working on the house – an electrician, a carpenter or a decorator – Alec was not there all day every day, but he was there most afternoons, which was just as well as there was usually something or other about which she wished to consult him, and he always seemed to value her suggestions. 'Did you realize you had a real gift for interior design?' he had asked her one day.

'Of course I haven't!' she'd said, flushing slightly. 'You flatter me!' Nevertheless, she'd been pleased by the compliment and since then she'd put forward several more ideas.

'I don't flatter you,' he'd said, looking at her steadily. 'It's true. You have style – your own style. And you see things through a woman's eyes. Think of the differences you've made in this house.'

She knew what he said was true.

She enjoyed the discussions with Alec. She would be sorry when everything was done and there would be no further need for them. In fact, she would miss just seeing him, sharing a pot of tea in the afternoon, or a glass of wine if they had worked into the early evening. 'You know, you should think about interior design as a job,' he suggested one day.

She had laughed at him, feeling pleased in spite of herself. 'I'm not qualified for that!' she'd said.

'But you have the gift,' he'd insisted. 'For instance, you've chosen light fittings I might never have thought of – and they're exactly right. And you seem to be able to seek out the relatively inexpensive things and combine them in ways that are smart, and work well.'

151

'Thank you kindly, sir!' Caroline said. 'The thing is, it's quite simple. I just love doing it.'

Her thoughts turned now to Roger Pym. She owed so much to him. In addition to seeing her through the sale of the house in Bath, which had gone through without a hitch, to the delight of the Matthews, he had also been there to help with her parents' house. There he had advised her to use a local estate agent. 'They'll be there to hand,' he'd said. 'And they'll know local conditions. They'll know what they're talking about. It will make things easier for you.' But it was when she came to buying number seventeen that he had most truly been a guiding light, and not only in the transaction with the truculent Frank Teasdale. When that was signed and sealed to Roger's satisfaction he had talked with her at some length about prospective tenants. 'It's imperative,' he'd said, 'that you have legal agreements with the tenants of each flat, as well as about the building in general. What they can do, what they can't do. What *you* can do and can't do. What your obligations are. It must all be laid out, signed, sealed and delivered, so to speak. And this is for the convenience of all of you, living closely together in one building, as you will be.'

'You mean things like not practising on the saxophone at four in the morning?' Caroline asked.

'You may smile,' he said, 'but yes. That sort of thing, and more besides. Who keeps the hall and stairs clean – which you do. What you must insure for – very important, that. You'll be amazed by what landlords have to consider – and tenants too, of course. It cuts both ways. And word of mouth will not do.'

'I'm not expecting to have trouble,' Caroline had told him. 'I shall choose my tenants most carefully.'

'Of course you will,' he'd agreed. 'And it's possible you won't have any difficulties. But the best way to ensure that is to draw up good, workable agreements. Which, my dear,' he had added, 'I will be pleased to do for you if you'll let me!'

'Of course I'll let you!' she'd said. 'And I can't begin to tell you how grateful I am.'

'I'm enjoying it,' he'd said. 'And I'm enjoying seeing you more often than I've done for a long time.'

'Me too!' Caroline assured him.

He had also sorted out a reliable letting agency. 'Much better than sifting out the applicants for yourself – though only initially, of course. You yourself must get proper references from the would-be tenants. You must meet them, satisfy yourself that they'll be compatible. After all, they'll be living in your house, and so will you. You'll not be an absentee landlady.'

She had told the letting agency that she would inform them as soon as any particular flat was ready for occupation, and this week she had been able to tell them that the lower-ground-floor one was now available. 'But preferably for one person only,' she'd said. 'It's really not suitable for more – and certainly not for a family.'

'There'll be no difficulty about that, Mrs Denby,' the agent had said. 'We always have single persons looking for accommodation.'

She had been down earlier today to inspect it, see that the windows were clean, that everything was working which should work, and so on. She had sprayed it with air freshener – there was still a slight smell of new paint around. She had even thought of putting a small plant on the windowsill, but had decided that that was going a bit far. Really, all she could do now was wait for the phone call. She hoped it wouldn't be a long wait.

Sitting here, her thoughts drifted back to the day she had finally moved up into her own flat. Knowing that she had to go to work, Alec had said, 'Don't worry! I'll get help from one of my men. It will all be done when you get home.'

When she'd reached number seventeen Alec had opened

the door to her. 'I saw you from the window,' he'd said. 'Come and check that we've got everything in the right places.' He'd gone first into the living room, and she had followed him. She thought now that she would never, ever forget the surprise which awaited her. There, side by side, were the two chairs: the William Morris chairs which he had discovered in her parents' loft, the chairs that had meant so much to Caroline's grandparents and her mother, too. There they were: polished, lustrous, totally beautiful. She had been forced to blink back a tear.

'I can't believe it!' she'd gasped. 'I had no idea . . . !'

'A flat-warming present,' Alec had said. 'Not that they're not your own chairs.'

'They look totally different!' she'd said, smiling. It was so wonderful to have these chairs. Not only were they beautiful to look at but they represented a vital part of Caroline's life – her beloved grandparents, their loving marriage and all the happiness that sprang from it.

He'd smiled. 'I'm glad you're pleased,' he'd said.

The phone call she was waiting for came fifteen minutes later. She rushed inside and spoke to the agent. The first potential tenant would come to look at the flat at half past two the next day. As she replaced the phone she felt a shiver of anticipation.

154

FOURTEEN

At two thirty precisely the bell rang. Caroline ran down the stairs and opened the door. A woman was standing on the step. She was small, about five feet one, Caroline guessed, and probably in her seventies.

'Good afternoon!' the woman said. 'My name is Eleanor Grayson. I've come from the agency. And you, I hope, are Mrs Denby? I understand you have flats to let?' Her voice was deep and mellifluous, her accent cultured. She had an air of confidence, inborn confidence, as of a woman used to wielding authority; brought up to it, Caroline thought, which her appearance belied. Her skin was pale, with the pallor of age, her eyes were bright blue and, though puffy beneath and surrounded by a network of fine lines, gave the impression of missing nothing. Her lips were fuchsia-pink from not-too-carefully-applied lipstick; she had smudged over the edges. She wore a pillar-box-red coat, which had seen more fashionable days and a round, black felt hat which perched on the top of her head as if it had been carelessly dropped there from a height. Locks and tufts of white hair escaped from the hat and hung down over her forehead and ears. Her stockings were beige, and wrinkled; her shoes

155

black leather, with buckles. And yet, Caroline thought, how does she manage to look so awful, and at the same time, aristocratic? And sound immediately in charge?

'Good afternoon, Miss Grayson,' Caroline said. She knew instinctively that the lady would only wish ever to be called by her name and title, and guessed that only the chosen few would ever address her as Eleanor. 'Only one flat, so far. But do come in.'

'Lower ground floor, I understand,' Miss Grayson said. 'When I was a gel . . .' This is the first time I have ever heard anyone pronounce it 'gel', Caroline thought '. . . we called it the basement. The maids lived there. I always rather envied them. It was cosy and warm in the winter, while we shivered upstairs.'

Caroline led the way down from the hall. 'Though there are steps outside which lead down to your own front door,' she said.

'Ah!' Miss Grayson said. 'The tradesman's entrance. They used to call every morning for orders, and deliver them by lunch time. We lived in London, but it was the same everywhere – at least for some.'

'It's quite compact,' Caroline said as they went into the flat. Good heavens, she thought. I'm using estate agent's speak! Compact indeed! It was small. 'But I think you'll find it has everything you need,' she added. 'Living room, one bedroom, kitchen and bathroom. As you can see, it's newly decorated, but I'm waiting for new carpeting, which will be here in a few days. I've been living down here myself, and quite comfortably, while I was waiting for my flat on the top floor to be ready. And on this floor there are store rooms and a laundry room which any of my tenants may use if they wish to do so.'

Miss Grayson followed Caroline around, from time to time nodding what seemed like approval. 'And how many more flats are there to let?' she enquired.

'Three,' Caroline said. 'One on each floor before you get to mine. All larger ones. They're not quite ready yet, but they soon will be. So I'm afraid that means there will be work going on in the house until then, though I don't think it will disturb you. It's past the very noisy stage.'

'It all seems quite quiet at the moment,' Miss Grayson said.

'Yes,' Caroline agreed. 'My builder isn't here this afternoon.'

Miss Grayson had turned away and was looking out of the window. 'And a small patio, as one now has to call them,' she observed. 'I suppose that goes with this flat?'

'Oh yes,' Caroline said. 'It's been neglected – or at least the plants have. I reckon they hadn't been watered until I moved in. But it could be a pleasant place to sit out if one wished to.'

Miss Grayson turned back from the window and glanced around the room again, rather more intently. 'Yes,' she said, after a pause, 'my bits and pieces of furniture will fit in nicely here, even though they are all of another era. Inherited, you see. Though what they will think of ending up in a basement flat, who can say?'

Caroline smiled. 'Well,' she said, 'if you think one's furniture has feelings, as you seem to . . .'

'Oh, I do!' Miss Grayson interrupted. 'I feel *that* when I'm polishing something, making it look it's very best. In fact it's the only bit of housework I actually like doing.'

'Well then,' Caroline said, 'they'll know they're being cared for, looked after. They're not being abandoned, ending up in a saleroom.'

Miss Grayson gave her a look. 'How wise you are!' she said. 'You are not thinking – or if you are it doesn't show – why is this old woman going on about bits of furniture which have seen better days. And now there are one or two further questions I'd like to ask. Ground rules and so on.

157

I think one must always get that kind of thing sorted out, don't you?'

'Of course!' Caroline said. 'Why don't you come up to my flat and we can sit down and discuss things? Can you manage the stairs?'

Miss Grayson drew herself up to her full five feet one. 'Of course I can!' she said. 'I'm very fit, you know. Scarcely ever ill! I shan't need any looking after!'

Nevertheless, when she reached the top floor she was clearly breathless. 'Do sit down,' Caroline said. 'It's a long haul, isn't it? Would you like a glass of water?'

'Thank you, I would,' Miss Grayson said.

As she sipped it, Caroline told her of her plans for the rest of the house, and mentioned the agreement which all would have to sign. 'Including me,' she said. 'I will have responsibilities to my tenants, as they will to me. But it's all quite straightforward and sensible. My solicitor has drawn it up. And it's for the mutual convenience of all of us. I don't have a spare copy right now, though I will have in a day or two, and in the meantime I can tell you what's in it – which will give you time to think over whether you might or might not want to take the flat.'

Miss Grayson nodded at intervals as Caroline outlined the terms and conditions, then quickly said, 'I don't need to think it over. It's a nice little flat, and when I put my own things in it I daresay it could be quite cosy. And I like the area. It's remarkably unspoilt.'

'Even so,' Caroline said, 'do go away and think about it, at least for a few days, Miss Grayson. I won't let anyone step in ahead of you.'

When Miss Grayson had left, Caroline went outside and watered the plants at the front. They looked almost past it, she thought. She should have replaced them before now, and before anyone else came to look at any of the flats she would do so. They were not a good advertisement, though they hadn't put off Miss Grayson. She had rather taken to the old lady, and somehow 'old lady' seemed a derogatory way to think of her, though both words were true. I'll phone Roger and tell him about her, she decided as she walked back upstairs. Unusually, it was two or three days since she had last spoken with him. She wanted to tell someone about her first would-be tenant, and who better than Roger, who had been so encouraging all along?

As she went back into the house the phone rang. 'Talk of the devil . . .' she thought as she rushed to pick up the phone – but it was Alec.

'I'm calling to tell you I'll be a bit late in tomorrow,' he said. 'I have to be in Hove to take a delivery of some stuff. Is everything OK with you?'

'More than!' Caroline said. 'I've just got my first tenant! For the basement.'

'Wow!' Alec enthused. 'Wonderful! Didn't I tell you you wouldn't have any difficulty? And you'll have even less with the other flats.'

'I could hardly have less,' Caroline said excitedly. 'She wanted to make up her mind there and then but I told her she must think it over.'

'Quite right! What's she like?' Alec asked.

'Elderly. A bit posh, but nice with it. I reckon she's been used to more than a basement flat, but she seemed happy enough and she'd like to move in fairly soon.'

'That's wonderful!' Alec said warmly. 'And I'm sure you'll find the same will happen with the other flats. They'll be snapped up. Anyway, see you tomorrow!'

She put down the phone, hit suddenly by mixed feelings. He was probably right, she thought. The flats would go quickly, almost as soon as they were ready. And when they did, that would be the end of seeing Alec, which she did almost every day. She would miss him. She would miss their conversations, the way they pooled their ideas. They always had something to talk about. He had become a friend, but, she told herself firmly, their friendship was based on the work in the house. She had no other claims on him. And he had a girlfriend, though he seldom talked about her. Well, she would meet all that when she came to it, but for now she would phone Roger, which she had been about to do when Alec's call had come.

Roger was also delighted by her news. 'I was about to ring you. However, I would like to meet the lady myself,' he said. 'And of course I will do that when we discuss the agreement.'

'You mean you don't trust me to pick the right people?' Caroline said. She said it lightly, half teasing, though she was not totally pleased.

'Not at all. It's not like that,' Roger replied. 'But you don't know her, she's appeared out of the blue – and the same will apply to the other tenants.'

'And as we agreed earlier, I shall ask for references – not to mention a month's rent in advance.'

'I know,' Roger said. 'But one can't put all one's trust in references, though of course one has to ask for them. Look, you don't really mind me taking a hand in this, do you? A second opinion can do no harm and, as you know, I do have a good deal of experience of dealing with people in business matters.'

'Of course you do. I'm sorry, Roger! And it's good of you to care.' In a way, she thought, it might not be a bad thing if would-be tenants met with her in the company of her solicitor. 'Though you can't be zooming down from Bristol at a moment's notice,' she said.

'We can work something out. We'll see how it goes, shall we?'

'And don't think I'm not grateful,' Caroline said. 'Of course I am! You do so much for me. But you were ringing *me*. Was it something special?'

'I just wondered if it would be convenient if I came down to Brighton next weekend,' he said. 'See how you are, and so on. Bring the final agreements. I'd come on Saturday and stay overnight. I can easily book myself into an hotel.'

'Sure!' Caroline said. 'I'm sorry it's not convenient for you to stay here – not yet, at any rate. And perhaps I can arrange for you to meet the new tenant, if that's what you'd like.'

'That would be fine,' Roger said. 'Until Saturday, then.'

She had hardly put the phone down when the doorbell rang again. Another would-be tenant, she asked herself as she ran down the stairs? But if that were so, then wouldn't the agency have rung her first?

She opened the door to a young woman: tall, slender, probably in her mid-thirties, with straight blond hair, shoulder-length, beautifully cut. She was casually but, Caroline thought, carefully dressed in faded denim jeans, a white T-shirt and a short, soft black leather jacket. The woman smiled, and spoke first.

'Hi, you must be Caroline. I'm Paula. I came to see Alec's mistress!'

Caroline knew who Paula was; but what in the world had he said to her?

'I am Caroline,' she said, feeling flustered and wrong-footed. 'But you've got the rest wrong.'

Paula gave her a puzzled look, then burst into laughter. 'Oh, my goodness! Oops! Sorry! I didn't mean *you*! I meant this house! Hasn't he told you I refer to it as his mistress? He spends half his life here and talks about it for the other half. Not that it matters. When it comes to my job I'm afraid I'm just as bad. And that's what I need to see him about. I tried his mobile but I couldn't get a reply; all I got was voicemail. It must be switched off and he hasn't checked it. I didn't know your phone number here, only the address. It's all rather urgent.'

'I'm sorry,' Caroline said. 'Do come in, though he's not

161

here. He might be in Hove. He's working there part of the time. But I do have the number and you can ring from here if you wish.'

She couldn't help but feel a slight sense of indignation at the idea of her as Alec's mistress being quite so hilarious.

Paula followed her to the telephone, and dialled the number. 'Oh, Alec, thank goodness you're there,' she said. 'Your mobile's not working. Look! I have to leave in a hurry. It's the Sledges. Something's come up and we have to be in Sheffield for a gig this evening at nine o'clock. They'll be opening for the XLs. Well, yes – isn't that fantastic – and even *you* have heard of the XLs! The band they'd booked has let them down without any notice, more or less fallen apart, or so it seems. I don't know the details. Anyway, their agent had seen the Sledges and called me to see if we could step into the breach. Seems we're getting known a bit, isn't that great? And that's not all. How about this? From Sheffield they're booked to go on to York, Leeds and Newcastle! All university towns so they'll be perfect audiences. A week's bookings altogether, and we've nothing else on right now. It's a great chance. I've already alerted the boys. We'll have to set off within the next hour or two to get to Sheffield and give us time to do a sound check and all that. It's a four-hour drive, mostly up the M1, thankfully.'

There was a pause while she listened, then she said, 'No, Alec! I simply can't afford to turn it down, and I wouldn't for the boys' sakes. We *must* take it and I must go. It's a great chance. And there's the association with the XLs. Who knows what that might lead to? It's important to the boys *and* to me.' There was another pause. 'Yes, I know I always put work first,' she said. 'So do you. Look, I can't argue about it. I have to go now. I'll ring you tonight when it's over. I've no idea where we'll be staying. They'll fix up something. Bye, honey!'

She rang off. 'Thank you,' she said to Caroline. 'Nice

meeting you, but I must fly. I have to pack the van, pick up the boys and the equipment, and get to Sheffield. Hope to see you again some time.' She blew out of the house almost as quickly as she had blown in, leaving Caroline feeling confused and a little jealous of this vibrant, successful young woman.

Roger arrived shortly after twelve noon on Saturday. 'A lovely day here!' he said. 'It was raining when I left Bristol. How are you?'

'I'm fine!' Caroline told him. 'And you?' She was always, these days, surprised anew by how good he looked. He was one of those men who were, unusually, she thought, more handsome in middle age than they had been when they were younger. His thick, dark hair was greying in exactly the right places. Or not greying but, better still, turning silvery. She supposed he must always have been good-looking, but when they'd all been young together she hadn't thought about it.

'I thought we'd have lunch here,' she said. 'Something very simple. I've made a good, old-fashioned shepherd's pie, if that's all right.'

'Couldn't be better,' Roger said. 'But I thought you might like to eat out.'

'We can do that this evening,' Caroline said. 'And since you want to set eyes on her, I've arranged for Miss Grayson to pop in this afternoon. Around three o'clock.'

'Fine!' Roger said. 'And now tell me everything you've been doing – and show me, of course. It looks fine up here!' He glanced around her flat with approval. 'But then you were always good at making the place you lived in seem special.'

'Was I?' Caroline said. 'I never knew that.'

'Oh yes, you were,' Roger said.

'Thank you!' Caroline said, smiling at the unexpected compliment. 'And is it all right if we eat first and I show you around afterwards? The pie is in the oven and the vegetables are only going to take minutes.'

'Fine by me!' Roger agreed.

When they had eaten – ('It was delicious!' Roger said. She wondered what he usually ate if he found a run-of-the-mill shepherd's pie delicious?) – she showed him around the whole house. 'I'm impressed,' he said. 'It's all come on a lot since I was last here, though that's not all that long ago.'

'Oh, it has. But then that tends to happen at this stage. The main fittings are all in, the last of the decorating will be done at the beginning of next week and the carpets go down on Thursday. I also have rather nice blinds going up at all the windows. The last thing I wanted was a variety of curtains, especially where they face the street. And they won't be needed now.'

'It's going to look really good,' Roger said. 'So when do you expect the other flats to be ready for letting?'

'Very soon,' Caroline said. 'In fact, I don't see why I shouldn't give the agency the go-ahead for viewing. People can see what they'll be like when they *are* ready. And the sooner I start taking rents, the better. I seem to have spent an awful lot of money.'

Miss Grayson arrived on the dot of three. Caroline suspected that she did this with every appointment she ever made. 'So, Mr Pym,' she said good-humouredly when she was introduced to Roger and it was established that he was Caroline's solicitor, 'have you come to look me over?'

Roger grinned. 'Not exactly, Miss Grayson. It's good to meet you . . .'

'But wise to do so!' she said with a mischievous glint in her eye. 'Tell me, are you related to the Shropshire Pyms? My family knew them quite well at one time.'

'No,' Roger said. 'I don't think so. But it might be interesting to find out.'

She waved her hand. 'I wouldn't bother. They weren't the nicest people. I never liked them, nor did my father, and he was a good judge of character. I once read that we are all probably related to everyone else, if we dig deep enough. For what it's worth.'

'And, Miss Grayson, do you think you will be happy here?' Roger broke in. 'Forgive me for stating the obvious but it's a far cry from London. You live in Kennington, don't you?'

'That's right,' she said. 'And I've had enough of London.'

'Well then . . .' Caroline said. 'Perhaps we can—'

Miss Grayson interrupted whatever she had been going to say. 'There is one more thing. It hadn't arisen when I spoke to you earlier, but now it has, and it's very important to me.' She sounded nervous, not a quality Caroline had observed in her up to now.

'And what is that?' It was Roger who asked.

'Well,' Miss Grayson said, 'the thing is . . . would I be allowed, could I possibly bring a dog?'

'A dog?' Caroline said. 'You didn't mention this earlier.'

'I know,' Miss Grayson agreed. 'As I've just said, I wasn't sure about the circumstances, but now I am.'

'And what are they exactly?' Roger enquired.

'The thing is,' Miss Grayson said, 'my neighbours in Kennington have informed me that they have at last made up their minds to emigrate. They have this dog – the dearest dog you could ever imagine – and they will not be allowed to take her with them. They were therefore hoping and expecting – not without reason – that I might take over the dog. I have known her since she first came to them as a puppy. She and I have always been great friends. She is now six years old.'

There was a silence. Caroline, though she was not averse to dogs, imagined it at once, and for no good reason, to be a German shepherd. Very large; possibly fierce.

165

'What kind of a dog?' Roger asked. 'Your flat is not particularly large.'

'Oh, my goodness!' Miss Grayson said. 'Not a *large* dog. I wouldn't dream of asking you that. No, this one is a Bichon Frisé. Particularly small, as perhaps you know. Her name is Frizzie. She is totally housetrained and exceptionally beautiful. Naturally, I would make sure she was no trouble to anyone, and of course I have my own front door so she wouldn't need to come into the rest of the house.'

She sat there, having made her plea, her face creased with anxiety.

Roger and Caroline looked at one another. 'It's up to you,' Roger said.

Caroline hardly hesitated. Miss Grayson suddenly seemed rather small and defenceless and she felt sorry for her. 'Very well,' she said, 'you may bring Frizzie!'

Miss Grayson's face was instantly suffused with relief and happiness. 'God bless you!' she said. 'Not that I am in the habit of invoking God. Not at all. But I think, having heard of Frizzie's situation, if you had said no, then I couldn't have come without her.'

They discussed when she and the dog might move in, and agreed that a couple of weeks ahead would be fine. 'I shall arrange for a van to bring my bits and pieces,' Miss Grayson said. 'And I will bring Frizzie on the train.'

Not long after Miss Grayson left, Alec arrived. It was a surprise to Caroline: she didn't usually see him on a Saturday. Alec himself seemed equally surprised to see Roger. 'I was in the area,' Alec said. 'I thought I'd just call in and see if everything was OK.'

'Fine!' Caroline said, hurriedly composing herself. 'I enjoyed meeting Paula yesterday. Were you pleased by her news? I'm sure you were.'

Alec turned to Roger. 'My girlfriend is the manager of

166

a band – the Sledges. You probably won't have heard of them, but if Paula were here she'd probably say you will, and before too long. They're going places, she tells me, and I expect she's right. I can't judge – I'm not into bands – but they've had a few good write-ups. Paula's a professional photographer, magazines and so on, and she started out doing PR stuff for the Sledges – and now she manages them. Which is why she rushed off North. Anyway, if everything's OK, I'll shoot. I'll see you Monday afternoon,' he said to Caroline. He left as quickly as he had arrived.

'It's a lovely afternoon,' Caroline said when he had gone. She suddenly felt a bit flat and needed to cheer herself up. 'Shall we go for a walk? Would you like to go down to the marina?'

'Why not?' Roger said, offering her his arm.

FIFTEEN

Caroline, with Roger, called in at the letting agency before making for the marina. 'You've just caught us in time, Mrs Denby,' the agent said. 'I was about to close up. We usually keep open on Saturday afternoon as long as there are customers around. So what can I do for you?'

'I hoped to catch you,' Caroline told him. 'Mr Pym and I have just seen Miss Grayson. She's very keen to have the basement flat, and Mr Pym has checked her references.'

'Which are fine!' Roger said.

'So I think we can finalize that one,' Caroline said, 'and I've also decided that the other flats can now be offered – certainly they can be viewed.'

'No problem,' the agent said. 'I'll put out the details first thing on Monday. I reckon you won't have the slightest difficulty in letting.'

'I hope you're right – and I do hope you send me some nice tenants,' Caroline said.

'I'll do my very best,' the agent promised. 'I won't send anyone I think isn't suitable. They're lovely flats, in a decent area, and you'll be living on the premises, so you need tenants to match.'

There was a narrow path below the level of the seaward side of the road which led to the marina. 'I discovered this only recently,' Caroline said, 'which surprised me. I suppose it was always here, it looks well trodden.' In spite of that they met only one walker – a man pushing a child in a buggy – and one cyclist, for whom there was scarcely room to pass, and he had no intention of dismounting. Reaching the marina Caroline thought she might have liked to look at the shops, but Roger was immediately taken by the scores of craft which crowded the waterways. 'I'd no idea there was so much going on,' he said. 'Some of them are exceedingly smart, aren't they? There must be millions of pounds bobbing around on the water here! As a matter of fact, I always rather fancied having a boat but I never got around to it.'

Caroline smiled. 'That's where you and I would part company!' she said. 'I prefer to keep my feet on dry land.'

They walked around, looking at everything. 'Actually,' Roger said after a while, 'we could eat down here. There's no shortage of restaurants.'

'If you like,' Caroline said. 'But I'll need to go back home first, pick up a coat. It will be chilly when the sun goes down.'

Roger smiled at her. 'Did you notice you said "home"? Is that how you feel?'

'I hadn't noticed,' Caroline admitted. 'I said it without thinking. But yes, I do feel like that!'

'Good!' Roger said.

They lingered a while longer, Roger still looking at the boats, then he said, 'I think I'd better book a table. Saturday evening and all that. Do you know anywhere?'

'I don't,' Caroline said. 'But there's a restaurant which belongs to the new hotel. I've heard it's good.'

'Then let's try it,' Roger said.

'Or I could cook something,' Caroline offered. 'I promise it won't be shepherd's pie again . . .'

'Whatever it is, I'd much prefer it,' Roger said quickly. 'I eat out far too often. I think one does, living alone. Do you find that?'

'Not really,' Caroline said. 'I'm guilty too often of living on snacks, not making proper meals. Perhaps women like having someone to cook for?'

'Then I'm happy to oblige, at any time,' Roger said. 'I remember how many meals we shared when we were younger, you and Peter, Bettina and me. You made the best *boeuf bourguignon* I ever tasted.'

'Gosh, that takes me back. It was one of my party dishes,' Caroline said. 'I haven't made it for years.'

'They were good times, when we were young,' Roger said. 'While they lasted. And you don't look any different, not the least bit.'

'Oh, Roger, of course I do!' Caroline said, flattered none-theless. 'How could I not? But thank you kindly all the same.'

They wandered around a little longer until, suddenly, the wind changed and a chilly breeze blew from the water. Caroline hunched her shoulders against it. 'You're cold!' Roger said. 'I think we should go back.'

They returned at a brisker pace. 'I've really enjoyed this afternoon,' Roger said when they reached number seven-teen. 'You really have chosen a pleasant area to live in.'

'I think so,' Caroline agreed. 'All I need now is some nice tenants. I do hope I get them – nice ones, I mean.'

Back at the house, later on, she made mushroom omelettes and they drank a bottle of white wine, sitting at the table, placed in the window so that there was a glimpse of the sea. It was too chilly now to sit outside. They lingered over their coffee until the night was quite dark, then Roger said, a touch reluctantly, 'I suppose I must go! I've really enjoyed my day – and I'll see you tomorrow before I leave.'

'I've enjoyed it too,' Caroline said. 'It was good of you to come. I do feel I'm being taken care of.'

The agent was as good as his word. He put out the details on Monday and on Wednesday afternoon Caroline – she had not long been home from work – received a call from him. 'I have a Mr and Mrs Winslow here with me, from London. They are very interested in seeing your flats. Would it be convenient for them to come around now?'

'Of course!' Caroline said. She would like to have asked him more about them, but since they were almost certainly sitting opposite to him, it was not possible.

They arrived fifteen minutes later. Mr Winslow was tall, good-looking, well spoken. His wife was tiny, well dressed, and proved enthusiastic about everything Caroline told them and showed them. 'And I particularly like the ground-floor flat,' Mrs Winslow said. She turned to her husband. 'What do you think?' she asked him.

'I agree with you, dear,' he said. 'And if that suits you, then that's it! How soon could we move in?' he asked Caroline. 'The thing is, we've sold our place and the buyers, who have recently returned from abroad, are anxious to take possession.'

'They're living in an hotel. With two small children, poor dears! They can't even unpack properly!' his wife added. 'I feel so sorry for them.'

Caroline showed them a copy of the tenancy agreement. 'I think you ought to read through this,' she said. 'See what's expected. Just the usual things, of course.'

Mr Winslow read quickly. 'It seems straightforward to me,' he said. He turned to his wife. 'Do you want to read it, dear?'

'Oh no!' she said. 'I'll take your word for it, darling. You understand these legal things.'

171

'So what shall we say, dear? Shall we think it over?'

She shook her head. 'I don't need to,' she said firmly. 'It's exactly what we want.'

Mr Winslow gave Caroline a broad smile. 'So there you are!' he said. 'You've got yourself two new tenants!'

'Wonderful!' Caroline said – and then, remembering Roger's instructions, said, 'Subject to references, of course!'

'Of course!' Mr Winslow agreed. 'We'll let you have them as soon as we can. In fact, we'll get our referees to telephone you.'

'I'm afraid my solicitor will want written ones,' Caroline apologized. 'But I'll give you his address and telephone number, and I'm sure he'll do everything he can to deal with things quickly. Perhaps you'd like to give me the names of your referees while you're here. That might speed things up.'

Mr Winslow wrote down two names and addresses. 'And your bank details,' Caroline reminded him.

'Absolutely!' he said. 'Well then, I think all that seems satisfactory.'

'I shall so look forward to living here,' Mrs Winslow said. 'It's a lovely flat, and for some time now I've wanted to live in Brighton. One can tire of London.'

Caroline showed them to the door and watched them walk away. What a charming couple, she thought. And how lucky I am, yet again. She would phone Roger, she decided. He would be in his office but he probably wouldn't mind.

'That was quick work,' he said. 'So what did you think of them?'

'I liked them,' said Caroline. 'They were very friendly and easygoing.'

'Actually, I would like to meet them myself, but I can't get down this weekend. However, when they let me have the references I'll get on to them quickly. And how are you?' he added.

'I'm fine, absolutely flat out though. And I really did enjoy last weekend.'

'So did I,' Roger said. 'So did I.'

On Friday afternoon the agent phoned again. 'Well, Mrs Denby,' he said. 'Things are really moving, I have two more prospective tenants. Adam Carter and Eric Foster. Nice young men, who both have jobs in Brighton – but they'll give you all the details. Could you see them tomorrow morning, say at ten o'clock?'

'Sure!' Caroline replied. Again Roger would be disappointed that he couldn't be there to meet them, but really, she thought, she was quite capable of making her own judgements. It was kind and thoughtful of him to want to guide her, to be protective, but while she wasn't averse to that she was not sure that she needed it. She could trust her own judgement.

The two young men arrived on Saturday, a pouring wet morning. 'What a day!' she said. 'Do come in!'

They were, she judged, in their early thirties, or perhaps the taller of the two was a little older. 'I'm Adam Carter,' he introduced himself in a pleasant, confident voice. 'And this is my friend, Eric Foster.' Adam Carter was tall – six feet or more; thin, red-haired and cleanshaven. Eric Foster was shorter, dark-skinned, thinner and the quieter of the two.

'The agent said you had three flats to let,' Adam Carter said, following her into the house, with Eric Foster a step behind him.

'I did have, until a few days ago,' Caroline agreed, 'but now I've let the ground-floor one. Subject to confirmation, but I don't think they'll change their minds. However, the flats are all similar in layout and there's still the first- and

173

second-floor ones to choose from. I'll show you both of them. The first-floor one has the rather nice iron balcony at the front. Perhaps you noticed it?'

Adam Carter nodded. 'We did,' he said. 'It's attractive – and typical of the period, isn't it? Other things being equal, that's the one we'd like to see.' He looked at Eric, who nodded in agreement.

'Other things are *almost* equal,' Caroline said. 'The living space is the same in both flats, but the balcony flat is a little more expensive.'

Adam nodded. 'That makes sense.'

She led the way upstairs. 'Do you live in Brighton?' she enquired.

'We do,' Adam said. 'But not together. This will be our first shared home. I'm a radiotherapist at the hospital and Eric is a librarian. Actually, Eric lives in Hove and I live in Patcham, so there's quite a distance. This area would be perfect for both of us.'

Caroline wondered if Adam always spoke for them both – but it didn't seem to bother Eric. He continued to smile, and nodded assent in the right places. 'It's so well thought out. And I *love* the kitchen, which is just as well because I'm the one who does the cooking.'

When it seemed they had inspected everything Caroline said, 'And now I must show you the basement. There is a small flat at the front, for which I have a tenant, an elderly lady. She'll be moving in quite soon, and then there are a couple of storerooms and a laundry room. There's also a small garden, which has been neglected and must be put to rights. Any of my tenants can use the garden if they wish to. Are either of you gardeners?'

'Not so far,' Adam said. 'But who knows?'

'I might quite like to do that!' Eric said suddenly. When he does speak, Caroline thought, he has rather a nice voice. Deeper than one would have thought.

174

'Thank you for showing us around,' Adam said. 'We'll talk it over.' I wonder what Eric will have to say, Caroline asked herself. 'And we'll get back in touch, probably later today,' Adam promised.

What very pleasant young men they were, she thought as she closed the door on them. She would be very happy to have them as tenants. And now she would phone Roger yet again. She was sure if he'd met them he would have liked them. It was all happening, she thought happily. And so quickly!

She rang Roger at once, but there was no reply and she left a message. 'More good news!' she said. 'Call me back' – which he did, but not until Sunday. She wondered, in the meantime, what he had been doing with his Saturday evening. For her part she had watched wall-to-wall television: two documentaries, both of which she'd seen before, and a whodunnit, of which halfway through she'd guessed the end. After that she had gone to bed.

'More good news?' Roger said when he rang. 'So what is it?'

'Another two tenants – first floor. Two young men. They were pleased with everything. They'd like to move in as soon as you get the OK on their references.' She told him everything she so far knew about them.

'They sound all right,' Roger said. 'I look forward to meeting them.'

'Which I'm sure you'll do soon,' Caroline said. 'Anyway, I have a good feeling about them. In fact, I've been lucky with everyone I've seen so far.'

'And you're very trusting. In a way, I'm pleased you are. It means you're a confident person. Even so, I'll follow up their references right away.'

'Thank you. I'm glad you're doing all that part. I shall owe you a small fortune by the time all this is finished!'

175

'Don't worry,' Roger said. 'I shall give you a very special discount. So if this goes through you now have only the second floor to let. That's pretty good, isn't it?'

'Wonderful! I'm delighted,' Caroline admitted. 'I never thought it would go so smoothly, and so quickly.'

It was not to last. On the following Tuesday afternoon Roger telephoned.

'Not good news this time!' he announced. 'The Winslows! I've had a letter from his bank. Short and to the point. "We regret we are unable to give a reference for the above-named" is precisely what it says.'

'Unable to give a reference?' Caroline said. 'But why? Whatever for?'

'The bank is not obliged to say why, and they haven't done so, but it's not the first time in my life I've come across those words,' Roger said. 'The long and short of it is, the Winslows are clearly not financially sound.'

'What about their other referees?' Caroline asked. 'Have you heard from them?'

'Not yet,' Roger said. 'But the bank reference is the important one. You can't – you definitely *mustn't* – entertain these people in the face of this.'

'But I'm astonished!' Caroline exclaimed. 'And rather sad. They seemed such *nice* people! Both of them.'

'Con artists usually are,' Roger said. 'It's part of their stock in trade. They probably have a load of debts in London. But don't worry, you'll find someone else. And most people, in my experience, *are* decent.'

'But obviously not all. And it's certainly shaken my faith in myself as a good judge of character. I might have said yes to them without turning a hair! And now, of course, I'm wondering about the two men.'

'Don't!' Roger said firmly. 'Wait and see. They'll probably be fine – though of course I haven't seen them, any more than I did the Winslows. But they sound genuine.'

'So did the Winslows.'

The next morning she rang the agent and gave him the news. 'Well, I'm truly sorry about that!' he said. 'And surprised – though I suppose I shouldn't be, it does occasionally happen. I do regret that I sent them to you, but I was taken in – as you were – and in my case in spite of my fairly long experience in the job. They seemed quite genuine.'

'They certainly did to me,' Caroline said.

'But thank goodness you found out,' the agent said. 'That will have saved you a great deal of trouble, not to mention money.'

'Or thank goodness my solicitor found out,' she said. 'I know he thinks I'm too trusting, but what else can one do? I don't want to be suspicious of the whole world.'

'Well, never mind, Mrs Denby,' he said. 'And I'm sure we'll very soon find someone who *will* suit you. It's early days yet.'

He was as good as his word. He called her the next day. 'I saw someone today who might well fill the bill,' he said. 'Though it's rather a sad story. A Mr Thomas Downey. His marriage is on the rocks – though he and his wife are not divorced – and as a result of this his wife and sixteen-year-old son are to remain in the matrimonial home while he has chosen to move out and seeks a place where his son could spend every other weekend with him. Mr Downey has a business in Brighton, so he needs to be somewhere fairly local. Would you like to see him? And I imagine he's solvent, unlike the unfortunate Winslows.'

'Yes, please do send him my way,' Caroline said.

Mr Downey came later that day, on his way home from work in the early evening. He was smartly dressed in a dark suit, and seemed gentle and was softly spoken. 'I'm told you have two vacant flats,' he said. 'One on the second floor and the other on the ground. I'd much prefer the ground floor. The thing is, when my son comes to stay with me I think he would feel happier on the ground floor. He's at a difficult age. As far as I can I want to do what's best for him.'

'Of course,' Caroline agreed. 'I'll show you the ground-floor flat and you can see what you think of it.'

He walked around with her, nodded approval of everything, but said little.

'Would you like to see the other one, while you're here?' she asked.

He shook his head. 'This will do fine.'

She felt sorry not only for the son, but for the father too – and then she told herself quite firmly that she must not let her heart rule her head, and since Roger was due to come to Brighton at the weekend, and also because she was not totally sure of herself, she decided she would involve him. It was what he would like anyway.

'There's just one other thing,' she said, 'my solicitor likes to meet my prospective tenants and he will be here on Saturday. So if you decide you're interested in the flat, would it be convenient for you to meet him then? I'd hold it for you if you wish. And perhaps you might like to bring your son with you, let him see what the place is like?'

'That would be a good idea,' Mr Downey said, 'but would it be possible for us to come in the afternoon? Greg plays football on Saturday mornings and I wouldn't want him to miss that. Nor would he. It would start us off with a black mark.'

'Afternoon is fine,' Caroline assured him.

She had no sooner got up to her flat than the phone rang. It was Rosie. 'This isn't the first time I've tried to get you,' she said. 'You always seem to be on the phone these days. It's not like you!'

178

'Sorry about that,' Caroline said. 'I was with a would-be tenant.'

'And did you clinch it?' Rosie asked.

'Not quite. He's coming again on Saturday. But I think I shall. And that's not all!' She told Rosie about the other tenants. 'Or prospective tenants,' she said. 'If the references are OK.'

'Do let me know,' Rosie said. 'But in fact I was ringing to ask if I could come down for the weekend fairly soon. Say Saturday fortnight, arrive lunch time and leave some time on Sunday. Would that be OK?'

'Of course!' Caroline said. 'I shall look forward to it. In fact, Roger will be here this coming Saturday. He's going to give a prospective tenant the once-over.'

'You seem to be seeing a lot of Roger these days,' Rosie said warily.

'He's being very helpful,' Caroline answered, trying not to let a defensive note creep into her voice.

'I did wonder,' Rosie said, changing tack, 'whether I should pick up Aunt Patience and bring her with me? It's a while since we saw her. What do you think?'

'I think that would be great,' Caroline said. 'I'd love to see Patience, so will you get in touch with her? And I'll see you on Saturday week. I'm really looking forward to showing you what's been done since you were last here.'

'Well, I'm glad it's all going well,' Rosie said. 'I'll have to ring off. I'm calling from the office and we're rather busy. Lots of love!'

It was lovely hearing from Rosie, Caroline thought. She hoped that the prickly period they had been going through would soon be over. Things were already improving between them.

SIXTEEN

Tom Downey arrived, as arranged, on Saturday afternoon. Caroline introduced him to Roger.

'I'm sorry my son isn't with me,' Downey apologized. 'He couldn't make it. Something cropped up unexpectedly.' It was not true. The truth was that Greg had not wanted to come, he had dug his heels in and flatly refused to do so. 'Unfortunately,' Downey continued, 'my son is not taking any of this well, and of course he blames me.'

'That's a shame,' Roger said. 'But it might be better once you move in, once he's spent his first weekend here. And I gather he will be here only at weekends?'

'That's right,' Downey said. 'And not every weekend, perhaps no more than alternate ones. But if he doesn't do at least that I stand to lose touch with him, perhaps almost completely. I don't want to do that.'

'Don't worry,' Caroline said. 'It's early days; he'll get used to it.' She was not the least bit sure, but no way would she show it. 'And other things being equal, do you think you'd be happy here?' she asked him.

He shook his head. 'It's all to try for,' he said. 'And it's up to me to try it, and to make a go of it. I suppose I will.

Other people do. So yes, I'd like to take the flat, and if it's agreeable to you I'd like to move in within a couple of weeks. Would that be all right?'

'I don't see why not,' Caroline answered. She glanced at Roger and he nodded agreement.

'I'll need a little time to sort out my possessions and decide what I'll bring,' Downey said. 'That's something to be agreed with my wife. As far as I'm concerned she can keep the lot . . . except . . .'

'Except?' Caroline prompted him.

'Except for my music and my CDs. I wouldn't want to be parted from those. Or my books.'

'What kind of music?' Caroline asked.

'Classical,' he said. 'But don't worry. I won't fill the house with it. I almost always listen through headphones. It's better that way.'

'That's all right, then,' Caroline said. 'Not that I'm averse to hearing music, but there'll be the other tenants to consider. Anyway, let me tell you about them.' She mentioned Miss Grayson. 'She moves in next week,' she said. 'And there will be two young men above you, on the first floor, and me here on the top floor. The second floor is ready and I'm sure we'll have someone for it soon. So far, they all seem very nice people and I imagine you'll get on with them.' Whether his son would, she thought, was another matter – but not of great importance. He wouldn't be here much. And come to that, her tenants didn't have to mix with each other if they didn't want to.

'And I'll have to furnish the flat,' Downey said. 'Tables, chairs, beds, kitchen stuff.' He remembered, as he was saying the words, the excitement he and Myrna had felt furnishing their first home when they were newly married. They'd been short of money then; every piece of furniture had been a small triumph; but they had been happy days.

'If I can be of any help in that line, please do say,' Caroline offered. She felt sorry for him. He seemed uncertain which way to turn, though possibly in normal circumstances he was a very decisive man.

'Right!' Roger said. 'Then it all seems satisfactory. I'll check your references, of course, and then we'll deal with the tenancy agreement. I do hope you'll enjoy living here.'

'And I hope your son will grow to like it,' Caroline said. 'Will he bring some of his possessions do you think? I mean, to furnish his own room?'

Downey shook his head. 'I'm fairly certain *not*,' he said. 'There's no way he intends to make anything of a home here. I hope that doesn't sound rude. I don't mean it to.'

'Of course not,' Caroline said. 'It's understandable, especially to begin with.'

'I do hope,' Caroline said after Tom Downey had left, 'that I'm not going to end up with a number of people who don't fit in anywhere else. I don't see myself in the role of counsellor or adviser, or even a shoulder to cry on. Does that seem harsh?'

Roger smiled. 'Not really,' he said. 'And it's not inevitable. But in the end it's largely up to you, isn't it? All the same, if you have a number of flats in one house you're also bound to have a disparate number of characters – and you will be living in the middle of them.'

'On top of them, actually,' Caroline said. 'But I know what you mean.'

'You must set the boundaries yourself,' Roger said. 'If it's a case of a blocked sink, or the lights on the stairs suddenly don't work – that kind of thing – then you have to do something about it, but otherwise you're not responsible for other people's difficulties, however sympathetic you might feel. Indeed, you have no right to be.'

Caroline nodded. 'That's true,' she said. 'I must bear it in mind. It's just that at the moment I feel so sorry for Mr

Downey's circumstances, not that I know the full story, of course . . .'

'. . . And no doubt for Miss Grayson's possible loneliness, and whatever difficulties your tenants might have,' Roger said. 'None of which are your responsibility, or even your business. They are all grown-up people. You're not running a home for the bereft and the bewildered.'

'You're right! Of course you are!' Caroline conceded.

The following week Miss Grayson moved in. Everything exactly to plan, Alec said to Caroline afterwards. He had a few odd jobs to do in the house and, since Caroline would be at work in the morning, had offered to coincide them with the arrival of the furniture van, which was due around noon, and turned up on the dot. When Caroline reached home Alec was still there.

'I've put everything in what I hope might be the right places, where I think it should go,' he said. 'If I've got something wrong, then I'll probably still be around when she arrives, but if not I can drop in tomorrow and deal with it. No need for you to do so, let alone Miss Grayson. As you can see, it's good, solid old-fashioned stuff, and quite heavy.'

'Thank you!' Caroline said. 'You're very kind. It all looks fine to me. Have you eaten? If not, I'm going to have some soup, so would you like to join me?'

'That would be lovely, it seems like some time since we've had a chat,' Alec said. 'What time is Miss Grayson due?'

'Around two thirty,' Caroline told him.

She heated the soup and served it with bread rolls she had bought on the way home.

'How is everything going?' Alec asked.

'Very well,' she said. 'I have a new tenant moving into the ground floor in the next fortnight, then the two men I told you about will be here next week, and today Miss

183

Grayson. That leaves only one flat unoccupied. And how about you?'

'I'm fine,' Alec said. 'Quite busy.'

'And Paula?' she asked, trying to keep her voice casual.

'She's also fine,' Alec said. 'Not that I've seen a great deal of her. The Sledges have really taken off. Paula's feet hardly touch the ground these days.'

Less than an hour later Miss Grayson arrived by taxi from the station. When Caroline answered the bell there she was, standing on the doorstep, a large bag in one hand and in the other a dog lead, attached at the other end to a not-very-happy-looking small white bundle of fur.

'This is Frizzie,' Miss Grayson said. 'She was all right on the train but she didn't care much for the taxi. The driver did throw us around a bit, and she's not used to it. What she needs is a nice long drink of water. I've got her bowl in my bag.'

'She shall have it at once,' Caroline said, leading the way down to the flat, Alec following, carrying Miss Grayson's bag.

Stepping inside the flat, Miss Grayson looked around, then nodded. 'You've kindly had a go at putting everything into place,' she said. 'Not quite in the right places, of course, but I'll soon sort that out.' She turned to the dog, who was staying close to her feet. 'And now, Frizzie,' she said, 'you shall have a nice long drinky!' She fished the water bowl out of her bag and handed it to Alec. 'Would you be so kind?' she asked him.

He jumped to her assistance. Caroline had the feeling that everyone jumped to Miss Grayson's assistance, also that Miss Grayson would have been surprised had they not done so.

Frizzie lapped at the water as though she would never stop, nor did she until the bowl was empty. 'There, Frizzie!'

Miss Grayson cooed, 'you *were* a thirsty little girl, weren't you? And now we'll sort out your basket and you can have a proper sleep.'

'I've already sorted that out,' Alec said. 'I didn't know where you'd want it but I've put it in the living room.'

'That's quite right,' Miss Grayson said. 'Living room by day, and I'm afraid on my bed at night. She's not fond of sleeping alone – are you, my dear?' she said, turning to the dog, which was now sniffing out every inch of its new home.

'If you want me to give you a hand with moving your furniture to where you want it,' Alec said, 'I'd be happy to do that.'

Miss Grayson hesitated. 'That's most kind of you,' she said after a moment. 'Actually, I rather think I need to take a little rest. Today has been quite an experience, *quite* an experience, physically and in other ways also. I shall make up my bed and have a lie-down for an hour or so. And Frizzie needs a little peace and quiet after her journey. We are neither of us as young as we once were, though you wouldn't think that to look at her, would you? So she will lie down with me. The furniture will have to wait.'

She looked all in, Caroline thought. Her face was pale and her body sagged with weariness. 'At least let me get your bed ready for you,' she said. 'I always think making up beds is quite exhausting.'

'How kind you are,' Miss Grayson said. 'And I accept with pleasure.'

'While Caroline is doing that, shall I take Frizzie for a short walk?' Alec offered.

'That would be wonderful!' Miss Grayson said. 'She needs her exercise, even though she is so small.'

Alec clipped on the lead and he and Frizzie made for the door. She showed no reluctance to go with him.

'I'm afraid she would go with the biggest crook in the

world if he offered her an outing,' Miss Grayson said. Then she shook her head. 'Oh dear! I'm sorry,' she said. 'That doesn't sound very complimentary, does it?'

'That's all right,' Alec said. He was halfway out of the door by now, being dragged by the small, white dog. It was an amusing sight. 'I won't be long!' he called back.

'In the meantime,' Miss Grayson said, 'I brought a flask of coffee and a sandwich so I shall have a little snack before I lie down.'

'You're very organized,' Caroline said.

'My father taught me that. "Always think ahead, Eleanor," he used to say. "That way you will never be caught out." It was good advice and I try to follow it.'

'So I suppose you know exactly which box your bedlinen is packed in?'

Miss Grayson nodded. 'I do indeed. And you will find all the boxes are labelled with the contents.'

Caroline made up the bed, Miss Grayson had her snack, and Alec arrived back with Frizzie. 'She seemed to enjoy that,' he reported. 'Dozens of new smells!'

'All of which she will explore in the days and weeks to come,' her owner said. 'She is going to be a very happy dog.'

'We'll leave you to your rest now,' Caroline said.

'And when you're ready to have your furniture put in place,' Alec added, 'Caroline can tell me and I'll come. I'm often in the area.'

Alec went upstairs with Caroline to her flat. 'I think Miss Grayson is going to be all right, don't you?' he asked.

'I do,' Caroline agreed. 'I shall keep an eye on her, though I shan't let her know that. She wouldn't appreciate it. She's far too independent.'

'You're probably right,' Alec said. 'Anyway, how's your job going? I mean, with Doctor Freeman.'

She didn't answer immediately. When she did she said, 'It's difficult to decide. I can do it all right, it's actually much easier than my job was in Bath, though that's partly because there isn't as much happening – at any rate for me. No hurry, no bustle, no sudden problems. Nothing like that. Of course Doctor Freeman is fine – charming, in fact – but it's all at a more leisurely pace – at least it is in his consulting rooms. He's busy enough in the hospital. And I'm on my own a lot. Not enough to do and the phone doesn't ring all that often. It never stopped ringing in the Bath surgery.'

She realized, not for the first time, how easy it was to unburden to Alec. He was a wonderful listener.

'I'm sorry to hear all that,' Alec said. 'Though actually not totally sorry, because it may have a bearing on a suggestion I have to put to you.'

'Really?' Caroline said. 'It sounds mysterious. So what is it?'

'Well,' Alec said, 'I've been busy on another job in Hove. Reconstructing this house. And it's going fine so far. At least my side of it is – the reconstruction, the building part – but it's now reached the stage where it calls for the kind of ideas which don't come so readily to me. I mean things like fittings, equipment, design, decoration. All those things which, if you look around here, were so much your contribution, what you took care of.'

'Not really,' Caroline protested. 'It was a joint effort. I discussed everything with you.'

Alec nodded agreement. 'That's exactly what I mean,' he said. 'I can do all the practical work; I can install things, even build them if necessary, but I don't have the ideas. Interior design isn't my thing, but it is yours. You've got a wonderful eye.'

'I never knew it was – not until I came to do it,' Caroline said. 'And then, I must say, I really enjoyed it. So what are you saying?'

187

'I'm asking you if you'd like to do the same kind of thing in this other house that you've done so well here,' Alec said. 'You design; I carry out the practical part. Also, you advise on the finishing touches – fabrics, window treatments, lighting, decorating, colour schemes and so on. Even items of furniture. You have a real flair for all that. I think especially for colour.'

Caroline gave him a long look. 'You astonish me,' she said. 'You really do! It was just something I enjoy doing. I really don't have any expertise.'

'You have the gift,' Alec said. 'So you supply the ideas, the client – in this case it's a couple called the Comptons – makes the choices and I'll provide the expertise where it's needed.'

'And what would the Comptons say to all this?' she asked. 'It wouldn't be free, would it?'

'Certainly not,' Alec agreed. 'They'd expect to pay, and probably pay well. Such things don't come cheap. And as a matter of fact . . .' He hesitated.

'Yes?'

'I did mention you. I told them what you'd done here and they were interested. Naturally they wanted to see something you'd already completed. So I'm afraid I told them I'd ask you if they could look over number seventeen. I'm sorry I didn't ask you first, and you can always say no – though I hope you won't. For a start, we work well together, the two of us.'

Caroline was hesitant. 'I don't know what to say,' she admitted.

'Well, think about it,' Alec said. 'But not for too long. Since they seem keen on the idea, if you don't give them an answer then I think they'll look for someone else to do it.'

'If I were to agree, it would have to be soon,' Caroline said. 'The tenants will be in before long. I'd rather not disturb them.'

188

'The tenants might not mind,' Alec said. 'They might quite like the idea that they were all occupying designer flats, so to speak. But you still have one flat empty. If the Comptons came soon they could look at that. And perhaps your own, if you agree.'

'Very well!' Caroline said. 'I'll consider it. I'll let you know in a couple of days.' The truth was that, though the idea appealed to her, and certainly boosted her ego, it was unexpected. But it would be lovely to work side by side with someone like Alec. She would like to ask Roger what he thought. He had both feet on the ground. He would see the pros and cons. 'Would you mind if I discussed the idea with Roger?' she asked Alec.

'If you must,' he said, 'but don't take too long, will you? The Comptons are keen to make a decision.'

'I'll ring him this evening,' Caroline promised.

'I don't see why not,' Roger said when she told him that evening. 'As long as it's what you want to do. And if you have the time. I agree with Alec, you've made a good job of number seventeen.'

'Time won't be a problem,' Caroline said. 'Once my tenants are in I don't expect to have much to do for them—'

'I wouldn't count on that,' Roger interrupted.

'But it was you who told me I wasn't here to look after them,' she reminded him.

'I didn't say *quite* that,' Roger protested. 'But it will be good for you to do something for yourself. At least you could meet with the Comptons, see how it goes and, of course, note their reaction to what you've done here. Did Miss Grayson move in as planned?'

'This afternoon,' Caroline said. 'Complete with Frizzie. A dear little dog, and her name suits her.'

'Any enquiries on the remaining flat?' he asked.

189

'Not yet, but I'm sure there will be. And I'm happy not to have everyone arrive at more or less the same time. Adam Carter and Eric Foster are due next week, and the week after that, Mr Downey.'

'I'm sorry I can't be down for the next two weekends,' Roger said. 'But you will keep in touch, won't you? Let me know what's happening?'

'Of course I will,' Caroline promised. 'And now I'm going to check that Miss Grayson is all right, and if there's anything she needs. Oh! don't worry. I won't make a habit of it! But it *is* her first night here, in a new place. She might be feeling a little strange.'

A little later she went downstairs, carrying a bottle of red wine, two glasses, and a corkscrew. When she knocked on Miss Grayson's door Frizzie immediately barked.

'There you are!' Miss Grayson said as she opened the door. 'She's settled in! She already knows she lives here, and she's guarding the territory. Who's a clever dog, then!'

'And she's guarding *you*,' Caroline said. 'I'm pleased she's settled so well. Did you both have a good rest?'

'We did, thank you.'

'I've brought some wine. And the glasses and a corkscrew, in case you couldn't lay hands on yours – though I expect you could. I thought we might have a welcome drink.'

Miss Grayson's face split into a wide smile. 'What a splendid idea!' she cried.

Caroline opened the bottle and poured the wine. 'Now,' she said, 'let's raise our glasses and drink to your health and happiness in number seventeen!' I'm not sure I shall do this for all the tenants, she thought, but Miss Grayson was old and alone. On the other hand, she reconsidered, why not?

They drank a glass of wine, then followed it with a second. Miss Grayson was quite flushed, and smiling more widely than ever. Frizzie lay asleep at her feet.

190

'I think . . .' Miss Grayson began. Then she picked up her glass and drained it. 'I think . . .' she continued, carefully enunciating her words and with even more than her usual precision, 'I think you should call me Eleanor!'

'Thank you! And you should of course call me Caroline!'

'Eleanor and Caroline,' Miss Grayson said, rather slowly and thoughtfully. 'Two beautiful names!'

A few days later Adam Carter and Eric Foster moved in. They had both taken a day off work to do so and it all went with great efficiency, so that when Caroline knocked on their door early in the evening, enquiring if there was anything they needed, she was invited into a totally orderly flat, complete with cushions on the sofa, pictures on the wall, fresh flowers in vases and a smell of coffee in the air. 'Good heavens!' she said. 'I can see you don't need any help from me!'

'Nevertheless,' Adam said – it was, she had noticed it before, always Adam who spoke the words and Eric who nodded a smiling assent – 'thank you for asking, and do please stay and have a cup of coffee with us.'

'That's kind,' she said. 'Thank you. I will.'

'Any news on the empty flat?' Adam asked a little later.

'Not really news,' Caroline said. 'I don't have a tenant in view yet, but it's possible that I might be showing it to a couple from London in the next day or two. Oh, not prospective tenants! It seems they're interested in what's been done here and they might, just might, like me to do one or two things for them in the house they're having converted in Hove.'

'Great!' Adam said.

'It might come to nothing,' Caroline said. 'Naturally, when I do get a tenant I'll tell you. Anyway, I won't take up any more of your time. I'm sure you must have things to do, even though it does all look spick and span.'

Back in her own flat, there was a phone message waiting for her, from Alec. 'The Comptons are coming down from London the day after tomorrow. Would it be convenient for me to bring them to see you in the afternoon?'

She called him back. 'Fine!' she said.

SEVENTEEN

When Alec, as planned, brought the Comptons to number seventeen, Caroline found herself surprised. They were much younger than she had expected them to be. Though Alec had probably never said so, she had thought of them as a couple on the verge of retirement, which, she had assumed, they would spend in the house in Hove. She quickly realized it was not so. Mr Compton was possibly in his early fifties, and his wife several years younger. It was Mrs Compton, without being asked, who gave the reason for the move. 'It's not that we don't like London,' she said, 'of course we do. But we also, in fact more and more, like to get away from it, certainly for the weekends, and sometimes for longer periods. And we both enjoy being by the sea – and James has his love of sailing. Fortunately, he doesn't *have* to be in London for his work. He can work just as well from home, and often does. So we shall be spending much more time in Hove than we do in London.'

Mr Compton nodded agreement. 'And we don't need two properties,' he said. 'Eventually – sooner rather than later – we shall sell the London house and then we would live here permanently.'

'The house has been neglected, I'd think for quite some time,' Mr Compton said. 'But we liked the fact that it was basically well built and roomy, and of course the position, only a hundred yards or so from the sea, is fine. Alec has done a good job on it for his part, but now it needs fixtures, fittings, decorations, floor coverings – all the things to give it life and atmosphere. The kind of things you have here. The right colours—'

His wife interrupted him. 'All these things make such a difference,' she said. 'It's no use asking me what to do. I don't have those kind of ideas in my head. And it's no use me saying I know what I like because until I see it, or at least see a picture of it, I don't!'

'So we'd be pleased to have your ideas,' Mr Compton said. 'So what's the next step?'

'Well,' Caroline said, a little nervously, 'first and foremost I would need to see the house; look at everything quite carefully, decide what was possible and what wasn't – and then I would want to talk to both of you, together: find out what you like, and also what you dislike. The latter is important. You might hate certain colours, or maybe some small things, like blinds at the windows. Anything. The big things are important, but so are the little ones.'

'I'm sure that's true,' Mrs Compton said.

'And I'd want to know a bit about your lifestyle – are you party-givers, for instance, or do you have hobbies which need to be catered for? Photography? A dark room?' They shook their heads. 'What do you want the house to do for you? All that sort of thing. It probably sounds intrusive, but if you want something really tailored to you, which I imagine you would, then I'd need to ask questions, and listen to the answers before I could put my final ideas to you.'

'It sounds quite exciting, actually,' Mrs Compton said. 'And really personal – I mean, in the nicest way. But you would have to come up with the ideas . . .'

'Or a choice of ideas,' Mr Compton said. He turned to his wife. 'So what do you think?' he asked.

'Well, dear, I'd certainly like to take the next step, which I presume . . .' she said, turning to Caroline, 'is to ask you to come and look at the house.'

'I'd be pleased to do that,' Caroline said. 'After that I can put forward some proposals, and we can see where we go from there. No obligation on your part, of course. You might not like my ideas, in which case, you don't have to go ahead.' She turned to Alec. 'I'd like you to be there when we do this,' she said *sotto voce*. 'You can keep me on the straight and narrow about what's possible within the structure and what isn't. I daresay there'll be several things we'd need to sort out together.'

Alec had kept quiet so far. Caroline, he thought, needed no help from him at this stage. Talking to the Comptons she sounded competent and businesslike, no sign of the nervousness she'd shown when he'd first put the idea to her. Now he nodded his assent.

They made a date, an afternoon in the coming week when the Comptons could come down again from London and Caroline would see the house at first hand.

'Good! I look forward to it,' she said. 'And while you're here would you like to see what I've done with my own flat? You might get a better idea, seeing it furnished, though, naturally, what you want could be quite different from what I've chosen for my place.'

She showed them around. They admired everything, especially the colours she had used. It was interesting, she thought, seeing her surroundings through the eyes of strangers. After that she and Alec took them downstairs and saw them to their car, parked near by. 'See you soon, then,' Mr Compton said.

★   ★   ★

195

'Well, what do you think?' she asked Alec as they went back upstairs.

'I think you might be on to something good there,' he said. 'They were clearly interested. I think they'd be reasonable to deal with. And I reckon that, fortunately, they might be able to afford whatever you suggested.'

'What is his job?' Caroline asked.

'He's a financial adviser, he has his own company,' Alec told her.

'I'd want them to like what I did,' Caroline said firmly. 'I'd want them to be happy to live with it.'

'Of course you would,' he agreed. 'That's why it's important to discuss it thoroughly. I think they realize that.'

'Are you in a hurry – I mean, now?' Caroline asked. She didn't really want him to go. 'Or do you have time to stay for a drink?'

'Thank you. I'd like that,' Alec said.

She served the drinks. Alec raised his glass. 'To our first job together!' he said.

'I never expected to find myself doing this,' Caroline said. 'I'm really nervous.'

'You didn't sound so when you were talking to the Comptons,' Alec said, touching his glass to hers. 'In fact, quite the reverse. I was impressed by how sure, how confident you sounded.'

'Ah!' she answered. 'But what I said was the theory – well, that's too grand a word. Common sense, really – though I do stand by it. But now I have to get down to the nitty-gritty, I have to come up with the ideas.'

'Which you will,' Alec said. 'I don't doubt it for a minute. I've seen what you've done here – and now so have they.'

'I pleased myself here,' Caroline pointed out. 'I had no one else in view. Still, I'll put it all to you first. We'll pool our opinions. And I don't just mean the things I need to ask you about, like what's possible and what isn't. I mean our ideas. It's going to be an interesting project to work on – not least because they don't seem to have many ideas of their own – or at least they haven't expressed any. It will be like starting a painting on a totally blank canvas. Of course I'll listen to them. I want to end up with what's right for them rather than for me.'

They finished their drinks, and Alec got up to go. 'I'll pick you up on Tuesday afternoon,' he said. As she saw him out Caroline thought that she could easily have asked him to stay for supper, she would have enjoyed his company, but too late now. She sighed and decided to make a start on the Comptons' job right away, insofar as she could without having seen the house, and going only on Alec's description. She sought out a new notebook and labelled it 'Comptons' and began to write a list of questions for discussion.

She had filled several pages with jottings when the phone rang. Her first thought was that it was Alec, with some new idea. Instead it was Tom Downey.

'I'm sorry to disturb you,' he said. 'I'm ringing because I plan to go shopping this week to choose some of the things I'll need for the flat. Beds and bedlinen, chairs, kitchen things. One forgets just how much is needed. So I thought I'd better find out from you when it would be convenient to have them delivered, and also to bring over a few things from home.'

'If it's within the next week . . .'

'Which it will be,' he said.

'Then any afternoon except Tuesday,' Caroline told him. 'But let me know, and it would make sense if you were to be here, then you can say where you want everything to go.'

'Oh, I will be,' he assured her.

★   ★   ★

On Tuesday, Alec picked her up and drove her to the house in Hove. The Comptons were already there. It was a pleasant house and Caroline and Alec, between them, took measurements and made notes. Caroline asked all the questions she had in mind, and things began to take shape in her head.

'I shall give it all a lot of thought,' she said in the end to the expectant Comptons. 'And if there's anything else you think of, no matter how small, don't hesitate to let me know.'

Over the next ten days, though it took more than one occasion, Tom Downey had two single beds, two armchairs, a table and dining chairs, bedlinen and a television set delivered. And from the home he was leaving he brought, on car trips, his laptop, music things, the contents of his wardrobe, and so on. 'I think that's it for now,' he said, standing there, looking at it. It was not a great deal to be accompanying him from what he must now think of as his former life.

'I'll move in, not this coming weekend but the one after,' he said, 'if that's convenient to you.'

'Absolutely!' Caroline said. 'And will your son stay with you that weekend?'

'No,' he answered. 'But he will the one after. Just for the Saturday. Oh, and he would like a friend to stay overnight. Is that OK?' It might lighten the atmosphere, he had thought, if Greg had a friend to stay with him. In any case he was quite sure the boys would go off together into Brighton on the Saturday evening. It wouldn't be spent with him.

'Of course,' Caroline said. 'It's your flat, you must do exactly as you please.'

'Thank you,' he said. 'And I shall have to buy a camp bed for Greg's room – or perhaps his friend will manage with a sleeping bag? Anyway, I'll be off now.'

He said nothing whatever of why he was leaving his home, or about his wife and, she thought, it was not her place to ask. His references had been acceptable. There was something rather sad about his situation and she felt sorry for him, and his son.

For the rest of the afternoon, Caroline worked on her proposed plans for the Comptons' house. Immersed in what she was doing, she had taken no notice of the time, except to switch on a lamp or two as it grew dark. When she looked at her watch it was almost half past ten, and she had not yet eaten. She stood up, and stretched herself. She was quite tired but, in a way, exhilarated and she felt rather pleased with what she'd achieved. She left her drawings and her notes on the table – she would clear them away in the morning. She went into the kitchen, made herself a chicken sandwich then went to bed.

Although she was tired, sleep didn't come. Her head was too full of thoughts, chasing each other around, so when the telephone rang just before midnight she was still awake. Wrong number, she thought as she stretched out her hand to answer it. It was Rosie.

'Darling! Is something wrong?' Caroline asked quickly. 'Are you all right?'

'All right?' Rosie said. 'Of course I am! Why wouldn't I be?'

'Because it's midnight,' Caroline said crossly, relieved but annoyed at Rosie's thoughtlessness. 'You don't usually phone so late.' Not to mention, she thought, that her daughter had not phoned at all in the last two weeks.

'Oh dear! I'm sorry!' Rosie said. 'I've been to the theatre. I hadn't realized the time – or that you went to bed early.'

'It's not early,' Caroline said. 'But never mind that – as long as you're OK. Did you ring for something special?'

'To ask how you are, of course, and to talk about the

weekend. I thought we could be down for lunch and leave after tea.'

'That would be great!' Caroline said. 'I'd really look forward to that.'

'Will Roger be in Brighton?' Rosie asked.

'Not this coming weekend. Probably the following one.'

'Oh well! A pity! And have you let all the flats yet?' Rosie asked.

'All except one. You'll probably meet some of the tenants.'

'Great!' Rosie said. 'Any more news about anything?'

'Not really.' She would say nothing of what she was doing for the Comptons. It was too soon to discuss it with Rosie; better to wait until it was a fait accompli, cut and dried.

They chatted a little longer about this and that, then Rosie said, 'Well, I'm sure I'm keeping you from your beauty sleep, so I'll say goodnight.'

'Goodnight, darling,' Caroline said. 'Lovely to talk to you.' She put the receiver back, switched off the light, and settled down. It was nice to talk to her daughter, she thought, even if it had been at such an antisocial hour. Sleep, which had eluded her earlier, came almost at once.

The following afternoon – she had been home from work less than an hour – the agent phoned. 'How is everything going?' he enquired. That is not what he is calling to ask, Caroline thought. He is too busy a man for chit-chat. 'Quite well,' she answered.

'Good! Then I'm sure you'll be pleased to hear what I have to tell you! Another tenant – actually, a couple, not long married. Mr and Mrs Holby. They live in Crawley but he has recently taken a new job in Brighton and they're keen to move closer. Would you like to see them?'

'Of course!' Caroline said. 'Could they come this after-noon?'

'Yes,' he said. 'That's what they'd like to do. They're with me now.'

'Then ask them to come around right away,' she said.

Fifteen minutes later they were standing on the door-step. 'I'm David Holby,' the man said. 'And this is my wife, Brigid.'

He was possibly in his early thirties, tall, and fresh complexioned. His wife was a few years younger, dark-haired and plumpish. Her husband was smiling. She looked nervous.

'Do come in,' Caroline said. 'Have you had far to come?'

'Not far,' the man said. He repeated what the agent had already told her. 'We live in Crawley but now I've got a job in Brighton, so it seems better to move here. It's expensive, both of us travelling every day. I'm the manager at Johnson's and my wife's also on the staff there.' Johnson's was a well-known store in the town, not one of the giants, but long-established, and respected. Caroline had never shopped there. She was a Waitrose woman herself.

'I'm on the delicatessen,' Mrs Holby said. She had a shy voice and a soft Irish accent.

They were standing in the hall. 'I'll show you the flat,' Caroline said. 'It's on the second floor, immediately below my own.'

'This is a nice house,' Mr Holby said as they climbed the stairs. 'These old houses have style, don't they?'

Caroline agreed with him. His wife nodded but said nothing, though when they were shown around she made small murmurs of approval. 'So what do you think, love?' her husband asked her when they had seen everything.

'It's lovely!' she said. 'I like it very much.' Even so, Caroline thought, she still sounded nervous. They did seem a rather unlikely couple.

'Perhaps you'd like to think it over?' Caroline suggested.

'No! We don't need to!' Mrs Holby said quickly. 'I really do like it.'

'The rent's a bit more than we budgeted for,' Mr Holby said, 'but we wouldn't have travelling expenses as we do now. So we could manage it. Would it be possible to move in fairly soon?'

'As soon as you like,' Caroline told him. She was happy, she thought, to waive Roger's approval. She didn't think they would give her trouble as tenants.

She took them up to her flat. 'Sit down,' she said, 'and I'll show you the tenancy agreement. You must read it through. It's quite straightforward but I do ask for a month's rent in advance. In any case,' she added, 'perhaps you'd like to think it over for twenty-four hours or so?'

Mr Holby looked at his wife. 'I don't think we need to,' he said. 'What do you think, darling?'

Mrs Holby had looked apprehensive from the beginning; now she looked decidedly nervous, twisting her hands.

'Are you not quite sure?' Caroline asked her. 'If so, you probably *should* go away and think about it, talk it over with your husband.'

There was a short silence. Mrs Holby took hold of her husband's hand and held on to it firmly. 'It's not that,' she said hesitantly, 'it's exactly what we want. We'd be very happy here. The thing is . . .' The words came out in a rush, blurted out. 'The truth is, I'm five months pregnant! Would you be happy to have a baby here? I mean, are there any other children, or is it all adults?'

'There aren't,' Caroline said. 'I mean, any other children, as it happens. But I'd be happy to have a baby in the house.'

'I'd have the baby in the hospital,' Mrs Holby said. 'Not here. We wouldn't be any trouble.'

'I don't suppose you would be,' Caroline said. But little does she know that it's not the birth that's the main thing, she thought. It's everything that comes after. She wondered why Mrs Holby had looked so apprehensive, troubled even? Had she met with opposition in the rooms they now occupied? Not that she would ask. 'Well,' she said, 'subject to references, of course, the flat is yours if you want.'

Mrs Holby's eyes filled with tears. 'Oh, we *do* want it!' She turned to her husband. 'We *do* want it, don't we, love?'

'Of course we do,' he answered. 'I reckon we'd be very happy here.' He handed her his handkerchief and she dried her eyes.

EIGHTEEN

Miss Grayson was busy with her small collection of potted plants, Frizzie at her heels, when Caroline saw the Holbys off at the front door. She immediately raised her head and waved her trowel in greeting. 'Lovely day!' she called out, including the Holbys. Caroline gave her a nod. If she was waiting to be introduced, which she clearly was, then this was not the moment. 'We'll be in touch,' Caroline said to them. 'You'll hear from me in a few days.' She knew better now than to take anyone on without checking references, though she felt confident that all would be well.

'New tenants, were they?' Miss Grayson asked, as Caroline turned to go back into the house.

'Possibly,' Caroline replied.

Miss Grayson stood there, waiting for more information, which Caroline did not give. If her tenants wanted to know about each other, then it was up to them. They were not going to get the gossip.

'When are they moving in?' Miss Grayson asked. 'Do they live locally?'

'Nothing is fixed,' Caroline said. The rest of Miss Grayson's question she left unanswered.

'Then we shall have a full house,' Miss Grayson said. 'How very interesting! I do hope we will all fit in with one another.'

'My daughter and my sister-in-law are coming down for the day on Saturday,' Caroline said, changing the subject. 'You might like to meet my sister-in-law.' She knew Patience wouldn't mind, she liked meeting new people.

'Thank you! I shall look forward to that,' Miss Grayson said.

I have not been totally truthful to Miss Grayson, Caroline thought as she went back upstairs. Of course she knew the Holbys' date. 'Would it be all right if we moved in on Monday week?' David Holby had asked. 'Would that be convenient? It's the easiest day for both of us to take off work.'

'Assuming that everything checks, that's fine by me,' Caroline had agreed. 'Will you still be working?' she'd asked Brigid.

'Oh yes!' Brigid had said. 'I haven't told Johnson's I'm pregnant, not yet. I want to go on working as long as I can. It will make such a difference, money-wise. I had no idea babies had so many needs!'

Caroline had nodded. 'They do! Especially first babies. Everything's new, nothing handed down.'

'I'd like everything to be new,' Brigid had said.

Now, Caroline rang the agent. 'I liked the Holbys,' she said. 'I've agreed to let them have the flat.'

'So that's the whole house let,' the agent said. 'Not that I ever had any doubts about it. It's in a good position and you've made it look really attractive. I hope all goes well!'

'I'm sure it will!' Caroline said.

She rang Alec, brimming with excitement, dying to tell him her news. She would have rung Roger, she ought to have rung Roger, but he had been away and she could assume that he was not yet back. 'Good news!' she said to Alec. 'I've just let the second-floor flat. We're full!'

'Great!' Alec said. 'That was quick work! And by the sound of your voice I'd say there were no problems!'

'No problems,' she agreed. 'A young married couple.' She went no further into the circumstances. 'They'll move in on Monday week.'

'Good! And I'll be in during the next day or two – Mr Downey has asked me to put some shelves up – so at the same time I'll take a careful look around the second floor, see that every last thing's as it should be. Would Saturday be all right?' he asked. 'Right now I'm in the middle of a job, it's difficult to leave.'

'Saturday will be fine,' Caroline said. 'Rosie will be here, with my sister-in-law, Patience.'

'Then would you rather . . .' he began.

'No, it's fine!' she said, not wanting to put off his visit. 'You'll like Patience!'

Patience and Rosie arrived shortly before midday. 'How lovely to see you both!' Caroline said. 'I've been looking forward to it so much.' As she said the words she knew them to be absolutely true. She *was* pleased to see them both. Having members of her own family visit made everything seem suddenly like a real home.

'Are you going to show us everything?' Patience asked eagerly.

'Later,' Caroline promised. 'But first of all I'm going to give you a glass of sherry and let you relax.' She turned to Rosie. 'Was it a good drive down? You must have left quite early.'

'We did,' Rosie said. 'Certainly I did from London. But it was fine.'

'If we're going to have a drink, then this will come in handy,' Patience said. From the large carrier bag she had been holding ever since she arrived she took out a sizeable box, beautifully wrapped and tied with ribbon, and handed it to Caroline. 'This is a house-warming present,' she said.

'Oh, thank you! It looks exciting,' Caroline said, touched by the gesture. 'Whatever can it be?'

'Well, if you open it instead of playing guessing games, you'll find out!' Patience said. 'But put the box down on a table or something, don't try to do it holding it in your hand like that. And be reasonably careful with it.'

Caroline looked at her sister-in-law. Patience's cheeks were flushed pink and her eyes were as excited as those of a child. 'Go on then! Get on with it!' she urged.

Caroline untied the ribbon, removed the gold-pattern paper, then opened the box. She gave a cry of surprised delight.

'Oh, Patience!' she said. 'How wonderful! But how can you? Your beautiful Waterford sherry glasses! You can't possibly be giving them away. I know how you love them! Are you sure you can bear to part with them?'

'Of course I am,' Patience said. 'And I always intended you to have them in the end, so why not now?'

'And I've brought the sherry,' Rosie said.

'And you can tell us everything you've been up to here,' Patience said. 'I must say it all looks fine. Shall we be able to look around the rest of the building?'

Caroline shook her head. 'Not really,' she said. 'I already have tenants in most of the flats.'

'How many are still to let?'

'None!' Caroline told her with satisfaction. 'I let the very last one this week.'

'And all nice people?' Patience asked.

'I think so,' Caroline said. 'But quite different, one from the other. In fact, I did tell the lady in the basement flat, Miss Grayson, that I would introduce her to you, Patience. She's elderly and lives alone. She doesn't get to see many people. Would you mind, or are you too tired after your journey?'

'Tired?' Patience said. 'Not the least bit!'

A minute later Alec arrived. 'I'm sorry to interrupt,' he said. 'I've brought Mr Downey's shelves. If you'll let me have the key, I'll put them up. I know where they have to go.'

'Sure!' Caroline said. 'Do come in for a minute.'

She introduced him to Patience. 'I couldn't have done anything here without Alec's help,' she told her sister-in-law. 'And indeed, as you know, it was he who found this house for me.'

Patience greeted him warmly. Rosie gave him a perfunctory nod. It was partly her daughter's coolness which caused an embarrassed Caroline to say, 'Do have a glass of sherry with us, Alec, before you start work! Patience has just given me these beautiful glasses as a house-warming present.'

'Thank you!' Alec said. 'But I won't. I have some work to do downstairs, but they are lovely, aren't they?'

'I did promise Miss Grayson that I would introduce her to Patience,' Caroline told him. 'Would you mind very much going down and bringing her up?' She felt a little disappointed that Alec wasn't joining them for a drink and saw this as a good way to detain him . . .

'Not a bit,' Alec said. 'I have a soft spot for Miss Grayson. I'll be back with her in a jiffy.'

When Eleanor Grayson appeared with him ten minutes later it was obvious to Caroline that, relying on the promise to introduce her to her sister-in-law, she had dressed for the occasion and had clearly been to a hairdresser. She looked striking and elegant and Caroline could see how attractive she would have been when she was younger. For a moment, as Alec brought her to the door, Caroline was lost for words. In the end she said, 'How nice to see you, Eleanor! You're looking very well! Let me introduce you to my family!'

It was inevitable, she thought soon afterwards, that Patience and Eleanor should get on together like a house

208

on fire. They were two of a kind: educated, intelligent, independent; well brought up and socially competent in whatever situation they might find themselves. They were attracted to each other like a magnet to iron filings. It would be difficult to say which was one and which was the other.

For a little while everyone chatted, and then Alec said, 'I must go! I must get on with the job. But thank you.' And to Patience he added, 'It's been a pleasure to meet you!'

'And I must go too,' Miss Grayson said a little later. 'Frizzie will think I've left home. When I go out she expects to go with me.'

'You could have brought her with you,' Caroline said.

'I wouldn't have done that without permission,' Miss Grayson said. 'Not everyone likes dogs. But she would have enjoyed it; she's very friendly.'

'Another time then,' Caroline said.

'I would quite like to have company down the stairs, if you would be so kind, Caroline! I find it more difficult to go down stairs than climb up them.' Caroline, she thought, had made a lovely job of her top-floor flat and she had really enjoyed meeting Patience, she had quite taken to her. She had seemed an intelligent woman, a kindred spirit who would be unlikely to mind the cosy clutter of her own flat, should she come to visit.

Back in her flat, she submitted to Frizzie's ecstatic welcome, and then she surveyed herself critically in the mirror in her bedroom. Yes, her hairdo had definitely been successful; it did do a certain something for her, she thought, turning this way and that. Not that she could afford it often.

'Well, that was interesting!' Patience said when Caroline returned. 'Quite one of the old school, I'd say. Knows what's what. Has her own values and standards.'

'You're right,' Caroline agreed. 'But she's also quite

tolerant, and interested in other people even if she doesn't agree with them. A bit like you, Patience.'

'Thank you, my dear!' Patience said.

'Nosey, I'd think,' Rosie said. 'Wanting to know everything about everyone – not that I mean you are . . .'

But if the cap fits . . . Patience thought, and was aware that it did.

'I reckon next time you see her,' Rosie said to Caroline, 'she'll want to know all about me – what do I do for a living, how old am I, what's the boyfriend situation?'

'It's not necessarily being nosey, Rosie dear,' Patience said. 'Elderly people who live alone *do* want to know.'

'You're not like that,' Rosie said stoutly.

'Of course I am,' Patience disagreed. 'And I'd be more so if I lived in a basement flat in Brighton rather than in my own cottage in the middle of the high street in a very pleasant village where there's always something or other happening.'

'Are you both ready for lunch?' Caroline interrupted. 'I have a casserole in the oven, I only have to do the vegetables. Or if you're not yet ready, it can wait.'

'I'm starving!' Rosie admitted.

'And though I'm not starving,' Patience said, 'I think I should eat something solid. That delicious sherry has rather gone to my head!'

'Now, Caroline dear,' Patience said as they sat at the table, 'do tell us all about your tenants, all those people who are going to live under your roof. I must say, it's something I never would have thought of you doing. How *did* you come to think of it?'

'I don't really know,' Caroline admitted. 'One moment I hadn't any such idea in my head, and the next there it was, fully fledged! I owe a large debt of thanks to Roger of course.'

'I was hoping Roger would be here,' Rosie said, somewhat mutinously.

'Yes, I'm sure he'd like to be,' Caroline agreed. 'He's away on business. But I expect you'll see him next time you visit. It's no great distance from Bristol to Brighton, or Brighton to London, for that matter.'

'So who *is* living here?' Patience persisted.

'Let me see!' Caroline said. 'Well, in the basement, as you know, is Miss Grayson, and on the ground floor I have a Mr Tom Downey. He has recently split up with his wife. He has a son, a young teenager still at school, though he won't be living here, just visiting for the occasional weekend. I don't know the ins and outs but I think it's a rather sad situation.'

'Oh dear!' Rosie said. 'Another lame duck!'

'Nothing of the kind!' Caroline said. 'You do exaggerate! I would think he's a very competent man, though not in the best of situations at the moment. And then on the first floor I have two nice young men. And on the floor below mine a young couple, Mr and Mrs Holby. They've not moved in yet but they soon will.'

'So if their flat is still empty we could look at it, couldn't we?' Patience said eagerly. 'I love looking around new places. Did you have a great deal to do throughout the house?'

'A fair amount,' Caroline admitted. 'Alec and I between us, but Alec did the real work.' She was deliberately keeping from them the plans she and Alec had of working together on the Comptons' place. She was certain it would not meet with Rosie's approval. She was not sure why, except that her daughter clearly didn't take to Alec and it did bother her slightly.

'Well, it all seems very well done,' Patience said. 'Alec's a nice man, isn't he?'

'Very nice,' Caroline agreed, keeping her voice steady.

'And is he married?' Patience asked.

'No. He was once. And he has a girlfriend,' Caroline said. 'She manages a band.'

211

'A *band*?' Patience queried.

'A group,' Caroline told her. 'Four young men. Singers and musicians.'

'You mean like the Beatles?' Patience persisted.

'Sort of,' Caroline agreed, realizing she wasn't all that sure herself. 'But not quite. She travels around a lot with them, so she and Alec don't get to see much of each other.'

'What interesting lives young people live,' Patience said. 'I quite envy them. The only choices offered to me when I was young were nursing, teaching – or getting married and raising a family.'

'But you did rise to be a headmistress,' Caroline pointed out.

'I did indeed. And I loved every minute of it,' Patience said. 'Though, to be truthful, I was always happy to get home to my own house at the end of the day. I never wanted to take a child with me. Nothing domestic ever appealed to me. Still doesn't!'

'And what about *your* job with the consultant?' Rosie asked Caroline. 'How do you manage to fit that in?'

'Quite easily,' Caroline said. 'It's not onerous. In fact, it's a teeny bit boring. There's not enough to do. I might or I might not keep on with it. I'm not sure.'

They had a short rest after lunch. Indeed, Patience nodded off, then soon afterwards wakened suddenly. 'I would like to take a little trip down to the seafront,' she said. 'One doesn't come to Brighton and not go near the sea.'

'Do you feel up for a walk along the front?' Rosie asked. 'Or shall I take the car?'

'Walk, of course!' Patience said rather sharply. 'I walk everywhere. Legs were made for walking, my father used to say. As you know, I've never had a car.'

The tide was high, though not splashing over on to the promenade, which disappointed Patience. 'When I was

212

small,' she said, 'I used to enjoy running ahead of the incoming tide, to escape it. Beating the waves, I called it.'

'Then you must come in the depth of winter,' Caroline told her. 'You'd get enough of that then. But I know what you mean. I always enjoyed that.' She turned to Rosie. 'You did, didn't you?'

'I didn't particularly like getting wet,' Rosie said, slightly crushingly.

They walked a little way along the seafront, and then made their way back to number seventeen, slowly, since Patience – though she denied it – seemed short of breath. Caroline looked ahead and saw Adam Carter and Eric Foster a short distance away, walking down the road towards them. 'Your lucky day,' she said to Patience. 'You're about to meet two more of my tenants!' She paused while the men covered the last few yards, and they all came to a halt outside number seventeen.

'Patience,' Caroline said, 'let me introduce Adam Carter . . . and Eric Foster. They have the first-floor flat.'

'Oh, the one with the lovely balcony!' Patience said. 'I really like that.'

'So do we!' Adam said.

Rosie intervened. Any minute now her aunt would have elicited an invitation to take a closer look. 'I think we should be on our way,' she said. 'The longer we wait, the busier the roads will be.'

'Of course!' Patience said. 'You're right!'

They took their leave. 'What pleasant young men!' Patience said as they went up to Caroline's flat. 'I hope you'll be as fortunate with all your tenants.'

I think Patience sees this as one big house party, Caroline thought after everyone had left. All of us dashing in and out of each other's flats. It would *not* be like that. She hoped, and believed, they would all be civil and considerate to one another, but no way did she expect her tenants to live in

213

each other's pockets. She had her own life to live and no doubt they too would all value their own privacy.

Later in the evening the telephone rang. It was Roger. 'I got back an hour ago,' he said. 'How's everything?'

'Great!' Caroline told him. 'I've had Patience and Rosie here for the day. They were sorry not to have seen you. Oh – and I've let the second floor!' She said the words as nonchalantly as she could. 'A young married couple.'

'You've actually let it? That was quick work!' She sensed disapproval in his voice.

'Yes, wasn't it?' she said brightly. 'They're a nice couple. You'll like them. They've arranged to move in Monday week. But don't worry, I'll make sure everything's OK before they do.'

'Well, I'll definitely be down next weekend,' Roger said. 'It seems ages since I saw you.'

'I look forward to it,' Caroline said.

'And don't do anything rash in the meantime,' he said, slightly pompously.

She had hardly put the phone down before it rang again. This time it was Alec.

'I enjoyed meeting your family,' he said. 'I take it they've left?'

'A little while ago,' she said. There was a short pause during which Caroline asked herself exactly why Alec had rung and then:

'I wondered,' Alec said, 'if you'd like to come out for a meal? I mean, if you've nothing else planned.' He added this last hastily. Caroline thought he sounded nervous, which was rather endearing.

'Nothing at all!' Caroline said happily. 'And I'd like that very much.'

NINETEEN

Caroline, getting ready to go out for her dinner with Alec, surveyed herself in the long mirror in her bedroom. She was not entirely pleased with what she saw now, but nor was she dismayed. She was still too thin for her liking; she would have preferred more curves, though her legs and feet, she thought, were not bad; the former long and the latter slender. There was more grey in her hair. Not a lot more, but it was there, and she must do something about it, though there was no time for all that before this evening. Alec, she thought, had hardly any grey hairs, but then he was younger than she by a few years. But why am I fussing? This is only a dinner date with a friend. Nothing posh. She was not exactly going to a ball. Even so, she washed her hair.

The thing is, she asked herself, have I changed in other ways, not to do with appearance? She thought she had, especially inwardly. She felt more independent, less inclined to go along with the views of others, as she usually had done with Peter – not that she had ever minded that and not that he had been the least bit overbearing, but he had been the leader and she the follower. Now, she didn't feel the need to be a follower. She could make up her own mind as, indeed, the move to Brighton and the purchase of number seventeen showed. Nor, she felt sure, would that be the end.

It was hard to know what to wear. Naturally, she wanted to look nice but she didn't want the embarrassment of being overdressed. Despairingly, rifling through her wardrobe she realized she had bought nothing new since the dress in Marks & Spencer's sale. It was time she did. In the end she took out a straight-cut cream wool dress, above knee-length but not too short, with three-quarter-length sleeves and a lowish, scooped neckline, which she filled with the delicate triple-strand gold necklace Peter had once given her. Her hair had come up reasonably well but she must, she repeated to herself, do something about the colour.

When Alec arrived he looked at her with approval and she felt her labours had been worthwhile. 'You look lovely!' he said. When she offered him a drink he refused. 'Wait until we get there,' he said. 'I've booked a table. In any case, I'm driving.' She couldn't help but notice that he looked rather handsome himself, in a blue shirt that brought out the colour of his eyes, and then felt cross with herself for having such thoughts.

When he drove down to the coast road she expected him to turn right, towards the centre of Brighton – she had imagined they would eat somewhere in the Lanes – but instead he turned left along the Eastbourne road. 'We're going somewhere different! There's a good Italian restaurant, just the other side of Newhaven,' he said. 'I thought you might like it.'

'Here we are!' he said presently, drawing up outside a rather ordinary-looking single-storey building. 'It doesn't look much from the outside, does it? But I promise the food is good – *and* the service. The owners are Italian. Really, it's a place you have to get to know about. It's never advertised but it's always busy.'

The moment they entered, Alec was cordially greeted by

a short, rotund man, clearly the owner. 'Ah, Mr Barker!' he said genially. 'How nice to see you again. It's been a few weeks. We wondered about you. You are well?'

'Very well, thank you, Giovanni!' Alec said. 'And you? And Maria?'

'We are both well,' Giovanni said. 'My wife is taking an evening off for once. The children have something special on at school. They are both involved in a play. It is important for her to be there.'

'Of course!' Alec agreed. 'So who is doing the cooking?'

'Emilio. But do not worry – he is not only a good waiter, he is a competent chef. And I have been giving him a helping hand.'

'I'm not worrying,' Alec said as Giovanni showed them to their table and gave them the menu. 'The lasagne is good,' Giovanni advised. 'That I made myself. Sometimes my wife lets me in the kitchen! But I will leave you to make your choice.'

They studied the menu while drinking a white wine as an aperitif. 'I do like lasagne,' Caroline said, 'but I see there's veal Milanese on the menu and it's a favourite of mine. Would I hurt his feelings if I chose that?'

Alec laughed. 'If you do, he won't show it. In any case, I'll have the lasagne.'

While waiting for the meal to be served they chatted comfortably – about number seventeen, about the Comptons, about Tom Downey whom, Caroline confessed, she was not sure she liked, though she didn't know why. 'And it doesn't really matter, does it?' she said.

'And what about the son?' Alec asked.

'I haven't yet set eyes on him,' she said.

She moved on from Tom Downey to the Holbys, and then to Eleanor Grayson. In the end, Alec weaned her away from the tenants. 'It's all going to work out,' he said. 'Don't worry about it.'

217

'I'm not really worrying. I suppose it's just that it's new to me and I feel responsible. So how is Paula?' she asked, changing the subject. She imagined he must bring her here.

'I had a call from her yesterday,' Alec said, looking suddenly sad. 'From Manchester. They go from there to Liverpool – and I think Dublin is on the cards.'

'She's a busy lady,' Caroline said, injecting what she hoped was an admiring note into her voice.

'She certainly is,' Alec agreed. 'The Sledges are really making a name, and it's largely due to Paula. They have the talent, but it needed Paula to harness it. She's first-rate at the job. And tireless! And of course she loves it.'

The food came. 'This looks delicious.' By now the small restaurant was busy, every place taken. 'Is it usually like this?' she asked.

'Always!' Alec replied. 'And I reckon most of the people here are regular customers.'

'Yes, you can tell that by the way they're greeted.'

There was a slight pause in the conversation, then Alec said, 'Will Rosie be coming down again at the weekend?'

'Oh no!' Caroline answered. 'I don't think she'll be here too often. Rosie has a busy life, lots of friends, in London. But Roger is coming.'

'I suppose you've known Roger a long time?' Alec said.

'Ages! I met him when I first got to know Peter. They were in the same firm – Roger's still there. I don't know what I'd have done without Roger. He really looks after me. Oh, I don't just mean my legal affairs, but in many ways. He and his wife, and Peter and I, did lots of things together until he and Bettina divorced. We saw very little of Bettina after that, but Roger has always been there.'

'And still is,' Alec said.

'Yes. Still is,' she agreed.

There was another short silence while they continued to

218

eat, then Alec said, 'Have you made up your mind about your morning job? Are you going to keep on with it?'

'It depends on whether I could get work doing more or less what I'm doing for the Comptons at the moment,' Caroline said. 'I really am enjoying that.'

'I reckon you could,' Alec said. 'As I've said before, I could put you in the way of jobs and, hopefully, we could work on them together. I'm never short of work and there are always interior-design issues in addition to the construction; the kind of things you're good at. We'd complement each other. But if you wanted to go it alone you could advertise . . .'

'Oh, I don't want to go it alone,' Caroline broke in. 'It would be much more interesting working with another person, sharing ideas and so on, even if we didn't always agree.'

'In the end the work would come through recommendations,' Alec said. 'Most of mine does. And apart from what you've done for the Comptons . . .'

'What *we've* done,' Caroline interrupted.

'OK,' Alec said. 'And as well as that you can show what you've done at number seventeen.'

'Again, what *we've* done.'

'Agreed again. But your ideas have made a difference. We make a formidable team.'

What have I to lose if I give up the morning job, Caroline thought? It didn't pay enough to make much difference to her financially, and now that she had the tenants she could manage without it.

'I suppose I could give it a go,' she said. 'Let's say that once we've finished the Comptons, and if that goes well, I'll make up my mind.' She would, she thought, have to consider whether she and Alec could work together on other jobs. It had gone without a hitch so far, but she had happily played second fiddle – it had been *his* job, she hadn't been involved from the start – but she wouldn't continue to enjoy a situation where she was too dependent on him.

As if he could read her thoughts, Alec said, 'We'd have to pool our ideas right from the start of each job. It wouldn't be a case of I'd lead and you'd follow. We'd need to rely on each other, consult all the way. And of course that would be better for the client.'

'Well, I *will* – as I've said – make up my mind when we've finished with the Comptons,' Caroline said.

Neither of them wanted a pudding, though Caroline didn't want the evening to end. It had all been so lovely, so relaxed, so companionable.

He drove back, parked the car, and saw her to her door. She was about to unlock the door when his mobile rang. 'Excuse me!' he said to Caroline as he answered it. She could tell at once that he was talking to Paula. She paused on the doorstep waiting until he had taken the call, already feeling the pleasant warmth of the evening ebbing away.

'Yes,' he was saying. 'Yes! That's wonderful! Congratulations! I'm not at home. I went out to supper with Caroline. To Giovanni's. Yes, very good – as always!'

After a few more words – she tried her hardest not to listen – he rang off. 'Sorry about that. It was Paula,' he said. 'The Sledges have just been booked for a TV appearance, so she's over the moon.'

'That sounds great. Will you come up for a cup of coffee?' Caroline asked him, noticing that he hadn't sounded all that over the moon himself.

'Thank you, but no,' he said. 'I have to get back.' He seemed distracted.

'Well, thank you for a lovely evening,' Caroline said, feeling embarrassed and not wishing to detain him any longer against his will. 'I did enjoy it. See you soon.'

★　　★　　★

Back in the flat, she checked her messages. The only one was from Roger. 'I just wanted to say hello,' he said, 'and to confirm that Saturday's OK. Sorry to miss you. Give me a ring.'

She did so at once. He didn't ask where she'd been when he called, nor did she tell him, though she might well have done so except, she thought, that he still seemed slightly wary of Alec.

'So is it all right for next weekend?' he asked.

'Great!' Caroline said. 'I look forward to it.'

'So do I,' Roger said. 'I'll ring the hotel in the morning. Do you think I might get to meet the Holbys?' he added. 'I'd like to.'

'I'm not certain,' Caroline said. 'They both work on Saturdays. But I assure you they're OK.'

'Very well,' Roger said. 'I'll be with you around lunch time. We can eat out.'

'No,' Caroline said, 'we won't eat out. I shall cook for you.' It would be nice, she thought, to have a focus for the next weekend. But as she lay in bed later, trying to think about other things, her mind kept drifting back to Alec.

The following day, skimming through the local newspaper, she came across a notice of a classical concert. It was ages since she'd been to one, listened to real live music rather than to a CD, experienced the atmosphere of the concert hall. It was almost certainly something Roger would enjoy. The two of them had always had that in common, though Peter and Bettina had never been particularly interested. Why not give Roger a call, she thought? It would distract her from thinking about Alec; she really must forget about that one, she told herself firmly.

'So what do you think?' she asked when she had given him the details. 'It's mostly Beethoven. The main work is the fifth piano concerto, a great favourite of mine.'

'And of mine,' Roger said enthusiastically. 'Of course I'd like to go!'

'Then I'll get the tickets,' Caroline said.

The concert was everything they had hoped for, and more. Afterwards they elected to walk back rather than take a taxi. It was a fine evening.

'I shall see you safely home before I go back to my hotel,' Roger said.

Standing on the doorstep of number seventeen, Roger said, 'I really enjoyed that. Thank you for suggesting it.'

'So did I,' Caroline said. Then, remembering her manners, said, 'Will you come up and have a nightcap, or a coffee? Is it too late?'

'No, I'd like that,' Roger said.

He followed her up the stairs and into the flat. On leaving, she had left the curtains undrawn, and a low light burning. 'I seldom draw the curtains until I actually go to bed,' she said. 'I love the view from my window, and as much after dark as when it's daylight.' Though the daylight had long gone when they stood side by side by the window.

Looking east over the rooftops, she could see the coast road as it rose over the cliffs, still busy with traffic. It was a ribbon of white and red lights. And would be, she knew, until the early hours of the morning. To the right, down the street to the front, past the lights of Marine Drive, the view quickly gave way to the blackness of the sea at night, but for a triangle of bobbing lights, probably a yacht returning late to the marina.

After a minute or two she turned around, away from the scene. 'What would you like to drink?' she asked. 'Coffee? Whisky? Wine? A cup of tea?'

'I think wine,' Roger said. 'Does that suit you?'

'Perfectly!' Caroline said. 'And perhaps a sandwich?'

'A sandwich would be fine,' Roger said. 'Can I do anything to help?'

'You can open the bottle and take it into the sitting room,' she said. 'The glasses are in the cupboard, here. I'll make the sandwiches.'

He left her to it. She took cream cheese and a tomato from the fridge and a loaf from the bread bin. The door was open between the kitchen and the sitting room and after a minute or two Roger called out to her. 'I'm looking at the TV programmes,' he said. 'There's a classic Fred Astaire and Ginger Rogers film on BBC 2. I love those old films. Do you mind if I turn it on? It started a few minutes ago.'

'Switch it on,' Caroline said. Though old musicals were not to her taste – they had such improbable plots – she would be glad of Roger's company for a little longer and it was often more interesting to watch television with someone else. It was one of the things she missed. She took in the sandwiches and joined Roger, sitting beside him on the sofa. He poured the wine. 'I think we've missed a bit of the film,' he said, 'and I don't think I can fill you in from what I've seen so far.'

'Don't even try!' Caroline said.

The plot was, as Caroline expected, ridiculous. But the romantic sparring of the two misguided lovers was amusing and the dancing was, as always, captivating and exhilarating. She found herself enjoying it, despite her earlier misgivings. Perhaps it was because she was watching it in the company of such a dear, loyal friend. Roger only ever had her best interests at heart.

It was after midnight when the movie ended. 'Well!' Caroline said. 'It was entertaining, but what was it all about? If anyone had shown even an iota of common sense they could have solved everything in the first half-hour!'

'Of course they could,' Roger agreed. 'But without the

misunderstandings and miscommunications there'd have been no film! You are too logical, Caroline.'

They had been aware increasingly during the course of the film that, although it had been bright skies and sunshine on the screen, outside there in Brighton it was quite different. Heavy rain had started to batter, and was still battering, on the roof of number seventeen, interspersed with streaks of lightning and rolls of thunder, sometimes so loud that they had had to turn up the volume on the television.

'I must ring for a taxi,' Roger said. 'I'd be soaked, walking back to the hotel in this.'

She handed him the telephone and gave him the number of the taxi firm she occasionally used. After the shortest of conversations he put the phone down. 'Totally booked up!' he said. 'No idea when they'll have a car free. Oh well, give me the phone book and I'll try somewhere else.'

It was to no avail. No company had a car available for at least an hour, and even that was uncertain; nor would they take a booking beyond that time.

'You can't possibly walk,' Caroline said firmly. 'You'd be drenched in the first five minutes! But not to worry! I have a perfectly good spare room available, as you know. It's not very tidy, but the bed is comfortable. You're more than welcome to stay.'

'Well, that does seem to be the answer,' Roger said. 'If you're sure.'

'Of course I'm sure!' Caroline said. 'I don't have pyjamas, or a dressing gown, but I do have a spare toothbrush!' She had given all Peter's clothes to the local hospice shop soon after he had died. They had taken them away for her. She had been hardly able to look at his suits, hanging in the wardrobe, or his shirts, folded in the drawers. 'And I have a spare kimono, which is unisex anyway. You can have that for wandering between the bathroom and the bedroom, or wherever.'

He accepted. What else could he do, he thought? The rain was as heavy as ever, accompanied by shafts of lightning which lit up the sky, and echoing thunder as it rolled across the sea. They sat there. Watching or half-watching whatever came up on television. In the end, Roger said, 'I shall go to bed. And you must be tired as well.'

'I *am* tired,' Caroline admitted. 'So I'll also go to bed. You know where the room is. The bed's made up and I'll get you the kimono.' She was back with it in a few minutes. 'I'm sorry it's a bit flowery,' she said. 'Not really your style. But no one's going to see it. Is there anything else you want?'

'I don't think so,' Roger said.

'Then I hope you sleep well!'

'I'm sure I shall.'

In fact, he didn't. Though he had been quite tired until he got into bed, sleep eluded him for a long time. He heard a clock, presumably a church clock, strike three before he finally lost consciousness.

Caroline, tossing and turning in her bed, fared no better. It was the double bed she and Peter had shared, and by habit not by intention, she still occupied her own side of it. Would it have been sensible, when she'd moved from Bath, to have changed over to a single bed? But it had not even occurred to her, and if it had she would never have done it. It would have seemed like banishing Peter from her life. But you left me, she thought now. Even though you didn't want to, you left me. She missed having him in her bed, which had been their bed.

She thought about Roger. He was one of the nicest men she had ever known – and a good man, yet Bettina had left him, not by death but, perhaps more cruelly, by choice. Why had she done that? They had seemed so happy together – but to Bettina someone else had clearly been more enticing. And Alec's wife had left him. But perhaps, as he had intimated, they had married too young. By now the daylight was creeping through the gap in the curtains – the rain had eased off – and at last she fell asleep – and dreamed that Roger and Alec were getting ready to go on holiday, somewhere abroad, and Bettina was going with them while she stayed behind to look after Miss Grayson, who had tripped over Frizzie, fallen down the basement steps, and sprained her ankle. Peter was not in her dream, but he never was. It seemed unfair. It had been a relief to waken, and a surprise to find that it was almost half past eight, more than an hour later than her usual waking time.

It was the smell of coffee, and the fact that somewhere a radio had been turned on, which wakened Roger. Unshaven, his usually immaculate hair tousled, barefooted, and dressed only in the kimono, he went into the kitchen.

'Good morning!' Caroline said. 'I must say, you look rather fetching! Did you sleep well?'

'Well I . . .' He hesitated, not wanting to sound rude. 'I'm afraid I didn't,' he finally concluded. 'Did you?'

'No. I was ages getting off, and then I had the most stupid dreams. Are you ready for breakfast?'

'If you don't mind me half dressed,' he answered.

'The same applies to me,' Caroline said. 'How do you like your eggs?'

'As they come,' Roger said.

They had not quite finished breakfast when they heard footsteps on the stairs, and then a knock on the door.

'Who . . . ?' Roger began.

She went to the door, opened it and there stood Alec. 'Alec! What a surprise!' Suddenly she was all too aware of her dishevelled state, her ancient dressing gown and un-brushed hair. She raised her hand and tried discreetly to pat her hair down.

'Sorry, I know it's Sunday,' said Alec smiling, 'but I came round to pick up some tools I need that I'd left at the

226

Holbys' and, as I was here, I thought I'd stop by to give you some good news.'

Becoming aware that they were still standing in the doorway, Caroline hastily said, 'Why don't you come in for some coffee?'

Alec started to answer as he followed Caroline into the flat but stopped, as his glance immediately took in the whole scene.

'Oh, I'm sorry. I didn't know . . . that is . . .'

His eyes were drawn to Roger, resplendent in the floral kimono, but otherwise clearly a man who had just got out of bed, sitting at the breakfast table as to the manner born.

'Alec, how good to see you. How are you?' said Roger, rising awkwardly and extending an arm to shake hands, the deep sleeve of the kimono unfurling gracefully.

'Alec has keys because he has to be able to get in if I'm out at work,' Caroline said. She didn't know why she was explaining this.

'Of course,' replied Roger as the two men shook hands.

'Coffee?' Caroline asked again, looking at Alec, desperately trying to diffuse the awkward atmosphere.

'No, no thanks. I really must be pushing off. Got a lot to do today, Sunday or not. No peace for the wicked, eh? . . .' His voice trailed off.

'What did you want to tell me? You said you had news?' Caroline asked.

'Oh, that can wait for another time. Really I should be going. Well, bye then.' And Alec was off in a flash.

'Oh dear!' Caroline said in dismay. 'I'm afraid he's got totally the wrong idea!'

'I daresay he has,' Roger said, smiling happily. 'Shall I make some more toast?'

'As a matter of fact,' Caroline said as they lingered over breakfast, 'I'm considering teaming up with Alec on a few jobs – he to do the conversions, the building stuff, and I'd work with him on the interior design: kitchen and bath fixtures, decorations, lighting – that sort of thing. I'd enjoy that – and Alec thinks I have a flair for it.'

'Looking around, I daresay you have,' Roger conceded. 'But would that be wise? And in any case you already have a part-time job. And then there are the tenants.'

'I've been thinking of giving up my morning job,' Caroline said. 'There's not really enough for me to do. And Doctor Freeman would be able to replace me quite easily.'

'Well, don't rush into anything with Alec,' Roger said.

'I won't,' Caroline promised. 'But I won't dismiss the idea completely. I think I might like it.'

'Then promise you'll consult me before you do anything legally,' Roger said.

'I will,' Caroline said. 'But it hasn't come to that yet.'

TWENTY

They had spent the rest of Sunday doing ordinary things: reading the papers, taking a walk by the sea, and in the early evening watching television.

'I did enjoy the concert. I'd got quite out of the habit of concert-going but we must do it again,' Roger said.

'I agree,' Caroline replied. 'I would go alone if there was something I particularly wanted to hear, but it's so much better with someone else – especially a like-minded person.'

There was a short pause between them, then Roger said, 'And there is one thing I have to say to you. You might not like it, but it really is important.'

'It sounds mysterious,' Caroline said, slightly nervously. 'What is it?'

'Please think very hard before you get involved any further with Alec,' he said. 'I mean in any business arrangement . . .' Caroline started to protest, but he cut her short. 'No! I mean it. I'm serious. I have nothing against Alec, he seems a nice enough fellow, but you simply don't know him well enough to go into a business arrangement with him.'

'Oh, I'll be cautious,' Caroline promised. 'Of course I will.

But I think perhaps you're making too much of things. And I'm sure Alec wouldn't let me down. He's not that sort of person, and I do trust him.'

'That's one of your problems,' Roger said. 'You're inclined to trust everyone.'

'I daresay I am,' Caroline said tartly. 'And I'm not going to apologize for that. And don't forget, I've worked with Alec for quite some time on this house, and now we've all but finished the Compton house.'

'I don't want you to apologize,' Roger said. 'I just don't want you to get too involved, to risk being disappointed.'

'I won't,' Caroline assured him. 'Maybe just do one or two jobs together – always supposing we're fortunate enough to get suitable ones like the Comptons' has turned out to be – and see how it goes. Nothing more than that. Anyway, I'll keep you in touch.'

'Please do,' Roger said. 'And don't bite off more than you can chew!'

How do I know what I can chew until I try it, Caroline asked herself? The trouble was, Roger saw things through the eyes of a lawyer. Peter had been the same. For them it was inevitable, and sometimes necessary. They saw litigation a mile off. But this was different. She couldn't help thinking there was more to Roger's reaction to Alec than a simple concern about her business relationships. On the other hand, she thought, Roger is saying what he's saying for my sake. He's looking after me and I should be grateful.

'Don't worry!' she said. 'I'm sure nothing will go wrong.'

She walked down the street with him to where his car was parked. About to open the car door, he hesitated then turned towards her to give her his usual good-bye kiss. But it was not his usual kiss; not the friendly hug, the peck on the cheek, the 'Take care! See you soon!' Suddenly his arms were around her, holding her close, his lips on hers. And then, just as suddenly, he let her go, turned away, and got into his car. He said nothing. Nor did she. She had no time to react. She watched him drive away – he didn't turn around to give her a final wave as he usually did. She watched until his car was out of sight, then walked back to number seventeen, her mind, her thoughts, in turmoil. Was this what she wanted? She thought not. Had she done something to make him think it was? She had never thought of Roger in that light, and now she must find a way of conveying that to him. He was a dear friend – they went back a long way, they had shared experiences. But that was all, she thought, as she walked away.

Back at the house, Eleanor Grayson had popped out of her own doorway, ostensibly to put out crumbs for the birds. 'Such a nice man!' she said. 'So handsome! Such charming manners. Quite one of the old school!'

'I've known him for a very long time,' Caroline said, not wanting to go down this route with Miss Grayson. 'He and my husband were colleagues.'

'Is he married?' Miss Grayson enquired. She believed that if one wanted to know, then the sensible thing was to ask.

'Divorced,' Caroline said.

'I see,' Miss Grayson said.

You don't really, Caroline thought in exasperation. You see what you want to see. 'And now I must get on,' she said.

People did jump to quick conclusions, she thought as she went back upstairs. And very often the wrong ones, as Alec had quite clearly done. It had been written on his face, there had been no need to speak – and that silly kimono had not helped. The situation was not unlike that in the film she and Roger had watched on television: everyone assuming the wrong thing, no one contradicting it out loud. But being a film, it had all worked out in the end. There was nothing she could do. She couldn't say to Alec, 'Actually, I hadn't slept with Roger; it's not what you think!' She couldn't say it because Alec hadn't said what he was thinking,

231

though it had been clear from the look on his face, and from his embarrassment. To explain it would be even more embarrassing. The only thing was to let it go.

He had phoned at some point when she was out, and had left a message. 'The Comptons will be down on Monday afternoon. I've only a couple of small things to do before they come. I can finish those in the morning and finally hand over in the afternoon. I think it might be a good idea if you were to be there. I could pick you up from Doctor Freeman's shortly after two. If I don't hear from you to the contrary I'll wait outside in the van.'

At the door that morning, she thought, he had said he had news for her, but in his hurry to leave he hadn't got around to giving it to her. Perhaps this was it?

The next day she had a slow morning at the surgery. Doctor Freeman left at noon; he had to be earlier than usual at the hospital. At two o'clock she checked that everything was in order, looked through the window, saw that Alec's van was there, and went out to join him.

'Hi!' Alec said. 'You're very prompt!'

'It's been a quiet morning,' Caroline said. 'Which reminds me, when you arrived on Sunday morning you said you had news, but you never got around to telling me what it was. I suppose this was it, that the Comptons' job was about to be wrapped up?'

'Partly,' Alec said, 'but more than that. When they phoned about seeing us today they also said there was possibly another job in view – for the two of us, that is. Not certain, but promising.'

'Goodness!' Caroline said. 'Already? That sounds in-teresting. What is it? And where?'

'Good luck again,' Alec said. 'It's in Brighton.' He told her the name of the road but it rang no bells with her.

'It's an old house,' Alec said. 'Two-storey. And if they buy

232

it – their name is Benson – which isn't yet certain, they want to convert it into two flats; the ground floor for his mother and the upper floor for him and his wife as a *pied à terre*. They come down to Brighton fairly often.'

'Does the mother already live with them?' Caroline asked.

'No. She lives alone, in north London. She's widowed and her house is now too big for her. She knows Brighton well, absolutely loves it, apparently. Loves the shopping, the theatre, the sea,' Alec said. 'So the Comptons mentioned us, and as a result you and I will meet up with them any minute now. And then probably they'll take us over the house; tell us what they have in mind, get our views.'

'Yours particularly,' Caroline pointed out. 'Mine are only the trimmings, so to speak. So do Mr and Mrs Benson also intend to move to Brighton?'

'No,' Alec said. 'I don't know all the details, but the house in question appeals to them because it's near the station and they can come down by train. Quick and easy. I think Mr Benson wants to keep an eye on his mother. And it seems the present owner already had permission to convert into two flats but he changed his mind, decided to move away, and put the house on the market.'

'It sounds good,' Caroline said. 'I look forward to meeting them.' And what would Roger say to all this, she asked herself? Wasn't this what he had warned her against? He would no doubt tell her that she should be careful, she must not get too involved – though in fact he had quite approved when she herself had taken on number seventeen. Perhaps because he knew *he* would be involved.

It was less than fifteen minutes' drive to the Comptons' house. As they drove, Caroline felt relieved that any awkwardness between them following the encounter with Roger in the kitchen seemed to have dissipated. 'Here we are!' Alec said as he drew up outside.

Mr and Mrs Compton welcomed them warmly. They were delighted with all that had been done in the house, and were now bursting to take it over, everything completed. They introduced Alec and Caroline to the Bensons. 'We're down here for another two nights,' Mr Benson said. 'We'd like to go some time tomorrow to see the house we have in mind.'

'Or even this afternoon,' his wife put in. 'If you can manage that.'

'As far as I'm concerned we could go now,' Alec said.

'Then why not?' Mrs Benson said. She turned to her husband. 'That would be fine, wouldn't it?'

'We won't come with you,' Mr Compton said. 'We've already seen it and there's no point in six of us hanging around.'

Twenty minutes later they were at the house, together with the estate agent, who had insisted on accompanying them. The five of them walked through it together.

'It seems a straightforward job to me,' Alec said, when they had looked at everything. 'I don't foresee any problems,' he added. 'Certainly not big ones.' He described to the Bensons what might be done. 'If that sounds the kind of thing you want,' he said, 'I could draw up some plans. Would you like me to do that?'

They agreed that they would. 'And if we decide on the job, we'd like to have it done for next Easter. Would that be possible?' Mr Benson asked. 'I have to buy this one, but I don't foresee any delays there. I don't need a mortgage.'

'I daresay we could do that,' Alec replied. 'I could get the plans to you within a week and then it's a case of you making up your minds. There'll be details we can go into later. The basic conversion is down to me, and Caroline will come in with her ideas – fittings, decoration, equipment and so on. We work together, which will be convenient for you as well as for us.'

'That sounds OK,' Mr Benson said. 'And naturally you'll give me an estimate of what it's going to cost.'

'A basic estimate for the conversion,' Alec said. 'The rest will depend on whatever you choose in the way of fixtures, fittings, and so on.'

Mr Benson looked at his wife. 'How does all that sound to you, my dear?' he asked.

'Fine!' she said. 'I look forward to seeing the plans.'

'And if you want it to be completed by Easter, let us have a reasonably quick reply,' Alec repeated. He turned to Caroline. 'Is that all right with you?' he asked.

It was a courtesy question only, Caroline thought. She would have loads of time, especially if she gave up Doctor Freeman. 'No problem at all,' she said.

'Caroline and I will need to come in to take some measurements,' Alec said. 'And to get the feel of the house. I'd like that to be as soon as possible.'

'Whenever you like,' Mr Benson said.

'You can pick up the key from me,' the estate agent added.

'Then probably as soon as tomorrow,' Alec said. He turned to Caroline. 'Would tomorrow afternoon suit you?'

'Perfectly!' she answered.

The five of them parted company outside the house; and Alec took Caroline home. 'I won't come in,' he said, not quite looking at her. 'I have a job to go to. Last-minute details, actually, but the client wants to see the end of it – as all clients do. And I'll be pleased to have the cheque. Shall I pick you up from Doctor Freeman's tomorrow? Usual time?'

'That's fine,' Caroline said. She had by now resigned herself to the fact that their friendship was to be purely professional and she was going to make herself respect that.

Eleanor Grayson, with Frizzie in close attendance, was outside, attending to her plants. Frizzie barked as Caroline approached, but it was a friendly bark. 'She likes you!' Miss Grayson said. 'In fact, she gets on well with most people, even the postman, but she can't abide cats, and there are quite a few of those around. The one in particular she hates is a large, black tom – I call him the Black Panther. He's a frequent visitor. I don't know why. I don't feed him. Frizzie wouldn't allow it.'

'You look as though you're busy,' Caroline said. 'What are you doing?'

'Actually,' Miss Grayson said, 'I'm throwing out the plants which have finished flowering, and in any case are past it. I'm also going to plant a few outdoor bulbs. I aim to have some colour all the year round.'

'It sounds great,' Caroline said. 'And, really, I think I should bear some of the cost. I would like to. Everyone in the house benefits from what you do.'

'I wouldn't say no to that,' Miss Grayson answered. 'Plants are quite expensive – and then there's all the other stuff: compost, pots, plant food – so thank you kindly.'

'Perhaps we could go to a nursery together?' Caroline suggested. 'It wouldn't be easy for you to do it without a car. Too much to carry. What about Saturday? Would that suit you? I think it's the best day to go. They're always well stocked on a Saturday, especially if we go in the morning.'

'That would be splendid!' Miss Grayson said.

'And at the same time,' Caroline said, 'I'll make a start on buying a few things for what will be my roof garden. I must make plans – and we must both make lists.'

'Wonderful!' Miss Grayson said. 'I look forward to it.'

Frizzie, alerted by the enthusiasm in her owner's voice, gave an excited bark of approval.

'And how is everyone else in the house getting on?' Miss Grayson asked. She would have liked a regular report, indeed she would like to know everyone, to be on chatting terms with them, passing the time of day, hearing the snippets of news, but even though she spent as much time outside as she reasonably could, attending to her plants, or sitting in the window, watching the world go by, it seemed not to happen. People hurried by, with no time to spare, no inclination to pause for a little harmless gossip, which in her view was one of the things which made the world go round. 'When are the new couple arriving?' she asked now.

'Next Monday,' Caroline told her.

'Good! And the boys?' She always referred to Adam Carter and Eric Foster as 'the boys'.

'Very well, as far as I know.'

'I don't see much of them,' Miss Grayson admitted. 'They come and go quietly. But nice boys!'

'Very nice,' Caroline agreed and went upstairs thinking that her roof terrace could benefit from some plants growing along the walls and even a few tubs. A visit to the nursery was definitely in order.

The plant nursery was on the outskirts of Brighton, about twenty minutes' drive from number seventeen. Once there, they found almost everything they had listed, and also some things they hadn't thought about.

In the end, Caroline bought mostly shrubs, small enough to go in pots or small tubs: lavender, a berberis, a silvery-grey artemesia. Then she and Miss Grayson between them chose a variety of bulbs; hyacinths to force, tulips, lilies.

'Plant the hyacinths deep,' the salesman said. 'Four inches isn't too much.'

'Right!' Caroline said. 'And I rather fancy some grasses – especially on my roof, where I can imagine they'll move with the breeze.'

'A wise choice,' the salesman said. 'And with one or two exceptions you can put them in at any time of the year, and they need very little looking after.' He pointed out the area where they would find them.

'I think we'd better call a halt,' Caroline said to Miss Grayson when she had chosen the grasses. 'I'm thinking about the space in the car.' They pushed their two carts to the checkout, and joined the short queue there. In spite of Miss Grayson's protestations, Caroline paid for the contents of both carts. 'Anyway, you'll be doing all the work in the front. I shall stick to my roof garden.'

Caroline drove back home, found a parking space close to number seventeen and started, with Miss Grayson, to unpack the car. It was not easy. Some of the things they had bought were awkward to handle, as well as heavy. 'I don't think I realized we'd bought so much,' Caroline said as she struggled with a shrub which, no matter how she held it, persistently hit her in the face. It was with pleasure and relief that, over the top of the shrub, she looked ahead and saw Eric and Adam walking down the road towards them.

'What in the world are you doing?' Adam called out as they drew near.

'We've been garden shopping,' Caroline said. 'I think we got carried away.'

'Then if you'll stand to one side, we'll unpack it for you,' Adam said.

'And if you'll tell us where you want it all, we'll put it there,' Eric added.

'How very kind!' Miss Grayson said. 'And you've appeared at exactly the right moment!'

'Some of it goes in Miss Grayson's area, at the front,' Caroline said, 'and the rest, I'm afraid, goes up to the roof, where I'm planning to make something of a garden.'

'OK,' Eric said. 'Just sort out what goes where.'

The two women watched in admiration as the two young men picked up pots and plants and bags of compost as if they were no more than feather cushions. It was all done in no time at all. 'What very nice boys they are!' Miss Grayson said to Caroline when they had left.

'I agree. I'm lucky to have them. And now we must give everything a good watering. Would you like me to give you a hand?'

'No, I'll be fine,' Miss Grayson said. 'It's been a lovely morning. Thank you so much!'

For Caroline, the evening passed quietly and pleasantly; watching television, catching up with the morning's paper, which she never seemed to get around to until later in the day. She had enjoyed being with Eleanor Grayson. It was long since dark now, and a little chilly. She switched on the fire and soon afterwards, what with the warmth of the fire, the afternoon's fresh air and thinking over the excitement of the day, she fell asleep. It was the noise of her door buzzer which awoke her.

She jumped to her feet to answer it. It was Adam. 'Please come down quickly!' he cried. 'Bring our flat keys with you. I haven't got mine.'

She snatched up her duplicate bunch of the keys to their flat and ran down the stairs as fast as she could. 'I'm coming! I'm coming!' she called out. She reached the door, and opened it.

Adam was already on the front step, with Eric. Caroline gave a sharp scream at the sight of them. Adam was supporting Eric, who clearly could hardly stand. His face was swollen with crimson and purple bruises, blood had at some point poured from his nose and seeped into his collar. One eye was closed, and the area around it was livid and swollen.

'What in the world . . . ?' she began – but it was no time for explanations. Eric was clearly on the point of collapse. And then Miss Grayson's door opened and she appeared. 'Who . . . ?' she began – then shrieked at the sight of Eric.

239

TWENTY-ONE

'Oh, my goodness!' Miss Grayson cried. 'What in the world has happened? Oh, you poor boy!'

'He was attacked,' Adam said shortly.

'Bring him straight down to my flat!' she said. 'Can you manage that? I know it's several steps down from the hall, but still not as many as up to your own flat. And we can't do anything for him right here!' The hall was narrow, with only one upright chair, and an umbrella stand. 'Now if only Mr Downey were in . . . but I saw him leave earlier in the evening.'

Eric sat on the chair, Adam holding on to him to keep him from collapsing on to the floor. Caroline dabbed ineffectually at the blood on his face with her handkerchief, but he winced at that. Beneath the blood and bruises he was deathly pale. 'Perhaps a drop of brandy?' Miss Grayson suggested. 'I always keep a little in case of emergency.'

Caroline shook her head. 'I don't think so. In fact, definitely not. Not while he's still bleeding.' And who knows where else he might be bleeding from, she thought to herself. 'No! He should go straight to the hospital,' she said. 'He needs expert help. I'm sure of that!'

'I've already said so,' Adam put in. 'He doesn't want to go. I'm sure he should, but he's adamant.'

Eric tried to shake his head but the pain stopped him.

'I'll be all right,' he protested, though the weakness of his voice said otherwise. 'Just help me upstairs . . .'

'No way!' Caroline said firmly. 'I don't mean we wouldn't help you all we could, but hospital's the place for you. They can sort things out and do what's best for you. Adam and I will take you in my car.' She turned to Miss Grayson. 'Could you get something to deal with the bleeding? A clean teacloth perhaps? And a blanket or a rug. We must keep you warm,' she said to Eric.

'I'm cold,' he agreed. 'But I really don't want to go to hospital,' he said yet again. 'I'll be OK. I just want to go to bed.'

'Sorry, mate!' Adam said. 'Caroline's right. Hospital it is. They'll see to you, do whatever's needed. Don't worry, they won't keep you in. We'll bring you back with us!' In fact, he felt far from sure about that.

Miss Grayson returned quickly with a clean cloth and a blanket. 'And I've brought my hot pad,' she said. 'I heated it in the microwave. It will keep you warm in the car,' she said to Eric.

'I'll bring the car to the door. It's parked halfway down the road,' Caroline said. 'I'll be as quick as I can.'

In a surprisingly short time they heard her toot the horn outside. Adam helped Eric to his feet and led him carefully down the path. It was not easy. Eric had no strength in him. The over-large blanket impeded him and he seemed too confused to deal with it, while Adam needed all his own strength and skill to guide his friend. Miss Grayson followed a step or two behind, and when Eric was seated, and Caroline ready to drive away, she handed him the hot pad. 'Hold it against you!' she said. 'You'll find it's comforting. Heat usually is.'

She stood at the gate anxiously waving them off. Not until they were out of sight did she go back into the house. She would dearly have liked to go with them, but when she'd suggested that it had not been encouraged.

'Savages!' she cried out loud as she went back to her flat. 'Brutes and savages!' Frizzie, who had kept unusually quiet, picked up the anger in her mistress's voice and barked in agreement. 'Brutes, thugs and savages!' Miss Grayson repeated. 'No, Frizzie! I don't mean you!' She sat down on the nearest chair. She was deeply shocked. Eric had looked so awful, and it was not only physical pain, it was clear he had been badly frightened, and he had been right to be afraid, she thought. What was the world coming to when a young man as kind and self-effacing as Eric could be set upon in the street for no reason at all? Of course, she had read in the newspapers of such assaults. They were far from uncommon. But just reading about them was not the same. And Adam, though he had escaped whatever had happened to Eric, had looked deeply worried. How had he avoided it all, she asked herself? Why only Eric? Surely they had been together? But Adam, being bigger and stronger than Eric, would have been more capable of fending off the attackers.

She made a cup of tea, added the generous tablespoonful of brandy she had been forbidden to give to Eric, and settled down as best she could to calm her mind and await their return. She would wait up for them, no matter how long. She would certainly not think of going to bed until she saw them back, safe and sound. Not that Eric had looked anywhere near sound, poor boy!

Entering the Accident and Emergency wing, Caroline and Adam took Eric immediately to the desk, behind which the receptionist was talking to a nurse. At the sight of Eric they broke off their conversation. 'My goodness!' the nurse said. 'You've been in the wars! You'd better come with me. I'll

242

take you straight through. And one of your friends can go with you, though not both of them.'

'I'll do that!' Adam said quickly.

'Fortunately, the doctor is free,' the nurse said. 'I'm sure she'll see you right away.'

'I'd like to go in with my friend when he sees the doctor. Can I do that?' Adam asked.

'I expect so,' the nurse said. 'The doctor will need some details. I daresay you can help with those.'

The doctor seated Eric, gave him a brief, though sympathetic examination, and asked a few questions which Eric answered as well as he could, though his voice was weak and shaking. 'Well,' she said, 'no broken bones as far as I can tell, but we'll do an X-ray, just in case. And Nurse will clean you up a bit, make you more comfortable, after which you can tell me more about it.'

The nurse was skilful and gentle, though Eric winced and drew away when she touched his face. When she was through, the doctor examined him more carefully. 'So you were in a fight,' she said. 'And by the look of you, you got the worst of it.'

'No!' Eric protested. 'No, I wasn't in a fight! I was attacked. I didn't even have a chance to fight, even if I'd wanted to!'

The doctor turned to Adam. 'So you weren't together when this happened?'

'We weren't at that moment,' Adam said. 'We would have been. We'd gone into the pub together.' He mentioned the name of the pub and the doctor nodded, recognizing it. 'We'd had two halves each. Nothing more. In fact, we were just leaving. We don't often stay long. I went into the lavatory while Eric continued into the street. It all happened in the short time while he was waiting for me. No more than a minute or two.'

The doctor turned to Eric. 'And what did happen?' she asked.

Eric began to shake his head, but it hurt too much. 'They just came at me without any warning.' The act of talking through his swollen mouth, with his lower lip still bleeding, hurt him, as did the cut on his bruised cheekbone. In fact, he still felt shaken and bruised all over. His legs didn't belong to him. He made an effort to talk again. 'I was standing there, on the pavement, waiting for Adam,' he said. 'They appeared from nowhere. I hadn't seen them. There were three of them, all on me at once, hitting me hard, calling me filthy names. They knocked me to the ground. I didn't have the strength to move and they ran off. It was all so quick,' he repeated.

'Was there no one around?' the doctor asked. 'Did no one come to help you?'

'I don't know. There might have been people passing,' Eric said. 'I didn't see them, or they didn't stop. People don't want to get involved, do they?' He stopped talking, exhausted. The bruises on his face stood out against the pallor of his skin.

'I was there just in time to see the back of them as they ran away,' Adam broke in. 'It wouldn't have been possible to recognize any of them. I didn't see their faces. And I don't remember seeing a group of youths in the pub. It was mostly the regulars. But from what I saw from the back of that lot as they ran away, I'd say they were young. You could tell that.'

Eric found the strength to speak again. 'I did just notice they were standing there when I came out on my own, as if they were waiting. But I thought nothing of it.'

The doctor looked from Adam to Eric, and then back again to Adam. 'You must both know that the area this pub is in doesn't have a good reputation. I don't mean the pub. As far as I know, that's well run, but the area around is another matter. It's been in the news more than once. You must know that. Not that it's any excuse for what happened.'

244

'I suppose we did know that,' Adam admitted. 'But you never think such things are going to happen to you, do you? They just happen to other people.'

'That's true,' the doctor agreed. She turned to Eric. 'However, though I can see it's painful, and it's certainly regrettable, I reckon no serious harm has been done this time. We don't need to keep you in, but it could well have been otherwise. And you'll report it to the police, of course?'

'I'd rather not,' Eric said quickly. 'I don't have to, do I? *You* don't have to, do you?' He sounded anxious.

'No, I don't have to in this case,' the doctor said, 'because however painful, there are no serious injuries, nothing which is likely to be ongoing. If there were, then I would report it, and I think perhaps you *should.*'

Eric shook his head – or attempted to until, again, the pain stopped him. 'I'd rather not,' he said. 'I hate publicity. We both do. All we want is to be left alone to get on with our lives.'

'It's up to you,' the doctor said. Then she smiled. 'I could suggest you change your pub, found one in another area.'

'We don't like being driven out by thugs,' Eric said.

The doctor gave him an injection, plus something with which to bathe the most painful of his bruises, and two tablets to take when he went to bed that night. 'They'll help you to sleep,' she said. 'And take it easy. Don't go into work on Monday. Come back tomorrow and let the nurse take a look at you.'

When the two men came back into the waiting room to join her, Caroline thought Eric, under his bruises, looked as white as a sheet. 'Let's get you back home!' she said. 'Bed's the best place for you.'

Miss Grayson had naturally intended to be there to greet them when they returned; to hear what the verdict had been, to offer whatever help and sympathy she could. Unfortunately – no one could deny that it had been an eventful day, and she had a right to be tired – she had fallen into a deep sleep as, unusually, also had Frizzie – and the returning party had let themselves in so quietly that neither she nor Frizzie heard a thing. Indeed, when Miss Grayson wakened it was way past her usual bedtime and Frizzie was pawing at her to be let out.

It was bliss to be in bed, Eric thought. Or comparative bliss. He ached all over, it seemed from top to toe, though most of all in his head and shoulders. Adam, when he had re-heated Miss Grayson's bed-warmer and put it in the bed, had helped him to undress and had made him a cup of Ovaltine with which to wash down the tablets he'd been given. Adam, standing by the bed, now said, 'Is there anything else?'

'Nothing at all,' Eric answered. 'I just want to go to sleep!' If the pain will let me, he thought. But perhaps the tablets would take care of that. He was already a little drowsy. 'You don't mind that I won't go to the police?' he asked Adam. 'I daresay I should, but I really don't want to.'

'I don't mind at all,' Adam said. 'I agree, we don't want the fuss. But only as long as you think the same. What good would it do? Anyway, try to sleep.'

'I couldn't, could I?' Eric said. 'Not looking like this!' He tried to smile, but his face wouldn't cooperate. Earlier on he had seen himself in the bathroom mirror and had been horrified.

In the morning Caroline knocked gently on the men's door. 'I didn't want to phone,' she said when Adam answered it. 'I thought Eric might be asleep. How is he?'

'As a matter of fact, he *is* asleep,' Adam said. 'And the longer he sleeps, the better. I'll go with him to see the nurse later on. We'll get a taxi. I'm not on duty until one o'clock today.'

'I'd forgotten you worked in the hospital,' Caroline said.

'It will help,' Adam said. 'We probably won't be kept waiting. And thank you for everything you did last night. It would have been even more of a nightmare without you.'

'Well, I won't say it was a pleasure,' Caroline told him, 'but I'm glad I was around. And would it be a help now if I popped in on Miss Grayson, told her Eric was OK, but asleep – not to be disturbed? She means well, but . . .'

'A great help,' Adam said. 'And right now, the truth. He needs to rest.'

Caroline knocked on Miss Grayson's door and gave her the message. Miss Grayson was pleased to hear Eric was better – or 'no worse' Caroline said – but clearly disappointed not to go upstairs to see him. 'Better we leave him to rest and recover,' Caroline advised.

The Holbys moved in the following Monday, as arranged. Caroline had suggested an afternoon arrival so that she could be around in case they needed her for anything, and this was convenient to them. It all went reasonably smoothly. They didn't have a great deal of furniture, and what they did have was modern and light, and the staircases at number seventeen, at least as far as the third floor (from there up to Caroline's flat the stairs narrowed), were wide, so there was no difficulty in getting things up.

David would not allow Brigid to carry anything more than her handbag. He seated her on the very first armchair the men brought up, found a box which would serve as a foot-stool, and there she sat, directing where everything should go. She was only five and a half months pregnant, Caroline thought. What would it be like by the time she was due to give birth? Still, it was rather sweet, the way he cosseted her,

247

and as well to make the most of it while it lasted. She would soon have her hands full.

It was a satisfying feeling that they were here, she thought. Every flat was now occupied. She hoped it would work out – but why wouldn't it? In any case, she reminded herself, she wasn't responsible for everything and everybody. They were all grown-up people, free to come and go, do whatever they pleased, within reason. She provided the flats, and she had done everything she could think of to make them pleasant places to live in – and they paid the rent. They might go for days, weeks even – though she couldn't imagine that of Eleanor Grayson – without seeing one another, and maybe even then only going in and out of the front door or passing on the stairs.

It would be right, of course, and no more than neighbourly, to keep an eye on Miss Grayson. She was old, and seemed not to have anyone to turn to. And for the moment Caroline was also concerned about Eric, though that would pass. He was young, he would recover quickly. She also had the feeling that the boys – she had picked up Miss Grayson's manner of referring to them – agreeable though they were, perhaps preferred keeping themselves to themselves.

In any case, she had Rosie, whom she hoped to see more often. Brighton and London were so close. Also, she had enjoyed having Patience here and she would do that again. And there was Alec – a working colleague now, as well as a friend. And Roger.

She stopped short at the thought of Roger. She was so fond of him, but at the moment not totally happy about him. She'd realized when they'd parted, when he'd kissed her, that his thoughts about her were not akin to hers of him. There had been no time to show anything, let alone speak. He had called her since with a formal 'thank you' for a pleasant visit, and the hope that they would meet again soon.

She hadn't seen Alec this last week either, though, she told herself firmly, there was no reason why she should have. The Comptons were done with and the Bensons had presumably not been in touch about the Brighton conversion. She could call him, of course. Perhaps she would, just to see how the land lay. Or perhaps not.

Two more days went by. Where was everyone? And then, when she returned from a visit to the hairdresser there was a message waiting. It was from Roger. 'Sorry to miss you,' he said. 'Will you give me a ring?'

She put the phone down, then hesitated before picking it up again. But of course she would have to ring him, she couldn't just ignore the message, and if she were to do so he'd think she'd not had it and he'd call again. She wondered what he was going to say, and what she would say. The phone was not her thing, it never had been. If she had anything of importance to say to anyone she preferred to do it face to face. Or in some cases, in writing, but this was not a situation for writing. They were close friends, old friends. They must talk to each other. She asked herself again if she had read too much into his kiss, though she knew she hadn't. She took a deep breath, picked up the receiver, and tapped out his number.

'Roger Pym,' he answered. He had the pleasantest of voices, and indeed he was a very nice man. That was what made it harder. Why couldn't she fall for him?

'It's me! Caroline. You left a message . . . I've just got in. I've been having a haircut. I look like a long-haired curly poodle . . .' She was babbling, and she knew it.

'I rather like them,' he said. 'Poodles, I mean. And I'm hoping to get to see the haircut.'

Oh no! she thought. She didn't want him to come to Brighton again until she had sorted things out, decided what she would say, how she would say it. She knew – she was sure she did – what he was going to say to her. It had

249

all been there in the kiss. And Roger was not one for playing games.

'I'm not sure . . .' she began.

'I'm inviting you to a dinner party,' he said. 'I haven't done the other invites yet. I decided it was high time I did something sociable. And why would I have a dinner party and not invite you?'

'A dinner party?' she said. 'In your own home, do you mean?'

'Exactly!' he said. 'Much nicer than a restaurant. I'll get caterers in. Friday week, and of course you'll stay over. Too late for you to get back to Brighton.'

'I'm not sure . . .' she repeated.

'If you can't make the date, I'll change it,' he said. 'There'll be ten of us. Maybe one or two you know, maybe not.'

There was no escape, and in fact she wasn't sure she wanted one. She liked Roger and she liked dinner parties. And it would also, she thought, give her the chance over the weekend to make it quite plain where she stood. She didn't like the thought of doing that but she knew it would have to be done, and to do it not in a hurry, actually to talk, would be better, kinder. Oh, Roger, she thought when she had put down the phone, I do wish I wanted what you want, but I don't!

TWENTY-TWO

Caroline had still not heard from Alec. It had been two weeks now. She presumed that he was extra busy, also that he had had no word from the Bensons, or he would surely have let her know. But when it came to buying and selling houses, she reminded herself, delays were common, everyone waiting for everyone else to move. She missed being in touch with him though. She wondered if she would give him a call. And then, on Thursday evening, before she could put the thought into action, the phone rang, and it *was* Alec.

It was much as she'd thought. He was waiting for the powers-that-be to give consent to the extra alterations he had submitted along with the Bensons' existing plans. 'They take their time, and there's no hurrying them,' Alec said. 'I'm used to it, but fortunately I have enough small jobs to keep me busy for a while. Anyway,' he continued, 'that wasn't why I rang. I wondered if it would be convenient for me to come around at the weekend. I have a few ideas I'd like to discuss with you. Friday or Saturday? Whichever suits you. That is if . . .'

'Oh dear!' Caroline broke in. 'I'd love to but I'm sorry, I can't. I shan't be here. I'm off to Bristol for the weekend.

Roger's giving a dinner party on Friday evening. He's invited me, and naturally I shall stay overnight.'

'Oh, I see!' Alec said. 'Oh well . . . !'

No, you don't see at all, Caroline thought. 'I would have liked . . .' she began.

'Some other time,' he said. 'I'll be in touch. Enjoy your weekend.' He rang off. The tone of his voice said he was backing off.

On Friday afternoon she set off for Bristol, leaving early enough to avoid the weekend traffic. Driving was more convenient because she could leave whenever it suited her on Saturday. She would be able to choose the moment to say, if it came to it, what she had to say to Roger and then, if need be, leave. She would play it by ear. She had no wish to spoil her friendship with Roger. She was too fond of him for that.

She had informed Miss Grayson that she would be away for the weekend, and since the lady had waited expectantly for news of where she was going and why, she had told her that too.

'How wonderful!' Miss Grayson said. 'It's a long time since I went to a dinner party. My parents gave them, of course, but once you're on your own, and a spare woman, you're not invited as often.' She nevertheless sounded quite happy about it. 'A man on his own is different. A spare man is pure gold! Anyway, you must tell me all about it when you get back! What you had to eat; what everyone wore.'

'I will!' Caroline promised.

She enjoyed the drive to Bristol. It was a fine day, but not too sunny. She purposely bypassed Bath. There were too many memories, and this was not the day she wished to resurrect them. She had other things on her mind. She was exercised about what she should say to Roger, exactly how she would make known her feelings – or in this case the lack of the kind of feeling he was looking for – without hurting him. She knew – she had no doubt about it – that something would have to be said. She felt certain the subject *would* arise. And what a pity it was, she mused as, nearing Bristol, she was held up at traffic lights, that the ideal solution, the fictional one, was not at all what she wanted. It would have been such a neat one. Two couples, all four of them close friends together, liking and respecting each other: one woman leaves suddenly, by choice, and one man, not her husband, dies. The man and the woman left behind spend more and more time together, their liking blossoms into love. They marry each other, and live happily ever after. Perfection! But *we* wouldn't, she thought. We just wouldn't.

Roger's house was on the outskirts of the city, near to the top of Clifton Hill. It was a pleasant, solid-looking early-nineteenth-century house, built of Bath stone. Roger had heard her turn her car into the drive and was at the door the second she pulled up. For one moment she wondered how he would greet her. She needn't have worried. He embraced her lightly, kissed her on the cheek, took her overnight bag and led her into the house.

It was a house she had always liked, even more from the inside than from the exterior. In a way, it was not unlike number seventeen. It had possibly been built around the same time, but on a larger and more opulent scale. The hall was spacious, with an elaborately tiled floor, the ceilings were more ornate, the stairs to the upper floor were wider and less steep. It was a large house for one man to live in alone, but she had never heard Roger mention even the slightest possibility of leaving it, going for something smaller. And as a matter of fact, she thought, he seemed suited to it. Tall, gracious and attractive, with a strong yet warm personality, he had always filled it with his presence. She wondered, yet again, why Bettina had left him. But there was no accounting for the vagaries of love. People did not always love, or not love, exactly where they might have wished to, where it might be the most convenient. It was seldom a matter of will.

He showed her to her room. It was large, well-furnished and at the back of the house, overlooking the garden. Although she and Peter had visited many times, since Bristol was no great distance from Bath, they had never stayed overnight. 'What a lovely room!' she said now to Roger.

'I hope you'll find everything you want,' he said. 'Mrs Parkin prepared it for you. But if you don't, then just ask.' Mrs Parkin had been his part-time housekeeper since soon after Bettina had left.

'I will,' Caroline said. 'And for now I'll unpack my things, which won't take long – put my dress on a hanger and so on – then I'll come downstairs and give you a hand. I'm sure there must be things to do.'

Roger shook his head. 'Not really,' he said. 'Mrs P has stayed on – she usually leaves at lunch time but today she's here for whatever's needed. And as far as the meal goes, I have a caterer coming in. So you can relax, and do absolutely nothing! There's lots of time. My guests won't arrive until seven thirty. Perhaps you'd like a drink, or a cup of tea?'

'I'd love some tea,' Caroline admitted.

'Right!' he said. 'Come down when you're ready. Oh, it is so good to see you, Caroline!' he added. 'I can't begin to tell you . . .'

Please don't, she thought. I don't want to hear it. She was too fond of him to want to hurt him, though she would probably do so in the end.

The guests arrived promptly. There were eight of them. One couple she knew – Marcus Hayward was a partner in Roger's firm and she had met him in the past, together with his wife,

Cynthia, at more than one social function. The rest were new to her, and Roger introduced them in turn. The men greeted her politely, the wives were friendly and charming; smartly dressed, stylish, without being over the top.

'Such ages since we saw you!' Marcus Hayward said. 'You must tell us what you've been up to!'

Roger served champagne, assiduously keeping the glasses topped up, though apart from that he stayed close by Caroline's side. Then at half past eight he said, 'Why don't we eat?' and they all moved from the small room in which they were standing into the dining room. Caroline, of course, had seen it before, many times, though not recently. There were two quite modern still-life watercolours which were new to her. The long mahogany table, in the soft light from candles, gleamed with crystal and silver, most of which she knew Roger had inherited. Everything was there, on display. The evening, in fact, was beginning to feel like a special occasion, much more so than she had expected.

'I know we're only a small party,' Roger said pleasantly as they went in, 'but I've put out place cards. I think it works better that way.'

He took his place at the head of the table. Caroline, looking for her name, found it at the opposite end, directly opposite to Roger but with the length of the table between them. It might or might not mean anything to the other guests, but it did to her. Its significance struck her at once. He was the host, she was the hostess. What was more, she felt sure he had meant this. He had seated her where Bettina had always sat. Clearly, it had been deliberately arranged. Hesitating, though only slightly, before taking her seat, she looked down the length of the table to where he was standing, waiting for his guests to be seated. He looked straight back at her, unflinching, his eyes meeting hers, a confident smile on his lips. It was all there in his look. 'This is where you belong,' it said.

And then the food was served, the wine poured, and the general polite conversation continued.

It was a superb dinner: cooked and served by the caterers, of course, but doubtless chosen by Roger. He and Bettina had always known how to entertain. Caroline remembered many happy times around this table though then she had taken it for granted that Bettina had been the guiding hand behind such occasions, though Roger, she knew, had always chosen the wine. That was a man's job, something he took pride in, and he had lost none of his skill there. They were drinking a wonderful claret. And all this, she thought, for a small dinner party? But she sensed more to it than that. The feeling grew on her that this was both a signal and a celebration, as if he were saying, 'And all this could be yours!' A calculated sign of something more to come.

She turned to the man on her left, whom she had met for the first time this evening. He had been introduced to her as Councillor Tom Thornton. 'Tom, please!' he'd said at once. He was an affable man, inclined to flirt, she discovered, but in a pleasant way. 'So *you* are the reason Roger's been spending all these weekends in Brighton?' he said now. 'He's a dark horse! Of course we did wonder – and now we see why! He's a sly devil!'

'He's an old friend,' Caroline said. 'I've known him practically for ever. And recently he's been seeing me through the buying and selling of some property – nothing large, but it's an area of which I was quite ignorant, and he came to my aid. You know he was a colleague of my late husband?'

He shook his head. 'No, I didn't know! In fact I've only known Roger since he became interested in local politics. You'll find the same goes for one or two of us here.'

'Really?' Caroline said. 'Well, he was always aware of what was going on in the city, he took an interest in it, but we haven't talked about such things recently.'

'Oh, but he's very interested,' Tom Thornton said. 'Local affairs, of course. Not national. Some of us are hoping he'll eventually stand for the council. He'd be the ideal person for this ward, and the present councillor is due to retire at the next election.'

'And do you think Roger will do that?' Caroline asked. He hadn't mentioned it to her. Perhaps it was no more than wishful thinking on this man's part?

'We don't know yet,' Tom said. 'Perhaps you could persuade him?'

'Oh, I don't think so!' Caroline said quickly. 'I don't know much about politics and in any case I don't have that sort of influence over him.'

'Really?' he said. 'Well, I think you could have.'

With that he turned to his neighbour on his other side. 'I've just been saying,' he told her, 'how much we value Roger's interest in local matters.'

'Indeed we do!' she agreed. 'And are you interested in such things?' she leaned forward and asked Caroline.

'Not really,' Caroline replied. 'It's not something I've ever thought about.' She was aware that Roger had once been mildly interested, but it had not been mentioned between them recently. When he'd been with her in Brighton they had listened to music, watched a film, gone for walks, had meals together, but politics of any kind had never come into it.

'Then perhaps you *will* become interested,' the lady said. 'Who knows?'

I know, Caroline thought, but she was saved from replying when Tom Thornton broke in again on an unrelated subject.

The dinner continued pleasantly. Wonderful food, well served. Civilized guests. Roger at his most attentive, not only to her, but to everyone. He really was a charming man, and as she well knew, it was not just surface charm. Why shouldn't she go that bit further, she asked herself now? Why couldn't she take that step which she knew – she had little doubt about it – she was going to be invited to take? Everything since she had arrived had pointed to it: the way she had been treated, not just by Roger but by his guests, as if they knew something or had guessed at something which had not yet been stated but would be. And not least, where she had been seated. But it was not a step she wished to take. It was in the wrong direction.

When dinner was over Roger said, 'We'll have coffee in the drawing room, shall we?' Miss Grayson, Caroline thought, would have approved of the words 'drawing room'. She would have led an army against all who used the word 'lounge'. 'Lounges are for airports!' Caroline had heard her pontificate. 'Not for houses!'

Roger's drawing room lived up to its formal name. It was elegantly furnished, with comfortable chairs and sofas, lamps casting soft light in exactly the right places. Caroline was not aware of how Roger had accomplished it but she found herself sitting on the sofa, pouring coffee from the low table in front of them for his other guests, Roger hovering near, handing around the cups. Tom Thornton quickly sat next to her and continued his conversation about local politics.

'So do you think you can persuade Roger to stand?' he asked again.

'I don't think so at all,' Caroline said. 'Actually, I don't see Roger all that often.'

Roger moved back towards the table and was within earshot. 'That could be remedied,' he said.

'I'm settling very happily into Brighton,' Caroline said deliberately. 'In fact I *have* well and truly settled there. It suits me so well. I couldn't ask for anything better.' She hoped that Roger was taking this in, but he was smiling at her as if, for the moment, he was humouring her.

It was late, almost midnight, when the party broke up. It had largely, though not entirely, since they were a sociable lot, been kept going by Tom Thornton, who had a seemingly endless fund of small talk and stories. Aunt Patience, Caroline thought, would have had the right phrase for him. Caroline had heard her use it more than once. 'He could talk a glass eye to sleep!' she'd have said. But eventually his wife had, firmly but tactfully, put a stop to him and everyone had departed more or less together. Caroline, purposely, did not go to the door with Roger to see them off, and the moment he returned to the drawing room on his own she was on her feet.

'It's been a lovely evening!' she said quickly. 'Thank you! And now I really must go to bed. I'm dropping!'

'Oh please! Not just yet!' Roger pleaded. 'We haven't had much time to talk. Have another drink – or I'll make a cup of tea if you'd rather?'

She shook her head. 'No! Nothing. Honestly! It's been a great evening but I'm almost asleep on my feet!'

The disappointment showed in his face, but Roger was too well mannered to persist. Almost, she relented – but not quite. She knew what he was going to say to her and she knew what her reply must be, but it would have to wait until the morning. Knowing also how polite and considerate he was, she also realized that he would not press her any further at this precise moment, and she was glad of that.

'Goodnight, then,' she said.

Tired though she was – it had been a long day in more ways than one – she found it difficult to fall asleep, nor did she look forward to the morning. She knew what was certain to happen. In the end, for what was left of the night, she slept deeply then wakened late. When she went downstairs Roger was preparing the breakfast. 'Saturday is Mrs Parkin's day off,' he said. 'She has two grandchildren on whom she dotes.

259

She spends the day spoiling them. Would you like scrambled egg?'

'Scrambled egg would be fine,' Caroline answered, 'and after that I must make a move.'

Roger, again, looked disappointed. 'I hope not too soon,' he said. 'I'd hoped you'd stay at least for lunch, or even longer.'

'I'm really sorry, but I can't,' Caroline said. She searched around in her mind for an excuse for not doing so, but found none, and so was forced to give a rather helpless shoulder shrug instead.

'I'm sorry about that,' Roger said, 'I don't seem to have spent much time with you. Perhaps a dinner party wasn't the best idea?'

'Oh no!' Caroline protested. She felt so awkward. 'It was a lovely party. I enjoyed it.'

They sat at the table, eating the breakfast Roger had prepared. Halfway through it Roger pushed his plate away from him and leaned back in his chair. 'It's no use, Caroline,' he said. 'I have to say it. I love you, Caroline! You must know . . .'

She put up her hand to stop him. 'Please don't! Please don't say that!' she begged. 'You are a very dear friend, you always have been, always will be. But I don't love you – not in the way you'd want me to.'

'Why?' he asked. 'Why not?'

'I don't know why not,' Caroline said. 'You're worthy to be loved, of course you are! You're a wonderful man. But I can't do it. Not in the way you want, not in the way you deserve. And please don't ask me to explain, because I can't. There's no logic in it, no reason. We can't always love where we want to.'

'Perhaps you could come to it,' he said beseechingly.

She shook her head. She hated seeing this man – she had always thought of him as strong and proud – saying these things to her. 'No, Roger,' she said, gently but firmly. 'It's not possible. I love you as a friend, I always will. But nothing more.'

There was a long pause. Then he said, 'I see!' And then he added, 'Is there someone else?'

'No,' she said. 'No, there isn't.'

'Very well,' he said. Then he gave a rueful smile. 'But don't expect me to give up hope.'

'I think you should,' Caroline said. It was kinder to nip this firmly in the bud.

She left soon afterwards. Just before she drove away she looked at him. 'We'll always be friends, won't we?' she asked.

'If that's how you want it,' he said.

It was a beautiful day as she drove, too fast, to Brighton. She wanted to be back there. She wished she could have prevented what had happened, but she didn't see how she could. Reaching Brighton, she drove along the seafront and turned left into Kemp Town. She found a parking space close by, left the car and walked across to number seventeen. It seemed an age since she had left. Frizzie heard her approach and barked vociferously. Caroline hurried to let herself in. She would see Eleanor Grayson later, but not now. Not yet. She rushed up the stairs, as quietly as she could, let herself into her flat and closed the door behind her. Oh, it was so good to be home!

She checked her phone for messages and there were none. Though why should there be, she asked herself? What did I expect? Common sense told her there was no reason to expect any, but she had half hoped that Alec might have phoned. But why would he? He knew she was away for the weekend, that she was with Roger. If he'd thought about it at all he wouldn't have expected her back so soon. He almost certainly had the wrong idea about Roger. Should she ring

261

Alec, she wondered? He had said he wanted to discuss a few things with her, though she doubted they were urgent, and no doubt by now he would be busy with this and that or, it being the weekend, and if the Sledges allowed it, he would be with Paula.

She pottered around, unpacked the bits and pieces from her case, made a sandwich then ate no more than half of it. She went up to the roof garden, but there was nothing new there. Why would there be? It was not much more than thirty hours since she'd last seen it. She took in the view for a few moments, until the chill air made her shiver and she went back down. The whole house seemed uncommonly quiet, she thought, though of course it was Saturday afternoon and probably everyone was out, doing different things, shopping or whatever. The Holbys were no doubt still at work, Mr Downey she scarcely ever saw anyway, and there was no sign of his son so it was probably not his weekend for visiting his father. But why had she purposely escaped Miss Grayson? And anyway, why should she feel like she did? Hadn't she accomplished exactly what she'd been to Bristol for? Wasn't it how she had planned it? Roger was a disappointed man, but he would get over it. Women would fall over themselves to catch Roger. And I will get over what I'm feeling now, she told herself. I will stop feeling sorry for myself because there's no one here to hold my hand just when I want it. What a wimp she was! And what she should be doing, before anything else, was ringing Roger, telling him she was safely home, and thanking him for . . . for what? For inviting her for the weekend? For declaring his love? For almost proposing to her? No. She would have to wait and think about it before she called him. He was a wonderful host. He was a wonderful man. She wished she could feel differently about him.

She turned on the television. Saturday afternoon, and almost all sport. Determined, she sat down to watch a golf

match which, judging from the palm trees and the golfers'
clothes, was definitely not being played in England. Ten
minutes later the phone rang. She was slightly disappointed,
and chided herself for it, to find that it was Eleanor Grayson.
'I see your car's back,' she said. 'Come down and have a cup
of tea.'

Caroline hesitated only slightly, then said, 'Thank you! I
will!'

Miss Grayson poured the tea, served a plate of biscuits, then
sat back in her chair. 'Now tell me all about it!' she said.

TWENTY-THREE

Caroline did not spend long with Miss Grayson, long enough only to tell her about the dinner party, what they had eaten, what the women had worn, what the house was like. 'I can't stay,' she said in the end. 'I have to nip to the shops before they close. I seem to be short of a few things I need.'

'If there's anything I can . . .' Miss Grayson began.

'No, really!' Caroline interrupted. 'I'll go. Would you like me to take Frizzie with me, give her a bit of a walk?'

'That would be very kind,' Miss Grayson said. 'She'd love that.' She turned to Frizzie. 'There!' she said. 'Walkies! Who's a lucky dog then!' Frizzie leapt to her feet, barking with excitement, and allowed herself to be leashed. 'Perhaps I'll take a little nap while you're out,' Miss Grayson said to Caroline. 'I'm really quite tired!'

'You do that!' Caroline said. 'We might be a little while. I do have several things to buy.'

She set off with Frizzie. The company of the little dog usually, if it were needed, raised her spirits, but today it didn't. She was still worried about Roger. She wondered if she might have handled things better, though she didn't know how she could have, and it had had to be done. I will definitely write to him tomorrow, she thought. Apart from thanking him, she wanted to reassure him that the friendship they had, a friendship that had surely deepened over the last year, they would always have. She was better with words set down on paper than words spoken, especially words spoken on the verge of an awkward departure.

She did her shopping and then, passing the coffee bar, she was tempted by the aroma. She'd be allowed to take Frizzie in, she'd done so often. Frizzie entered with alacrity. This was the place where she knew she would be given a biscuit.

'A chilly day,' the owner said as she served the coffee. It was true, and by the time Caroline had finished her coffee – though she didn't hurry – the best of the day was over. It was already getting dark. She stood up, and gently pulled Frizzie from under the table where she'd settled, and left. Walking back, she wondered again why she hadn't heard from Alec. She had called him twice, and each time left a message, though saying no more than 'Hi, I'm home!'

As Caroline approached the house she saw two figures sitting side by side on the steps leading to the front door. As she got closer they appeared to be young men or teenagers. Both were dressed in dark sweatsuits with the hoods pulled up over their heads, the peaks of baseball hats sticking out from under the hoods. And each seemed to be drinking from a bottle or can held inside a paper bag. While the street was well lit, their faces were in shadow under their hats and hoods.

Caroline's heart started to beat faster. What were they doing there? Why were they outside her door? Were they going to be awkward when she asked them to move so she could get in? Of course she could avoid having to deal with them at all by simply going down the basement stairs to Miss Grayson's outside door, which is what she would normally do to return Frizzie.

No, I can't do that, she thought. This is my house. Those are my steps they're sitting on. I should assert my right to go through my own front door.

They didn't pay any attention to Caroline until she stood in front of them and said, in as firm a voice as she could muster, 'Excuse me, can I help you?' Two teenage faces, younger than she had expected, looked up at her and Frizzie, tail wagging, head cocked on one side, obviously expecting to make new friends, looked up at them.

'I live here,' said one of them, not moving.

'I beg your pardon?' said Caroline, taken aback. Then, almost immediately, she recognized him. She'd seen him briefly a couple of times going in and out of the house, but had never actually spoken to him.

'Oh,' she exclaimed. 'You must be Tom Downey's son. I'm sorry, I didn't recognize you in the dark with the hoods and everything. We haven't met and I'm afraid I don't remember your name. I'm Caroline Denby. I live on the top floor.'

Neither boy seemed disposed to join the conversation, so she went on, with more confidence than she felt, 'I'm sorry, what is your name?'

'Greg.'

'Right, well, pleased to meet you, Greg, and . . .' Caroline looked pointedly at the other boy.

'That's my friend Dylan. He's staying with me.'

Still neither boy moved. 'Well, I need to get in,' said Caroline nodding towards the door. Both boys rose slowly, moving to either side of the steps – still holding their paper bags, which Caroline could not swear to, but strongly suspected, contained beers.

Their movement made Frizzie bark sharply several times and both boys straightened quickly and stood even further to the side. 'Quiet, Frizzie,' commanded Caroline. 'Thank you,' she added as she went past them and up the steps, only to realize she had not taken out her keys and had to rummage in her bag to find them while both boys looked on impassively.

As she closed the door behind her she heard one of the boys let out a loud and practised burp and both of them broke out in snorts of laughter.

As Caroline crossed over to Miss Grayson's hallway door she wondered whether she should have said something about them drinking on the steps. But she might have made a fool of herself. They might have had Cokes or apple juice in the bags for all she knew. She rang Miss Grayson's bell. 'Who is it? . . . I'm coming.' Caroline heard her say as she climbed the stairs to reach her door.

'Oh my dear, it's you. Why didn't you come in through my front door? Hello, Frizzie, did you have a good walkies?' she said, bending down to Frizzie, who was on her hind legs pawing Miss Grayson's knees in greeting.

'We didn't walk all that far,' Caroline admitted. 'We stopped for a cup of coffee, rather longer than I meant to.'

'I'm sure Frizzie enjoyed that,' Miss Grayson said. 'Will you come in and have a wee drink, or whatever?'

'I won't, if you'll excuse me,' Caroline replied. 'I have a few things to do. But can I ask you if you know Tom Downey's son?' Caroline briefly described the doorstep encounter.

'Yes, I've seen him coming and going occasionally. He doesn't seem to be here that often. But I do hear him. Sometimes he plays this loud music with what I think is referred to as a strong beat. I've been thinking I should say something to him or his father, but as yet, I haven't.'

'You should tell me if something like that happens,' protested Caroline. 'It's my responsibility to make sure the house runs smoothly and tenants are not disturbed. Please, promise me, next time you are disturbed by his music, call me and I'll talk to him and his father.'

'Well, thank you, my dear. I will. Now, are you sure you won't come in?'

'No, thank you. I really do have things to do.'

Caroline went upstairs to her flat. It was not true that she had things to do. But now she had something else to think about. She made a mental note to ask Adam and Eric, who lived right above the Downeys, if they were ever disturbed by Greg's music, and if so, to let her know. Where she was, two floors above the Downeys', she was blissfully unaware of any noise. She hoped Greg and his friends were not going to become a problem.

The rest of Saturday evening stretched before her with nothing in view – not even anything interesting on television. She had checked her messages, but still no word from Alec. I'll try him once more, she thought. When she picked up the phone, to her pleasure, it announced that there *was* a message. 'Hi!' his voice came over. 'Sorry I didn't get through to you sooner. I knew you were in Bristol and I did call your mobile once, but you must have switched it off.'

That was true. She had switched it off when she got to Roger's and had forgotten to put it on again this morning – she was clearly not yet part of the mobile generation. She was always forgetting to switch on her phone and some-times forgetting even to take it with her. 'I'm away,' Alec was saying now. 'Paula had a few days' freedom from the Sledges and we decided to take advantage of it.' There was a slight, uncomfortable pause in the message, then he went on, 'And I have a bit of news which isn't so good: the job with the Bensons is off. I'll fill you in on the details when I get back. But don't worry. I've no doubt that something else will come up. Anyway, I'll be in touch. We get back Tuesday night. Bye.'

That was all. Nothing about where he and Paula had gone. On the other hand, Caroline told herself firmly, there's no reason why I should be told, though I would like to know. But was it really her business? No, Alec was simply a friend. But she couldn't help the sudden feeling that she would have much rather have been with Alec this weekend than with Roger. She shocked herself at the unkindness of the thought and immediately dismissed it from her mind. But she couldn't suppress a cautious sense of pleasure that, if all went well, Alec and she would be working partners and would be seeing a lot more of each other. But would they? Would the right projects come along? Was it a partnership which would flourish – or even settle down? Alec had sounded confident enough, but did he really feel as committed as she was to the idea of their working together? Then she told herself not to be silly. Nothing had changed between her and Alec. He had simply gone off for a few days' holiday with his long-standing girlfriend. No – more than that, she corrected herself – his partner. He would be back on Tuesday.

On Sunday, in a fit of domesticity which was foreign to her nature, she went through her flat from stem to stern, cleaning, vacuuming, dusting, polishing, rearranging the contents of cupboards, cleaning what few bits of silver she had, moving furniture into new places. Nothing was left untouched, and by the end of the day – she had not heard a peep from any of her tenants, not even from Eleanor Grayson – she was exhausted. She soaked in a hot bath, then went to bed though, in spite of her fatigue, not quickly to sleep. Questions, suppositions, doubts, theories, none of them with reasonable answers, chased each other around in her head. In the end tiredness took over and she fell into an uneasy sleep.

Alec, unusually for him, phoned her at work on Wednesday morning. 'We were back very late last night and I didn't want to disturb you,' he said, 'but there's something I want to show you and talk to you about. Would it be OK if I popped round this afternoon?'

'Fine!' Caroline said. 'But if it's urgent you can tell me now. I'm not busy.'

'No,' he said, '. . . at least it's not *that* urgent. But I hope it might interest you. This afternoon will be fine. See you then.'

He arrived just after three. She found herself terribly pleased to see him, as if he had been away for a much longer time. 'Did you have a good break with Paula?' she asked. 'Where did you go? Would you like a cup of tea?'

'Yes, to France and yes, I would like some tea,' Alec laughed.

While she made it they chatted, or rather she did, about something and nothing most of the time. What was the weather like? Did you have some good meals? Did you take the Chunnel? Your car or Paula's?'

'Paula's,' he told her. 'It's bigger and flashier than mine. And the weather wasn't bad. A bit chilly in the evenings. And, yes, we ate very well. And how about you?' he asked abruptly. 'How was your weekend with Roger?'

'Oh, fine, fine,' said Caroline vaguely, handing him his tea. And before he could probe for more details she asked the question that was really on her mind, 'So, what was it you wanted to talk to me about?'

'I've had an idea which I think you might be interested in. I came across something, in one of the trade magazines I read, about an exhibition in Harrogate next week. It's the New Kitchen and Bath Show. It's all about approaches to interior design using innovative types of materials and fixtures with a major emphasis on "green" issues.'

'You mean like saving energy and water, and using recycled materials and that sort of thing?' she asked.

'That's right! It's a really important movement and I think

going to be even more so in the next few years – especially in a place like Brighton, which attracts a lot of trend-setting people. The sooner we know more about it, the better. I think it could be very important for the business. Something that would set us apart – for the right sort of client.'

'But at the moment we haven't even any jobs in view, let alone jobs for trend-setting clients,' Caroline pointed out.

'That's why this is the time to go to something like this. When you have projects on you can never get away. So you have to seize the moment when there's a break. And we will have more jobs!' Alec insisted. He paused and looked at Caroline. 'You haven't gone off the idea of working with me, have you?' he added suddenly.

'Not in the least,' Caroline assured him. 'And this sounds really interesting, something I'd very much like to do – and, as an extra bonus, I've never been to Harrogate.'

'You'll need to take off Thursday and Friday of next week. We'd have to leave right after you finish work on Wednesday. It should take us about six hours by car,' Alec said. 'We'd need to get past London before the rush hour. I've driven to Whitby so many times, going to Harrogate will seem like a breeze. I'd pick you up from the office. We'd spend all day Thursday and probably Friday morning at the exhibition and drive back Friday after lunch. We'd get back to Brighton late in the evening. My only concern is, do you think you can get the time off? And, of course, you may already have plans for the Friday evening . . .'

'It is rather short notice,' said Caroline, 'but I'm sure I can get the time off.' She was in fact resolute that she would. 'I think Mrs Freeman would be happy to stand in for me for a couple of days. In fact, I'm sure I could take Wednesday as well. I haven't taken any time off since I started there. That way we could leave in the morning and do the whole drive in daylight. Wouldn't that be better?'

'If you can do it, that would be much better,' Alec agreed,

pulling a magazine from his bag. 'Here, I've brought the details with me.' He handed her the magazine, open at the page. 'If we do want to go we'll have to decide quickly. It'll be a popular affair, and being in Harrogate it'll soon get booked up. In fact, it might be even now.'

She read the details. 'It sounds wonderful,' she said. 'I'm ready and willing. I'll have a word with Doctor Freeman in the morning, and give you a call.'

'I might ring today and make a provisional booking,' Alec said, 'which I could hopefully confirm tomorrow when you were sure.'

'Why not do that?' Caroline agreed.

'Is it OK for you to leave here?' Alec asked.

'Of course!' Caroline said. 'I'm not tied hand and foot, I'm not a nanny! I'll ask someone – probably Adam and Eric – to keep an eye on things, to give me a call if anything should go wrong – not that I expect it to.'

'Good!' Alec said. 'In fact, why don't I phone from here? In any case, I'll need a list of hotels, we can't hang about for that.'

Caroline picked up the telephone and handed it to him. 'Go right ahead.'

Five minutes later he put down the phone. 'They'll put all the stuff about the exhibition, plus an accommodation list, in the first-class post this afternoon,' he said. 'They warned me places were filling up. Apparently, and as I expected, it's proving to be a very popular exhibition. So if I get the details tomorrow, shall I go ahead and book the rooms? Or would you like me to check with you? Situations and so on?'

'Oh, go ahead!' Caroline said. 'I don't know a thing about Harrogate – in fact, I don't know a thing about the north of England. You'd be much more competent to make a choice.'

'Right!' Alec said. 'And you'll like Harrogate. Of course, it's a place I've always known. It's not a million miles from

Whitby, where I was brought up. And by the way, this is a business "do" so the expenses go down to me, or at any rate to my business.'

'Are you sure?'

'Absolutely!' said Alec firmly. 'All above board! Quite legitimate.'

'Well, what can I say but thank you. It's something really to look forward to.'

'No, thank *you*. I know it's short notice. But I really think this will be a great opportunity and I think you'll really enjoy it,' said Alec, pushing the magazine back into his bag. 'And in the meantime,' he said, pulling out a bottle of wine from the same bag, 'I brought back this very tasty wine from France. Why don't we open it?'

'Lovely! What a treat!' exclaimed Caroline.

He drew the cork and poured the wine. Lifting his glass and smiling, 'To the future. And to Harrogate!' he said. She was unable to suppress a small shiver of excitement.

All the information Alec had requested arrived in the following day's post. He rang Caroline at work. 'Are you sure you don't want to see it first, or shall I go ahead and book?'

'Oh, please do! There's no problem about taking the time off work,' she said.

'Right! I'll call you this evening and confirm all the details. And, when you start thinking about clothes to bring, pack something warm. It will be cooler in Harrogate than Brighton. And, bring some comfortable walking shoes. You'll be on your feet for most of two days, walking round the exhibition halls. Talk to you later.' And with that, he rang off.

True to his word Alec called that evening with all the details. He had booked into a small hotel just out of the centre, but within walking distance of the exhibition halls if they felt like walking. Otherwise, the hotel suggested using the frequent buses or a taxi, as parking was always a problem during popular events.

Caroline pointed out that she should really pay her share, but Alec, again, firmly rejected her offer. 'No, this is all a business expense. The rooms, meals, petrol, transportation, everything. I'll cover it all,' he insisted.

After she put the phone down Caroline could hardly contain her pleasure at the thought of the trip. She bounced into the kitchen and uncorked what remained of the bottle of wine Alec had brought with him the previous evening. Then the thought struck her: Roger! She *must* write to Roger. A task she had been avoiding. What kind of friendship is that, she chided herself? How rude and thoughtless!

She had spent quite a bit of time during the last few days turning over in her mind what she would say to Roger. How she would phrase it. But now she must do it. She decided the best approach was to imagine Roger was sitting here with her and to write to him as if she were talking to him; explaining her feelings and her hopes for both of them in as simple and direct a way as she could. She owed him that.

She fetched several sheets of notepaper, settled at the table, looked for a few moments at one of the empty dining chairs, then began to write.

When Alec and Caroline left Brighton on the following Wednesday morning the weather was overcast and blustery. The forecast called for rain showers, heavy at times, across most of the country for the next few days. But Caroline was in high spirits. She had not, except for her visit to Roger, been on a trip away from home since moving to Brighton. And here she was going somewhere she hadn't been before, to do something she had never done before and with a new travel companion. And she did so enjoy spending time with Alec.

She got into the car with an enormous bag of provisions for the journey, which had made Alec laugh. 'We're going to Yorkshire, you know – not on the Monte Carlo Rally. But thanks. I still plan to break the journey for lunch and to get petrol, but this is all very welcome.'

Early on the previous Sunday evening Caroline had called Adam and Eric to say she would be away for a few days and to ask them to keep an eye on things and to make sure they had her mobile number in case of emergencies. They had immediately asked if she would like to pop down for a glass of wine and some nibbles. Caroline gratefully accepted, having kept company with herself for most of the weekend, except for taking Frizzie for a long walk on Saturday afternoon, followed by tea with Miss Grayson. She had called Rosie's flat and left a message, but not received a reply.

Eric was getting back to normal, though a scar was still clearly evident on his face. 'Nothing hurts any more,' he said, 'and the headaches went away. The doctor thinks the scar will also disappear over time. But the worst part is that I still occasionally dream about the attack and wake up in a sweat of panic.'

'But,' interrupted Adam, 'we went back to the pub a couple of weeks ago with a group of friends. Had some drinks and some laughs.'

'I think that really helped,' said Eric. 'Mind you, I made sure we all left together! But we'll go there again. It's still one of our favourite places. It would certainly be adding insult to injury if I felt I couldn't go back again.'

'So what's happening with you?' Adam asked, turning to Caroline. 'Where are you off to in the middle of the week?'

Caroline told them about the trip, the exhibition, and why she was going with Alec. Of course, she realized, they had been unaware of her plans to work with Alec and just telling them about it made it seem more real and more plausible.

'It sounds fantastic,' said Adam enthusiastically. 'And I agree that green building is the wave of the future. I think you're both very smart to be thinking that way. We shall want to hear all about the exhibition and,' he added with a smile, 'all about the fleshpots of Harrogate when you get back.'

'The Moorland House Hotel, two AA stars, doesn't sound likely to be the scene of any wild parties,' said Caroline, laughing.

'Oh, don't you be deceived by those dour Yorkshire exteriors,' said Adam.

Caroline, changing the subject, told them about her meeting with Greg on the front steps and learned that they, like Miss Grayson, had been disturbed by his music. 'Next time it happens, please call me,' she said. 'I can't hear anything upstairs. But I will deal with it. I'm not sure how, but I will.'

'You are an amazing landlady,' said Eric. 'We feel very lucky to have found this place.'

TWENTY-FOUR

The weather did not improve as Caroline and Alec drove north. Once beyond London and on to the M1 they picked up speed, but the intermittent rain kept the road wet and they seemed to be driving constantly in the dirty spray kicked up by other cars and lorries.

Alec, Caroline observed, was a good driver. He drove as fast as conditions permitted, and for the most part stayed in the right-hand lane. He was obviously a man who liked to concentrate on his driving. Apart from occasional comments about something they saw out of the window, they didn't talk. The silence was totally comfortable and Caroline was pleasantly lulled by the rhythm of the engine and the warmth of Alec's car.

'Let's listen to some music,' Alec said suddenly. He reached across and flipped open the glove compartment, revealing a messy assortment of battered-looking CDs. 'Whatever takes your fancy!' he said grandly.

Caroline pulled out a few of the CDs and saw immediately that one of them was by the Sledges. 'Oh!' she exclaimed as she opened the case. 'The Sledges! I've heard so much about them, but never actually heard them.'

'Ah, yes, well . . .' Alec hesitated. 'Maybe not now. I don't think they're your type of music. And they're certainly not mine.'

'But couldn't I listen to a couple of tracks? Just to know what they sound like?' she asked.

Alec sighed. 'OK, if you must. Skip to track three. That's the song that first got them noticed. But this is not background music. It's meant to be played loud, so turn up the volume!'

Caroline did as she was told. The blast of music seemed to hit her physically, and it was, indeed, not her type of music, but what it lacked in melody was more than made up for by a driving energy. 'The singer is Craig,' Alec shouted over the music. 'He has a remarkable voice, if he doesn't destroy it too soon singing at this volume. And the lead guitar is Sean. He's a brilliant musician. He's really the soul of the band.' They listened to two more tracks, which were just as loud but rhythmically quite different – driven along by the pounding bass. 'That's enough,' said Alec, hitting the eject button as the song ended.

'Yes,' Caroline laughed. 'Well, I did ask for it! And you're right, I'm not going to run out and buy it. But I'm glad I finally know what they sound like.'

'And now,' Caroline said, rummaging in her bag, 'for something completely different.' And with that, she pulled out one of the CDs she had brought with her and popped it into the player.

Eventually they drove into Harrogate and found the hotel. The Moorland House Hotel was set back from the road by a generous semicircular driveway, guarded at each end by solid stone gateposts. It did, Caroline had to admit, have a somewhat drab exterior – perhaps, she thought, some former Yorkshire industrialist's weekend mansion. But once inside it proved to be warm and lively. The bar and the dining room, just off the reception area, were both busy with people. The drive had taken longer than they expected so, on the way to their rooms, they agreed they would have a quick meal in the hotel and get a good night's sleep.

Sitting down to dinner, Caroline, looking around, noted that the prevailing dress code for both male and female guests seemed to be tight and black with, for variety's sake, the occasional flash of grey and white. 'I think,' said Alec, following her gaze, 'we're surrounded by a bunch of architects and interior designers up here for the show.'

'Oh dear,' Caroline replied. 'In that case I think I'm going to need a whole new wardrobe – and possibly a new body!'

Alec laughed. 'Don't even think about it,' he said, 'on either count,' and she blushed at the unexpected compliment.

Over dinner they looked at the list of exhibitors, who were set up over several exhibition halls, discussing which they would like to see and in what order. There was a great choice. In the end, both of them tired, they agreed to meet for breakfast at eight, after which they, gratefully, went to their rooms and to bed.

Caroline found the exhibition exhilarating. She couldn't remember when she'd ever been introduced to so many new ideas in such a short period of time. They looked at brightly coloured flooring made from recycled rubber tyres and at gorgeous patterned bathroom tiles recycled from glass bottles. 'I'm beginning to feel a lot better about sorting my rubbish if this is how it ends up!' she said to Alec as they studied one of the displays. He spent quite a bit of time at one stand learning about cabinets made of wheatgrass board, while Caroline, close by, examined elegant light fittings made entirely from recycled plastic bottles and aluminium. She was always aware of Alec's presence, no matter where he was in the room.

By the end of the day Caroline was more than grateful that she had heeded Alec's advice to wear comfortable walking shoes. Several of the more elegantly clad women were by this time perched on chairs, pained expressions on their faces. Apart from short breaks for morning coffee, a lunch-time sandwich and an afternoon cup of tea, she and Alec had been walking around since they'd arrived. They looked at each other. 'Shall we call it a day?' Caroline said. 'I'm exhausted, not to mention filled to the brim with ideas.'

'I agree!' Alec said. 'Time to leave!'

'I'm *dying* to put my feet up!' Caroline laughed.

'You're not the only one,' Alec told her. 'Let's go back and rest for a while before dinner.'

The hotel was a welcome sight as they trudged up the driveway, both bearing carrier bags weighed down with brochures and samples.

Later they met in the bar and agreed to eat at the hotel rather than go out to a restaurant. 'I thought the food last night was very good,' Caroline said as she stirred the ice in her gin and tonic, 'and there are several other dishes I'd like to try.'

'Cheers,' said Alec, raising his pint of local bitter. 'Cheers,' Caroline replied, 'and, once again, thank you for including me in this trip. I can't tell you how much I'm enjoying it.'

With that the conversation turned to what they had seen that day: what had interested them most ('Just about everything,' Caroline had to admit). What materials they could see using almost immediately in any renovation they might do. Which products they wanted to learn more about. Which they thought clients might be more interested in. 'Of course, we have to get some clients first,' Caroline reminded Alec.

'Of that I'm confident,' said Alec. 'But bear in mind that some of the things we saw today aren't widely available yet and they'll often cost more. Two things clients never want to hear – it will take longer and it will cost more! So what we've seen won't be everyone's cup of tea. Shall we go and eat?'

As they walked through the reception area towards the dining room Caroline stopped to look at the series of water-colour paintings on the walls. 'These are lovely,' she said. 'I didn't really take the time to look at them earlier.'

Alec looked at each painting. 'Actually, I know all these places. They're all in Yorkshire. I reckon I've visited every one of them at some time or another.'

There were more paintings on the walls of the dining room and, after they had ordered and the waiter had poured a glass of wine for each of them, Alec looked around the room. 'Most of the scenes are of the Yorkshire Dales,' he said. 'A lot of these places won't have changed since I was a kid.'

'Do you miss Yorkshire?' asked Caroline, quite keen to get the conversation on to a more personal level.

'If I thought I wasn't going to be able to visit Yorkshire again, yes, there are things I would really miss,' replied Alec. 'Of course Whitby and the surrounding coast, where I grew up. The moors. And definitely the Yorkshire Dales. I don't think there's anything like the Dales anywhere else in the world. And I would miss Yorkshire people: their friendliness and their frankness. They're not afraid of letting you know their opinion! And the Yorkshire sense of humour: very dry, straight-faced and usually right on the mark.'

As they ate Caroline asked about some of the places in the paintings close by their table. Alec seemed to have a story for each one of them; when and how he had been there, and with whom. 'They all look beautiful,' Caroline said. 'Peter and I used to love watching that TV show a few years ago about the vet in the Yorkshire Dales. I don't know why we never went there.'

'Well, sitting in Harrogate, it's hardly "there", it's right

281

on our doorstep,' Alec said. He took a sip of his wine then, abruptly, he stood up. 'Excuse me,' he said. 'I'll be back in just a second!'

'Are you all right?' Caroline called after his disappearing back. But no sooner had he left the dining room than he returned with one of the newspapers left out for guests in reception.

'Listen,' he said as he sat down. 'This may make no sense at all to you, and of course you may have plans – maybe Roger is visiting or something. But we're right here and I just suddenly thought that maybe, instead of driving back to Brighton tomorrow afternoon, we could – if you'd like to – drive into the Dales. And I mean, stay overnight, spend Saturday there, perhaps go on a walk, and drive back to Brighton on Sunday. But just let me look in here.' Alec opened the paper and found the right page. 'Yes, excellent! The weather looks good for the weekend. Clouds clearing out tomorrow afternoon, Saturday and Sunday should be sunny, and not too cold.' He stopped suddenly and looked at Caroline. 'I'm sorry, I'm rambling on. But what do you think?'

Caroline knew exactly what she thought. 'But what about you?' she asked. 'Don't you have to get back? Won't Paula be expecting you?' Alec shook his head. 'Well then,' said Caroline slowly, 'I think it's a lovely idea and I don't have any plans for the weekend' – she paused – 'so I would like to do it. But on one condition. I insist on paying my full share of everything: for the petrol, the food and of course for my room.' Caroline paused again, then added, 'And I'll have to pop into a Marks & Spencer's before we leave Harrogate. I hadn't packed for the weekend!'

'Agreed!' Alec said. 'Let's do it! First thing tomorrow I'll call some bed and breakfasts. I'm sure at this time of year I'll find something open. It'll be great!' he added, full of enthusiasm.

***

After they had finished breakfast the next morning Alec excused himself from the table to call the bed and breakfasts and to check his messages. 'You never know. Maybe someone has called about the next big job!'

As Caroline watched him go she suddenly realized that she had, once again, completely forgotten to turn on her mobile. Checking that she was not going to disturb other guests – one or two of whom were themselves speaking quietly into mobiles – she turned her phone on.

There were three messages, all from Rosie. They were essentially the same message, but increasing in tones of frustration: *Why* did Caroline have a mobile if she never turned it *on*? That was the *point* of mobile phones. Where *was* she? She was not answering the phone in Brighton or her mobile. *Please* call.

Rosie would probably be on her way to work, Caroline thought, but to show, if belatedly, that she too was prepared to use her mobile to reach people anywhere at any time however inconvenient to them, she called Rosie's phone.

'At last!' Rosie's voice answered. 'I was getting worried. Where have you *been* the last couple of days? I've been calling and calling!' Caroline could hear the sound of traffic in the background.

'Hello to you too,' said Caroline coolly. 'Actually, I'm in Harrogate.'

'Harrogate? What on earth are you doing in Harrogate?'

Caroline explained as briefly as she could. Rosie seemed grudgingly impressed. She approved of everything green.

'The reason I was calling,' Rosie went on, 'was to see if I could come down to Brighton this weekend. It's been a while since I saw you and I thought we might have a real girls' weekend together. Go and see a film, maybe two films, perhaps do some early Christmas shopping, go out for a really nice meal – my treat. When will you be back?'

283

Caroline, again as briefly as she could, explained her weekend plans. This time Rosie was not impressed. 'You're going on a weekend jaunt with Alec?' she asked incredulously. 'Doesn't he have a girlfriend? Where does she figure in all this?'

'She's away with her band this weekend . . . I think.'

'You think?' cried Rosie. 'Mum! I know I thought Alec was taking you for a ride over the house conversion and I was wrong about that. But it sounds like he really is taking you for a ride this weekend, in every sense!'

'It's not like that at all, Rosie,' Caroline protested tartly. 'You have to trust me to be able to look after myself. And I'm really sorry about the weekend. That would have been so much fun.'

At that point Caroline saw Alec coming back into the dining room. 'I'm sorry, Rosie, I have to go. Alec is coming back to the table. I'll call next week and please, please, I want to have that weekend with you. Whenever. Bye for now and lots of love.' Before Rosie could protest, Caroline hung up.

After settling the bill and loading the car, they returned to the exhibition and spent the morning visiting the stands they had not seen. They had a quick sandwich, made an even quicker dash into Marks & Spencer's, picked up the car and were on the road heading for the Dales by two o'clock.

Alec had booked a bed and breakfast in Kettlewell. 'One of my favourite villages,' he said, 'but I thought we'd stop and look at Bolton Abbey on the way, while it's still daylight. Then we'll head up into Wharfedale.'

It was fully dark when they crossed the stone bridge over the river and came into Kettlewell. Earlier they had strolled around the ruins of Bolton Abbey, stark and grand against the winter sky, taken a short walk along the river then set off again as dusk gathered in.

Now, he pulled the car over to get his bearings and then, turning on to a narrow street, they crossed over another, smaller, bridge and followed a winding road up a steep hill. He swung into a cobbled driveway and stopped the car. 'This is it,' he announced. In the headlights Caroline saw a neat stone house, set back behind a low wall. The windows glowed in the dark and as she got out of the car Caroline saw the front door open and a small, well-rounded woman in a floral apron waved and came down the path to greet them, introducing herself as Mrs Perkins.

TWENTY-FIVE

Mrs Perkins showed them to their rooms and in a seamless monologue pointed out the facilities, described the breakfast and the hours it was served, suggested where they might eat that evening, asked if they would like a cup of tea – and then added an update on her visit to the doctor earlier that afternoon to 'see to' her sciatica.

They took Mrs Perkins's suggestion and later that evening, by the light of a full moon, walked downhill to the pub she had recommended. It was by no means crowded. A handful of people, mainly men, sat at a dark wooden bar with drinks in front of them. From the conversation that passed between them they were regulars who all knew each other. After a short discussion with the barmaid on the merits of the various bitters on offer, Alec ordered drinks and told her they would be having dinner. The barmaid waved toward the few tables set along the walls of the bar. 'Take your pick, love, we'll not be that crowded tonight.'

They selected a table near the fireplace, not far from the bar. No sooner had they sat down than one of the men, who looked to be the oldest in the group, turned to them. 'You'll be staying here then?' he enquired.

'Not here exactly,' Alec replied. 'We're up at Ghyllhead Farm.'

'Oh aye, with Bessie Perkins. Well, you'll get a grand breakfast there. They keep their own pigs. And hens!'

'As long as you get your feet under the table before Jack!' another voice chimed in, setting off a round of laughter from the other drinkers.

'Jack's her husband,' explained the man. 'He farms Ghyllhead ever since his dad passed on, oh, near fifteen year ago by now. He's up and out before dawn most days getting a start on things. Goes into breakfast about eight, hungry as a hunter. And you'd never mistake him for a small fella. But don't worry, Bessie won't let you starve. So where might you be from then?'

From that point on Caroline and Alec became, at first the centre of, then just a part of the conversational circle. Discussion ranged from farming to football and, when they learned of Alec's connection to Whitby and of his current 'line of work', talk shifted to commercial fishing and the best way to frame a roof. When they found out Caroline was a landlady she was questioned closely about her property and there were appreciative whistles as she answered their disarmingly direct questions about 'what one of her flats would fetch'.

Caroline was aware that, as he talked, Alec's voice was taking on a decidedly more pronounced Yorkshire accent. And as she watched him she was struck once again by how attractive he was – by the warmth of his smile, his keen sense of humour and his easygoing manner as he traded stories and jokes with the locals around the bar.

They ate well: lamb stew and grilled brook trout followed by apple pie and Wensleydale cheese, after which they left the bar to the cheery good-byes of the other patrons. The

287

road back up to Ghyllhead Farm rose steeply out of the village. They walked briskly, both breathing heavily in the crisp air. 'Am I going too fast?' Alec asked.

'No,' Caroline puffed, 'and I think I need this walk to prepare myself for Mrs Perkins's breakfast.'

'When I booked, I also ordered two packed lunches for tomorrow so we could spend the day out,' Alec told her. 'You're going to make good use of those walking shoes!'

As they parted to go to their rooms, Alec turned and gave Caroline a quick peck on the cheek. 'Sleep well,' he said. 'See you at breakfast.'

Caroline did sleep well. She had felt absurdly happy when she'd fallen into bed. When she appeared, hurriedly and a little rumpled, at breakfast Alec was already seated at the large farmhouse table in deep discussion with Jack Perkins about repairing an old plumbing line.

'There you are,' he smiled as soon as he saw Caroline. 'I was just about to come and knock on your door.' He introduced her to Jack, who was indeed a large man, with a round, ruddy face and shock of unruly black hair.

'Sorry,' said Caroline. 'I haven't slept as soundly in a long time.'

'Well, that's what you get away for!' Jack boomed heartily, as he stood up from the table. 'Now I've got to be off. Nice meeting you both, and thanks for the advice, Alec. I reckon I'll do what you suggested.'

After breakfast, which lived up to all expectations, Alec and Caroline gathered their jackets and carried their packed lunches out to the car. 'I can't imagine I'll ever be hungry enough to eat again,' Caroline said as she peered into her lunch bag, 'let alone by lunch time.'

'Oh, we'll see about that,' said Alec. 'We haven't come up to the Dales to loll about by the pool. We're off to do some serious walking.'

Catching Caroline's questioning look he quickly added, 'But not too serious. You won't need your ice pick. But walking is the best way to experience the Dales. It's a fabulous day and there are some lovely walks around here. Mrs Perkins gave me this,' he said, waving a photocopy of a local map. 'Far better to walk than drive around in the car all day.' He rummaged around in the car boot and pulled out a rather dilapidated and paint-spattered rucksack. 'This is usually a tool bag, but today it'll be our picnic hamper.'

They drove a few miles out of Kettlewell along the banks of the river then pulled into a parking area, and left the car.

'We'll walk along the river a little way, then climb up the fell, cross over the top, and take a look down on Littondale; then back along the top till we pick up the path that will bring us right back down to the car again. How's that?'

'Sounds wonderful,' Caroline said uncertainly. 'I hope I can make it!' She couldn't help thinking that Alec was probably used to hiking with Paula, who was a decade or more younger, and probably fitter, than she was.

'Don't worry,' Alec said. 'We'll take it at an easy pace.'

The countryside and the day itself were both magnificent, Caroline thought as they walked now along the bank of the swiftly flowing river. The bottom of the valley to either side was green meadows with cattle grazing, and then the land rising, at first gently, then quite steeply until it finally broke out into high open moorland which now glowed a golden brown against the sharp blue sky. Ribbons of pale limestone wall ran up and across the hillsides. And all over the slopes the white dots of grazing sheep moved slowly across the land.

Despite the cool air, the sun was warm and after a short distance both she and Alec shed their outer jackets, which he rolled up and stuffed into the rucksack.

Caroline found the climb hard, but not as bad as she had feared. Maybe I'm fitter than I give myself credit for!

she thought to herself. Even so, they stopped frequently to turn round and admire the view, which seemed to go on for ever, with ranges of hills stretching into the distance. Kettlewell was just visible, nestled into the folds of several hills. Caroline felt a wonderful sense of triumph when they finally reached the top and the ground levelled off.

'This is so beautiful,' she sighed. 'It's dramatic and imposing and yet so intimate, all at the same time. Those stone houses and barns look like they've been here a thousand years – as much a part of the natural landscape as the hills and rivers.'

But now, on the top of the fell, there was a cool breeze blowing. Putting their jackets back on, they walked over the moor then downhill a little until they found a wall facing the sun, and there they sat down on the thick tufted grass, their backs against the warm stones, sheltered from the breeze.

'It's really so lovely to get away like this,' Caroline said. 'Even though I love Brighton, and I really do, this break is doing me a world of good. Everyone should be forced to take regular breaks from their routine as a matter of public health!' she pronounced. 'But maybe not as frequently as you,' she said with a smile, before adding cautiously, 'You've only just got back from a holiday with Paula. Did that recharge your batteries?'

Alec was silent for a few moments, his eyes focused on the view. 'Not exactly,' he said slowly. 'As a matter of fact' – he paused again – 'well, you should know, I just didn't know when to tell you' – another pause – 'Paula and I are splitting up.'

Caroline was momentarily speechless. Alec continued to stare into the distance, and then he said, 'Paula was the one who initiated the idea, while we were away. At first I was shocked, but as she talked about it I realized she was quite right. We haven't really been a couple for quite some time. Her life is completely bound up with the Sledges these days and I've been so busy trying to get my new business off the ground. That didn't leave much time for "us". We both had to admit, we've drifted apart. And now the Sledges have been offered an American tour. So, after a couple of gigs in Brighton in the New Year, Paula will be off to the States, for at least six weeks. So, Paula suggested we both face facts and think of that as a time to end things. Not to end our friendship,' he added quickly, 'there are no recriminations on either side, but the end of our—' He broke off. 'I'm not sure what the word is . . . "relationship"? "Partnership"? "Long-lasting affair"?'

As he spoke Caroline's mind was racing. Was Rosie right? Did she really not know what she was doing? Was this whole weekend carefully engineered by Alec in the full knowledge that he was breaking up with Paula? What was he playing at? Yet part of her couldn't believe he was playing at anything. It just didn't seem like him.

'Well, I'm shocked, and really sorry to hear that,' she managed to say. 'There may be good reasons for it, but I always find it sad to hear of people breaking up. And I'm glad you told me. Not that it's really any of my business . . .'

'But it is your business,' Alec said firmly. 'You must be asking yourself what am I playing at. Inviting you away on this weekend. Taking you all the way up here and then dropping this on you!'

'Well . . .' she began.

'Believe me,' Alec interrupted. 'This was not planned. The trip to the exhibition was something I thought we should do for the future of the business. It had absolutely nothing to do with the state of things between Paula and me.'

'And coming up here? Also nothing to do with Paula?' Caroline asked a little sharply.

'Nothing at all! I had no plans for this trip until the idea occurred to me at dinner on Thursday. It really was a spontaneous suggestion. In fact, if I had had to get home to see Paula this weekend I wouldn't, couldn't, have suggested it. But, as usual, she's off with the band . . .' His voice trailed off. 'But I asked you here as a friend, to do something I thought we would both enjoy. No ulterior motives.'

'Why didn't you tell me then, at dinner?' asked Caroline.

'I almost did,' said Alec, turning to look at her. 'Then I thought, if I tell you, *"Oh, by the way, I'm breaking up with my girlfriend, how would you like to come away for the weekend with me?"*, what would you be likely to say? And I told myself, which was true, that I was inviting you on the trip as a friend, not because of Paula, and I didn't want to start to complicate the whole thing.' Alec shook his head. 'But I think I've really messed it up, haven't I?'

'I don't know what I would have thought if you'd told me that night at dinner,' Caroline said, ignoring his question. 'But you're right, I might have said no.'

But even as she said it, Caroline was thinking: Would I really have said no? I might have felt I *ought* to say no, in the circumstances. But in truth I'd still much rather be here with Alec than be anywhere else.

'Do you regret coming up to the Dales with me?' Alec asked quietly.

Caroline thought for a moment, then smiled at him. 'No. I can honestly say I don't regret it at all. I just wish I had known . . . I can't explain why, but I just wish I had.'

'Well, I hope now you do it won't prevent you from enjoying being here. And thank you for listening to me. And I'm sorry if I appeared to mislead you, or to be not entirely open with you,' Alec said.

'That's OK,' said Caroline. 'I see that you didn't intend it that way. And, strictly speaking, what's going on between you and Paula is none of my business. Might I also say,' announced Caroline, raising her voice, 'that, much to my surprise, I feel quite hungry! Do you mind if we eat our lunch?'

Alec laughed, as much in relief as amusement. 'Nothing like a little fell-walking to work off a Yorkshire breakfast,' he said as he brought out the lunch bags Mrs Perkins had made up for them.

They ate for a while in silence, then Alec said, 'Do you mind if I ask you a personal question?'

'Go ahead,' Caroline replied, intrigued.

'I know it's really none of *my* business, but, I'm taking advantage of the fact that we're here in Yorkshire where us Yorkshire folk tend to ask direct questions.' He paused. 'What are your and Roger's plans? Do you have plans?'

Caroline sighed. 'I thought you might have got the wrong impression.' She looked at Alec. 'We have no plans. We're just good friends. And that's it.'

'Oh,' Alec said, 'but I thought, with him coming to Brighton so often, and when I burst in that Sunday morning and he was there in that ridiculous dressing gown, looking very much at home . . . One of my more embarrassing moments.' He smiled. 'And you off to Bristol for week-ends . . .'

'For *a* weekend,' Caroline corrected him.

'Well, I just assumed, you know, that you and he . . .'

'No. As I said, we are just good friends.' At least I hope we are, Caroline added to herself.

The sun had begun to move off them and they felt the air cooling. 'Best we get going,' Alec announced. 'It will warm us up and we want to make sure we get back to the car before it drops dark.'

Walking down the fellside, with breath to spare, they talked more and found themselves sharing more intimate thoughts and feelings about their personal lives. The conversation continued all the way back to Ghyllhead Farm, and into the evening, when they decided to eat at a restaurant rather than return to the pub. Caroline talked more about her relationship with Roger and what had happened in Bristol. Alec asked her about Peter and she found herself talking about him more freely than she ever had since his death. Alec also asked about Rosie, how she was doing, how she and Caroline were getting along. Caroline decided not to tell Alec about her most recent conversation with her daughter.

Caroline questioned Alec more about how difficult he was finding the break-up with Paula. Alec admitted it was going to take him a little while to come to terms with it emotionally, but he and Paula were already starting to deal with the practical issues of separating after almost seven years of being together.

Despite the increased intimacy of their conversation, Caroline had the distinct impression, throughout the afternoon and evening, that Alec was going out of his way to demonstrate that what they shared was a friendship, nothing more, and that his intentions were entirely honourable. She noticed he was avoiding even the slightest physical contact. On the way up the fell that morning he had offered his hand, and even held her waist at one point, to help her negotiate some of the trickier stone stiles they had encountered, but on the walk down in the afternoon, while standing close in case she slipped, he did not touch her. And when they returned to the farm after dinner and said goodnight at the top of the stairs, this time there was no peck on the cheek.

Caroline lay in bed listening to the soothing sounds of the ghyll that gave the farm its name. As she drifted off to sleep she tried to make sense of the thoughts and feelings the events of the day had stirred in her.

Hadn't Alec suggested the weekend simply because he wanted to share his love of the Dales with a friend? But how did she really feel if that was all it was . . . ? Why should he want me to be anything other than a friend and work colleague? Why should he be interested in me? I'm a lot

294

older than Paula. On the other hand, she told herself, I'm no older than Alec! . . . But just supposing there *was* more to it and he *had* tried to take advantage of the situation . . . would she have protested? Probably. But deep down, would she have minded? And what would something like that do to their hopes of a future working relationship? . . . Was that why Alec was now being so careful? . . . Did she really want him to be so careful? . . . And now Paula was leaving . . . what did she really want from Alec . . . ? Be honest, she told herself, What is it you really want? The answer was simple. She knew it; she just hadn't let herself think, let alone say it. 'I want,' she said aloud, 'Alec'. . .

TWENTY-SIX

The following morning, having enjoyed another of Mrs Perkins's memorable breakfasts, Caroline and Alec drove back to Brighton, arriving in the early evening. They agreed that Alec would not even try to find a parking spot, but would simply drop Caroline off at number seventeen. Lifting her bag out of the boot he said, 'I don't enjoy the thought, but I am going to be a bit preoccupied for the next two or three weeks. You know, working things out with Paula. Of course I'll call you at once if any jobs come into view. And I'd like to get together with you and go through all this,' he indicated the shopping bags full of materials from the exhibition. 'We need to decide what we should keep, what we should follow up on or learn more about.'

'Then why don't I make a start on that,' Caroline said. She summoned her most efficient-sounding voice, though efficient was the last thing she felt as she contemplated the possibility of not seeing Alec for several weeks. 'I could organize it all into various categories,' she offered. 'Flooring, wall covering, lighting, appliances, that sort of thing.'

'Are you sure?' Alec said as he lifted out the carrier bags.

'That would be great. But I can't leave you to carry all these upstairs.'

'I'll be fine,' said Caroline. 'If you could just help me get them into the front hallway, I'll do the rest. Clearly you can't leave the car here.'

Between them they carried the bags up the front steps and deposited them in the hall. 'Then that's it, I think,' Alec said a little awkwardly as he stood there.

'Thank you,' Caroline said, surveying the bags. Then she looked at Alec. 'And, thank you for the last few days. I really have enjoyed myself.'

'No, no,' Alec protested, 'thank *you*.' He paused, 'Well,' he said, 'I suppose I'd better be on my way.'

Caroline summoned up a smile. 'Yes, I suppose so,' she said.

He moved to go down the steps but Caroline, putting her hand on his shoulder, turned him to face her and, leaning towards him, gave him a gentle kiss. 'Goodnight, Alec,' she said, 'I'll see you soon.'

He stepped back, looked at her for a moment, holding her eyes with his. 'Bye then,' he said, and skipped down the steps to his car.

Caroline made a determined attempt during the following days not to think too much or too often about Alec. She knew she had to give him time and space to deal with Paula. And she was sure he would be in touch if and when any work came into view.

She had to be sensible about this, she told herself, but what she told herself and what she felt were quite different. Now that she had allowed herself to admit fully to her feelings for Alec, she found herself being swept by unexpected waves of desire – as she lay in bed, as she sat behind her desk in Doctor Freeman's consulting rooms, as she rode home on the bus. When this happened, *all* she could do was think of Alec, imagining where he was at that moment, what he was doing, wondering whether he was thinking of her at all, wondering whether he *ever* thought of her when they were not together and, if he did, what were his thoughts about her? She was consumed by the kind of feelings she'd not had since she was a teenager. What was happening to her?

She forced herself to focus on some of the practical, day-to-day tasks which were there before her. First she had called Rosie.

'How did it all go? What did you do?' Rosie was full of questions.

'Oh, it was just fine!' Caroline said. 'I had a lovely time. Now, why don't we make a date for you to come down to Brighton?'

When the date for Rosie's visit had been decided, Caroline turned her attention to Christmas. It would soon be here, her very first Christmas at number seventeen. Should she decorate the house in any way? She would, she decided, certainly buy an evergreen wreath with red berries to hang on the front door. And in Brighton she had seen a beautiful garland made of exquisite glass snowflakes which would look stunning draped around the central light in the hall. She wondered if Adam and Eric might do something with their balcony overlooking the street? A simple string of small white lights outlining the curve of the railing would look lovely. She would ask them if they had planned anything.

As for her own flat, she most definitely wanted a Christmas tree. She had brought with her from Bath a box containing all the tree decorations that she and Peter had collected over the years. She had not had a tree since he had died. In fact, since then, she had spent each Christmas with Rosie in London, neither of them able to face all the memories that a Christmas spent in their family home in Bath would trigger. But now she wanted to spend Christmas in her new home, and she wanted a tree.

But a tree was not enough. She also wanted to celebrate the season with more than that. A party, she decided! Why not? She would have a party for number seventeen! The more she thought about this, the more she warmed to the idea. It would have to take place before Christmas; people might well have plans for the Christmas period itself – visiting family or, as increasingly seemed to be the case, off on a holiday to some exotic location in the sun. But she *would* have a party. She would invite all the tenants. Should she invite Greg Downey? Yes, she decided. The chances were he wouldn't be around and if he were it was highly unlikely he would want to attend. She would invite Rosie, Patience – and Alec of course. She would also invite Roger – but, she wondered, would he accept?

When she had returned from Yorkshire, in addition to Rosie's frustrated messages on her home phone, there had been a message from him. 'Hello, Caroline,' he'd said, 'I was hoping to catch you at home, but as you're obviously not there . . . I was calling to thank you for your letter. Not something I can do properly in a phone message! I do hope to be able to talk to you and see you soon. Bye for now, and please call when you have a chance. Bye again!'

Caroline had not called Roger immediately, but now she had her own reason to speak to him, to ask him to the party.

The call was warm and friendly, both of them making an effort to maintain the easygoing style that their conversations had always had. Roger thanked her once again for her letter and assured her that he too hoped they would continue to be part of each other's lives. 'Actually,' he said, 'I have another bit of news. I've finally succumbed to the pressure from Tom Thornton – you remember, the city councillor you sat next to at dinner? – and been persuaded to stand for the council myself in the next round of elections. I have to say,' he admitted, 'the seat I'll be contesting is a bit of a long shot, but Tom has convinced me I have a fighting chance!'

'I'm delighted!' Caroline said. 'You'll make a wonderful councillor. You'd have my vote any day!' She went on to tell him about the party. 'You'll be getting an invitation soon,' she said. 'I do hope you'll be able to come.'

'So do I,' Roger replied, 'but forgive me if I can't say yes right now. I don't know my exact schedule, and most of my evenings and weekends are going to be taken up with meetings, speeches, visiting constituents and, as someone once said, generally "putting myself about". But I'll let you know. Anyway, we'll speak again soon, and I'm looking forward to seeing you.'

For the first weekend back home Caroline set herself a full schedule. She would write the party invitations and get them in the post. She would buy the Christmas decorations and scout out the best place to get a tree. And she would sort all the materials she and Alec had brought back from Harrogate. In addition, she had agreed to have tea with Miss Grayson on Saturday.

The weather now couldn't have been more different from the weekend in the Dales. There it had been glorious, here it was wet and windy, with a gale forecast for Sunday. Once back from her shopping she was happy to have a list of indoor tasks to attend to.

Everything seemed to take longer than she had planned and by the time she turned to the bags of brochures they had brought back from the exhibition it was late on Saturday afternoon. Looking through them she felt a strong urge to call Alec. The excuse would be to ask whether the categories she was planning to use to sort everything made sense to him, but the real reason, she knew, was that she just wanted to talk to him, to hear his voice, to hear his laugh. She knew she must resist the temptation. He had – hadn't he? – said he would need time to work things out with Paula. She must respect that. But as she began to review the contents of the carrier bags, she found herself reliving everything that had happened in Yorkshire – her own feelings for Alec welling up more strongly with every recollection and, at the same time, her uncertainty about Alec's feelings for her.

In the evening, around seven, she decided to take a break. She would pour herself a drink and start to make something to eat. That was when the first call came. It was Adam. He was very apologetic about disturbing her, 'But you did say we should. It's about the music coming up from the Downeys' flat, it is unbearably loud. Sorry!'

'Oh dear!' Caroline said. 'Well, leave it to me. I'll do something.'

No sooner had she put the phone down when it rang again. It was Miss Grayson with the same news. 'I don't know what to do,' she said. 'I hate to make a fuss. I remember as a girl our neighbour used to practise the piano for hours at a time and my parents never complained. But that didn't seem as oppressive as this steady boom, boom, boom I'm hearing now. It is really quite unpleasant.'

'I'll go down and see them,' Caroline promised.

Caroline, not quite sure what she was going to say, set off immediately. As she approached the ground floor the thump, thump, thump of the music grew louder and louder. This is quite unacceptable behaviour, she told herself as she got to the Downeys' door.

She knocked. There was no response. She knocked again, harder. This time the music, some vaguely familiar rock number, was turned down a little, so she knocked again as hard as she could. After a moment the door was opened by Greg Downey.

'My dad's not here,' he said, without any greeting.

'Hello, Greg,' Caroline said. 'Actually, it's not your dad I want to talk to. It's you.' At that moment the song in

301

the background ended and another one started which, to her amazement, she recognized. She was listening to the Sledges!

'I have to talk to you about your music,' she began.

Greg visibly stiffened.

'It's the Sledges, isn't it?' she said. 'From their first album.' Greg's eyes widened. 'You're a fan of the band?' she asked.

'Yeah. They're awesome,' Greg replied. He looked at Caroline with a mixture of surprise and curiosity on his face.

Caroline pressed on. 'You must know they're a Brighton band. But did you know they're off on a six-week tour of America starting in January? It's a really big break for them.' This, she thought, is not really what I came to say.

'Are you one of their mums or something?' Greg was bemused.

'No,' Caroline laughed, 'I suppose I'm what you might call a friend of a friend of the band. But' – she paused for effect – 'though I presume we both want the Sledges to make it big and to be around a long time, I have to ask you to turn your music down. I'm afraid you're disturbing other people in the house. Maybe you could use earphones? I know their music has to be listened to loud, but it's not on to be broadcasting it to the whole building. So, could you please turn it down?'

Greg hesitated, then shrugged his shoulders. 'Oh, sorry. Yeah, I'll turn it down.'

'Thank you, Greg. We'd all appreciate that,' Caroline said.

With that she turned and went back up the stairs. As she did so, the sound of the music began to fade.

She knocked on Adam and Eric's door as she passed. 'I think that's sorted out,' she announced, 'but let me know if it happens again.'

'What did you say to them?' asked Eric.

302

'Him, actually – oh, we discussed the Sledges,' Caroline said airily. 'That's who you were listening to.'

'We were?' Adam laughed. 'Well, Caroline, you never stop surprising us. Do you have time to come in for a quick drink? You can tell us all about the goings-on in Yorkshire.'

'Thank you,' said Caroline, 'that would be very nice.'

No one had predicted the strength of the gale that blew in the next day.

Caroline worked most of Sunday continuing to sort the contents of the bags. As she worked she was aware of the sound of the wind picking up, but this was as forecast, and was no different from other storms she had experienced since moving into number seventeen. In the mid-afternoon she had even taken a quick walk along the front, feeling the windborne spray on her face. She walked towards the marina and watched the waves exploding over the sea walls in spectacular clouds of white water. She had known these storms since childhood and had always felt exhilarated by them; the raw power of nature on display, reminding us of who or what was really in charge. Of course, she told herself, it was easy to enjoy the spectacle when it was just a short walk back to her cosy flat and the promise of a hot drink to warm herself up. Had she been out on the Channel she would undoubtedly have a different reaction.

Finishing her tea she continued with the task at hand. It had started to rain and, as she got up to draw the curtains, the wind, which had clearly picked up more strength, was battering the rain in noisy gusts against her windows.

By half past six she had finally sorted all the materials into one or other of the categories she had created. Whether they were the right categories she would have to discuss with Alec but, she decided, that would be it for the day. She would reward herself with a glass of comforting red wine and defrost a portion of homemade beef stew she had in the freezer – perfect food for such a stormy night.

She ate on the sofa in front of the TV. She tried to concentrate on the programme but found herself instead listening to the noise of the wind, which had risen to a level she had never before experienced. In the end, she went over to the window and peered out between the curtains. The air was filled with flying rain and spray whipped off the sea. And, even from this distance, she could hear the steady roar of the waves pounding the beach as the wind, racing up the street, jerked the streetlights back and forth. A sudden burst of wind and rain slammed against the windowpane making Caroline jump back, expecting to be showered with water.

At the same moment she heard a loud dull thud above her head. She looked up at the ceiling. The wind rose again in a burst of fury and again, another heavy bang above her head, followed this time by a low rumbling noise which rolled across the ceiling.

Caroline froze: something heavy was loose on the roof! But what? She always brought down or secured anything she judged could be blown around in a storm. And now the wind howled again and once more the rumbling sound crossed the ceiling.

Was it possible, she asked herself, that one or both of the round tree planters had blown over? Surely not, they were so heavy, and the trees were not that big – one a small coastal pine tree, the other a taller, slender mountain ash. And now there was another blast of wind, another thud, then more deep rumbling noises from overhead. She realized she would have to go up and see what was happening. She could not ignore it. Heaven knows what sort of damage was being inflicted on the roof garden, and on the roof itself. And, horror of horrors, she thought, could this wind be strong enough to blow the tree planters off the roof entirely and down into the street?

She pulled on a thick pullover and her rain jacket, grabbed a torch and climbed the stairs to the roof. She drew back the bolt and pushed open the door. A blast of wind and water hit her full in the face. She cried out in shock and another burst of wind slammed into the door and banged it shut, almost knocking her over.

She knew now she could not go out on to the roof. If the door was blown shut when she was out there, which it certainly would be, she would be trapped for the rest of the storm. But it was imperative to find out what was happening. She put her shoulder against the door, braced her foot on the corner of the jamb and pushed hard. The door opened, but it took all her strength to hold it open against the force of the wind. She was doused in a blast of salty rain, but wiping the water from her eyes and placing herself between the door and the jamb she surveyed the roof. Immediately she saw one of the tree planters, on its side, rolling around, driven here and there and spun around by the force of the wind, banging into the brick parapets at each edge of the roof. Far worse, the taller tree had also been blown over, and now its narrow trunk was lying across the parapet, its branches hanging over the street. The weight of the planter itself was holding the tree on the roof, but with each ferocious burst of wind the branches of the tree flexed down, threatening to lift the planter up, like a giant seesaw, and flip the whole thing over the parapet and on to the street below. Caroline stared unbelievingly at the scene, the noise of the wind and rain filling her ears. She could hold the door open no longer. She stepped back on to the small landing at the top of the stairs and the door was immediately slammed shut by the wind.

Caroline sat at the top of the stairs, her head in her hands, water dripping off her. A feeling of helpless desperation welled up in her. 'What can I do? I can't handle this. I don't have the strength. What made me think I could live alone

and manage a house like this? I was crazy to take all this on
. . .' Another savage blast of wind, followed by a loud bang
as the loose planter rolled into the door behind her, brought
her to her senses. Alec! She must call Alec. He would know
what to do!

She ran down the stairs, grabbed the phone and called
his mobile. He answered immediately. 'Caroline! How are
you doing over there? Quite a blow, and you're on the front
line!'

The words poured out of Caroline as she described what
was happening and what she had seen on the roof. Alec
finally interrupted her in mid-sentence, 'I'll be right over.
We have to secure those planters. Have you seen the news?
They expect the winds to get even stronger before the storm
passes. It will take me a bit of time to get over to you in this
weather, but I'll call when I get close and you can meet me
downstairs. We'll need to carry some things up to the roof.
And don't attempt to go on to the roof by yourself. I'll be
there as soon as I can.' With that, he rang off.

TWENTY-SEVEN

Caroline was at the door to meet Alec. He was dressed from head to foot in foul-weather gear, his hooded head hunched over against the wind and driving rain as he thrust some coils of rope into Caroline's open arms and returned a few moments later with several lengths of wood.

They carried everything up to Caroline's flat, and then up the stairs to the roof-door landing. Raising his voice over the sound of the wind and the rain drumming on the outside of the door, Alec said, 'I'm going to open the door now and, while I hold it against the wind, I want you to jam it open by pushing in the pieces of wood exactly where I tell you. OK?'

Caroline nodded. 'Then, you bring those two coils of rope,' Alec said, pointing to them, 'and I'll take the rest. Follow me, but stay low. If you feel at all unstable, crawl on your hands and knees. Don't stand up, whatever else you do, and don't go near the edge. Are you ready?' Caroline nodded again, trying hard to show a confidence she did not feel. She was amazed at the way Alec just seemed to assume she was capable of handling any kind of situation that presented itself.

He pushed open the door and they were both met by a blast of wind and stinging rain. They quickly secured the door and, crouching over, stepped on to the roof and into the full force of the storm.

Afterwards, Caroline had no idea how long they had been out on the roof. Her world had narrowed down to the few feet in front of her that she was able to see through the rain and spray being blown into her face. The wind seemed to snatch her breath away with every angry gust and the noise of the storm enveloped her.

She focused all her attention on following Alec and doing what he indicated by gesture, or occasionally by shouting into her ear. Using their combined strength they wrestled the taller tree off the parapet; then, both of them on their hands and knees, they rolled it towards one of the brick chimneys rising above the roof. They stood the tree up and Alec motioned for Caroline to lie across the planter, holding the tree trunk. Then, kneeling down beside her, his arm over her shoulders, he shouted, 'Can you hold it here while I get the ropes to secure it?'

'I think so,' she shouted back. 'I'll try!'

Alec scuttled across the roof to get the rope as Caroline felt the force of the wind tearing at the tree. She held on grimly. Then Alec was there, passing the rope around the chimney and, kneeling behind Caroline, feeding the rope between her and the planter. After several more turns around the tree trunk he deftly tied a knot. 'That's it for this one,' he shouted over the roar of the storm.

Caroline, in relief, started to stand up and was hit by a body blow of wind. She let out a startled cry as she was knocked off balance and fell backwards. Alec caught her, and held her for a moment. 'Are you OK?' he shouted as he released his hold on her. 'Yes,' was all she could say. The truth was she felt weak from the physical effort of fighting the wind and wrestling with the heavy planters. The hood of her rain jacket had been blown back off her head and her hair was plastered to her face. Water was running down her neck and she was horribly cold.

Alec indicated the other planter which, at that moment, was pinned to the further parapet wall by the pressure of the wind. He motioned for her to follow him. 'Stay low!' he called. It took them less time to secure the second tree as, each now knowing what to do, they worked more quickly and efficiently. But Caroline was aware that she couldn't hold the planter much longer. The wind was beating at her, the rain lashing at her head and face and the tree bending and straining, trying to break away from her. It was with immense relief she saw Alec tie the final knot and signal for them to get off the roof.

They half crouched, half crawled, over to the door, and while Alec held it against the wind, Caroline removed the pieces of wood. Alec let the door slam shut, then threw the bolt.

Both of them dropped to their knees on the little landing. Then, like survivors rescued from some great danger, they threw their arms around each other in celebration – holding each other tight and rocking slightly side to side. 'Wow!' said Alec, 'that was quite something, and you were absolutely amazing!'

Caroline pulled back a little and looked up at Alec. Suddenly they were kissing – the cold of their faces in stark contrast to the heat of their mouths and the warmth of their breath – the taste of salt on both of their tongues. They kissed again and again, the sound of the storm still raging behind the roof door. Caroline felt a deep warmth returning to her body.

Alec took her head in his hands and gently pushed some strands of wet hair off her face. 'I feel like I'm kissing a mermaid just emerged from the sea,' he said, smiling at her. He leaned towards her and they kissed again, this time more tenderly.

Caroline threw her arms around his neck and hugged him to her. 'Oh, Alec,' she sighed.

'Come on,' said Alec, standing up, lifting Caroline with him, 'we've got to get you out of these wet clothes.'

'I thought you'd never ask!' blurted out Caroline, then, shocked at her own words, 'Oh my God, I can't believe I said that.'

Alec laughed as the two of them stumbled down the stairs together, refusing to let go of each other.

But they did not make love that night.

As they kissed and held each other Caroline said, 'I can hardly find the words to tell you how I feel about you, how much I want you, in every possible way. But I know, at this moment, that you still have to return to Paula. Even though you're breaking up with her, until it actually happens, she is there. And much as I want to keep you here with me, I know I can't. You will have to go, whether it's tonight or tomorrow morning. Do you understand? Does it make any kind of sense that I want so much for you to stay, and at the same time I'm asking you to go . . . but only for now?'

Alec left a little later. They kissed good-bye at Caroline's door. 'Be careful, my love,' she whispered into his ear. Alec zipped up his storm jacket, picked up the pieces of wood and headed downstairs, back into the storm.

In the days that followed Caroline had no reason to wonder whether Alec was thinking of her. He called her frequently. His calls were usually brief, from his mobile as he criss-crossed Brighton responding to pleas to deal with storm damage. 'There's lots of work cutting up and clearing fallen trees, repairing roofs, fixing badly built extensions, that sort of thing,' he told her. 'It's mainly small jobs, but it's putting some extra money into builders' pockets right before Christmas, so no one in the trade is complaining!'

After the storm blew over Alec had instructed Caroline to check the roof and the outside of number seventeen, just to make sure there was no visible damage. She reported back that everything looked fine – and that there had actually been some dried out pieces of seaweed on the roof!

One afternoon, just as she was getting ready to leave work, the phone rang. 'Can I give you a lift home?' Alec's voice said. 'Your luxury limo is right outside.'

'Oh my! A girl could get used to this,' Caroline laughed as she climbed into the front seat of Alec's well-worn work van.

As he pulled away from the kerb he said, 'I have some good news. But, don't get too excited . . . yet.'

Caroline looked at him with raised eyebrows, then quickly composed herself into an expression of exaggerated seriousness. 'All right, I'm not excited. So tell me.'

'I had a call this morning from a woman called Jackie. She and her husband have just bought a flat in Brighton and want to do a complete renovation before they move in: new kitchen, new bathrooms, the works.'

'Oooh!' exclaimed Caroline, then immediately added, 'Sorry. I am not excited.'

'Good,' said Alec, smiling, 'because right now she is just calling around to see who might be available. She wants to get down to serious bidding for the job after the New Year. But,' Alec went on, 'here's the best thing. About three years ago – right before I set up my own business – I was in charge of the renovation of a flat in Hove, for Jackie's sister. That job went very well, so apparently I come highly recommended!'

'But that's wonderful,' cried Caroline. 'Please let me be a little excited!' And, as the van drew up at a red light, she threw her arm around Alec's neck, pulled him towards her and placed several wet kisses on the side of his face. Alec continued to look straight ahead, but couldn't stop himself from breaking into a broad smile.

When they arrived outside number seventeen, they sat in the van holding hands and talking – neither of them wanting to say good-bye. Finally Alec leaned over and gave Caroline a kiss. 'I feel a bit as if your parents might open the front door at any moment and tell you to come in!' he joked.

'It's more likely that you're going to get a ticket for double parking!' Caroline said.

'You're right, my love,' he said. 'And work calls. I promised to go and check out a damaged conservatory before the end of the day. I'll speak to you soon,' he called after Caroline as she got out of the van.

Caroline had begun the preparations for her party. Roger had called on Monday to tell her he wouldn't be able to attend, but first he had asked about the gale and Caroline assured him that both she and number seventeen were fine. 'Good!' Roger said. 'And as I suspected, I do have to be at a local community meeting the evening of your party. I'll be really sorry to miss it.'

But, by the end of the week, everyone else – except Greg, who was with his mother that weekend – had accepted the invitation. And, much to Caroline's delight, Rosie had offered to come down the day before to help with the food preparation and, most importantly, to help Caroline put up and decorate the Christmas tree.

Patience was also coming. She would stay over in the spare room and Rosie would sleep on the sofa. The three of them had agreed to spend the following day together in Brighton.

With about ten guests Caroline really wanted to make it a dinner party rather than a buffet meal that people would have to eat on their laps. She much preferred the intimacy and intensity of everyone round a table. But her table was too small. When she discussed it with Alec he said he could easily make an extension for her dining table using plywood and trestles and she could cover the whole thing with a large tablecloth and create whatever size table she wanted. That settled it; it would be a dinner party.

Caroline's Christmas plans were also falling into place. Rosie said that of course she wanted to be with Caroline at Christmas, but had then asked if she could invite a guest. 'Matt: he's an American, currently working over here. He can't get back home for Christmas, so I would love to invite him. He's terrific. I really like him. And I know you'll enjoy his company. He's a lot of fun,' she said enthusiastically.

Caroline had immediately agreed, and had resisted the temptation to ask Rosie about just how much she really liked Matt. She knew how prickly Rosie could become if questioned too closely about her relationships with men.

Caroline had also invited Miss Grayson for Christmas. She was clearly touched and delighted by the invitation and offered to do whatever she could to help with the preparation of the meal.

And Alec would be there! When she had asked him about his Christmas plans he told her that in the past few years he had gone with Paula to her parents' place near Guildford. 'But obviously not this year,' he had added. He too had immediately accepted Caroline's invitation. 'But what about Rosie?' he asked. 'How will she feel about the two of us and about me being there at Christmas?'

Caroline agreed that she would have to talk to Rosie. 'But, for the moment, does it seem deceitful to ask that we keep our feelings under wraps – especially at the party? I don't want to have to explain it all to Rosie just yet. But I will have to before Christmas.'

'I'll do whatever you feel is for the best,' Alec replied, smiling. 'I shall be the soul of discretion at the party. There will be nothing even the most inquisitive gossip could seize on.'

When the evening of the party arrived Caroline had to admit that the flat did look lovely. She had turned on only the side lamps then placed some large candles in strategic places around the main room which, together with the coloured lights on the Christmas tree, cast a warm and welcoming glow. The long dining table, between the main room and the kitchen, was covered with a deep-red cloth. The newly polished silverware and the wine glasses sparkled in the candlelight. At each setting Caroline had placed a name card and down the centre of the table were several small bouquets of holly and juniper, the red and blue berries offset by the deep-green foliage.

As each guest arrived they were handed a glass of champagne – except for Brigid Holby, who looked ready to deliver her baby at any moment and asked if she might have sparkling water.

Caroline, where necessary, introduced her guests to each other as they came in and Rosie introduced herself to those she didn't already know as she circulated with plates of hors d'oeuvres. Alec took over the job of making sure everyone's glass was kept filled and it wasn't long before the room was a buzz of lively conversation and laughter.

Caroline had stored extra bottles of champagne and white wine in the cool air on the roof and, as she noticed Alec was opening the last of the champagne from the fridge, she excused herself and went quickly up the stairs to bring down a couple more bottles.

The air on the roof was cold and the sky was clear. She went over to the bottles lined up under the front parapet. Suddenly she was aware of someone behind her. She turned and Alec drew her into his arms. 'Sorry,' he said, 'I can't go all evening watching you but not allowed to touch you, or hold you, or show any sign of affection. It's more than a man can stand!' He kissed her, at first gently, then as she tightened her hold on him, more deeply.

'You must go back down now,' said Caroline, running her fingers through his hair. 'Here, take these two bottles. At least try and look like you were simply seeing to our guests' needs.'

'*Our* guests?' said Alec, raising an eyebrow.

'Yes, that's exactly how I feel. *Our* guests,' replied Caroline. 'Now please, go down. I'll follow in a few moments.'

Alone now, with the light from the doorway spilling on to the roof and the sounds of the party carrying up the stairs, Caroline took in the view. The lights of Brighton stretched out to the right and left and, from the bottom of the street, she could just hear the faint sound of the waves breaking on to the beach.

She shivered, suddenly aware of the cold. She took one last look around, then crossed the roof and, closing the door behind her, went back downstairs to join the party.

315

ACKNOWLEDGEMENTS

To Stephen, for his ever-present (though sometimes from a long distance) love and encouragement. He helped me so much with many details in this book.

As always, I wish to say thank you to my agent, Mary Irvine, to my secretary, Shirley Hall, and to my publishers at Transworld, and especially to Linda Evans for her encouragement when I most needed it.